STRANGE CASE

AN URBAN FANTASY

BOOK III

LAUREN STEWART

Cover design by Olivia Rivers
Edited by Red Adept Publishing
Formatted by IRONHORSE Formatting

Other Titles by Lauren Stewart
Darker Water, Once and Forever #1
Unseen, The Heights Vol. 1
Unearthed, The Heights Vol. 2
Hyde, an Urban Fantasy
Jekyll, Hyde Book II
Strange Case, Hyde Book III
The Complete Hyde Series Box Set
No Experience Required, a Summer Rains Novel
Second Bite

ReadLaurenS@gmail.com
www.ReadLaurenS.com

ISBN-13: 978-0-9881701-6-2

DEDICATION

Merci beaucoup to the crazy and wonderful readers and bloggers who've supported me by spreading the word, leaving reviews, and being just plain awesome.

To my kids, my BFF, and my mom: You brighten each day of my life and remind me that there still are amazingly good people in the world.

"...everything happens for a reason. People change so that you can learn to let go, things go wrong so that you appreciate them when they're right, you believe lies so you eventually learn to trust no one but yourself, and sometimes good things fall apart so better things can fall together."

Marilyn Monroe

PROLOGUE

Control yourself and you can control others. "I want the good news first."

"Uh...Two days in Florida have made me a prouder Texan, and I can't wait to go home. That's about it for the good news. Other news? I cleaned up what I could, but the cops are still hanging around."

"I have someone working on it." *Too damn slowly.*

"That's what you get for trusting a woman to do a man's job."

"Lesson learned." *First Jolie Cabot, then Alex Bertram— both very good teachers.* "Did you talk to the guards who were there that night?"

"Most of them high-tailed it as soon as it went down, but I spoke to a couple. They didn't tell me anything new. Some stuff about the fight, but they all ran before Hyde01 got out. Bertram's already on her way to Dallas."

"I'll be talking to her as soon as her plane lands. What about Turner and Colfax?" *The two Abnormals who always seem to do the exact opposite of what I need them to do.*

"Haven't found them yet. Looks like they went back to

Turner's house at some point, but they're gone now."

"They have to be somewhere close. From what was left of Hyde01, Turner isn't Turner anymore—no human would've been able to rip him into that many pieces. And there aren't many places strong enough to secure a Hyde." Sigh. *What a fucking mess.*

"So what now?"

"Find them. Get the guards that are left to help."

"There *are* none left. A bunch of them went AWOL and the others are...unavailable."

"As in *permanently* unavailable?"

"Yep."

"You were supposed to talk to them, not kill them."

"You hired me to get it done, but get it done quietly. Those men would've spilled everything after five seconds with a cop."

"You're not getting paid by the body." Sigh. "What about the scientists?"

"I'm meeting with Steve Harris again tomorrow. He's scared, but I think he gets how deep he is. A couple others are being tracked and..."

"And what?"

"Bradford, I think his name was."

"Was." *Not good.* "*Lou* Bradford? What did you do to him?"

"He said he wanted to disappear, so I helped him disappear. In the Everglades."

Bradford. Shit, of all people... "You have just created a huge problem for me. Huge." Deep breath. Then another. *Yelling shows weakness. You are not weak. Control yourself and you can control others...Control yourself and you can control others...Control yourself and you can control others...*

"Whittley? You still there?"

"Yeah. I was just wondering if there's a way this can get

any more fucked up than it already is." *And I came to an unpleasant conclusion.* "I've given you a lot of leeway here, Newman. But no more casualties unless you talk to me first or we are going to have some serious issues."

"How much leeway do I have if you're tying my hands?"

"You know, I'm beginning to think it's me—that I'm just not speaking clearly enough. My instructions seemed so simple: Find and subdue Colfax and Turner, or whatever he is, until I know what I want to do with them. Keep the ex-cop alive just in case I need leverage. And now I'll add: Don't kill anyone until we're absolutely sure we don't need them anymore."

"When I meet Harris tomorrow night, exactly how tight is that rope around my wrists gonna be?"

"Provided he can keep his mouth shut, he's still useful. Once he gets up to speed, I'll need him to start work on what Bradford was doing for me. So try not to kill him."

"I'll do my best...sir."

Ryan hung up by overhanding his cell phone right into the wall. "Control yourself and you can control others..." He said it over and over until he was just moving his lips. His hands were cramped from gripping the armrests of his chair.

Control yourself and you can control others... It wasn't working, not anymore. Too much going wrong in too short a time period. *Control.* He took a deep breath and let it out slowly. He could handle anything—the project, his employees, the Board. He'd be fine.

And, as soon as he controlled that little bitch, Ryan would control *everything*.

CHAPTER I

Eight days. Eight of the worst days of Eden's life. Seven of the longest nights of her life.

She hated being around him even more than she hated herself—for what she had to do, for what she'd done, for who she was becoming. She'd thought she was finally balanced, whole, a blend of her two sides.

Maybe it was just another lie The Clinic wanted her to believe. *No.* Alex believed it too—that kind of excitement couldn't be faked. The Clinic's Employee of the Month had caught and caged the pureblooded, potential broodmare who'd integrated her Abnormal side with her human one. And now Eden was a stronger, better person.

Stronger? Absolutely. Better? She didn't know anymore.

Her obsessions were taking over her every thought and action. Finding a way to bring Mitch back was priority number one. Number two was making absolutely sure The Clinic paid for everything they'd done. And murder, rape, kidnapping, and deceit were expensive hobbies.

Her rage and volatility were seeping out of her pores, leaving her agitated, aggressive, and pretty darned irritable. Kind of like the beast in the cage.

"Is it time for another cocktail, bitch?" Hyde growled. "How 'bout you add a little pineapple juice this time, maybe an umbrella?"

Of all the drugs they'd taken from The Clinic, Eden was still sure their best shot was the one marked 'J-0026.' She felt it in her gut, and her instinct had been right on lately. Aside from Landon, it was the only thing she trusted now. But neither of them were chemists, and they had no idea what a large dose would do to him. So they'd started out slow, a small amount of the powder mixed with saline injected into Hyde's massive arm. Then wait to see if anything happened. Mix up a bit more with a stronger ratio, inject and wait. Over and over. Day after day.

Today made eight days of *nothing*. Eight days since Mitch had given himself over and they'd brought the facility down.

Since it wasn't safe to stay at Mitch's house, their only option had been the brothel they'd stayed in before. But its cage was only for play, not holding back a monster, so they'd maxed out Landon's credit cards on some serious reinforcements and new locks on the doors. Unfortunately, credit cards could be tracked, if they weren't already. So she knew there was a very small window in which even this place was safe. The Clinic would need a little time to regroup, grease palms, and hire new employees. But they'd be back, and they might be as desperate to find Eden and her boys as she and her boys were *not* to be found. Not until they were ready to fight back.

But moving Hyde was no picnic and finding somewhere strong enough to hold him was next to impossible without any money, resources, or friends. She almost laughed at the ridiculousness. Almost. They were fighting with the devil, two devils really. Transform one back into a man and bring down the other, and the thing stopping them was cash flow.

That alone would keep this out of the history books—the brave underdogs defeated by an empty wallet.

They were running out of time. So in desperation, she'd

whipped up a batch heavy on the J-0026, filled a syringe, and prayed. If nothing happened, they'd move on to one of the other drugs. Then do the same regimen. Over and over. Day after day. Until Mitch came back. Until she saw a glimpse of humanity in Hyde's eyes. Like she'd seen in Hyde01's.

Her father.

When Landon had told her who Hyde01 used to be, she hadn't reacted. Just one more piece of bad news to stack on top of so many others. She knew her lack of emotion made Landon uncomfortable. But what did he expect? That she fall to the ground in tears? Shake her fists at the sky and scream, '*Why?*' Lots of emotion made for great TV, but it was useless in real life. It wouldn't get her closer to her goal. Plus, she was out of tears, out of answers, and would soon be out of time. So someday she'd deal with it. Maybe. But not now. Now, her plate was so full, she couldn't lift it.

Hyde was still Hyde, still strapped down, still angry. If he was in pain, he never mentioned it. Thankfully, it seemed like his metabolism had slowed or his body worked in a completely inhuman way. Like hers. She barely ate and was never tired. Well, mentally she was beyond exhausted, but physically, she felt ready to run a marathon. But since running away wasn't going to happen, that energy just simmered inside of her, made her more impatient, more agitated, and more bitchy. Like a meth-head suffering from PMS.

And poor Landon had to deal with it.

She unlocked the cage and went inside. Hyde watched her every move, an ugly smirk on his face, his hate disguising the natural beauty of Mitch's face.

"Listen, bitch. Get it over with so I can go back my daydream. I was at the part when you're screaming for mercy while I fuck you. So either let me get back to imagining it or let me *do* it."

She'd stopped responding to his threats a few days ago. It only made things worse…for her. He, of course, got pleasure from her frustration or when she lashed out. The truth was that she was afraid of him. When he took apart Hyde01, she'd seen what he was capable of. But more than that, he was holding Mitch hostage right in front of her, and she couldn't do anything about it.

They kept the bastard strapped to a bed, but he still held all the power. He was the one who controlled them, and they all knew it. The only way she could save Mitch was to get past Hyde. And he was so damn strong.

She didn't touch him—he was pain, made from thorns or razor blades. When the needle punctured his thick skin, she pushed the plunger down as quickly as she could, sending the highest dose yet into his vein.

"You're getting good with the poisons," he grumbled. "Didn't feel a thing. Maybe you should be a nurse, or at least dress up like one. That might make things more fun."

"It's so strange—I can see your mouth moving, but can't hear a word you're saying."

"Oh, you hear me. You hear every fucking word I say. Especially when I talk about him. Poor little Mitch. Gone and buried. And the best part is that he did it to himself. To get away from you and your perky little ass."

"Do you realize that every word you say only confirms how stupid you are?" Mitch had given himself over to save her, not to get away from her. It was still infuriating, but he'd thought he was doing the right thing.

The idiot.

Hyde laughed. "I'll be free soon, and then we'll see who's stupid."

She backed up and watched him for any reaction. Any sign of Mitch—his tell, his eyes, anything. In Hyde01's eyes, she'd seen humanity. Just a quick glimmer, but she'd seen it. And she would see it in this Hyde too—the warm, trusting look of Mitch as he called out to her. As he begged her for help. She had to be patient, had to hold on to the surety that, eventually, he would come back.

Hyde grimaced, and then shook it off. "You could make

him feel better."

She flinched. It was the first time he'd said anything about Mitch still being around.

"Does it hurt?" she asked.

"What?"

"Having him inside of you?"

"Nothing hurts me."

"Do you feel him like he felt you?"

Landon had told her how Mitch had struggled more and more to keep control over Hyde. Even when Eden had been two different people, she'd never felt Chastity trying to take over, other than a few ill-timed lustful moments. Maybe it was because both of Eden's parents were Abnormals, or maybe because Jekylls didn't experience the same violent urges the Hydes did.

"Does Mitch play with your mind like you did his?"

"Like I said, nothing hurts me. And no one plays with me unless I want them to." He paused. "And I want you to. Come over here and make both of us feel better. Fuck me. Fuck him. Maybe that would wake the bastard up."

"That's a really sweet offer. I'll keep it in mind for those lonely nights after hell freezes over."

Then she remembered the only time Mitch had forced his way through Hyde. Hyde had pushed her up against the bars of his cage and ripped off her clothes. Mitch came back when Hyde had his mouth on hers—not in a kiss, in possession, in taking something just because it belonged to Mitch. And the physical contact angered Mitch enough to be able to stop him.

Oh God. Would it work a second time?

As much as the idea repulsed her, there was little she wouldn't do to bring Mitch back. But could she put herself in that position again? There was no guarantee he'd save her. Just a deep-seated belief that Mitch would never allow Hyde to hurt her. Or have her.

She wasn't sure she could. *Do it. Do it for Mitch.* Her silent laugh was bitter. Doing someone else for the person you love.

How ironic. But she and Landon had nothing—no leads or help or knowledge. But Hyde did. He knew what was going on inside him—if Mitch was there, alive, in pain. He knew. And she needed to know too. To know her hope wasn't in vain, her goal was possible, the love of her life hadn't died so that she could live.

Maybe she could tease him to keep him talking and make him admit Mitch was there banging on the walls that trapped him. If it made Hyde open up and express himself, it was worth swallowing a little bile over.

She pushed down the doubt, the fear, and walked to the bed, locking her facial expression down and touching him for the first time since she'd closed the cuffs.

"Would it wake him up?" Eden asked, running her fingers along his thigh, up to the edge of the camouflage-colored shorts she'd bought just for him. If the woman at the store had any idea they were for a monster, she'd have probably suggested another color. But they were the only ones that would fit someone as broad and muscular as Hyde.

"You're going to have to do better than that to find out."

She tugged the shorts down, his erection freed and ready. Her tongue moved out of the way just in time for her teeth to slam together. *Calm. Control. Don't throw up.* She could do this. To get Mitch back, she would do worse things. If there were any.

"That's the spirit," he growled.

"Is he in there with you?" Whatever he said might be a lie, another manipulation to weigh. But she had to take the chance.

"He's buried as deep inside me as I'm going to be in you. So get to it."

She caressed him lightly, knowing it would piss him off. Hopefully he'd be annoyed enough to tell her something, or Mitch would return before this went any further. If not, she'd keep going, praying that she'd walk away knowing more than she did now.

And then she'd deal with the shame.

She cleared her throat so her voice wouldn't betray her. "As much as I enjoy our time together and as impressive as your dick is, I want to be with *him*. Could you call him back? Just a little bit. So that you both can have me?"

"I think you'd be more disappointed if I did. 'Cause he might not be interested." He sneered, lifting his hips up, pressing himself into her hand. "Take off your fucking clothes."

She kept her reaction to herself as she pulled off her underwear, keeping her dress down. Because he'd just admitted it was possible, and if it was possible, then all she had to do was find a way. And how hard could that be?

Really, *really* hard.

"Let me smell them."

She stopped, her underwear still in her hand, unable to find a happy enough 'happy place' to stay in, wishing this wasn't happening, wishing Mitch would save her again, wishing Hyde didn't exist. But he did. And she couldn't rely on anyone but herself.

"I'll do this," she said, "but only if you tell me about him."

A feigned look of sadness appeared on his face. "And I thought you wanted me for *me*. Whaa."

"Is he inside you? Can you sense him there?" When he didn't answer, she touched him again, her leg brushing his thigh.

"Let me see your tits."

Her stomach turned. How could he be part of the best man she'd ever known? "First tell me."

He blew out a breath of air, his body flattening against the mattress instead of reaching towards her. "I'm not going to tell you shit until I get something."

"Quid pro quo, Clarisse?"

"Huh?"

"Right. You don't get out much, do you?"

"I have all I need here." Though he shared a body with Mitch, they were so different. Hyde had none of the softness, the love and the care that Mitch showed her. This was how Mitch had always seen himself—cruel, vicious, evil. But he was so wrong.

"If I agree to this," she said, stalling, still hoping she could find a way out of it, "how do I know you'll tell me anything?"

"Because I can't move. Because you can. Ask whatever questions you want while you ride me. And if I don't answer, then you'll get off...before I have a chance to. And I want to get off. Really fucking badly."

She relaxed her jaw when she tasted blood, freeing her lip from between her teeth. "That's not good enough. Tell me something *now*."

His brow and biceps tightened and then relaxed completely. She waited silently until he spoke. "Your boy doesn't understand it because he pretends I don't exist when he's in the front seat. But I *do*. I watch everything he does. I accept him. And I want everything he has. Now it's your turn."

"That's not enough."

"I know how it works between us. And I remember things he's probably blocked out. Because he's too fucking weak."

"He was strong enough to keep you down for a very, very long time."

His mouth tightened. "That cunt, Jolie, helped. But I'll admit the asshole's got his talents. Just like I got mine. I said it's your turn."

Her legs shook as she moved to straddle him. He was so big, her knees might not even be able to touch the mattress. Unless she was flush to him, unless he was inside of her.

Oh God. How had Jolie done it? If she loved Mitch like she'd claimed to, how could she have used Hyde as a substitute? Eden tried to understand what Jolie might have been thinking or feeling. But the only thing going through her mind was that there was no way she could keep going.

For him. You'll do it for him. She threw her leg over him as if she were mounting a horse. *To get him back, you'll do whatever you have to.* Her foot came down just in time to avoid falling on top of him.

He twisted his hips, brushing his cock on her calf.

"If you move again, this is over"—her voice was so shaky, so filled with fear—"and I'm walking out. Got it?"

"So you expect me to just starfish it?" He wiggled his feet and hands as much as the cuffs allowed. "Already happening. But if you think I'm not going to move everything I can once I feel that pussy around my cock, you're in an alternate universe, baby."

She cleared her throat. Her fear wasn't helping. The deal was already struck, so it was better to go into it with strength, not terror. Control, not weakness. "The only way this happens is if you do what I say you do. And that means no moving at all." So that she could focus on disappearing, on pretending it wasn't happening, or maybe clenching her eyes tight enough to be able to imagine it was Mitch underneath her and not Hyde. She jumped up on the mattress before her courage waned too much, standing over him with a foot on each side of his hips.

"I need an incentive. Tell me what you know about him."

He smiled up at her. "How about the incentive of feeling my cock so far inside of you, you'll never be satisfied with anything less."

"Yeah, that's not going to work. Unless you're trying to incent me to throw up."

"Oh, my little peach," he said in his cruel falsetto. "Don't be afraid. I won't hurt you…unless you loosen the chains."

"Your threats are such a turn-on."

He chuckled and made a sound from deep in his chest, almost like the purr of a wild cat after a large meal. "Take off your dress and I'll tell you how it works between him and me. How different it is this time. How I always used to feel him just under my skin, wanting to wake up, but this time…" He waited, one eyebrow raised.

She yanked her dress over her head and dropped it on the

floor, wishing it was her falling there instead. With her hands on her hips, she looked down at him, watching his eyes dart all over her body, stopping in one expected place before moving to another. She inched her feet in closer to keep her legs from shaking, using his hips for support. It was either that or tumble down on top of him.

"Well?" she said impatiently.

"Well...now I envy the bastard. How many times has he had you?"

If she lost it, all of this would be for nothing. And she wasn't sure she could live with that.

She took a deep breath and closed her eyes. Withdrawing from him, the room, this moment, she looked for the void inside her. A place that held no fear, no emotion, no doubt. Her empty place—a gift enhanced by Chastity but created by others.

She hadn't thought she would ever need it again, but it was still there for her—the protective void where she felt nothing, saw nothing, *was* nothing.

"Tell me about this time." Her voice held no inflection or fear or pain. "What's different?"

"This time he's awake. And he's deeper. So deep I don't even feel like he's part of me sometimes. So deep that sometimes I stop hearing his screams."

She clenched her eyes tighter, trying to hold on. But the grief she'd felt for the last eight days grew beyond what she could handle. It was all she could do to cut her whimper off before Hyde heard it. If he wasn't here, she would let herself cry. A thousand tears, a million. Until what was left of her soul was completely gone.

"Hey, wake up," he said. Then he called her a few degrading names he probably thought were endearing until she opened her eyes again. "He isn't gone entirely. You want him back? Stop his pain? Then maybe we can work something out. But I like being out of the pit, and letting him take over would mean giving up a lot. So I need proof you're in."

"Standing here naked isn't proof?"

"Not enough."

She didn't know if he was telling the truth, if he would really let Mitch take over. But options weren't something she had a lot of. Mitch had come back when she needed him before. He could do it again. He would fight his way back to her before anything actually happened.

He will.

Her quads trembled as she started to bend her knees. She couldn't look at his erection, didn't want to see it or feel it push inside her.

She understood the mercy of facing away from the blade of the guillotine. When there is no escaping something, it's better not to see it coming.

"I need proof too," she said. "Give me something so I know you're not just conning me." Her muscles burned from holding her legs locked in a sitting position above him with nothing to hold onto.

No, that wasn't right. She was holding onto something. In her mind, she held onto Mitch and he gave her strength. He would come back. But would it be in time?

Please, Mitch. Come back to me. Come—

"He's here with us, my pretty little bitch. Come on down and maybe you'll feel him too. Or maybe he just wants to watch."

She knew Hyde had said it as a sick, twisted tool of seduction, but his words did exactly the opposite. She froze, knocked out of the void, almost seeing Mitch's face. She'd thought it would make her stronger, but imagining his expression as she took Hyde inside of her brought her nothing but shame.

What the hell am I doing? In her mind's eye, he looked furious. Maddened beyond belief that she would share something that was his, *theirs*, with someone else, let alone the thing he detested most.

Weakened and miserable, she stood up and opened her

eyes just to stop seeing Mitch's wrath. His disappointment. If she went through with this, he would never forgive her. Never forgive himself. Neither one of them would ever be the same.

She couldn't betray Mitch any more than she already had. He might be watching her from inside Hyde right now, seeing what she was doing but not understanding that she was doing it for him. Feeling betrayed. The thought tied her stomach into a knot, her brain into another. She couldn't do it.

I'm sorry, Mitch. Though she wasn't sure if she was apologizing for how far she'd gone or that she couldn't go further—either way she was letting him down.

She jumped off the mattress and grabbed her dress from the floor, disgusted with herself for how close she'd come to giving away something only Mitch deserved.

She was his. Only his.

"Are we moving too fast?" The condescension dripped from his words. "Should I tell you that I love you and have never seen a more beautiful ass? And that if I could, I would lay out a bed of roses and tell you all about your love and how to bring him back from the pit of hell." His smile was wicked and made what was normally a truly stunning face ugly and hateful. "And then I'd fuck that tight ass and listen to you scream out to your God for mercy."

She held her dress in front of her. "Is that your version of foreplay?"

"You want him, then you take me." His fury was apparent in a simple exhalation. "Fine. Then if you're too afraid to sit on it, suck it."

"You say the sweetest things." She rolled her eyes, her voice gaining strength as she came back into herself. But she kept her words and her movements very calm, very controlled. "How can I say no? Oh right, like this: *No.*"

As she left the cage, she ignored the curses and the names he called her. They were nothing new.

And they were nothing she wouldn't call herself.

CHAPTER II

The water ran down Eden's face, blurring her vision, creating a shield against the world outside. But she couldn't hide in the shower forever. There were things to prepare, a man to save, answers to find...somehow.

By the time she'd washed away Hyde's scent, Landon was back. She avoided his eyes, as if looking directly at him would expose what she'd done. It was the same reason she hadn't looked in the mirror while brushing her hair and teeth—she was afraid of what she'd see.

"I can't stay long," Landon said, scratching his eight-day-old goatee. Between that and the worn-down expression, he looked like a different man. "I'm meeting an old cop friend. Hopefully I'll find out if there's been any movement on anything." He followed her into the brothel's tiny kitchen. "Of course, if you ever answered your phone, I could've told you that on my way there."

"I need to keep myself busy." In a different way than Landon.

Because he was able to blend in better than she was and still had a few contacts in the police department, he did the legwork—talking to people and checking out the apartment

Carter had lived in while he worked for the people who caused his death, stuff like that. And like a good little wife, Eden stayed home to take care of Hyde, mix up most of the injectables, and do the Internet research.

They were both in charge of the most important job—mindlessly staring at the unreadable files Landon had grabbed from The Clinic's facility. As if suddenly one of them would be able to understand the jargon and codes. Of course they would.

Eden flipped through the files. Again. Files she'd practically memorized, telling her a whole lot of nothing useful. But she was grateful Landon had thought to take them. Eden's blinders had been tightly focused on finding a drug that might bring Mitch back. And without the documents, they'd know even less than the minuscule amount they *did* know.

She skipped over the ones in Carter's file that mentioned her—notes he'd taken when she thought he was her best friend, her greatest supporter. She pushed aside the envelope with his confession in it. The asshole had apologized in a *letter*. That was addressed to Landon, someone he barely knew, instead of her. Maybe because a stranger would be the only person who could possibly forgive him.

Landon leaned against the counter. "I'm not judging. You can hang out upstairs and stare at him all you want. Just keep your phone with you so I can reach you if I need to."

"Understood." *And moving on.* "When I was going down the list of pharmaceuticals from the files, there was one that kept coming up." She spread out a bunch of pages to find the right one. "Glycusaminamine-121 or something."

"I think that's an over-the-counter cold medication," he said, smiling.

"Whatever. Anyway, it's hardly a smoking gun, but there's a fight over who owns it. Somebody named Danvers mentioned it in a medical journal and then a university freaked out, claiming the drug was theirs." She ran her hands through her hair. "Of course, a bunch of labs are testing the other drugs we're looking at. So, basically, the only way we'll know anything is if one of us gets a PhD in bullshit decoding."

"I'm guessing none of the labs are named 'The Clinic,' either. How many are there and are any of them in Florida?"

"Five and no. Two are umbrellaed under a company named Malvers Labs in Washington and Texas. Then two individual ones in California and...somewhere in the middle. Indiana? Iowa? I wrote it down here somewhere."

Unfortunately, organization was something neither she nor Chastity excelled at. Too bad she didn't have *three* sides that blended—the good, the bad, and the one suffering from a severe case of OCD. Shove them all together and she'd be a hell of a gal.

"I doubt they will lead anywhere," she said. "The drug isn't approved for human testing. And anyway, I don't think The Clinic would want public credit for anything they've done. So the chance that they'd fight to claim it...?" She shook her head. "Not high."

Whoever was in charge at The Clinic was a genius with lying, secrets, and doping people without their consent. Sure, their motives were still fuzzy, but it probably wasn't to win the Nobel Peace Prize.

"Considering how little we actually have to do," Landon said, "I'll try to speak to them. Maybe my detective tone will work better than your..." He rubbed his lips together.

"My what?"

He hesitated, as if he couldn't find a word that wouldn't be insulting. "Your detached one."

She lowered her head so he wouldn't see her expression. He thought she was detached? Then he had no idea. Every cell in her body was engaged, filled with this moment, this situation, this ordeal. She couldn't be more connected to its outcome.

She wasn't sure if it was a good or a bad thing to be hiding her emotions so well. All she knew was that as long as Mitch was in his cage, she was in hers. Solid bars around her chest and body, holding her up, making her strong enough to stand. Until he was free. *Then* she'd worry about her emotions.

"Whatever," she said, once her moment of pathetic self-reflection was over. Seriously not helpful. Examining her feelings only made her weak, just like regret and fear did. And she didn't have time for weakness. Later maybe. Much, much later. "Any information is a good thing, I guess. Because I used up all my brilliant ideas when I suggested Chinese food last night."

"That was a brilliant idea, though." He gave her a pity smile. "Did you shoot him up already?"

She nodded. "With a much higher dose."

"And…?"

"And nothing. Absolutely no reaction." She shrugged. "Well, he got a hard-on, but that's not new. Although he made a sarcastic comment that I haven't already heard a dozen times, so my fingers are crossed that it was Mitch's creativity coming through."

Landon tossed a bottle of water to her. "I was going over scenarios on the way here. You know, what he'll be like if he comes out of it."

"When."

"On the way here."

She shook her head. "You said, *'if* he comes out of it.'"

He took a long swig of his water. Long enough to create a silence so dead, Eden's mind started to drift to places she never allowed. What if he was right the first time—if instead of when? What would she do if Mitch never returned? Keep him caged for the rest of his life? Be chained to him, reality killing both of them little by little?

"Right," he said, nodding. "*When* he comes out of it."

She and Landon didn't really talk anymore. Not unless it was about their current troubles. Everything had become so serious and unfriendly, and it was completely her fault.

But it's really hard to be lighthearted when your heart is

broken. When every moment of the day is painful. When a constant reminder of all you've lost is chained up in the next room.

When you have a hard time believing someone respects you...because you aren't sure there's anything left inside you that deserves respect.

But none of that was Landon's fault. So she took a sip of water and tried to shake off the angst. Because *nobody* likes an angsty Abnormal.

Then she said, "So tell me your scenarios."

"The best one I came up with was that he comes back and Hyde is truly gone."

"I love it."

"Yeah, but the funny part would be if he was so gone that Turner was actually nice. Polite. Not sarcastic. Think about it. Without the bad jokes and moodiness, he'd be a hell of a lot easier to live with." He waited, possibly until she smiled back.

She tried. She really did. And she knew he was just trying to make a crack in the wall between them, but he was missing the point of why they were doing this by at least three miles.

"I like the old Mitch."

"I do too," he said quickly. "I didn't mean anything by it."

She blew out a breath. "Sorry. Neither did I." She was being too sensitive. Too bitchy. Landon was amazing, and she would end up pushing him away if she wasn't careful. So she forced a smile. Because as long as he helped her, it didn't matter if he didn't understand. To not know who you are. To wake up being someone else. It wasn't smile worthy. Not even a little.

"We'll find a way to bring him back, Eden."

She nodded. "The real him. Not a faux version. He's in there, Landon, crying out for help. And we're the only ones who can help him."

"We're the only people who *will* help him. You were right—it's a 'when,' not an 'if.' I'm sure of it." Bless him for sounding so confident, so much like she did most of the time.

But being so close to Hyde had made her weak. She'd betrayed Mitch by touching his evil, teasing it. Even if intent mattered, her actions left her feeling used, dirty, and traitorous.

Not exactly good for the old morale.

"I went to see Fields' new place," Landon said. "And yes, I took the long way."

"It's never even crossed my mind that you wouldn't." They couldn't risk leaving a trail to where Fields had taken his daughter Alicia, Justin, and a few other Abnormals who needed a safe place to transform every few days.

"He's got a nice setup there. Not surprisingly, the security is great, but he wanted me to test it. A gated community can't stop anyone halfway determined, but the house itself is impressive. He's still planning on moving out of state, though."

"He told me the last time we spoke," she said. "How are Justin and Alicia?" She hadn't seen any of them since that night and she missed them, Justin especially. Seeing the pain in his eyes when she had told him the truth about Alex had created both a permanent bond and a little pocket in her heart. A Justin-sized pocket was about all it could hold. She'd already given the rest away.

"It's a good thing Fields got that long nap, because, more than likely, it will never happen again. Not with teenagers around." It had been touch and go with Fields for the first few days. Since the narcotic Alex had injected him with was meant for Eden, their prize broodmare, it wasn't lethal. But it was still a huge dose, drawn up for an Abnormal.

"I don't know how Fields hasn't killed one of them yet," Landon said. "It probably helps that he's got enough Velcro straps in the place to hold half of Fort Lauderdale down.

"Oh, and Fields remembered another one of the scientists' names. Dr. Lou Bradford." He took a folded piece of paper out of his pocket and smoothed it out against the wall. "Dr. Bradford wasn't an easy guy to find."

Hardly surprising. Eden didn't have much hope in the list of names Fields had given them. As soon as the facility had gone down, every guard and scientist must have run for it. But some of them didn't run fast enough. So far, all Landon had found was a lot of empty apartments and a few dead bodies.

"But..." Landon said. "I found him."

Her hopes shot up...

"In the Everglades. With a hole in his head the size of a 9mm bullet. Not self-inflicted."

...and then plummeted right back down.

"So, the case will probably be closed soon," he grumbled. "Because obviously, he was shot in self-defense by an alligator."

"It happens...in cartoons." Yes, the death toll was mounting, but she couldn't focus on that. Those guards had known what they were doing, what kind of people they were working for. The whole 'we don't kill people' thing had either *never* been true or was yet another rule that had changed. It was a good thing they'd never claimed to not have people raped, because then they'd have to admit they weren't angels.

"With the gator victim out"—he crossed the name off his list—"we have one more shot. Dr. Steve Harris. But he's in really deep—I haven't found anything on the guy. No house, no life. Just a name."

All she wanted was someone who could tell her how to bring Mitch back. But somehow The Clinic was in complete darkness and everyone who worked for them did it blind. Because if they could see, they would see the truth. Fields did it to protect his daughter. Eden understood how love could make you do things you wouldn't otherwise, but she doubted the rest of the employees could use that excuse.

"How can that many people avoid asking any questions for so long? No one wondered what they hell they were part of?"

"Responsibility is a funny thing. Something I learned a long time ago is: If you're not ready to hear the answer, then don't ask the question. Because once you know, you might have to do something about it."

Eden nodded. They all either hadn't asked the question or had asked the wrong one. And they each paid for it differently.

Landon wasn't much closer to the truth about his girlfriend, Tara, but his career and his pride had been stripped away and replaced with danger. Fields' daughter, Alicia, had been raped in the name of twisted science, and both of them were dealing with the aftermath of that truth. Justin was just a sixteen-year-old kid who believed The Clinic was trying to help him, and the wound caused by that deception would probably never heal. And because Carter closed his eyes to what he was doing to Eden and then what The Clinic was doing to him, he had paid for it with his life.

Eden was no different, no wiser or savvier. She had gone back to them with no idea of what they really wanted, thinking that if she played their game, Mitch would be okay. And look where that had gotten them—in a worse place than where they had started.

They all should've made better choices. But all of that was in the past, so it didn't matter. Only what was real, what was happening today mattered. None of them were who they'd been a week ago, and change wasn't always good.

Eden thought she heard someone yell and shushed Landon.

"What?" he asked, immediately palming his weapon and looking at the door.

"I heard something."

They waited a moment, both listening intently.

"It must have been Hyde," Landon said, putting his gun back in its holster.

"No, I don't even notice that anymore." She held her hand out to stop Landon from talking. After another minute, she relaxed. "It was probably just the voices in my head."

CHAPTER III

Mitch's back arched through the agony. It felt like he was being pulled out of quicksand...if quicksand had teeth.

He was proof that, yes, a tree *would* make a sound even when no one was in the forest. Because he'd screamed for what seemed like years. But he couldn't do it anymore—there was nothing left inside him. He was hollowed out, unable to breathe, to think, to feel anything other than pain. So unlike the good old days when he could nap through Hyde's turn with their body.

And then the pain stopped. So quickly, he didn't trust it. The demons were probably just teasing him with a moment of relief while they geared up for something else. He waited, unmoving, knowing that when it hit, it would be even worse than before.

Any second now.

Or now.

Or—*please, just let it be over.*

When he dared open his eyes, he saw a dark ceiling. Then the bars. Then the mattress he was lying on. Soft. Hard cuffs on his wrists and ankles, but a soft mattress. And a fucking pillow—thin and cheap and the most amazing thing he'd ever felt. Almost.

"Holy. Shit." He lay there for a few more minutes, or maybe an hour, who knew? Time wasn't something he could grasp any better than he could figure out if this was real or not. It felt real, looked real.

In fact, it looked just like that ugly-ass brothel Landon had taken them to years ago, back when Mitch was human. The last time he'd held Eden in his arms. Yeah, it had been years, hadn't it? *Had* to have been years.

If this was even real.

After another chunk of time—minutes or hours or decades—Mitch decided there was a definite possibility that he wasn't insane, this wasn't a mirage, and this *was* the same shithole he remembered. The place they'd gone after The Clinic's assholes broke into his house and tased the crap out of him.

He yanked against the cuffs, shaking as if he was still being tased. Not surprisingly, there was no way out. Because his karma sucked shit. He should've worked on that more before everything went to hell. Literally.

Give it up, asshole. You know what's more pathetic than flopping around on your back, knowing you have zero chance of getting loose? Nothing. Nothing is more pathetic than that. He took a few deep breaths, giving himself a moment to contemplate which arm he should gnaw off first.

He would give anything to have his hands free. Except his cock. *That* he'd like to keep, just in case he was ever lucky enough to need it again. But his head was going to explode any minute, and all he wanted was to push against the pain. At least he was somewhere warm, somewhere different than where he'd been—an unknown place for an unknown amount of time.

There might even be a chance he was alive. And if he was, hopefully it would continue. Of course, that was something that seemed to be out of his control lately. But his body and his mind were his own—no pain from Hyde, no physical reminders other than the headache.

Maybe the bastard threw our head into the wall a few dozen times. Yeah, that sounded about right. Sad. Because it was a perfectly good head. The stuff inside of it was shit, but the head itself was fine.

When he heard the door slam into the wall, he lifted his head. *Fuck that hurts.* But it was worth it. Because he saw *her*. His love. His life. His afterlife.

Oh shit. Maybe he really *was* dead. Sure, it was still a shitload better than the last place he'd been, but how motherfucking ironic to be strapped down in hell, too. With her image just across the room to torture him. Damn it, that was so poetic he wanted to kill someone. Again. He closed his eyes, because he was too much of a wuss to deal with it.

Open wide and take it, asshole. When he did, she was unlocking the cage door, staring at him. Her expression was unidentifiable, stoic, blank, but the tears running down her cheeks stung.

"Don't cry, babe."

She didn't listen to him. In fact, she did just the opposite. More tears, redder eyes.

"Is this real?" he whispered.

She nodded but said nothing as she undid the cuffs binding his wrists and ankles.

Being free was great, but his muscles still weren't happy...or unusable. As if he'd been in the same position for so long, they'd forgotten what they were for. The universe had a sick sense of humor—Congrats, you're back! And free! *But*...you can't move and there's a good chance this is all just a mirage.

"Can you say something, please?" he asked. "So I know I'm not just imagining this? 'Cause I'm pretty sure I told Landon to kill me."

"I..." She swallowed. "I didn't let him."

"Huh. I forgot how beautiful you are. But even *that* doesn't excuse your crappy judgment."

"Shut up."

When she kissed him, he came to life. Because there was no way in hell the devil would allow him this. He wanted nothing more than to put his arms around her and never let go, never eat, never think, never live anything but her ever again. And if he could have moved, that's exactly what he would've done.

Thankfully, she helped by throwing her leg over and straddling him, never letting her lips leave his. The moistness of her mouth, the fierceness of her kiss gave him strength to finally lift his arms and wrap them around her. Perfect enough to pretend that the *severe* case of pins and needles in every part of his body was just the devil giving him a little acupuncture.

"God, I hope that's really him," Landon said from across the room.

"It is." She pushed through Mitch's weak hold, climbed off, and helped him sit up, her eyes lowered the entire time.

"Am I really here?" When Mitch had let Hyde out of the gate, he assumed it would be for good. Or for evil, in sickness and in heath, i.e., forever. So it was probably normal he was having a little trouble figuring out what was happening. Or a *lot* of trouble figuring out what was happening.

"It seems so," Landon said, grinning ear to ear like a prepubescent girl at a boy band concert. A prepubescent girl who had a goatee.

Mitch stood on shaky legs, still doubting this was real. But he'd take it any way he could—her arm around him, his best friend looking shocked and happy, no cuffs. Yeah, he'd take it. Not even heaven could be this nice. So until his flesh started peeling off or purple mushrooms danced through the door, he'd take it for reality and be content.

"I like the facial fuzz, cop. It covers a lot of your face." He ungracefully staggered out of the cage, smiling. "So are you just going to stand there or come over here and give me some sugar?"

Landon grimaced and glanced at Eden.

"What? She's not the jealous type," Mitch said, nudging her side and then letting his hands wander wherever they may. "Are you?"

"It might not bother her, but the idea sure as shit is freaking *me* out."

"It's your turn." Eden pushed Mitch into the cop's arms. "But I get him right back."

What started out as something for balance turned into a sincere-but-not-too-weird hug, kind of like Mitch imagined brothers would do. Made sense. Good comparison. Constant fighting, except when a bigger threat showed up. Then it was time to shut their mouths long enough to kick some ass. Which reminded him…

"Hey, asshole," he whispered. "While I'm glad to see you, you were supposed to fry my ass with the Taser." Not that he minded not being dead, but it was a risk he hadn't wanted them to take. "I thought my directions were very clear on that. So what happened?"

The cop pulled back and then nodded towards Eden. "*She* did."

"You're going to let a girl push you around? Bros before—" *Everything but her.*

She smacked him on the arm.

"I was kidding, babe. It's just part of the cop's and my witty repartee."

"Can we repartee from farther away?" Landon asked. "Because you stink, my friend."

"Damn, I was hoping that was you." He looked up at the ceiling. "Please tell me the bastard didn't shit himself. Because if he did, I need you to strangle me to death and forget I was ever here."

"You're in luck," Landon said, chuckling. "I have no idea how his metabolism works, but he doesn't expel waste at all. He sweats—"

"Great news and let's stop talking about it." He tilted his

head toward Eden. "I want her to keep thinking I'm as hot as you do."

"Oh yeah, that. It lasted right up until I met you." He turned to Eden. "Do you remember how much you gave him?"

"I wrote it down."

"We should make up some of the same dose right away since we don't know how long this one will keep him pretty."

"You think I'm pretty?"

Landon groaned. "Now that he's back, can we sedate him?"

Mitch practiced using different muscles while they discussed dosages and filled in little snippets of information he should probably be paying attention to.

He still felt *apart* from what was happening, still afraid to believe it. He'd spent the last who knew how long living inside a fairly horrific dream. Giving in to Hyde had given Mitch one moment of pure relief, of overwhelming peace. And then the pain kicked in. Like he was being devoured by piranhas from the inside. Like they were hollowing him out, leaving only his skin. And his pain receptors, of course. Wouldn't want to get rid of those. And it never stopped.

The pain could be handled. It wasn't as much fun as having your fingernails yanked out and he'd sure like to avoid going through it again, but he could deal. His life had always been painful—from all directions.

But the most traumatic part was being able to see things and not understand them. Thinking it was reality but not believing it was real. A complete mindfuck—so emotionally draining, the physical pain affected him more.

It was almost like watching a movie from the electric chair. Sometimes it was a horror flick and other times it was a really fucking tragic drama, with tears and other girlie crap. He hated both kinds. Because he couldn't stop himself from yelling at the characters when they made a lousy decision or didn't see what was coming for them. And yelling was useless.

They never hear you. And even if they could, they'd never

listen.

Now it was different, more like a waking dream. One he couldn't quite get a handle on or trust. His memory of that other place was already fading, though. Maybe his mind was finally getting something right—forget about the bad stuff, 'cause that shit isn't healthy to keep around.

Things were fuzzy in this world, too, blurred and out of focus. But every second brought more clarity. And Eden was here, so it was a whole lot better than death. He detested how disgustingly sappy he felt. *Back off, idiot. You're being clingy.* She was going to regret giving him the dose that worked. But he couldn't stop looking at her, touching her, just to make sure she was real and tangible and by his side.

"What are you smiling at?" she asked with a smile of her own.

"I don't know where to begin." He had a second chance. No matter what happened now, no matter what drugs he had to take, he'd do it. Because she was worth anything. *Everything.* And nothing would make him fuck this up. Including him.

"How about we start with food?" she asked. "Are you hungry?"

He thought about it. "Very. Need a shower too. And someone to scrub my back—someone who isn't Landon. Sorry, man."

"I'd do a lot for you, asshole, but I got my limits. And touching your naked body is at the top of my 'Things I'll Never Do' list."

Mitch turned to Eden. "Then can I count on you?"

"Touching your naked body is at the top of my 'Things I'm *Dying* to Do' list."

"Excellent. Although I may not be up for much more than that. I feel like I just got back from a too-long vacation in hell. And it was nothing like you'd imagine—no heavy metal, cloven hoofs, or sulfur-scented morning breath."

A look of concern passed over her face, her arms falling to

her sides. "What do you remember?"

Shit. Downplay, man. Downplay. Because there was a good chance he was going back there, and he didn't want her to have anything else to worry about. She already looked so damn fatigued. As if she'd felt everything he had.

"Completely different than anything I've ever felt before, but it wasn't too bad." He shrugged. "No picnics or barbecues." Unless you counted the times it felt like he had a skewer up his ass and was on a spit being roasted alive. "But not too bad."

"Anything else?"

"Just images. Feelings. But they didn't quite touch me, if that makes sense. I was just an observer and felt...detached." A simple explanation that meant nothing at all. What he'd felt was empty. Dark. Cold. Like he was falling down an endless hole with no 'eat me/drink me' signs, no red queens, and no white fucking rabbits. But he didn't want to tell her that. *Couldn't* tell her that.

She lowered her head and sighed. A long, relieved sigh that made him anything but. It set him on edge for a reason he didn't quite understand. He lifted her chin and looked into her eyes, ones that he trusted and knew. Didn't he? Did anyone ever know anyone? Something was missing. They were open without being open, as if she was hiding something.

"What happened?" he asked quietly, brushing her cheek. "What'd I miss?"

When Landon cleared his throat loudly, Eden shied away from Mitch's hand, turning towards the cop.

"I want to be out of here before you guys have a happy reunion that will probably take a few hours. So let's take care of business."

"Good idea." Without making sure Mitch followed, she left the room. There was no *'I want to hold your hand'* or even *'Because you're such a weakling, I'll help you get down the stairs.'* Something had definitely happened and he needed to know what that something was. The conversation might have to wait, but they would have it.

"How long was I him?" he asked Landon, taking each stair like a hundred-and-fifty-year-old man would.

"Eight days."

Eight days. Making it officially the longest week he'd ever spent in hell.

"We plan for every contingency," she said as soon as they were downstairs. "He's back, but we don't know if it's permanent." She spoke differently—more matter of fact, less emotion. But then again, the last time he'd seen her was in the middle of a high-stress couple of days, so what the hell did he know?

Well, he knew she'd never felt this distant before. Neither one of them was in a cage, but there was empty space between them. That didn't happen. At least, it didn't *used* to happen.

He pulled her towards him. "I was out for eight days and you guys didn't hogtie every Clinic employee, make up a PowerPoint presentation of answers, and bake me a 'Welcome Home' cake? What the fuck have you been doing?"

"Unsuccessfully attempting all of the above," Landon said. "And looking for another place to stay. It's too risky to stay in South Florida. But if Hyde comes back, we need a place to hold him, and that complicates things."

He nodded. "The cage is a 'just in case he gets through one system' thing. If we can't duplicate it somewhere else, we should have a plan B." He should've set something up, back when time wasn't such an issue, back when he had no idea he was being doped and manipulated. Another cage in another locale.

It was almost funny how ill prepared he was, how content to spend the rest of his life believing what he believed and thinking he was untouchable. Funny, but not enough to laugh. More like, funny enough to slap yourself repeatedly, hoping like hell you're not the idiot you used to be.

"Enough chain will hold him down," Mitch said, "provided he's on a sturdy surface. So a big truck would work.

Thread some heavy-duty chain through holes in the floor and attach them to the truck's frame. It'll be just like home. A mobile home." He cocked his head. "A shitty mobile home."

"I should've thought of that." Eden stared at him with those big beautiful eyes of hers. "Why didn't I think of that?"

"Don't feel bad, babe. Even if you hadn't spent the last week babysitting the big, mean guy, I still have you beat by about ten years."

"As long as you have"—Landon rubbed his fingers together in the international sign for 'the green stuff everyone wants and no one ever seems to have enough of'—"you're useful. We're tapped. And yes, I tried to get into your account, but the password didn't work."

"Your skills are slipping, cop." Mitch took his cell phone from Landon's outstretched hand. "My hint wasn't big enough for you?"

"Your favorite four-letter word, right. But I tried 'fuck' and it didn't work. Then I tried 'Eden.'"

Mitch gave him a look, a mixture between doubt and WTF? "First off, I'm not that sappy." He opened the bank app. "Second, I'm not that organized—it was set up years ago and I never changed it. And third, I never said it was my *favorite* four letters." He winked at Eden, feeling a stupid-ass smirk of adoration on his face, but unable to avoid it. What'd he expect? Cold and aloof? He'd just gotten back from hell—it made sense he was still feeling a bit warm.

"You gonna tell us or what?" Landon asked impatiently.

Mitch spoke each letter as he punched them in. "E-V-I-L."

Landon chuckled. "Money is the root of all..."

"You got it." He handed the phone back to Landon. "Since there's a good chance I will be indisposed, big, and beastly soon, you should set up your own account, something they won't already be tracking, and transfer a lot into it. Actually, set up a couple—different names at different banks. And as soon as possible, take out as much cash as you can without throwing up any flags."

Landon's eyes widened when he looked at the phone. "You keep *that* much in cash?"

"Dude, I'm a monster. Setting up a retirement plan has never been a priority. So…are we done with the business portion of the day?"

"We need to powwow about what happens next."

"Can it wait a little while?" Mitch asked. "I got someone I need to do."

Landon's mouth closed, stopping whatever he was about to say as Mitch's words sank in. "Some*one*." Then he tilted his head, a sour look on his face.

When you come back from death, every moment matters. And as much as Mitch knew they needed to leave here, as much as he wanted them to be safe, he wanted Eden more. To feel alive. He wasn't asking for forever, just a little time. Putting off the move until he could reconnect with her wouldn't kill anyone. So, with his eyes, he asked the cop for his help. Again. To allow him this moment with her.

Landon wiped a hand across his face and then nodded. "We'll reconvene later."

"I think we should talk now," Eden said. Both men looked at her quizzically. Her whole body was tense, on edge, as if she expected the worst to happen within the next few seconds.

To say Mitch was disappointed would be like calling the sun a campfire, but he could deal with it. After all, while he was in hell, unsure about what was real and what wasn't, she was walking through it entirely aware.

"I'll set up the accounts." Landon glanced at his watch. "Shit, I'm late for my meeting. Hopefully, Joe will give us something to go on. But now that you're back, all our goals have changed. We still need a long-term solution, but we're a lot closer to the top of the mountain. So we can take it slower and be more careful."

Could they *do* 'slow' and 'careful'?

"I should go with you." As much as Mitch wanted to call it a night and crawl into bed with Eden, Landon shouldn't be the only one doing something. And right about now, Mitch was severely lacking on the 'getting shit done without making things worse' front.

Landon spoke with one eyebrow higher than the other. "I'm just talking to a friend, so no babysitter necessary. Plus, you look like shit. I'm going to blame it on the last eight days...*this* time. Take a little time to recover."

"But—"

"Do you think there's a bar chart somewhere with our names on it, so we can keep track of who does what? Whose bar is the tallest? If there is, then I think you're ahead. Because *I* didn't tell you to off me if a monster didn't do it first so that you'd be safe. That was you."

"I also fucked a lot of stuff up that put you in positions you wouldn't have been in."

"If you want to keep on living, never say 'fucked' and talk about positions you've put me in." He smiled. "I'm a big boy, Turner. I look before I jump, especially when I'm with you. Because I know who I am and I know who you are. All I'm doing is meeting a friend. Not a big deal. Not something I need a partner for. Understood?"

"Understood. For now." But there might come a time when that bar chart looked a lot different than it did right now.

"While you're gone," Eden said, "I'll fill him in and look for a truck."

While Landon and Eden spoke about plans for the day, their phones, and normal shit, Mitch stewed in his thoughts, still watching things from a distance, as if he no longer belonged. Here or anywhere else.

He knew he'd been out of it, knew he'd missed a lot, but something wasn't right. She wouldn't look at him. Her hand was limp in his, and her body was stiff. Everything they felt for each other couldn't be gone. Not in a few days. Not in a few *years*. The kind of love they had lingered, changed you, implanted itself in your soul for the rest of your life.

"Right?" she asked.

"Yeah, right." He wasn't sure how much of their conversation he missed while he was freaking out about what he might have missed. *Very productive, idiot. Highly impressive.* He redirected his mind to what she was saying.

"I know they're good at covering things up," Eden said, "but it would take a lot of shovels to scoop up what was left of Hyde01."

Mitch gawked at her, not believing what she'd just said and the blasé way she'd said it. Hyde01 was her father. Mitch hadn't been able to stick around for the main event, but it couldn't have been pretty.

"A lot of shovels," he repeated, not wanting to imagine what Eden had seen him do to her dad but feeling like he should. For a half a second he wished he'd actually died, just so he didn't have to face her now.

He looked at Landon. "Did you...does she know about him?"

Landon nodded. Saying thanks would have made an impossibly awkward moment even more so. But Mitch was thankful. Having to say those words to her? Nope, he couldn't have done it. He would have stuttered, hemmed, and hawed until his lips were numb. And he still wouldn't have gotten the words out.

But he had to say something. And it better be something good. He looked at her, swallowed, and wiped his hand over his mouth. Maybe it was better that she wasn't making eye contact. No, not better—easier. For him. *Very empathetic, asshole.* Another thing he had to atone for.

"I'm...really sorry." *Yeah, not good enough.* "If there had been another way, I would've done it." *Still sucking.* "Hit me if you want to. Kick my ass." *Great, Mr. Sensitivity. Skip right to the violence—hope she doesn't believe in an eye for an eye.* "Whatever you want."

"There are so many reasons I want to kick your ass, but that isn't one of them." She looked so calm, so controlled. He almost *wanted* to see her lash out, throw something, yell something. "You did what you had to."

When your boyfriend kills the dad you never knew, it has to sting for a while. Unfortunately, it seemed like that sting was being shoved into the 'I don't want to deal with this' section of her mind.

He was emotionally unhealthy enough for both of them. She deserved better. "It doesn't change the fact that I killed your father." *Oh shit, I just said the words.* But he was more concerned about her lack of reaction than feeling her wrath. 'Cause holding that shit in was not productive. He knew. All too well. "You gotta have some feelings about that. Anger. Disappointment. Anger. Sadness. Anger. Or maybe—I don't know—anger?"

Landon shook his head at each word.

She adjusted her hair as she spoke. "You did what you had to—he was a monster."

"So am I. But he was also your father."

"He stopped being my father before I was born."

Okay, this is a problem. Mitch looked at Landon. "Has this been going on the whole time I was him?"

Landon didn't answer, his face rigid, his jaw locked. She seemed relaxed, as if they were discussing something that had no bearing on her at all.

This is a big fucking problem. "Either of you want to fill me in on what the hell's going on with you two?"

Landon threw up his hands. "We're not supposed to talk about it. But she's totally okay with what happened, no feelings about it at all." Then he slapped Mitch on the shoulder. "I'm glad you're back, man. Now *you* can deal with her." He walked to the door. "I'm surrounded by people with so many frigging issues, I'm beginning to think Carter did the right thing."

"Carter *never* did the right thing," Eden shouted to his back, the first sign of fire Mitch had seen in her.

"I meant by dying." He threw the door open. "I'm glad you're back, asshole. See you soon."

CHAPTER IV

After a minute of staring at the door Landon had just slammed behind him, Mitch turned to face her, twisting her shoulders until she did the same. "I thought he'd never leave." Because now he had a chance to find out what the fuck was wrong.

She kept her eyes lowered, as if his feet were the most interesting part about him.

"I thought that we were past the eye contact thing. Actually, that was my issue not yours. So what's wrong? Besides all of the obvious."

"It's not a big deal." She brushed past him and headed for the stairs. "I'll go start the shower for you."

He grabbed her arm to stop her, feeling small vibrations of nervousness or fear or some other emotion he didn't want her to have. "Are we lying to each other now?"

"No. I'm just...It's just hard to believe you're here and he's not."

"Okay, I get that. But don't you think we should talk about what happened to your dad? What I did to him?" No one could walk away unscathed after watching a man/beast be torn apart in front of them and then discovering it was their long-lost father.

"He wasn't my dad. He was a sperm donor. You did what you did to save me. I understand that and I'm fine."

He wasn't sure what to believe or what to say. People grieve in different ways, and the last thing someone wants is to be told they aren't doing it right.

"If you want to talk…" Empty fucking offer. As soon as the latest serum wore off, Hyde would want out. So Mitch would check himself back into the cage and wait. But if she changed her mind, maybe they could talk through the bars until the inevitable happened.

She looked up at him briefly, opening her mouth as if she was about to speak, to confess something to him, but then she clamped her lips down. "I don't."

"Really? 'Cause it looks like you have something to say."

Her hands fisted. "Not about Hyde01. About your Hyde. He—" She shook her head. "Later, okay? I'll tell you later. Can you let me go now?" As soon as he released her, she was off and running. "I'll start the shower for you."

"What did he do, Eden?" he called. She didn't answer. She didn't slow down. She didn't even look back.

What did the bastard do this time? It was always about him. Hyde. The way Mitch dealt with him wasn't the same as she and Landon had to. Mitch never had to look at him, listen to him, or take care of him.

When he heard the water start, he took the stairs slowly, giving her time and giving himself time. He didn't know what for, but it seemed like a fairly sane thing to do. And when that rare type of thought happened, he paid attention.

When he walked into the bathroom, she pulled her hand out of the steaming water. The room was larger than he imagined a brothel would need. Maybe it was another fantasy room—geishas, Dominatrix, Wild West, and…a nice big bathroom for those who want naughty and probably painful things done to them with a scrub brush. And someone had provided towels, soap, and shampoo. Damn, this place had everything you could possibly want in a dump.

"It's still a little hot," she said, scooting her ass onto the vanity.

Was she serious? Did she really think he cared about the temperature of the water?

"I'm sure it's fine." It wasn't. It was really fucking hot. But with a quick twist of a knob, he could handle it. What he couldn't handle was seeing her across the room and knowing she was keeping something from him.

"Wanna join me?"

"Maybe later."

His hand clamped down on the soap, sending it shooting up to the ceiling. But it was fine. He was fine. Completely fine. He bent down to pick it up and proceeded to wash off the stench of his own personal demon. Maybe if he didn't smell like Hyde, she would realize they weren't the same guy.

Because if there was *another* reason she wasn't looking at him, surely she would tell him. Right? He kept his voice calm while he talked about stupid, trivial things and washed his hair. She mumbled a few answers, and everything was just dandy. In another place...with other people...with other issues. But here, in this place, with these two people, nothing was dandy.

He blew out a breath, reminded himself to be patient, and then turned the water off. His lip was bleeding from the last few minutes of gnawing on it, but that was better than going outside and making someone else bleed.

She handed him a towel without looking at him. So he wrapped the towel around his waist without looking at her.

Give her some time and she will tell you about whatever it is. 'Patience is a virtue' and all that crap. He wiped the condensation off the mirror and saw his reflection. Aside from desperately needing a shave, he looked human. Not too bad. Pretty much the same as he always did. Same hazel eyes, same dark hair, same body.

"Is it the beard?" He ran his hand across his jaw.

"What?"

"Does the beard make me so ugly that you can't stand to look at me?"

She swallowed, still looking at her feet. "No, the beard's fine."

He stared at the reflection of her back for one more minute.

And then he snapped. Blame it on his extended nap, or his near-death experience, or whatever the hell had happened that he *wasn't fucking privy to*. But every road led to his un-goddamn-raveling.

He spun towards her and grabbed her arms. "Then have the decency to look at me and tell me what the hell I missed." Not his proudest moment, but his proud moments were infrequent and very, very short. "Talk to me, Eden. Please."

"It's nothing."

Even though his experience with actually caring about anyone was limited, Mitch knew a couple of things. And one of those things was that there are a few situations in which a man has every right in the world to call 'bullshit' on what his woman says.

'*I'm fat.*' Definitely high up on the list.

'*You don't have to get me anything.*' Equally high, regardless of the holiday.

But the big daddy of them all, the one sentence that's a guaranteed lie and, if the man wants to keep her, he *must* ignore:

'*It's nothing.*'

And there it was. Coming from a woman who didn't lie. From *his* woman. Who'd told him every awful thing Hyde said to her the first night she saw him. Who knew what it felt like to be lied to, how raw it left you, how filled with distrust and doubt.

So whatever had happened in the last eight days had to be beyond what he could imagine. And it was his fault.

"What did he do to you?" He pulled back, ashamed of what he'd allowed Hyde to do, whatever it had been. Everything was a blur behind Hyde's walls, and Mitch didn't know what was real, what was fantasy, or how much of the message coming in was skewed by evil's perceptions.

Tears brimmed. "It's not what he did to me."

The emphasis was subtle, and if he hadn't been straining so hard to pay attention to every move she made, every word she uttered, afraid he wouldn't be there to see them for too much longer, he wouldn't have noticed. But he *did*.

'He' and 'me.' Two little words changed the temperature of the room, the density of the air. A thought bloomed in his mind, an unpleasant I-don't-want-to-believe-it thought.

"I won't blame you if you beat the shit out of him. Repeatedly." He knew there was desperation in his voice, hope that she'd simply tortured the bastard. That'd be okay.

"I didn't."

With another two words, the air was drawn from his lungs, leaving him unable to take in more.

"What *did* you do to him?" He knew. He'd been told by the little voice in his head that pumped out paranoia and enjoyed his anguish. He'd been told, but he needed *her* to tell him. Because she was the only thing he trusted, beyond the little voice, beyond himself.

He trusted her. Funny, that. Ironic.

She looked away, a blush coating her cheeks and chest, a quiver in her jaw.

He shouldn't blame her. He shouldn't. There were a handful of people he could blame for the last fifteen years of his pathetic life. His own name was at the very top of the pile. Hers was nowhere near it.

He'd been gone, probably never to return. She'd been confused, maybe looking for comfort. Not that he'd ever imagine her going to Hyde for comfort, but in a sick sort of way, it made sense. He and Hyde shared the same body—was it so terrible to share the same woman?

Yes. Yes, it was. Because Mitch didn't share well. And he would never, ever share her.

"Tell me what you did." He stepped back, needing the

space for all of his rage. Because it was just about to burst out of his chest.

"It was nothing."

Thankfully, he flinched backward, because if he hadn't, he'd have even more to regret. His ass hit the wall, stopping his retreat. "Ooooh, babe." He whistled through clenched teeth. "You've got about zero chance of me believing that."

"It was something. Something I regret." Her voice was frail, as if one misplaced word would break her. "But I didn't sleep with him."

"Okay, no sleeping." He took a deep breath, knowing he had no right to feel wronged—after all, he was supposed to be dead. But he was unable to stop feeling it, quaking from it. "What *did* you do?"

"I don't want to talk about it."

"Really? Well, that's too bad because I do and we will." Anger clawed at him, frustration close at its heels. He needed to know. Everything. So he could start thinking clearly. Stop imagining her head tilted back in ecstasy. Get rid of the high-resolution picture in his mind of her face as she came. As Hyde made her come.

Goddamn it, he wanted it gone. He ran his hands through his hair, yanking as if he could pull the images out by their roots.

"Do you really need to know?" She looked at him. "Really need to hear about it? Can't you just believe me? I didn't have sex with him."

Could he? He paused, determined to say the right thing so she would understand without having the shit scared out of her. "Okay, you didn't have sex with him. But since there are so many other things leading up to that, I need to know more. From your mouth." He was chewing on his lip so hard again, he tasted metal—like an iron bar was holding him back.

"The thing is…even if I believe you, part of my mind is a bit of a trickster and thinks it's funny to mess with me. It sets up little doubts to nibble on my ear and put unfunny thoughts in my head about all the things you *don't* say. And if those doubts have a chance to take root, no amount of trust will loosen them.

"So you tell me *exactly* what happened," he continued. "Everything. And then we can move on." He bit his upper lip so it didn't lift into a snarl.

Jealousy was new to him. Probably because he'd never cared about anything that could be taken away. But now he did. And it bit the big one. All the times he had told people to suck it up and deal with it, to not care, were instantly bullshit. Because jealousy had reared its ugly head and was enjoying the view from Mitch's shoulder. And unless she started talking, its mouth would be the only one smiling.

"Fine," she said. "I thought he would give me information about you, so I teased him."

Teasing isn't too bad. He could deal with teasing. "He was strapped down, I hope."

She nodded.

So his ability to touch her was limited. But not impossible. "How did you tease him?"

She shrugged.

"How did you tease him?" he snapped. He hated having to ask, to drag it out of her. Because it made him think she was holding back, only answering the questions he asked and offering nothing more. And if he asked the wrong question, she would leave something out. And it would start to rot. It would stay between them and grow until it reached them both. And then it would eat away at them, at their love, until there was nothing left for it to consume.

She squirmed under his stare. "I took off my clothes...and I touched him."

Mitch's stomach flipped, his mind imagining her stripping for Hyde, for anyone. "Show me." That way he'd know. He'd know exactly what she did and not have paranoid delusions dancing through his mind.

Her head popped up, her brow furrowed. "No. It's not like

I did it for fun."

But she had done it. Why? "Did you kiss him?"

"No. I didn't want to do any of it."

It was like a nightmare set on repeat—she didn't want to, but Hyde was strapped down. She had a choice, but she did it anyway.

She touched him, teased him, traded her body in. For what?

"Why? Why would you give yourself away like that?" He wasn't screaming, but she scooted farther back on the counter as if he were.

"Because I needed to know if you were still inside of him. And being with him was the only way I could find out."

No fucking way.

CHAPTER V

Impossible. She'd traded herself in for him. *Exactly* what Mitch didn't want to happen, why he should be dead right now. But he wasn't. Right now he was standing in front of the only person the world had ever given him to love, and all he could think about was someone else taking her.

The need to claim her, erase Hyde's touch, take his darkness off her skin was overwhelming. When Mitch took a step towards her, she jerked back, her head smacking the mirror behind her.

"Mitch?"

He moved in quickly, scooping her up into his arms, and carried her out of the bathroom. He headed straight for the closest room and threw her onto the futon, grabbing her ankles before she could scramble away.

"Mitch, stop!"

He couldn't. There was no way to stop it. No way to undo what had been done.

Blinded by the idea, he needed to know exactly what she'd done with Hyde, so that he could do the same thing. And then more. So that he could take her in a way no one else ever could. Wipe away the stain and the scars the bastard had left her with. Make everything she'd done with him disappear, leaving only Mitch's touch, his scent, his lips behind.

"Mitch!" She looked confused as she kicked her legs, but he held them firmly.

She could be as confused as she wanted to. Right now, he didn't give a shit. Until his heart stopped beating, she was his. *Only* his. That's what she needed to learn and what he had to prove to her.

He ran his hands up her legs, pulling her pants down and tearing her panties off with them. Anger flashed in her eyes before being overrun by heat.

Did she wear the same look when she was with Hyde?

No. Please, no. "Did you want him? Even a little bit?"

"No," she spat. "I only did it because I needed to know if you were still inside him. Why can't you believe me?"

His towel came off as he climbed on the futon and dug his fingers into her thighs, forcing them apart. He leaned over her until his hips held her legs open, but no further.

"Then you touched him." He brushed his fingers against her core, first lightly, then with more pressure, feeling how ready she was. When she arched her hips up, he wondered if she even noticed she'd done it. He could see she was fighting herself. Just like he was but for different reasons.

He kept his cock away from her. He would have her when he was ready to have her. Not before. Not when she wanted him. Not until he knew everything there was to know.

"Did you touch his cock?"

Her brow tightened with the memory. "Just for a second. But it was too weird. Too...wrong."

"Because he wasn't me."

"Yes." Her breath was quick, her breasts lifting towards him. He yanked her shirt over her head and pulled the cups of her bra down.

"Did he do this?" He ran his teeth across her collarbone, tasting her, imagining other lips doing the same.

"No. Definitely not."

"Did *you*?"

"No." She gasped when he took her nipple into his mouth, not playfully or seductively. Hard. He stopped as soon as he heard her moan, felt her arch her back in need, her hands in his hair. He slipped his fingers between hers and pinned both her hands to the bed. She writhed underneath him, bending her knees, and curling her hips towards his.

Not yet. "Did he put his mouth on you? Any part of you?" Then he kissed her. With everything he was.

"Never," she groaned as their lips separated briefly. "Because he's not you."

"Promise me, Eden," he begged. "Promise me that's all. And that it's the truth."

"I promise. I swear. I stopped because I knew it was wrong. I couldn't go through with it. I'm sorry I couldn't…for you."

He covered her mouth with his fingers to stop her lips from trembling. "No." He traced her lip with his thumb. "You can't be sorry. I don't want you to trade yourself in for me. Not to him, not to anyone. Understand?" He shouldn't have left her. He should've been strong enough to find a way back.

"All I wanted was for you to come back to me."

"I'm here." His doubt erased, his desire for her multiplied, his guilt almost more than he could bear, he forced himself away from her. It was their first time together post-hell and he was acting like he had a *right* to this. To her.

What the fuck was he thinking? "I have no right to take–"

"Yes. Whatever it is. Yes. Take it."

"I need to be inside of you."

"Yes." She wrapped her legs around him and pulled the tip of his cock into her incredible warmth.

"Wai—"

He groaned, she moaned, and *noooobody* moved. One breath. Then another. Then her legs tightened around him.

"Stop. Eden, stop. Now." He reached over to the box of condoms that was still on the nightstand from the last time they had been here. But in doing so, he slid a fraction more into her. *Motherfucker.* She felt amazing, and it took everything he had not to drive himself all the way in.

If there were no condoms in that box, he was going to hurt someone. Badly. Thank whoever was listening that there were a few left. Maybe not enough, but he'd worry about it later.

Pulling out of her was impossibly hard because *he* was impossibly hard. But even his cock knew protection was nonnegotiable.

"Mitch, you don't need—"

"Believe me, I *need*. Badly. So unless you *really* mean it, don't tell me to stop and don't tell me to slow down. Because that time is gone." As soon as his bases were covered, he lowered himself onto her, covering her body with his.

Damn it, he wanted in. But not yet. "Look at me, Eden." He was impatient the whole two seconds it took her to do it. "You need to be clear on something. No one else touches you and you don't touch anyone else. Do you understand me? As long as I am breathing—in whatever form—it doesn't happen." He paused. "Do you understand me?"

Her nod was immediate. "I understand."

"Ever." And then, in one fluid motion, he was inside her— his tongue, his cock, his heart. All inside of her. Where no other man or beast would ever be. Knowing he'd die a second time to make sure no one would ever touch her again.

$$\text{---}\!\!\!\!\lambda\!\!\!\text{---}\!\!\!\!\lambda\!\!\!\text{---}\!\!\!\!\lambda\!\!\!\text{---}$$

There was no chance Eden could hold her emotions back. With him, she felt everything. She handed herself over to him—to scorn or to accept. To hate or to care for. He was the only one who could take away the chill that seemed to always surround her, an arctic wind that she could never escape.

But Mitch kept her warm, inside and out. She trusted him with her everything. *Everything.* No one else. She'd do anything to keep him. But she would keep her promise. So that both of them could live. Do more than just breathe or hate or drown in anger and betrayal.

An hour ago, the strand of hope she had so desperately clung to was so thin, she'd felt herself lose her grip. But it strengthened and was made thicker every moment he was inside her. Ever deeper, ever more powerful.

She'd missed him so much. She'd missed this so much. Even thinking about being with someone else was wrong. Because no one fit her as well as Mitch did. No one could possibly make her feel this close to perfection, give her so much of himself, even when he was angry. Even when he had every right to be angry.

He held her down—pinning her hands to the bed and pressing her deep into the mattress with every thrust. And she'd never felt more free.

"You feel incredible. I don't..." Giving up on what he was about to say, he took her mouth again. He was unrelenting, demanding she open herself up to him. She would. She'd give him anything she had, no matter how he asked or what he demanded.

Her heart pounded to the rhythm set by his hips, each stroke bringing a spike of pleasure, almost painful in its intensity. But she wanted more, needed more. And he gave. Until the sensations overwhelmed her and she couldn't control it anymore. As she came, she cried out, his name tucked in between less important words.

He slowed down and wiped the hair out of her eyes, kissed her forehead. The tenderness of the movement caught her off guard and she laughed. Just like she'd planned to. Because he was back. And he was hers.

"Wanna tell me what's funny before I get a complex?" he asked breathlessly.

She wrapped her legs around his waist tighter. "Don't stop."

"Oh, I have no intention of stopping." He slammed into her. "I just wanted to know what the laugh was about."

Her body was already gearing up for the next round, tightening each time he pushed inside her. She swallowed, trying to focus on speech and not sensation. How was he doing it? "I'm happy. I'm really, really happy."

"Let's keep you that way, shall we?" He cupped her chin in his hand and kissed her again. Sliding his other arm under her back, her lifted them both up, changing the angle of their bodies, thrusting deeper, proving how much pleasure he could give her, how much she needed him.

"Come with me, Eden." His voice and those words were enough to topple her. A bolt of electricity went through her and then hit him. She dug her fingers into the sheets, his ass, whatever she could reach.

Because she had to hold on. So she would never lose him again.

CHAPTER VI

"I can't risk losing my job, man," Joe said. "Maybe if you spoke to the chief directly."

"Yeah, maybe." After a quick 'thanks and see ya,' Landon walked away from the meeting with nothing new except a cup of overpriced, bitter coffee. So once again, one of his hands was empty and the other had something useless in it. He dumped the coffee.

Joe had to look out for his family, and the chief was threatening to fire anyone he even suspected of leaking anything. So Landon couldn't blame the guy—if he had had a family, he'd be careful, too.

As it stood, the only people relying on him were a half-human, totally obstinate woman and the monster who'd finally turned back into his best friend. Were they family? Yeah, they were.

He pictured the Christmas card they could send out this year. He and Eden standing in front of the cage smiling uncomfortably, with Hyde growling at the camera through the bars. *Nice*. Unless he could figure out a way to make sure Turner stayed Turner. Then the Christmas pic could be of the two of them, their arms wrapped tightly around each other with him two feet away, his arms wrapped around nothing.

Equally as nice.

Equally as painful.

It wasn't that Landon resented their happiness. He was thrilled to have the asshole back and would do almost anything to make sure he and Eden had a chance to be happy. But seeing them together was bittersweet, leaving him with the dull ache of envy. A reminder of what he didn't have. Not since his ability to love had died when his love did.

Tara. Her memory brought a different kind of ache— indescribable longing. He hadn't had enough time with her before she died, so he'd never know if they could've made a future together. If he was everything she needed. If they could share something like Eden and Turner did.

Landon hated that he hadn't been there when she died, that he hadn't prevented it from happening. He hated that he had doubted their relationship. Sure, he'd said the three little-but- glacially-significant words, but looking back on it, he wondered if it was really love or just a more naive man's desire to be someone's hero.

A desire he didn't fulfill. A failure he was still paying for.

Maybe the shame would go away if he could avenge Tara's death and help his friends have what he couldn't. That had to be enough, didn't it?

So the case had turned into an obsession. But obsession wasn't love, nor was revenge or even justice. It was filler— something to focus on so he didn't have to think too much. Didn't have to remember too often.

Looking forward instead of back.

He glanced at his watch. With Turner and Eden doing exactly what he would be doing after waking up from limbo or wherever Turner had been, Landon needed to be somewhere else for a little longer.

What could a single guy do to kill another hour or so?

I could fill up the gas tank. He sighed. His life was so weak, he wasn't even sure it could be *called* a life.

Maybe he should go directly to the chief, the one who had seemed to really like him all the way up to the moment he fired him. Or was told to fire him by someone who knew someone who knew someone who was tucked deep into The Clinic's pocket.

A career he'd spent his entire adult life cultivating had been stripped away faster than a Band-Aid, but a thousand times more painfully. Then any police resources he had were gone, followed closely by his pride, his sense of self-worth, and a whole bunch of other shit that was probably useful.

His only solace was that he'd stopped his liquid diet before his liver gave out. So much to be proud of these days.

Knock it off, shithead. He had an hour to either play in the pity pool or do something he could pretend was productive. One stop before going back to the house and packing up. Before Hyde tried to claw his way out of Turner again.

They needed help. Because there was no way Landon would lose his friend again. But the kind of help they needed either didn't exist or was so well hidden, it was a bigger mystery than a woman's mind.

Back when Landon had been legit, Chief Fuller liked, trusted, and respected him. *Remember those days?* He missed his job, a sense of purpose, and protecting people. After this shit with The Clinic was over, he'd get it back and have everything he used to have. Which wasn't actually that much. But even his sad nothing of a life was better than all this fighting.

With a sigh came a decision—he'd talk to the chief and keep his fingers crossed. Because that was just as productive as anything else they were doing.

When he pulled up to the chief's house, he spotted two American-made cars in the driveway and a high-end import parked on the street right in front.

One of these things is not like the others. Out of habit and without breaking stride, he noted the plate and took a picture with his cell phone on his way up to the door.

A woman holding a baby answered. "Can I help you?"

He recognized her from a picture in the chief's office. With an ability that only women possess, she balanced the child on her shoulder and used both hands to snap up the little outfit he wore.

"Evening, ma'am. I'm Nick Landon. We met at a few station events you probably wished you didn't have to attend."

She smiled and nodded. "I remember you, but I'm assuming you came here to see my husband, not me."

"Yes, ma'am. Is he available?"

"Available?" She tilted her head, annoyed, before shrugging the baby into another position. "Very rarely, but he's here. Come in. Is this about a case?" She led him through the foyer.

"Yes, ma'am." Landon waved at the baby, wishing he would stop staring. Then the kid burped and puked up the most frightening thing Landon had ever seen, and that was saying a lot. The stuff shot out of the kid's mouth and down Mrs. Fuller's shirt as if someone had just thrown a can of paint on her back.

"Please tell me he didn't just do what I think he did," she said.

"I wish I could." *And I wish I hadn't just witnessed it.*

She adjusted the child and looked at her shoulder. "Dang it, Matthew!" Then she turned to Landon. "Third time today I've had to change my shirt."

"Would you like me to hold him a sec?"

Her eyes narrowed for a moment as she considered it. She didn't seem angry, just wary, which was appropriate. She was the wife of a police chief and had probably heard enough stories to make her want to keep the kid in a bubble.

She yelled, "Robert! Matthew needs to be changed, and one of your detectives is here to see you."

"I'm not a—"

"Thanks." She shoved the child at Landon and flicked her head down the hall. "They're in the living room." She called out, "Robert, hurry up!" and then went upstairs.

Landon held the child at arm's length, watching a drip of goo fall off the kid's chin. "Hey." The baby smiled, completely undisturbed by what he'd just regurgitated. "Don't do that again, got it, little man?"

Chubby legs kicked playfully as Landon headed down the hall, hoping he'd encounter the kid's father before anything more disturbing happened. If there *was* anything more disturbing that could happen.

Chief Fuller flinched when he saw them. Maybe because he hadn't expected to see Landon in his house or maybe because Landon was holding his kid. After his initial reaction, he came forward with a smile and took his son from Landon's outstretched arms.

"Good to see you, Landon. Unexpected, but good. How've you been?"

"I've had my ups and downs, but I'm fine, sir. Thanks."

"You don't have to call me 'sir' anymore."

"Old habits... Could we talk for a minute?"

Fuller hesitated a moment before nodding his head towards the room he'd just come out of. The room was large, with a playroom at one end and a grown-up area on the other. A little girl was handing a plateful of plastic food to a man sitting on the couch. The man was in his forties, thin, probably about 5'11", but it was hard to know for sure.

After he'd finished his professional observation, he felt something tighten in his gut. Was it...envy? Everything was so normal here. A long time ago, he had wanted a life like this one—nice house, cute and messy kids, a wife who yelled at him and thought he worked too much. But he'd forgotten. Or maybe he didn't think about it because he knew it would never be. Not with the path he'd chosen.

Along with Tara had gone everything he thought his life would be. Normalcy. Happiness. A legacy. The only legacy he'd leave now would be the end of the organization that had killed her. And even that was far from a sure thing.

He swallowed and started moving again. "I didn't know you had children, sir."

"Enough with the 'sir' sh—stuff. Call me Robert. And I'll call you...What's your first name, Landon?" Big emphasis on 'Landon' with a quick glance towards the man across the room.

The guy's hand froze, the plastic cake inches away from his mouth. Then his face paled and his smile disappeared. Landon knew that some people found him intimidating, but this guy was sitting in the chief's house. And he hadn't reacted to Landon's size or demeanor—he'd reacted to his *name*. As if the guy knew he'd just shown all his cards, he ducked his head down and spoke to the little girl quickly, thanking her for the feast.

What the hell? "My first name is Nick. But everyone calls me Landon." He spoke his name slowly, so the guy wouldn't miss it. And he didn't, adjusting in his seat and looking at Fuller nervously.

As if he needed the chief to rescue him.

Heat radiated out of Landon's chest, filling every part of him. It was like walking into your grandmother's house and discovering that, instead of brewing sweet tea, she's brewing meth.

Chief Fuller? No, that wasn't possible. Sure, it would explain every single thing the department had done regarding anything The Clinic was involved in, but...

Every single thing. Landon slowly let out the breath he'd been holding. Emotional reactions could happen later. Smart reactions need to happen now. *Hunches are wrong all the time.*

Fuller laughed, his back still to Landon. "Yeah, that might be easier. I can barely keep track of my kids' names." He set the baby down on a changing table. "What's your name, champ?" he cooed, leaning forward. The baby smiled again and Landon readied for another waterfall of unknown mush to shoot all over Fuller's face. Sadly, it didn't happen.

"Uncle Steve," the little girl whined, "you didn't finish your dessert."

"Yeah, eat your dessert, Uncle Steve," Fuller called out, still smiling at his son. With his back turned, he couldn't see how uncomfortable 'Uncle Steve' had become, but Landon could.

He crossed the room with his hand out. "I'm Nick Landon. I used to work for the chief."

The man shifted his plate of fake food into one hand and shook. His palm was sweaty. So either he was allergic to plastic food or Landon being there was making Uncle Steve nervous. And in times like these, Landon would bet on the latter.

Somehow he was involved with The Clinic. He might even be the disappearing scientist, Steve Harris. Because he was here, in this house, with the man who had enough clout in the police department to make anything disappear.

There were no words that could express what he was feeling. Coincidences happen. Accidents happen. But not for Landon. Not for Eden. And not for Turner. Part bad luck and part because The Clinic loved to screw with them too much.

And maybe Fuller had helped them out with that. It would have been so easy for him to lose files, close cases, and take away Landon's job. And no one would ever look that high for someone to blame. Because human nature is to look down.

Calm down and stop seeing red everywhere. He could be completely wrong. His gut was screaming, '*No, you're not,*' but starting from a conclusion didn't work.

"Should I call you 'Uncle Steve?" Landon asked, hoping to solicit a last name.

When Steve hesitated, the little girl helped him out. "Daddy just calls him Steve."

Landon bowed to her. "Then that's what I'll call him too." He sat down in a wingback chair. It wasn't right to have the kid here, standing next to someone who'd ruined so many lives. "Do you have any food left? I'm starving."

The little girl smiled and ran back to her kitchen to fix him something just as Mrs. Fuller came in and took over baby cleanup from her husband.

Fuller seemed calm, but the job had taught Landon that some reactions couldn't be controlled. No matter how good a liar someone is, the evidence is there if you look hard enough.

He knew he was sending out a billion subtle messages through his body language—that he wanted to put his hands around Fuller's throat and shake him until the truth fell out, and that it was taking everything he had not to channel Turner's mouth and start screaming obscenities.

But since that would get him nowhere fast, he focused on controlling the things he could. Hands open—unlike theirs. Legs uncrossed and slow, deep breaths—unlike Steve's. And he looked for the ones no one could control—eye dilation, increased blood flow to the cheeks, and micro-expressions. These were the things he focused on—his own and those of the other two highly uncomfortable men in the room.

"So what's up?" When Fuller sat down on the couch instead of asking him to step into another room for the discussion, Landon wondered if he was deliberately using the kid to stop any unpleasantness.

I didn't know the department was using children as shields now. Interesting. "I wanted to talk to you." *You piece of shit.*

"You could have called me at the office."

"Yes, sir. But my mother told me there are three things you should never do over the phone."

"And those are…?"

"Don't break up with your girlfriend, don't ask for a favor, and don't accuse someone of wrongdoing." He let the words linger, let them wonder whatever evil people wonder about. He took the plate of plastic fruit and a steak from the little girl. "Thank you. It looks delicious."

"You're welcome," she said shyly.

"So which is it?" Fuller asked as he motioned her over and pulled her onto his lap.

"Well, I'm not here to break up with you, so you can cross that one off the list." Landon created another pause by taking a pretend bite of a strawberry and winking at the girl. It also provided enough time to tell her to run upstairs so she wouldn't see him beat the shit out of her daddy. But he didn't do that, as tempting as it was. "I need to ask you for a favor, sir."

"What kind of favor?"

The little girl wiggled unhappily when Fuller pulled her closer to him.

It took all of Landon's strength not to say exactly what he wanted, to see Steve's reaction and watch both men squirm in front of the kids and Mrs. Fuller as they tried to lie their way out of everything.

But while it would be satisfying, it wouldn't get him anywhere but into more trouble. Panic might make Steve do something stupid, but not Fuller. If what Landon believed was true, the man had been lying for years, using the system to lose files, close cases, dump condemning information, and get rid of people who asked too many questions. All at The Clinic's discretion.

"I'm looking for work—private investigations. I was hoping I could put your name down as a reference. Sir." Again, he let the silence linger as the men considered what that meant for them.

"I hope it's something more interesting than cheating spouses or insurance fraud."

As Mrs. Fuller brought the baby over, the chief's eyes moved to her, and then back to Landon. "Come on, Sydney," she said to the little girl. "Quiet time." The girl grudgingly got off her father's lap and went to her mom with a frown on her face. "Detective, I'm sure my husband was just about to offer you something to drink."

Be smart. Not impulsive. "I'm not a detective anymore, ma'am, and I can't stay. Could I use your bathroom before I go?" He'd get more info if he let them converse in perceived privacy for a little while.

"Down the hall on the right. Say goodbye, Sydney."

"Goodbye. Uncle Steve, bring me back a good present. I don't want a key."

"A key?" Landon asked as he stood.

Mrs. Fuller laughed. "My brother is going to Key West."

Steve's wide eyes darted from Landon to Fuller. "Just for a week or so." Liars overexplain things. They feel the need to convince in a way honest people don't. So Landon let him talk, let him go as deep as he would. "Going to drive down…" He kept talking, but Landon stopped focusing on the words as much as on everyone's reactions.

Mrs. Fuller looked directly at her brother, smiling slightly, adding a few comments of her own. She believed him, bought his story of a short trip to the Keys.

But Fuller knew better, eventually cutting the man off midsentence. "Sydney needs to say goodbye, Steve."

"Oh, sure." He held his arms out for Sydney to jump into. "Come here, kiddo." He squeezed her tightly, not letting her go even after she unwrapped her arms from him and wiggled her way to the ground, the whole while explaining that she really didn't need any quiet time today and could keep playing. Then little Matthew was shoved into Steve's arms for a bon voyage hug. For a short trip that Landon was ninety percent sure was more of a three-hour cruise to an island with lots of mai tais and no extradition.

"You'll stay until I've finished putting them down?" she asked Steve. "Twenty minutes."

"Sure," he said, glancing briefly at Landon.

Great news all around. With everyone focused on goodbyes, Landon opened a recording app on his cell and put the phone facedown behind a big box of Legos.

When Mrs. Fuller left to take the kids upstairs, he walked down the hall with her.

"Is Steve your only brother, ma'am?" Landon asked her quietly.

"God, no. We're two of six."

"That's insane," he said, smiling. He asked her about her family, her ancestors, where they grew up, all to get one more piece of information—Steve's last name.

"Harris."

And Harris was his name-o. "Hmm…I think that's English or Irish or one of those places." Landon didn't know, and he didn't care. After thanking her, he excused himself, keeping a polite grin on his face until he closed the bathroom door behind him.

Then he growled.

Little kid toys were scattered around the bathroom—on the vanity, the floor, in the tub. Either Steve kept a bag of toiletries at his sister's for the hell of it or the guy was staying close to the chief for safekeeping.

He leaned against the wall and waited, giving the men a chance to talk, come up with a devious plan, or let something he needed to know slip. Hopefully by then he wouldn't be shaking with rage anymore.

As he picked some kind of bath toy off the ground, another pang of jealousy hit him, harder this time. Along with a fairly large fistful of hate. Fuller didn't deserve this. None of it. If he was moonlighting for The Clinic and was directly involved with Landon's life being taken away, then he deserved nothing.

And that's exactly what Fuller would end up with.

CHAPTER VII

After both Eden and Mitch were sated, at least temporarily, they talked. In the shower, with his arms wrapped around her, she came clean. She told him everything, never lying but softening a few things slightly. When she explained what he'd done to her father, he knew the violence in Hyde well enough to read between her lines.

When she told him what Alex really wanted from her—a baby created by her and a Hyde, *any* Hyde—he broke a few tiles. Luckily, he didn't break his hand.

Once he calmed down and she saw his eyes fill with need again, they tumbled back into bed. They both knew their time was limited and the war would start again soon, so they used every second to remind themselves and each other what they were fighting for.

He rolled over and grabbed the box of condoms off the nightstand. "We're going to need more soon, honey."

Her head popped off the pillow. "Did you just call me 'honey'?"

His brow crinkled and he looked at the ceiling. "Yeah, I think I did."

"Honey is really…sweet."

His eyes widened with amused horror. "Oh my god, you're right! It is! It *is* sweet!" Then he brushed his lips down her neck, tasting her. "Just like you are...right here. And, if I remember correctly, in a few other places as well. Though I should probably check to make sure."

She laughed as his unshaven jaw tickled and scratched her skin, his lips moving down her body. "It's just...I don't feel sweet."

"Oh, you are," he said, his teeth grazing her hipbone. "But if you don't want me to call you that, I won't. What should I call you instead? Baby?"

"God no."

"Honey is already out, so...sugar? Molasses? Drumstick?"

"You're terrible at this."

"Huh." He ran his hand over her belly and lower. And lower. Until she couldn't feel anything but his touch. "I thought you liked it when I did this." Then he used his mouth.

"I do," she said breathlessly. "That, you're very, very good at. I meant the pet names."

"Maybe that's because I've never had a pet."

"Never?" Why the hell was she distracting him?

He looked up from between her legs and shook his head. "I think animals hate me. Well, it's probably Hyde they hate because *everyone* loves me."

"So true. I've never had one either—foster care and all." Her hips curled towards him, aching. "But I want our kids to have a dog, so we'll have to find one that likes you." *Oh, shit.* She cringed and let her head fall back on the pillow. "I just said that out loud, didn't I?" Her eyes stayed glued to the ceiling because she didn't want to see his expression. Because she hadn't meant to say that. Or think it.

I can only imagine what he's thinking. Great, now she had to look.

His face was blank, all color gone. As if he'd just been shot and was bleeding out. "Are you...?"

Her head shook so fast, it probably looked like there was

an earthquake inside. "No, I'm not."

He blew out a quick breath of air. "Okay. It's not that I…" He sat up, blinking a lot and looking a bit shaky.

"I know. It's fine, Mitch. Don't have an aneurysm over it."

"Maybe…someday...I…" He shrugged helplessly.

"It's okay. It's not even something I think about anymore. Just pretend I didn't say anything. I'm not even sure why it came out of my mouth."

"I do." He scooted up beside her and tucked a strand of hair behind her ear. "Because having kids is something you want and is normal and is—"

"Impossible," she said, pulling away slightly, but he didn't let her go far. All true things. She wanted a normal life, a calm and boring life with him. But they'd never have it.

He kissed her lightly. "A few months ago, I thought I would never feel this way about anyone. A few weeks ago, I thought I'd never see you again. A few days ago, I thought I'd never take another breath of freedom. So how the hell do we know what will happen tomorrow?"

She held his face, pulling him closer to kiss him for a good, long while. "You're wonderful."

"Yeah, yeah. Tell me something I don't know." He gave her a quick peck. "Now, I need to work on my karma."

"Karma?"

"Karma. Payback. Whatever you want to call it." He spoke as his lips wandered down her body again. "You do something nice for someone and it cosmically comes back to you in another way."

"I know what karma is, but I don't get—Oh!" She gasped when she felt his tongue. "Sure. You work on that." And she'd very happily pick up some good karma of her own later. They were going to need all they could get.

─╫╌╫─╫╌

After not enough time, Mitch realized that she might need

a little time to recover. This brilliant realization occurred right after she said, "I need a little time to recover."

He stretched out alongside her, way happier than he deserved to be. As she napped, he caressed her hair and enjoyed the way her breath warmed his chest. He wondered how long it had been since she'd slept this peacefully. He'd put money on eight days. At least.

He had been so sure she'd be okay—Landon would be able to protect her and she would wipe her hands of Mitch and move on. But she was so thin, so fragile-looking, despite her physical strength. The bags under her eyes were a clear sign that, no, she wasn't okay.

Boyfriend of the Year, for sure. Congratulations. The only thing your big 'sacrifice' did was drag out her pain. Made it more of an emotional death than a physical one. *Nice work, asshole.*

Even though he had left her, she didn't leave him. She hadn't given up on him, instead becoming so focused on rescuing him that she didn't see the damage it was doing to her.

Not good. Really, really not good. In fact, it was really fucking bad.

All he wanted was for her to be free and have a chance at a life. A *good* life. Another instance of him not getting what he wanted. Maybe he should start wishing she'd be miserable and see if that worked.

He would do anything for her—he knew that down to his marrow. He would give up his life a thousand times over to keep her safe. Live in the black hole of pain inside Hyde for eternity if it would give her a chance. If he had fifteen minutes left, he would use them to help her. If he knew how. How many ifs did that make? Too many.

But on the bright side, or on the dark-but-if-you-squint-really-really-hard-you-can-see side, Mitch felt great. Coming back from hell changed a man, made him reprioritize. He had a second chance and wouldn't screw this one up as badly as he had the last one.

And evidently, the one time you're guaranteed to keep your shit together is when the person you love is losing theirs. Eden was the priority and she wasn't doing well. He'd already had his turn at being a mess—the whole time she'd been at The Clinic and the fifteen years before that. So whatever happened, whatever disappointments or crap came his way, he would suck it up and deal with it, so that she didn't have to.

And how healthy was that?

When he kissed her forehead, she felt his happiness, his faith in her. Deserved or not.

"Go back to sleep," he said quietly.

"I don't want to sleep." Because she didn't want to miss a moment with him. This was her reprieve from the obsessing and worry and fear. She'd changed in the time he was gone. But she could change back. She would respect herself again and let go of the anger that simmered under her skin. It wouldn't break her. Not now. Not now that Mitch was back.

"Well, if you're not going back to sleep and Landon will be here eventually, what do you want to do until then?"

"Before you showed up, I was planning on doing my nails," she said. "So I'll probably do that."

"You think you're funny, don't you?" He rolled on top of her, his smile something she'd never tire of seeing. "You have a terrible sense of humor. It's embarrassing." He spoke into her neck, nibbling, kissing. "Thankfully, you're good at other things." He reached for a condom off the nightstand. "Like…calculus and using the telephone and—"

"Being on top." With his arm extended towards the nightstand, she had just enough room to twist, grab his shoulders, and use her leg and both arms to flip him over to pin him down.

"Damn, I love it when you do stuff like that."

"Is that all you love?" she teased as she took the condom from him and ripped it open.

In only a few seconds, he was sheathed by latex and then by her body. He sat up, leaning on one hand and brushing her cheek with the other. They remained perfectly still as they looked at each other.

"No, that's not all," he whispered. "I love you." Then his eyes widened as if he was shocked he'd actually said it.

"I know." She smiled. "But I'm glad you finally caught up."

He blinked, his lips forming the words as if he was trying to get comfortable saying them.

When he was ready, he spoke. Perfectly. "I love you, Eden Colfax."

"I love you too." Each of the four words in her response was lengthened as he curled his hips, pushing himself deeper inside of her. She dug her fingers into his shoulders and rocked against him until she couldn't breathe anymore.

When he kissed her, she clung to him, her hands in constant motion across his chest, his jaw. Just to make sure he was still there. And that he'd never leave again.

Chapter VIII

Landon had become a cop because he believed in justice. After everything was taken away, he still believed. So as badly as he wanted to kill Fuller, he wouldn't. He'd feel sorry for Fuller's kids when they went to visit their daddy in jail, though.

The bastard had made his own goddamn bed, and Landon wouldn't feel guilty about pulling off the covers and showing the world what was underneath. He tried not to think of it in selfish terms, but he wanted his damn job back. He wanted his pride back, his reputation, his life. He wanted a chance at normalcy when this was all over. No hiding, no espionage, no frigging cages. Was that too much to ask?

When he got tired of his mind turning in circles, he splashed some water on his face and headed back to the living room.

Fuller and Steve were standing on opposite sides of the room. Not a good sign. It's tough to do any heavy-duty whispering from across a room.

"I should get going." He leaned against the wall next to the Lego box. With a flick of his wrist, he sent the box and its contents flying all over the floor. As the two men looked down in shock, Landon grabbed his phone and stuck it into his pocket. "Shit, I'm sorry." He bent down and started picking up the pieces.

"Leave it," Fuller said gruffly.

"I don't want your wife to hate me."

"Leave it, Landon."

"Okay, but if she asks, I'm blaming you." Landon dropped a handful of blocks into the box and stood. "Thanks for the recommendation."

"Good luck, Landon. And stay out of trouble."

"I'll try, but sometimes trouble appears right in front of you and you can't get around it." After a quick handshake with Fuller and a nod to Steve, Landon shoved his hand into his pocket, making sure the phone was still there, and walked outside.

He parked about a block away to wait for Uncle Steve to leave. Until then, he had his phone to occupy him. But only moments later, he saw the man walk briskly to his car, yank the door open, and get in. Evidently Steve wasn't big on long goodbyes.

Landon knew how to follow a suspect—how far to stay behind, how many cars to keep between them, how to anticipate each turn. But it didn't matter—Steve gave no indication he knew he was being followed.

As he drove, he listened to the recording.

"Why is he here?" That was probably Steve—nervous, fairly weak-sounding voice.

"It doesn't matter. Just keep your head down and let *them* deal with him." If only Fuller could be a little more specific about who 'they' were.

"Do you think that's why he's here?" Steve again. "To go after Landon and the other ones?"

"Specifics, guys," Landon said to the phone. "Fewer pronouns and more names."

"I don't know and I don't want to know." That was Fuller. "When did he get here?"

"Five-thirty, Monday night. He wants to meet again in about an hour."

It was silent for so long, Landon checked his phone's display to see if the recording was over.

Then Fuller spoke, his words clipped and tight. "Be careful. Answer only the questions he asks and don't offer anything."

"Give me a name," Landon grumbled. "My miserable, nonexistent kingdom for a name."

"And be smart, Steve, don't mention Landon coming here."

"He just wants to talk to me again, right?" More anxiety in Steve's voice. Maybe this nameless guy wasn't particularly good natured.

"Yeah. Yeah, of course." Not convincing. Fast speech meant to cover doubt. "I'd send someone with you, but if Newman noticed...I don't know what he'd do." His pause gave Landon a moment to rejoice about finally hearing a name—Newman. "But you'll be fine, Steve. You're valuable to them. Call me after the meeting."

"What if he knows I'm leaving?"

"If you don't tell him, he won't know. And once you're gone, it won't matter."

"What about you, Marnie, and the kids?"

"I'm the chief of police. Do you seriously think he's going to do anything to me?"

Landon heard his own voice, the thud and scatter of the Legos, and that was it. Damn it, he should've given them more time. But at least he had a name and an arrival time. He'd check out flights that arrived at 5:30 on Monday. How many could there be? Forty. Fifty, tops. And how many people named 'Newman' could there possibly be? Two, three million?

Shit. It wasn't nearly enough, but it was something. And as long as the pieces kept coming, crumb by frigging crumb, eventually Landon would end up with something that resembled a cupcake.

He considered calling Turner and Eden to give them the big news about his ex-boss, but he wanted to listen to Fuller and Steve's conversation a few more times. Maybe he'd notice something he hadn't already. He'd call them later. Plus, the guy deserved a little time to enjoy life. And maybe somewhere in the middle of all that enjoyment, he could get through to Eden. Because Landon sure as hell hadn't been able to.

Steve turned his car into the parking lot of a strip mall. One of the thousands in South Florida, all of them looking roughly the same—a bank, a nail salon, a café in one long building, then a pharmacy, a dry cleaners, and an ethnic food place in the next. Landon watched Steve get out of his car, glancing around nervously, and sit down in the café's outdoor seating area.

Landon did a loop around the strip mall, noting every exit and gate. The café was on a corner, a thin alley separating it from the next row of businesses. The gate at the back—a wire job with wooden slats fed through the holes—was padlocked. No escape there. He moved on, continuing around until he came out front again and pulled into a spot hidden by a row of parked cars. Unfortunately, it was also under a streetlight, but Steve was facing away from him, so he wasn't too worried. Until the alarm of the car next to his went off at the same time as the one in front of him backed up.

"Damn it." Bad time to lose focus on his surroundings. All eyes turned in his direction, including Steve's.

Landon was out and running before Steve had even stood. To avoid having twenty witnesses who would be able to pick him out of a lineup, he went slower than he'd have liked. With loose pants and a thin jacket that hid his weapon, he looked like a jogger as he wove in between two moving vehicles, trying to corral Steve into the dead-end alley.

It worked. Instead of going straight, Steve turned left around the side of the building. Then he broke from a speed-walk into a full-out run. But Landon was faster, even keeping it slow enough to look natural.

Steve slid to a stop when he saw the fence. He glanced back, breathing hard, and scrambled for a foothold on the metal dumpster. Landon grabbed his collar to haul him down and then shoved him into the brick wall. This was definitely not what he thought he'd be doing today.

"I didn't do anything," Steve shouted.

"That's great. Then we can just talk for a second." Landon knew what a mess he was in, and everything he did was only making things messier. Being spotted had forced the move, but it had also blown any chance he had of seeing this 'Newman' guy.

"What about?"

"You worked for The Clinic."

Steve kept his mouth shut, eyeing the only way out of the alley.

"It wasn't a question, just a statement of fact," Landon said. "I know you worked at their facility. And, after seeing your smooth reactions and your brilliant escape attempt, I'm pretty sure you weren't a guard." He took a deep breath. "So I'm really hoping that you're the guy in charge of prescriptions."

When Steve still didn't respond, Landon added, "I took down a few of The Clinic's fairly well-trained guards with my hands. If it turns out that you're tougher than you look, I also have a gun. And...I left my patience in my other jacket. So let's skip the bullshit and your empty protestations and cut straight to you telling me what I need to know."

One more chance and then he gets hit. Landon stepped forward, speaking very slowly. "Okay, we'll do the yes-or-no thing. I ask the questions and you nod for yes or shake your head for no. Until I get tired of being so accommodating. Then all bets are off." He shrugged. "I get grumpy when I'm hungry. And no offense to your niece's cooking, but plastic fruit and steak just aren't enough for a guy my size. So...were you in charge of the pharmaceuticals?"

"Just do it." Steve closed his eyes "Do it!"

"Do what?"

"Shoot me. Like you did to Bradford. Do it!"

Bradford—the guy they found in the Everglades. "I didn't kill Bradford."

Steve opened his eyes to glare. "So he, what, *fell* on the bullet that was lodged in his forehead?"

"My theory was a run-in with a gun-toting alligator. Either way, the guy's dead." They'd sent a cleaner in. Had to be. Newman, maybe? "Who are you meeting?"

"Someone you don't want to meet in an alley." He looked around them. "He'll be here any minute."

"We have a little time." Not a lot but, according to Steve and Fuller's taped conversation, they had at least another half hour. Plenty of time. "Let's get back to our discussion."

Hate radiated from him. "It doesn't matter anymore—the facility was destroyed by you people, and the drugs were confiscated by the police." And would be released by Fuller any day now, no doubt.

"Not all of them. In fact, I have a friend who, until a little while ago, lived in a cage. Now you get to tell me how much we use to keep him that way."

Steve blinked. "Turner's alive?" So much for the guy being in the know.

Too late to deny it now. "Yep."

"And he's human?"

"Yep."

"For how long?"

"You tell me. What's the going dose these days and when will he need it again?"

"Another dose won't help him." A smile crept onto Steve's face, slow but steady, until it was a full-blown sneer.

"Tell me why you're smiling or things are about to get very unpleasant, very quickly."

The expression slipped. "Turner has been without any

serum for a long time—long enough to allow his Hyde to completely take over. That's what happened, isn't it?"

Landon didn't nod, but something gave him away.

"Giving a large dose of J-0026 to a Hyde makes them revert to their human form."

"I know that," Landon said. "Now tell me something I don't know."

"The reversion doesn't last. And when it ends, it ends *very* abruptly."

"Define 'abruptly.'"

"To use a method of measure you're probably more familiar with, he'll go from 0 to 60 in forty-five seconds." That damn smile was back, as if he saw the ripple of panic move through Landon's body. "With a standard deviation of 15 seconds, of course."

Landon's mind flashed to Eden and Mitch happily doing some postcoital, sappy shit. Together. Outside of the cage. So *when*—not *if*—it happened, Mitch would have between thirty seconds and a minute to get into the cage and be chained down. "How long does he have before it happens?"

"The longest I've observed is twenty-four hours."

Landon sighed but didn't relax. When someone says, 'the longest,' it usually means the window is wide. "And the shortest?"

"Just over four hours. How long has it been?" He popped an eyebrow. "Maybe you should hurry home just in case."

Landon backed up, unsure of what to do. Taking a hostage was a pile of something he didn't want to step into. "We have more to talk about." When he tried calling Eden, like always, she didn't answer. Probably too busy to hear the phone.

Damn Abnormal hormones are going to screw everything up. Hopefully not permanently. When he was done with Steve, he'd try to reach her again. And again. And again.

"Tell me how the drug works, Steve. There has to be a way to stop the switch-back."

Steve looked at him innocently, confusedly. "We haven't

done enough testing to be sure of anything with J-0026, especially not with the Hydes. But we know they don't just 'switch back.' When the J-0026 stops staving Turner's Hyde off, he'll have a seizure." He paused. "A fatal one."

Fatal. No way could one man be *that* unlucky. Landon's mind went into 'will he or won't he' overdrive. Could he trust Uncle Steve or was this just more bullshit? "I don't buy it. There has to be more than that. You brought Hyde01 back repeatedly, right? That's what Fields said. So how did you do it?" He swallowed. "Tell me or I will drag you back to the house and have *him* convince you to talk."

"I need an assurance that you'll let me go."

"And you'll run straight to your bosses. Not going to happen." He spoke quickly because he needed to get back to the house to warn them. Before it was too late.

"I'm leaving Florida." He started to put his hand in his pocket.

Landon took another step backward and drew his weapon.

Steve slammed his back into the wall with his hands up, staring at the barrel that was inches from his face. "It's a plane ticket! Check my pocket. I stayed at my sister's because I thought it would be safer." With two little kids to shield him when the shit he wrought came down on him. "But it wasn't."

Landon reached into the man's pocket and took out a passport with a folded piece of paper tucked inside. He dropped the passport and opened the paper one handed, his other being occupied with something more important.

Sparing only a quick glance, he saw the boarding pass. London. He'd always wanted to go there. "Here's the deal, Steve. One-time offer. No negotiations. You talk and you talk fast. Then I let you go see Buckingham Palace." Maybe. But probably not. Because trust was a rare commodity these days. Too rare to waste on someone who'd already proven himself unworthy.

"But if you lie to me or Turner dies," he continued. "I won't hesitate. And I'll have enough time and motivation to find anyone, anywhere."

"London is a big—" His snide remark died in his throat as he realized he'd just given Landon a very good reason to kill him *now*.

"I wasn't talking about *you*. You're one of six kids, right? Uncle to how many?" He let the threat settle in Steve's mind. Gave him a moment to fully absorb it. Saw a new sense of terror on the face of an already-cowardly man. As hateful as the guy was, he loved those kids—Landon had seen it. "Tell me how to help Turner."

Tears filling his eyes, Steve nodded. "There's another pharmaceutical, but...I don't know if you have it."

"Pretend I do."

"It's called RLS-7. It encourages the Abnormal side to appear. If you want to keep Turner from dying, you need to force his transformation—the Hyde's physiology can handle what its human side can't. Your timing has to be right on— *while* he's seizing. If you wait too long, he'll die just like any human would."

"How much do we give him?" Landon went through a mental list of the drugs he and Eden had taken from The Clinic. They'd been tagged with undecipherable numbers and letters, but one of those number/letter combos was RLS-7.

"Don't hurt my family."

"Give me a reason *not* to. How much?"

"Fifty cc. Diluted in saline from the concentrated powder form to a ratio of 1:20. Injected directly into a vein, not muscle, not fat." The words kept coming, broken up by pleas for his family, for pity, mercy. Landon only listened to the information he needed, ignoring the rest because it didn't matter. He wasn't going to hurt the man's family. His threat was empty but, thankfully, it was also convincing.

"His Hyde can metabolize the rest, so an overdose is basically impossible with the RLS-7. Every Abnormal is different and every episode is different. There's no pattern to how long he will stay human—no way to predict it."

"That it?"

"We're talking about decades of research. But yes, that's what will keep him alive." A few tears escaped and rolled down his cheek.

"*This* time. And long term?"

"There may be something, but I don't know very much about it. Bradford was working on something outside of what the rest of us were doing, and he was in contact with the other lab that's conducting trials. But that's all I know, I swear. Too bad you—I mean, the gun-toting alligator murdered the only one who did."

"I didn't kill Bradford. Someone from your side did."

"*Please*. He was the head scientist, brought in from Texas and the *only* one reporting directly to the top."

"And he was killed by someone who isn't me." If Landon had to venture a fairly obvious guess as to why The Clinic would be killing their own people, he'd go with them having serious trust issues. He shook his head and focused on learning as much as he could before things went awry. Because things *always* went awry. "Someone else has to know."

"Maybe, but it isn't me. I had nothing to do with the other lab or the higher-ups."

Not a good enough answer, but Landon was out of time. And patience. And he was really tired of trudging through the labyrinth of lies, bogus rationalizations, and bullshit excuses. Thank goodness he knew two other people who would be happy to take over for him.

"I hope you bought a refundable ticket, Uncle Steve." He nodded towards the parking lot. "You can show me how to whip up the first batch."

With nonstop whining, Steve walked in front. Landon was just as unhappy about it—taking a hostage brought a whole new level of bad to the situation. Another liability. Another thing to go wrong.

There's always the chance of a hostage escaping. The more

you refuse to believe it could happen, the higher the probability that it will.

Although this was officially Landon's first kidnapping, he'd seen it from the other side more times than he had fingers. The more arrogant the hostage taker, the faster they dropped when everything came out from under them.

But he didn't have a choice. He had to get back to the house, and he needed all the information that was inside Steve's head. With it, they'd finally have answers, leads. They could set up an actual *plan* instead of rushing into things with nothing but crossed fingers and a strong desire not to get killed.

When he heard a popping sound, he pushed Steve to the ground and landed on top of him. Weapon raised, he spun to look around, knowing he'd probably just face-planted the guy because a patron at the café ordered champagne. Then he heard another pop and felt something displace the air a bit too close to his head. It wasn't a champagne cork.

"Move!" He grabbed Steve by the shoulder and yanked as he rolled to the side of the alley. All Steve did was flop over, exposing the hole in his forehead.

Shit. If they'd moved faster, argued less, or thought more, both of them would be better off. It seemed like Newman had arrived a little early, bringing a gift from The Clinic along with him. Landon was a simple man. He didn't like gifts. Or surprises. Or being shot.

And he probably wouldn't like death very much, either. He snapped the safety off, knowing he had thirteen chances to get out of here alive.

CHAPTER IX

Eden would never get tired of looking at him. Sure, it's the inside that counts and she loved every bit of his, but she'd be lying if she said she didn't enjoy his outside, too. She couldn't stop touching him, making sure he was still there and still himself, not knowing if or when he would transform again. Thankfully, he didn't seem to mind her hands or mouth on him at all.

They spent the time planning for each contingency and taking turns using their lips to torture each other while they spoke. Mitch looked at the files, asked questions, and listened intently as she explained every bit of information she and Landon had gathered. She watched him, answered him, and thought about how incredibly peaceful she felt. Finally.

A perfect blend of business and pleasure. As soon as Landon got back, they would pack and go check out the moving truck they had found. But this moment was hers, theirs. And she needed it.

A car pulled up outside, a door slammed, and footsteps pounded around downstairs. But it was one car, one door, one set of feet, and a lot of Landon mumbling.

Sadly, it was time to rejoin reality. She pulled out of

Mitch's arms and sat up. "Landon's back." And he was cursing to himself as he came upstairs, using words more commonly heard coming out of Mitch's mouth.

He yanked her back down. "He'll probably head straight for the liquor cabinet, so we have a bit more time."

"He hasn't had anything since we left The Clinic. Not a drop." Although she knew he wanted to, was aching to. Yet another reason to respect him—he put the team's needs ahead of his own. Because they were a team. Of three.

Dang, she owed him a big apology.

"Are you both alright?" Landon's steps were heavy as he went from bedroom to bedroom. "Where are you?" He slid to a stop in front of the door. The knob wiggled and then he pounded on the wood. "Open it! Now!" His voice was higher than normal, his speech faster.

Right. Only Mitch has changed—the world is still a cesspool. She'd almost forgotten. She jumped up and opened the door. "Do they know where we are?"

"No. But we need to leave. Now." He averted his eyes. "And you need to put on some clothing."

"What's going on?" Mitch asked, sitting up.

"I'll tell you downstairs. I need to mix something up. But we need to hurry."

"And again I ask: What's going on?"

"Bad things. I'll tell you after I have the second serum mixed. I'll be downstairs." He looked at Mitch for a moment longer, fear filling his eyes. "Yeah, downstairs. Hurry."

"What did he mean by 'second serum'?" She'd find out soon enough. Without much to pack and the duffel bag she'd thrown together for Mitch never even opened, all she had to do was get dressed.

He played with the row of safety pins attached to the belt loop of her jeans. "This is cute."

"I put them on every pair of pants I own." She shrugged. "Never know when they'll come in handy."

He nodded sadly. "Someday stuff like that won't be

necessary."

"I know." She held her hand out for him to take. "Ready?"

He stood in front of a small mirror, staring at her reflection silently for a moment, unmoving. "I…I need a minute. Okay?"

She wondered if he'd forgotten who he was, too. But looking in the mirror didn't help—she'd tried it.

"Sure, of course. I'll go see what spooked Landon so badly." It definitely wouldn't be good news, because Landon didn't spook easily. She found him in the kitchen. "What going on?"

He didn't look up from what he was doing. "Where's Turner?"

"Can you stop stalling, please?"

"I'm not stalling. I'm preoccupied by something that takes some concentration. But I'll try to multitask." He started by telling her about his old chief. There was pain in his eyes, just under the anger—things left behind by deceit.

By the time Mitch—now clean-shaven—came in, Landon was at the point of his story when he had the scientist up against the wall. And so far—minus the chief's involvement—it all sounded like great news. He'd learned more in the last few hours than they'd learned in days, maybe weeks.

But she knew a bomb was coming because, for a reason still unexplained, he was carefully measuring and mixing saline with one of the powders they'd taken from The Clinic.

"I'm all packed," Mitch said, shaking the empty box of condoms. "But we may need to stop off somewhere for supplies."

"Jesus, Turner, this isn't a goddamn pleasure cruise."

Mitch flinched. "Didn't think it was. But it's always darkest before someone screws in a light bulb, so I thought I'd keep things light. You know, until we get screwed."

After a pause, Landon went back to work, filling three syringes with the liquid. "So the guy Steve was supposed to meet shot him and tried to shoot me."

"Motherfucker!" Mitch stepped forward as if he could fight an enemy who wasn't there.

"Relax, Turner. I'm not dead. And I lost him. But he wasn't like any of the guards we've come across. So we need to be more focused now."

"I should have come along," Mitch growled.

"Because you can catch bullets? Or because you want to get shot?" The tone of Landon's voice was one she'd only heard him use once before—when they were huddled together on a cot, sprinklers pouring water down on them, talking about whether or not to electrocute someone they both loved. Frustration mixed with deep regret and hopelessness.

"Because I want to back you up," Mitch said slowly. Eden saw the guilt on his face—he would never have forgiven himself if Landon had been shot. "I swear, cop. If you die on my account, I'll—"

"I'm not doing this for you, Turner."

"You think I don't remember? I know you have your own shit to pay them back for, but I still don't want you to die, asshole."

Despite Landon's claims, Eden knew a big part of it was for Mitch, and, by association, her. He wanted payback for the death of a woman who might have made their team a foursome. But more than all of that, Landon was doing this for redemption.

"Well, the same goes for me," Landon grumbled. Then he popped needle covers and plunger guards on the syringes so they wouldn't accidentally be emptied.

"We're a team. Next time, call us." Although she probably wouldn't have called either. "Now can you skip to the part where you tell us what that is?"

He stood, tucking the syringes into his pocket and staring at Mitch.

Mitch waited silently, but the question never left his face, the tension never left his body. Finally he spoke. "Longing looks don't tell me anything other than you want me. But I already know that. So spill already."

Landon spilled. He hurried through the high points of his story, ending with a reiteration of the reason they needed to leave. But all Eden could focus on was a few words from the middle: 'seizure' and 'die.' Each swinging on separate pendulums in her mind, bumping into each other, ricocheting off in different directions, none of which made sense.

Seizure.

Die.

That couldn't be right. Mitch was back—they'd brought him back. *She'd* brought him back. With her whole being, she'd believed it was possible, and it was. He *had* to stay here. She could deal with occasional appearances from Hyde because she knew it would be temporary, but 'seizure' and 'die' were permanent. Things not even Hyde could come back from.

"Huh," Mitch said calmly. "That sucks. Did he mention how much time I'd have?"

"Between four and twenty-four hours."

"Big difference between four and twenty-four." He blew out a breath. "We should probably get moving."

She whipped around to face him. "That's it? 'We should probably get moving'?" Didn't he understand what Landon had said? What it meant for him?

"What would you prefer? That we have a snack and wait to see if this Newman guy will find us? Or just sit in a triangle with you two staring at me until I start to convulse?"

"Neither." What she wanted was for him to make it untrue. For Landon to continue his story and end it with a simple solution that had no downside at all. That Mitch's humanity didn't come with the risk of fatality.

She'd made things worse because she was so impatient to have him back. If she'd waited one more day, they would've known. If she'd gone after the scientists right away, instead of spending a few days staring at Hyde and wishing things were different, they would have answers.

If Mitch died, it would be her fault—her impatience, her desire to have him back overriding all thought. It would all be on her.

"I followed Steve's directions for the RLS-7 exactly." Landon touched her on the arm. "He was scared enough and stupid enough for me to believe him. And you know how cynical I am. One of us will shove a needle into him as soon as he twitches, and he'll be fine. Well, he'll be Hyde, which creates its own problems, but at least none of them will be death."

Mitch pulled her into his side. "I'm not sure how much you're helping, man."

"Yeah, well… Here." He held one of the syringes out. She took it without really seeing and slipped it into the pocket of her thin jacket. "Steve said another scientist might have been working on a long-term solution. Someone has to know what it is."

"We need to focus on that, babe. Moving forward. If the reversion stuff works, we'll deal. If it doesn't work, *you'll* deal." He paused. "That didn't help either, did it?"

"We should go while you're still you," she said, her voice hollow. The peace and happiness she'd felt a little while ago became just another memory. "Once we're in a safer location, we can figure out what to do next."

"Come here, drumstick." He smiled, lifted her into his arms, and then walked to the door.

"Put me down." She didn't mean to snap, but it came out that way. "Just in case we need to fight."

"Or run," Landon said.

"No more running." She wouldn't run anymore. Running away left your back exposed. And they'd been stabbed too many times already.

"We need to leave South Florida now that The Clinic is back on its feet and carrying guns."

"Now we have something to run towards," she said, "but

we still don't know which way to go."

"We find another one of their labs," Mitch said.

"Oh, is that all?" Landon rolled his eyes. "Unfortunately, they don't have a website, nor have they helpfully named any of their labs 'The Clinic.' So considering how many years it took me to find the one here—"

"They were holding the guy who started the whole thing here." Mitch spoke calmly and confidently, helping them feel the same, even though Eden wasn't sure they had reason to. "You'd think it would be the most hidden and probably the biggest. But there were no real power players there, no one making the big decisions. Alex was in charge and she buckled with some minor—yet painful—pressure. If companies that specialize in lying and torture are anything like companies that specialize in lying and business, then we aim for the funding. Once the decision makers are gone, the other labs will domino."

Eden agreed—when you're trying to kill something, you aim for the head or the heart. A strike anywhere else just drew things out. "Four labs are testing one of the drugs named in the files—GU-121. So if we assume whoever's in charge of The Clinic is associated with one of the four…"

Mitch looked at both of them with remorse. "I don't expect you to do anything more than what you've already done for me. Because that's—Yeah, that's already too much. But if I were going to stay human, I'd head straight for Dallas."

"Why Dallas?"

"I was a little distracted when you filled me in," he said to her. "So I guess I could've missed something or a lot of somethings. But a Texas university is the one claiming one of the drugs is theirs. And there was a note about that guy who published something about it—Danvers? He works out of Dallas, right?" He looked at Landon, whose eyes seemed to be getting larger by the second. "Eden told me you'd found a flight number in Alex's planner. Could it have been to Dallas?"

"Or a few dozen other places," Landon mumbled, but he *had* to know that things were stacking up way too neatly for them to have missed.

"True, but when I met Jolie, she'd just moved to Fort Lauderdale from—you guessed it—Dallas. I know it's not a sure thing, but every time we think something is coincidental, we're wrong."

Eden's sigh was long and tragic. "Fields mentioned it too. He thought Alex was from the Fort Worth area. Fort Worth and Dallas practically share a backyard."

Landon swore. "Steve said something about Bradford coming straight from Texas." He pulled out his phone and started checking something. "How the hell did we not put all of this together?"

Because she and Landon been taking things apart, not putting them together. If they'd actually been working together instead of separately—her fault—they might have noticed the forest instead of only focusing on cutting down trees.

"You've been looking at the same shit for a long time," Mitch said. "I heard it all back to back, with ears and a brain that haven't been used in over a week."

"So we go to Texas?" she asked.

Mitch's smile was sad, guilty even. "I don't get a vote because pretty soon I won't be able to do any of the heavy lifting. Or much of anything."

Eden looked to Landon. "You decide." Because, despite their differences of late, she trusted him and knew how smart he was.

"I think...I think we should go and see. It makes more sense than anything else we've got. And it's what I would do if I were still a detective and this was a normal case. Get someone inside the lab itself to see if there's a connection between it and the one here—money, people, whatever. Of course, I'd call the precinct there and have them do the legwork, but that was a different life."

"Sorry," Mitch said quietly.

She squeezed his hand. "We're all doing what we can."

"Yeah, well...I'm doing a fantastic job of being a weight on everybody's shoulders. Like a dumbbell, emphasis on 'dumb.'"

"I can carry it for a little while longer, man," Landon said as they began to gather supplies—food, water, files, syringes, and vials. "But you're going to owe me big, like *glacially* big."

"I thought I already did."

"I'll do it for your car." He smiled. "And a pony. Your car and a pony."

"Sounds completely fair. What do you want, drumstick?"

Just you. But she already had that. In as much as he could give her. "If we make it through this, I want you to take whatever drug you have to without argument. And I want a vacation on an island somewhere. And as many piña coladas as I can drink."

He nodded.

"I also want a house in the suburbs with a big bed and a picket fence and a dog. And you aren't allowed to scare the neighbors. And I want new shoes. Lots of shoes. And a new wardrobe because the one I have is tragic. And I want nowhere to go and nothing to do and no one to fight."

His eyes were warm. "You got it."

"I'm not done yet."

His smile grew. "Okay."

"I want a ring."

Landon snorted.

Mitch's eyes widened briefly and then he simply said, "Done."

They looked at each other in comfortable silence until Landon cleared his throat, reminding them that they could stare at each other some other time.

"I need to call Chief Fuller and warn him."

"And I need..." Mitch took a deep breath. "Some fresh

air." He held his hand up to Eden. "Alone. And I promise not to go far. Or die. I just need to think for a sec."

She didn't tell him he couldn't or ask him what he needed to think about. Instead, she forced herself to nod. He took the car keys from Landon and grabbed as many of the bags as he could.

Before he left, he said, "I'll be right out front. So both of you can ogle me from the door if you need to."

Peeking through the half-opened door, she watched him load the car and heard Landon tell his old chief that he should take his family on an extended vacation.

"And Fuller?" Landon asked. "If you say anything about us, I can't be held responsible for what happens. People say all kinds of things under duress—some true and some not. If they get ahold of me, the first thing out of my mouth will be your name and how helpful you've been."

After another quick warning, Landon hung up. The lines on his face seemed deeper somehow, in just a few minutes. "I threatened a police chief. No matter how much of an asshole he is...I threatened a police chief." Landon was a good man and, for the most part, played by the rules. Using the system for something outside of them had to be hard for him.

She didn't feel guilty about it, though. Not about anything they'd done or anything they would do. "It was necessary."

"Sure." He didn't *sound* sure. Or look sure. "There will come a time when they realize all these threats are bluffs."

She shrugged. "That'd be true if we were bluffing."

He looked at her in wonder, his mouth open slightly. "You're going after innocents now?"

"I was innocent once," she said. "So were Justin, Alicia, Shelly, Tara, even Mitch. And look what happened to us. Do you think The Clinic cared? Questioned if what they were doing was fair?" As much as she despised them, she also respected their ambition, their single-mindedness. They had a goal, they chose their allies, and they did what they had to. It's what Mitch believed, too. What he had done for a living before they took it all away. Why he gave himself over to Hyde to save her.

He did what he had to. And she'd do the same. One goal— to save him. After that she didn't care what happened.

A minute later Mitch came back inside, smiling. "Unfortunately, the air out there isn't all that fresh. Did I miss anything?"

Landon looked directly at her. "No. Everything is just fine."

CHAPTER X

Craigslist is good for finding all kinds of shit for all kinds of people. Someone who will give you their old, unwanted, broken crap for free. Or someone who wants a quick fuck and who uploaded a picture of his dick to prove just how quick he would make it. And most usefully, someone who was selling an old, possibly stolen moving truck and a piece-of-shit compact.

Being useful is a wonderful thing, and when you know there's an expiration date on it, you fit in as much as you can, as fast as you can. Sometime soon, Mitch would be completely dependent on the only two people he could stand. So yeah, knowing enough about engines to pick a truck and a car that would get them all the way to Texas without breaking down was a consolation. A really small one.

Mitch negotiated the incredibly unfair trade—the Jag was worth five times the truck, the car, and the guy's house. He didn't care about making a good deal, but he needed the outlet. Arguing with the guy gave Mitch something to focus on, other than the woman clutching his side as if he'd disappear any second. Which he might. Or worse. If he died right in front of her—again—he'd hate himself more than he hated The Clinic.

It was torture—knowing the game was about to change and there was a really good chance he wasn't going to make it off the field. Or if he did, it wouldn't be on a stretcher—it would be in a body bag. And then he could look up from hell to see his reason for breathing weeping over his ugly corpse.

After the keys were passed over, Mitch pried Eden off him and helped Landon transfer their stuff into the POS compact. The soft stuff like sleeping and duffel bags was tossed into the back of the moving truck. Anything that Hyde could damage or use as a weapon was packed in the car.

"You owe me a Jag." Landon put a cooler filled with The Clinic's dope onto the passenger seat.

"Are you kidding me? I just bought you this piece of shit, and you're already asking for more?" He smacked the cop on the shoulder before jumping into the passenger side of the truck. Eden hadn't taken her eyes off him since they left the brothel. He understood. He didn't like it, but he understood.

He waved at Landon to pull out first. "Next stop: Home Depot." He smiled, hoping she would match it. Because all he saw now was nervousness and paranoia. He leaned over and turned the key, squeezing her leg as he straightened. While they drove, he kept his hand on her. *Shit.* His comforting skills were legendary. Really. A leg squeeze and saying something stupid would make her completely forget about his impending death. *Sure.*

Lots of chain, a hacksaw, a few sheets of plywood, and a couple more man toys later, they were back on the road, following Landon through a labyrinth to get to Fields' place. They made so many turns and did so much backtracking, Mitch wasn't sure if they were in West Palm or West Virginia.

Eden needed to say goodbye to Fields and the teenagers, and a phone call wouldn't suffice. Anything long distance wouldn't cut it—their lives were so unstable that not being able to touch someone meant you never really knew they were there or that they were alright.

Plus, they had some time to kill before Mitch did the whole

seizure-injection-transformation thing, and it would be safer to shoot him up and strap him down in a nice, quiet suburban neighborhood than on the side of the freeway somewhere.

He kept his mouth shut and his eyes actively looking for danger. There wasn't much to say because, fuck, small talk was a bit too small for a situation like this. And he couldn't think of anything useful or encouraging to say. *'Nice driving'? 'Stop crying'? 'It'll be okay'?* All fairly disappointing phrases in terms of last words.

So he'd wait until he could think of something profound to say. Which would probably take about twenty more years than he had.

"I can't lose you," she whispered without looking at him.

Think of something deep, asshole. "If you had nothing— no money, no clothes, no me—you'd make it through. Because the other option is unacceptable. And if you think I'm an asshole as a man, just imagine what a fucking menace I would be as a ghost." *Not good*, he thought when he saw her flinch. As he undid his seat belt, she shot him a warning look. But *seriously*? As if something as mundane as a car accident was his biggest concern? Lightening can only strike you so many times before you have to realize that you just weren't meant to be.

"Keep your hands on the wheel and your eyes on the road." Not for him. So that she didn't get banged up if they hit something. He moved into the middle of the bench seat and put his arm around her. Legendary.

"It's different for me," she said. "I barely even feel Chastity anymore—she's too much a part of me. And it never hurt." She chewed on her lip. "It's painful inside of him, isn't it?"

If she didn't feel it, then it was *very* different for her. Whether it was for the same reason she'd been able to integrate the best parts of Chastity into her or because both of Eden's parents had been Abnormals, he didn't know. Either way, he was glad she was different.

"It's manageable."

"Ever since he took over, you've been awake inside of him, right? Not sleeping like you used to. He—" Her voice broke. "He said you were screaming."

Motherfucker. "You gonna believe him or me?" Maybe before he transformed, he should cut out his tongue. "It's like a nap." *A nap?* What a fucking liar. But if she knew how void it was inside of Hyde, how cold, how painful, she'd be even more upset.

"Eden, I need to know you'll be okay. I mean, don't get me wrong, I expect some mourning. Like…at least a few months. Maybe a year of heavy-duty sadness—wearing black, lighting candles, silent weeping, all that shit. But then I want you to come out of it. Do all of the shit on your bucket list, screw anyone—" *That's a topic best left untouched.* "Do whatever you want. Live. Maybe think of me whenever you watch a horror movie."

"Horror movies don't seem that scary anymore." Her lips were tight, her grip on the wheel tighter.

"You stick with Landon and let him be part of your life." *Oh shit.* What if the two of them got together after he croaked? Was he okay with that? *Noooooo.* If he was okay with anyone, it would be Landon. But since he *wasn't* okay with anyone, Landon was a no-go too.

"And you move on," he continued. "*Buuuut*, with that said, I have no plans for kicking it anytime soon. Unless it's with my feet up, a beer in my hand, and you sitting in my lap. So no worries."

"No worries?"

He tapped the pocket where she'd put one of the syringes. "If that shit is going to work, there's no one I trust to stick me more than you." This wasn't a good conversation to have side by side, doing seventy on the highway. This was one of those conversations that should be happening face to face, with deep, meaningful looks, holding hands, being able to see and touch each other. Without the threat of vehicular manslaughter if somebody needed to study their feet or their hands for a sec while they regrouped.

"I need you to try, Mitch. I need you to…live."

He didn't ask which way she meant that because both ways were pretty grim. "I'll try, babe. I promise you, I'll try harder than I've ever tried anything."

She needed him to live. He'd never felt necessary before— that his presence made anyone's life easier, let alone better. But she needed him. He thought he'd done the right thing when he gave himself over, sacrificed his life for hers. But all he'd done was put them both in a cage. Separate cages. Each of them with their fingers crossed that the person on the other side of Hyde's walls would be okay.

It was that damn reality that kept screwing things up. Because in reality, he couldn't stick around for much longer. She'd be alone and might not be able to move on. And didn't that just suck the big one.

What if she couldn't let go of him? What if she felt the same way he did—that without the other puzzle piece, nothing fits, nothing works, nothing matters? Hopefully it wasn't that way for her and he wasn't a necessity like water or air.

Funny. Someone finally gave a shit about him and all he wanted was for her to change her mind.

Landon led them through the winding streets of a gated community and parked in front of the smallest house on the block. While Eden backed the truck into the driveway, Landon went up to the door.

Mitch called out, "We'll start rigging up the back."

Even though she and Landon seemed to think all was kosher with Fields, Mitch didn't. Fields' hands had been very, very dirty for a very, very long time. Sure, he had done it for his daughter, but—

Huh. Wouldn't Mitch have done the same or worse to make sure Eden was alright? Hurt anyone he had to? Maybe. It might not be moral but, it was understandable. Human.

Goddamn morality is a fucking pain in the ass.

When he got to the back of the truck, Eden was staring at the roll-up door as if she was gathering her courage to see what was inside. As if she already saw the prison it would be. He flipped the locking mechanism and then pulled the chain hand over hand to open the door. With no ramp to walk up, he boosted himself onto the edge and then lifted her. Not that she needed the help. It was more because he needed to be able to help her any way he could, for as long as he could.

She started unpacking the tools, giving Mitch a moment to wander around his newest, and hopefully very temporary, home. Once they cut holes in the floor, put chains through them, and wrapped the chains around the truck's frame, it would be a cage. But until then it was just a cave, the sunlight only reaching about halfway in, leaving the area farthest from the door in complete darkness.

Mitch suppressed a girlie shiver. When you're planning on going into hell chained to the floor, a little sunlight on your face is a very welcome thing.

He shoved their stuff—sleeping bags, a couple folding cots, and bags filled with clothes and supplies—as tightly as he could to the far wall. Not that he cared if Hyde got slammed by something, but it would be nice not to wake up with a broken nose. They'd lay down some plywood over the metal so he'd be comfortable, if one *can* be comfortable while chained to the floor in the back of a truck.

"I want to be close to the door, if possible," he said as he stomped on the floor in different areas, looking for weaknesses.

"Sure." Her voice. Not scared, not sad, just cold. She was already starting to separate herself. Concentration was good, but full-blown lack of emotion wasn't.

"What are you thinking?" He crouched down next to her and started piecing together what they'd bought.

She took a deep breath, but without tears or any lip wiggles. "This is so far beyond life not being fair, it feels deliberate. Like the universe hates me and is punishing me with everything it can come up with." No, she was just an unfortunate bystander to *his* punishment. Collateral damage because she loved him.

"I don't have too many things to come back for." He lifted her chin. "But it doesn't matter. Because I only need one." He looked into her eyes, trying to take a mental picture of them so he'd have something to hold onto later. And then it got too overwhelming, and he had to break the tension before one of them—probably him—started bawling. "Make that two things—I really want to see Landon in a Speedo."

She laughed lightly. "He has a great ass, doesn't he?"

"Did you really just say that?"

"That he has a great ass? Yeah, I did."

"You're so cruel," he said, taking the hacksaw out of her hands and pulling her onto his lap. "But it's not as good as mine, right?"

"I had no idea you were so insecure about your ass, Mitch." God, he loved her smile. Her humor. Her teasing.

"Not at all. I just want to make sure I'm showing it off to its full potential. If not, I'll borrow a pair of pants from the cop."

"Your ass is amazing, don't worry." Her laugh was musical. "Do you know what I love about us?" She paused for only a second, just enough time for him to hope her next word would be 'everything.' "No matter what hell we're going through, we can be normal."

"We're never going to be normal, babe."

"Yes, we are. It's not all about war or revenge or fear or being what we are. When we're not fighting or having make-up sex, we're just regular people. It helps me deal with the rest."

"I hate the fighting, but I'm a big fan of the make-up sex."

"I promise that if you stick around, you'll be so content, you won't need the make-up sex."

"Deal."

"So you'll stick around?"

"As long as humanly possible." It was a safe answer. Nothing could drag him away from her while he was human. And when he wasn't? He couldn't control that.

There was a limit to how lucky one man could be. And he was maxed out. So, to keep the universe balanced, lots of bad shit had to happen. All he could hope for was that he got the brunt of it and it touched her as little as possible.

She held his face, traced his jaw, his lips, before leaning in and brushing her lips along the same path. "Any minute you could go, and he could come back."

"Yep. But we have more dope, so you won't get rid of me for long."

They'd decided not to waste his human time on the drive. So Hyde would enjoy the road trip in the back, *on* his back. Alone.

Along the way, Landon would try to find a way in, maybe through the rent-a-cop company that handled security for the lab. Then, once they got to Dallas, Landon could start poking around. And when they were ready, they'd tap into Hyde's vein and bring Mitch back for another go at it. Hopefully a long one. Possibly a violent one. Definitely a welcome one.

"We need to finish this," he said after a too-short but incredibly satisfying kiss. "But when you wake me up, be prepared to get naked immediately. And make sure you warn Landon because he shouldn't see what I'm going to do to you."

"What'd you just say about me?" Landon stood there holding an extension cord. A few of his new friends— including one of Eden's ex-captors—were behind him. All of them stared at Mitch as if he would go beastly any second and they couldn't blink until it happened.

A second later, Eden launched herself at the bastard from the three-foot-high truck bed and landed in his arms.

To stop himself from glaring at or assaulting Fields, Mitch focused on setting up his cage. What a fantastic way to spend what could be his last couple of hours. He turned away, wondering why she was so comfortable with someone who had spent a long time fucking them over. Ignoring their chatter, he just did the socially acceptable nodding thing as Eden introduced Fields' daughter, Alicia.

"Justin, come over here." She beckoned over the other friend who Mitch would never consider a friend. "I want to introduce you."

The kid shook his head, standing back from it all as if he was afraid to get too close. And for some unknown reason that hurt Mitch's feelings. *What the fuck?* With very specific and very recent exceptions, Mitch didn't *have* feelings, and he *never* cared what other people thought of him. And it was just his luck that the one time he did care—outside of Eden—it was a sixteen-year-old punk who—

Ah-ha. A sixteen-year-old punk who looked an awful lot like Mitch had around that age. Including the slumped shoulders, the drawn face, and the *'I don't give a shit about myself or anyone else'* expression.

At sixteen, Mitch had just killed his father and found out what he had to look forward to in a couple years. And at sixteen, Justin had just been clued in on the traitorous bastards who'd given him a place to stay and pretended to like him.

That's some deep-seated idiocy there, asshole. You better find time to work on those daddy/monster issues, or you might not be healthy emotionally.

Great angsty thing to bond over. If Mitch was interested. Which he wasn't. Even if he wasn't leaving both Florida and the human race very soon, making new friends wouldn't be high on his list.

Eden sighed. "Mitch, Justin. Justin, Mitch."

"It's Mitchell or Turner, not Mitch." After a final 'hey'-and-nod, Mitch turned on the jigsaw, wondering if he'd be electrocuted, thus sending everyone into a full-blown panic as they all assumed his shakes were really a seizure. Then they'd strap him up and inject him with serum *numero dos*. The 'going back to hell' serum. Really, he couldn't remember a time he'd had this much fun.

Once he verified that electrocution wasn't going to happen, he attacked the floor, cutting a hole just big enough to run a chain through—a bunch of chains really—estimating how far apart to make them. He laughed, realizing that he needed to lie down and have someone draw a chalk outline around his sorry ass to know how far apart to put the holes.

Since Eden seemed happy talking to the others, he called out to Landon. "Hey, asshole, I need some help."

Eden kept smiling, and everyone else shut up.

The asshole jumped in the truck. "It's a pet name. He has a deep affinity for assholes. *Aaand*...that came out wrong."

Eyebrows stayed up for another second and then everyone went back to talking and glancing repeatedly at the unlucky bastard who'd be spending all his free time in the back of a truck.

"I'm not really concerned with how comfortable he is." The argument about how spread-eagled he should be was one of the best and most ludicrous arguments Mitch had ever had.

"They're *your* muscles too." Landon marked the floor. "Do you want to wake up like da Vinci's man or have every appendage asleep?"

He smirked. "Not *every* appendage."

Landon grumbled something under his breath.

"You used to love my wit, cop. Have we lost some of our magic?"

"Do you think I like doing this, Turner?" He stayed focused on the line he was drawing on the floor, but his voice was sharp. "That it's fun for me? I don't want to laugh right now, so stop it with the jokes."

"I can't." Mitch moved closer so no one would hear the pussy-ass thing he was about to admit. "I need them. The bad jokes and the inappropriate or untimely comments. I need all of them because...I'm afraid."

Landon whipped his head up from the floor to stare at him. "You said it didn't hurt."

"I lied. It…" *is unimaginable torture.* "It's not the pain I'm worried about. I need you to do what I can't—to keep Eden safe. You fucked up the last time and I appreciate it, but my luck doesn't come in twos or threes. So next time, don't fuck up. And don't let *her* fuck up, either. She's changed…again. She's different, isn't she? Doing things that aren't who she is?"

The cop nodded, making Mitch wonder how many things she hadn't told him about. He'd noticed the tension between her and Landon—it was hard not to—but that was yet another conversation that would have to wait. "Please don't let her get away with it."

"I'll do my best."

"That's what I'm counting on. You have the stuff that will bring me back, the J-some number? If it comes to it, if you can't help her, bring me out so that I can. And I'll owe you two ponies."

Landon stuck out his hand. "I hate you."

"Me too, man. Me too." They didn't exactly hold hands, but it was close. A true bond built on who the fuck knew what, because Landon was *way* too good to him. There wasn't a single thing Mitch didn't respect about the guy. And all he could do was be thankful there was a reason—as warped and unbelievable as it was—that Landon seemed to feel the same way.

Before they let go, Mitch said, "Oh, and you need to get laid. ASAP. And ditch those pants. Your ass looks too good in them."

Landon's look of total confusion only made Mitch laugh more. "You're such a tease, you know that, Turner? And one hell of a sick bastard."

"Not only my opinion, cop. My woman—" She was. She was his woman. Forever. "My woman noticed first."

Landon glanced towards Eden, his eyes wide. "Really?" Then he smirked. "You best make sure you come back, then."

Mitch knew it was a joke, but his territorial side shot up a big fucking red flag and all he could do was slow his response down. "Touch her and—"

Landon held up a hand. "Relax, asshole. I'm not touching anything that belongs to you. Other than your vast wealth, of course."

"Enjoy it. Just don't blow it all on ice cream and hookers." He lay down and let Landon finish marking the floor around him.

Mitch felt Justin's eyes on him the entire time they worked. Eventually he gave up and told the kid to crawl under the truck. "Catch the chain as it comes down, preferably not with your face."

The kid did as he was told without comment. When Mitch went down to secure the chains on the frame, he backed up as if Mitch were a rattlesnake.

"Don't worry, I don't bite guys." He laughed, knowing he was probably causing some permanent scarring. But scars came with what they were. And the kid probably had quite a collection already.

After the cop double-checked everything, Eden triple-checked everything. Alicia came outside with sandwiches and a case of Heineken. Landon and Eden passed, the kids got a head shake from Fields as he took one for himself, and Mitch claimed the rest as coping aids. He felt fine now, but he knew what was coming. Any minute he'd get the shimmy-shakes and be strapped down, so he would celebrate his masculinity for as long as he could. And what better way to do that than with a gorgeous woman tucked in his arm and an almost-full case of beer?

CHAPTER XI

Once the truck was set up, the food was eaten, and plans were made, people got fidgety. They were just waiting for Mitch to seize or transform or die or…

Die. Eden's jaw slammed shut, and she stepped away from him. Claustrophobia wasn't new to her, but this time she wasn't in a small space or tied up. Her throat was so tight, she had to concentrate to get air through it.

Not working. She bolted for the front of the truck, away from the people and the chains and the fear.

Someone asked if she was alright, but she couldn't answer. She couldn't speak.

One foot in front of the other. Hurry. Find air.

From behind her she heard Mitch say, "Let her go. She can take care of herself." He somehow understood and was respecting her needs, even though they were probably the exact opposite of his.

She put her head against the cold metal of the truck's door, staring at the pavement, trying to calm down. The logical thing for her to do was hold onto him until everything went to hell, but she couldn't. He didn't need the distance, but she did.

Mitch knew where he was going and how he would get

there. But all Eden knew was that she was lost. Her feet couldn't find the ground, and her mind was a confused mess. He was leaving her again and she didn't know how to deal with that.

It wasn't self-pity—it was the kind of feeling that creates *nothing*. Being incapable of clear thought, of not knowing what might happen or remembering what had already happened. Of not knowing where you were or who you were. Just…nothing. She was so tired. And the only person who could snap her out of it would soon be in chains on the floor of a moving truck.

Fields and Alicia ignored Mitch's advice and followed her. Right after she slumped down on the truck's running board, Fields did the same thing. Landon and Alicia created the other two corners of the square. Justin stood back about ten feet and Mitch watched her sadly from where she'd left him. The conversation was incredibly awkward, everyone too tense to speak normally. They all knew what they were waiting for.

She looked over to Mitch, leaning against the truck that would be his home once he transformed back into Hyde. The only times his eyes left her were when he glanced at Justin, who was trying hard not to stare at Mitch.

The two finally met each other's gaze—man and boy—both with something dangerous and painful inside of them. Justin was who Mitch once had been, and Mitch was who Justin might be someday. Only seconds later, they broke contact.

Eden was disappointed. If they let themselves connect, it might be good for both of them. But to force a relationship would be useless or counterproductive, so she let it go. Maybe someday, if everything went their way, the man and soon-to-be man would have another chance.

A slim chance built on another slim chance.

"I'm gonna take off," Justin said.

"Can't it wait a few more days?" It hadn't been long since Fields had become Justin's guardian, but it was obviously taking a toll on him.

"No, it can't," he snapped. "I didn't agree to this. I can't go to school, can't see my friends, can't do anything. I'm so sick of sitting around doing nothing."

Fields sighed. "Where will you be?"

"A friend's. And yes, I'll leave his phone number," he said without provocation. "But I'm spending the night. Because if I have to sleep around freaks for the rest of my life, I think one night of freedom isn't asking too much."

Mitch closed his eyes for a second and then pushed off the truck. "It's a rare thing to have someone who actually wants to help you, kid. Don't fuck it up." Without expecting a response, he came towards the group.

"Whatever." Justin took off, knocking his fist on the truck as he went around the back.

"Are you sure it's a good idea to let him go?" Mitch asked.

Eden took his arms and put them around her, tucking herself into his chest. Because he wouldn't be here to keep her standing for much longer.

"He doesn't want to move," Fields said, shrugging. "His Hyde isn't due for a couple days, so I'll give him tonight. Tomorrow we start packing up, and I'm hoping we'll be ready to leave for Georgia in a few days. Hopefully we'll be there and set up by his next transformation. But teenagers are slow when it comes to doing anything you want them to do."

"Is he doing okay with any of this?" Eden asked.

"No. But then, which one of us is?"

Mitch flinched violently, his arms tightening around her like a vise, his weight falling forward onto her. Before she could turn around, he'd fallen to his knees.

He groaned. "I think the show's about to start. Let's…oh, shit…take our seats, shall we?"

The others helped Eden get him onto his feet and walked him to the back of the truck. Landon counted the seconds. The truck bed was illuminated for the first six feet. Then there was nothing but darkness. Like an abyss. Fields and Eden vaulted into the truck to pull him up and Landon pushed from the ground.

"Stop grabbing my ass, cop."

"Shut up and start helping, asshole," Landon grumbled before resuming his count. "20…21…"

She wished he would stop. It didn't matter if the count was up or down, whatever number it ended on wasn't one Eden wanted to know.

"22…"

"I don't feel so good." Mitch was trying to help, but his abs were spasming, his arms pulling against them uncontrollably. Even the curses coming out of his mouth were broken up.

As soon as his knee was on the floorboard, Landon jumped up and Eden stepped back to let the men drag Mitch the rest of the way. She took the syringe out of her pocket, gripping it so tightly she was afraid it would break.

He never got up from his knees, dragging himself to the chains. She knew he was furious, not at what was happening but at *how* it was happening, that there were witnesses to what he thought was his weakness.

He wasn't weak. He'd never been weak.

"This isn't normal," Landon said. "Seizures don't work like this."

"I'll try to get it right…next time." Mitch's body let go and he rolled onto his back. On top of the chalk outline he'd made Landon draw. His version of irony, she supposed.

Not funny.

"I need…" Mitch groaned. "Babe, I need…another beer."

"Damn it, Mitch! It isn't funny!"

As the men cuffed his ankles, Eden caressed his face, tears running down her cheeks. He yanked her towards him, his fist wrapped around her shirt. It may have just been an involuntary muscle contraction, but it didn't matter. She wanted to be close to him.

"Love you."

Landon pried Mitch's fingers off of her. He used his weight to pull Mitch's arm to the floor and his knee to hold it still. Then he attached the cuff around Mitch's wrist.

"29...30..." Landon looked close to tears, but he did what he had to.

"Stop this, Mitch," she moaned. "Make it stop."

His body answered with more powerful convulsions, but he mouthed, '*It's okay.*'

"Liar." She nodded, wishing he wasn't lying but knowing better. "I don't want you to go."

Landon took the syringe out of her hand. It was better that he do it. Because she couldn't move. There was no guarantee this would even work. All their hope stemmed from a Clinic employee—not the most reliable of sources. Just because he was right about the seizure didn't mean he was telling the truth about the remedy.

Then she felt hands on her shoulders and then was dragged backward. She threw her elbow out behind her and heard a grunt as she hit Fields. Without apologizing or thinking, she scrambled back to Mitch on her knees.

When the next spasm hit, Mitch cried out and his entire body lifted off the floor, the cuffs and chains snapping taut with the movement. And Eden understood why Fields had pulled her back. If she'd stayed where she was, with her head so close to Mitch's, one or both of their jaws would be broken.

"I'll figure it out, Mitch. I'll find a way to make this stop."

His beautiful hazel eyes disappeared, leaving only white as they rolled back in his head.

At Landon's count of thirty-eight, Mitch started to truly seize, full force, no takebacks. His body convulsed the way it had when he'd been hit with the Taser.

But this was worse. Because this was *now*.

"Hurry, Landon!" She held Mitch's head to prevent his skull from slamming into the floor. The skin on her knuckles opened up, the rough plywood shoving splinters into her flesh.

Landon popped the plunger guard and the needle cap off

and, with one of his hands and both of Fields', immobilized Mitch's arm. The rest of his body convulsed violently in the little give the chains allowed. His feet hammered the floor with enough force to shake the truck. To shake Eden's body and mind.

Landon shoved the needle in and pressed the plunger down hard. The cry Mitch released broke Eden in half. A few seconds of agony later, he went completely limp in her arms.

Her whimper echoed off the walls. A weak sound, a tragic sound, something that could only be caused by losing. They waited without speaking or moving or doing anything other than hoping. Thirty seconds. Forty-five. One of her tears landed on his cheek.

Then he started to transform, his body lengthening, thickening. His hair growing coarse against her fingers, his facial features more severe—similar to but so different from the face she could look at forever. His beauty was taken away along with everything good inside him. But he was breathing and, for that, Eden was happy.

"It's working," Landon said, standing up. "It *has* to be working."

She pulled away so she wouldn't be touching him when he opened his eyes. His heavy head thumped onto the floor.

Ice-cold blue irises stared into hers. "Hi, honey. I'm home." His laughter filled the air, guttural, horrible, chilling.

Numbing.

Nothing left to see here, folks. Mitch was gone now.

"Let's go," she said before jumping down and walking to the cab of the truck, not looking back. When Mitch had disappeared, her emotions had, too, tucked into her subconscious, useless. As if a light switch had been thrown— on to off in a matter of seconds. Maybe it was a good thing Hyde was here. She could put away her feelings for another day and focus on how to make sure there *was* another day.

Landon pulled down the back door and clicked the lock, muffling Hyde's cackling. She climbed into the driver's seat and turned the ignition, hoping the deep hum of diesel would drown his voice out of her head.

When Fields knocked on her window, she barely flinched. "Keep them safe, okay?"

"I will," he said. "You keep *you* safe, okay?"

This was probably how a father would say goodbye to his daughter when she left for college. Fields was more of a father than she'd ever had. But instead of clothes and plastic dorm furniture in the U-Haul, there was Hyde.

Not quite the same thing. But he might be the best she'd ever have.

CHAPTER XII

Ryan waited impatiently for Newman's call. The man was an imbecile, but how much brainpower did it take to kidnap and kill people? As much as Ryan didn't want to go back to Florida, it might be necessary. See the old neighborhood, get some good Cuban food, visit his father's grave.

Except that last one was never going to happen. Because his father didn't have a grave.

The Abnormal monster didn't leave enough to bury.

But Ryan would turn things around, make things the way they should be, create something good out of the bad. At least for himself.

When his phone rang, he poured himself a bourbon before he answered. It was important that underlings knew he had better things to do than wait around for them, a lesson he'd learned when Jolie Cabot had called him drunk and irritable because things with Turner and Colfax weren't going her way. How many days later did she die? He preferred not to think about it because it made him angry—at her, at the two Abnormals who were threatening everything he'd worked for, and at himself.

He took a sip and then accepted the call. "Good news first."

He really needed some good news.

"Not sure what's going on with the Hyde, but that police chief says the ex-cop and the girl are leaving South Florida. But he didn't know where to."

Ryan kept his voice calm, like always, but he set his glass down so it didn't shatter in his hand. "That's not good news, Newman. Not at all. How much do they know?"

"All I know is what the guy told me—they're leaving South Florida and if they get caught, they'll blame him."

People like Colfax, Turner, and Landon didn't run away, they ran towards. The idiots. "They're coming here." Ryan stood and walked to the glass wall of his office. The view calmed him, the pacing not as much. So he stopped doing it.

How the hell did they figure out where he was? "They are either very lucky or it looks like you did the right thing with Harris. Although I wish it had happened before he talked to Landon."

"Then can you untie me now and let me do what I'm good at?"

He would never know exactly what Harris had told Landon, but it would be stupid to assume he hadn't mentioned other things—like the names of their other labs, including the one here in Dallas, and how to make and keep Turner human. Thankfully, Harris didn't know much more than that. "It would have been nice to know exactly what Harris told them."

"Once they're all dead, it won't matter what he told them."

"I'll be sure to let you know the minute I want your advice, Newman. But for right now, you need to keep your fucking mouth shut and let me think."

"I don't like it when people are disrespectful to me. No matter who they are."

Ryan's stupid-radar must still be on the fritz, because there was no other explanation as to why everyone he hired was so moronic.

He sighed, running a hand through his hair. It needed a trim. "If you think I'm going to apologize, then you're even stupider than I thought you were. You do what you're told because I'm paying you to do it. However, this time there's a bonus involved."

"I'm still going to need that apology," the idiot muttered.

"Does fifteen more apiece make my insult sting any less?" He paused. "Yeah. That'll do."

Ryan had been so close to expanding The Clinic's mission—turning it from just the one facility in Florida that Ian had set up into two. Then four. Then as many as Ryan could manage, which by his figuring was as many as there was financing to build and people with enough intelligence to do what he told them to and nothing more.

Of course, now that plan would have to be delayed because of Colfax and Turner. The irony wasn't lost on him—while trying to gain control of their Abnormal sides, they'd lost control of their human sides. Double the irony, actually, because it was perfect little Eden Colfax who was fucking up his life again.

But once those two were muzzled, things could continue as he wanted them. He'd have Colfax and, if possible, they would continue the testing they were doing on Hyde01 with Hyde0016—Turner. Because there was something intensely poetic about that. And if Turner happened to die, there were others who could fill the position.

Newman cleared his throat. "I might be able to get to them before they hit Dallas if I move quick."

"And what? Shoot the men on the side of a freeway? And then hide three hundred pounds of dead Hyde, two hundred of dead Landon, and a hundred pounds of unconscious Colfax somewhere before anyone notices?" Before Newman could reply, Ryan added, "Those were rhetorical questions."

"Wha—?"

"It means you shouldn't answer them. And 'shut up' means you should be quiet until I say you can speak." He went back to his chair, sat down, and took a long sip of his drink.

Maybe this was a blessing. With the Florida facility being

unusable, he would've brought Colfax here eventually anyway. The lab was already set up, there were still a few empty cages, and he'd juggle the dorm rooms so she would have the nicest one. Once he'd chosen a scientist he could trust enough to replace Bradford, Ryan would be more hands on.

By the time his drink was gone and the ice hit his lips, he'd decided. "If they're coming here looking for me, then maybe I should let them."

"Not a bad idea to use you as bait," Newman said. "I can–"

"I'm not bait. Ever," Ryan snapped. "Bait is the little guy. The prey. The temptation for a larger fish. There *are* no larger fish, and I'm no one's fucking prey. If I have to flush them out, I will." *Like a falcon, not a dog.* "But I'd rather not. So here's what going to happen: I'll figure out a way to get their attention. Once we know where they are, you take care of Landon and the Hyde, if it's not already dead by then. Kill them only if you have to."

"And the woman?"

The woman who wasn't really a woman. Somehow she'd become more than that—not with pharmaceuticals—by her own nature. Within her was the solution to every question he'd ever had about the Abnormals, how he would go from answering to the Board to owning the Board.

The way it should be.

"Colfax doesn't die. I don't care how you make it happen, but I want her breathing when you bring her in." And if that plan failed as badly as so many others had, Ryan would still be more 'hands on,' but they would be bloody when he did it. He would kill Newman and any other throat he could get his hands on.

"And Newman? Whatever you do, if you see her with a man you don't recognize, don't shoot him. Because that'll be me. Got it?"

"Why bother with her?"

"Because she knows something I don't." *And I think our meeting is overdue.*

CHAPTER XIII

They drove straight through, only stopping for food, bathroom breaks, and a catnap. At every stop, Landon checked on Hyde, cracking the door a tiny bit to check his bindings, but not enough for any passerby to see their cargo. Along the way, they secured an empty warehouse in a sea of empty warehouses on the east end of Dallas. According to Google Maps, it looked safe and far away from everything.

Google Maps was right. Eden pulled the truck through the large roll-up loading door and parked in the center of the warehouse. Damn, there was a lot of space. A lot of hollow, cold, hard space.

"Think pillows and a few knick-knacks will brighten up the place?" When she heard the echo of her voice, she looked up, imagining she would see it being carried away. At least there was a lot of light from the windows near the ceiling. Not that they'd be around long enough to think of it as home. She hoped.

Garbage, a few old chairs, a three-legged table, and some old building materials were the only signs of civilization. Probably leftovers from when a building developer realized the place was a bigger shithole than he'd thought and no one would ever want to live here. She sure as hell didn't.

But there were a few things they could use—the table, some plywood, one decent chair. Off to the side was a small reception area with a long built-in desk, a separate office, and a truly disgusting bathroom. It was enough to make her miss the luxury of the brothel.

"This place is screaming for an extreme makeover," she said. "Or a wrecking ball."

Landon was already unpacking the car. "Think of it like camping. On cement. With a shitty view and stagnant air."

Despite Eden's desire to bring Mitch back *now*, she knew it was a bad idea. Hyde might need some more time to fully recover from the seizure before it was even safe for Mitch to use his body again. And it wasn't as if they could ask Hyde and expect the truth. In addition, and worse, was that bringing him back also brought the possibility of the RLS-7 not working. Their supply was already limited.

So angrily, disgustedly, and guiltily, Eden made the call. Hyde would stay in the truck, chained down at all times. Different city, different cage. Mitch wouldn't be revived until they knew more, had more of the drug, or had no other choice. Landon didn't say a word, maybe because he understood how much strength it took her to make a decision that condemned Mitch to more time in his prison.

She unlocked the back of the truck and pulled the chain to raise the door. The heat was almost suffocating. Texas weather was better than what they had driven through, but inside the truck it was still hellishly hot. Getting their sleeping bags and clothes would have to wait until it cooled down a little. They could do the supply run for flashlights, batteries, and food first.

Add air freshener to the list. "How you doing in there, big fella?" She climbed up and checked his bindings.

"I got an itch," Hyde muttered. "Need you to scratch it…with your tongue."

"I'll keep the door open to air the place out but, if you start yelling, I'm going to change my mind." She backed away from him—you don't turn your back on evil, even if it's strapped down.

"Hey," he called. "Take the toddler with you. He needs a snack. And a diaper change."

"What?"

"Come out, little mouse," he sang in a rough falsetto. "And go away. You're stinking up the place."

Eden stepped forward confused. "What—?"

Her suitcase slid forward by itself. Then a sleeping bag moved. And then she saw him.

Justin.

"Oh my god." She wanted to scream, 'What the hell are you doing here?' but she didn't. Because he looked so terrified. Shell-shocked from spending hours, days, trapped in here with Hyde. Alone. Because she didn't check...she didn't want to be close to Hyde...she didn't think...

"Come here," she said softly, moving towards him.

Small and shaky steps brought him out of the shadows, where it had been too dark them to see the boy who'd stowed away, hiding behind all of their stuff. He bumped into the wall, staying as far away from Hyde as he could get.

What did the bastard say to him? She could barely stand to be around him and hear his ramblings. Justin had been trapped in here, unable to get away, since they left Florida.

She remembered the first night she'd seen Hyde and the things he had said to her, so she knew the kinds of filth Justin must have heard. That moment, flattened to her chair by the weight of her new reality, had been the most frightening moment of her life. But she could have left, gotten up and walked out the door. Justin had been huddled in the back of a moving truck, no way to escape and nowhere to run.

"You're okay now. I'm going to take you out of here." She put her arm around him and led him to the edge, jumping out first and helping him down.

"Good talking to ya, little mouse," Hyde said. "Remember

what I told you."

"Shut up!" She yanked the truck door closed so that Justin wouldn't hear the laughter and called to Landon for help.

After they cleaned Justin up and gave him something to eat, he sat huddled on the ground of the reception area dressed in Landon's extra clothes and wrapped in a blanket, his eyes still huge—whites wide from fright, edges red from crying. Eden and Landon sat so close, all of their knees touched.

They watched him, saying nothing for a long time.

Eden spoke first, trying to keep her voice calm and quiet. "Why did you come?"

"Is that what I'll turn into?" he asked, as if he hadn't heard her question. "If we can't find more serum?"

"We'll find more." Fields had a decent supply, but eventually it would run out. So, yes, there was a chance it would happen, but she would make sure it didn't.

"What if you can't? What if there *is* no more?"

"There's more. That's why we came here—because there's another facility here."

Landon climbed to his feet. "I'll call Fields and see about a plane ticket for him."

"Let me stay!" Justin grabbed his pant leg. "Please."

"We can handle it, kid. You'll be safer with Fields."

"Please."

"Why did you stow away?" Eden asked, hearing the desperation in his voice, understanding and recognizing it.

Tears filled his eyes, his jaw shook, and he shivered despite the hot air and the blanket. Eden glanced up at Landon, silently asking him for more time, enough to hear Justin out.

"Look, if you don't have a reason to be here," Landon said, "then I have no reason to let you stay. As you may have noticed, this isn't a good place or time for rebellious shit. I already have enough of that to deal with as it is."

"I didn't do it to rebel."

"Then why'd you do it?"

"I heard what they did to Alicia," Justin said quietly,

dropping his head down as if he couldn't confess something and look at them at the same time. As if he was ashamed. "Fields didn't know I was there, but I heard every word he said. They were in the living room, and both of them were crying. Fields kept apologizing for not believing her. For believing Alex when she told him it was just a sick fantasy from her Jekyll." Then he glanced up at Eden. "But it wasn't. They had her raped. To get her pregnant."

"I know. They did a lot of terrible things." She tried not to think of what they'd done to Alicia too much because it made her nauseous made her own abuse seem almost paltry in comparison. To be raped by a monster at the goading of those you trusted, all so that *they* could have a baby. To hold in their arms, to sing lullabies to. And then to strap down and test as if the child were nothing but another lab animal.

"They'll be punished for what they did to Alicia, Justin. I promise."

He looked at her without more tears, but with a grief that she could barely look upon. "What if it was me?"

She didn't get it. Until she did. Until she felt his pain as if it was her own.

Oh God. She shook her head. "It—" They didn't know which Hyde had been used to rape and impregnate Alicia. It could have been Justin's.

Eden wouldn't lie. Not because of what she used to believe—you can't expect others to be honest with you if you're not honest with them. Because that was bullshit.

What she believed now was much simpler and more…honest. People lied because they didn't give a shit about your feelings and because lies got them what they wanted.

She didn't lie to Justin because he was strong enough to take it. Even if he wasn't right now, sugarcoating it wouldn't help or toughen him up. Being what they were, to live in their world, required a skin so thick that nothing could get through.

Not to mention that Eden was in a shitty mood about

eighteen hours of the day and lying took work, thought, and planning. She needed that energy for other things.

"We don't know who it was," she said, putting her hand on his leg. "But even if it was your Hyde, it wasn't *you*. It's not your fault. You didn't do anything wrong."

"Tell that to Alicia."

It didn't matter how many times they said it, he would never truly believe them. So eventually they stopped talking and stepped outside.

"We need to send him back." Landon started pacing. "Now. We'll get him on a plane and make sure Fields keeps him locked up until all of this is over."

Sending Justin back would mean forcing him away from his greatest fear. She'd done that. For years. And it didn't work. Pretending things weren't what they were and that nothing affected her.

Eden shook her head. "He should stay. We'll call Fields so he doesn't worry, but Justin stays here." He was so brave for someone so young. Sending him away now would negate that courage. If he didn't overcome this guilt now, he'd never be able to face who he was.

"We can't babysit him, Eden. He's just another complication."

"He's also another set of hands and eyes. How many trustworthy ones do we have? I count four of each. That's not enough." She grabbed Landon's arm. "I'm not saying we send him out to fight. But he could keep an eye on this place, make sure no one comes inside, and be here if, by some miracle, Mitch comes back without the drug."

"You want him to babysit the creature that put that look on his face? Whose greatest pleasure is to terrify a kid?"

"If Justin doesn't deal with it, he'll always be afraid. Not just of Hyde—of himself, of life, of everything. If we push him away now, emotionally, he'll never come back."

"We can worry about that later. Once all of this is over."

She was beginning to doubt it would ever be over. "We

don't know what's going to happen, so we prep him for every scenario. Give him a safe spot, make sure he understands what to do and what not to do. Please, Landon. He thinks he raped someone. It doesn't matter that it wasn't his fault—he thinks it is. Give him a chance to redeem himself in his own eyes."

All of us need that chance.

After staring at her for a minute that held an eternity, Landon yanked his arm away and stormed back inside. Justin scrambled to his feet, his eyes wary, his hands in front of him.

"How long until you transform?" Landon yelled.

Justin looked at Eden uncertainly. But she knew Landon wasn't going to hurt him. Of course, if she was wrong, she'd take care of it.

"Don't look at her. Look at me. How long?"

The response was so quiet, they had to read his lips. "Tomorrow night."

"Shit!" He started pacing again. "I knew it. What would have happened if we made another few stops? You could have been in the damn truck with Hyde when you transformed! What the hell were you thinking?"

"I want to know." Justin's voice picked up speed and volume as he spoke. "I *need* to know. I was so stupid to trust those people. I know I screwed up, but I had to come. I *had* to."

Landon fumed for another minute. "You'll be cuffed tomorrow, got it? No soft straps. *Cuffs.* Because we're not wasting time trying to find something softer. Then you have three days. *Three days.* At the end of those three days, you get on a plane and wave goodbye with a big-ass grin on your face. And then, I swear on all that's holy, if I hear you've made as much as an argumentative peep to Fields, you'll think back on the time you spent in that truck with fondness."

"But—"

"Three days," Landon said tightly. "Then you're gone."

Justin nodded. "Yeah, fine, whatever." His shoulders slumped as he said it, turning right back into a teenager.

"Okay, I'm glad we got that settled." Eden turned to Landon. "You want to do the supply run or should I?" As much as she'd like a chance to scope out the area around The Clinic's Dallas facility, it might be better if Landon had a chance to cool down. On second thought… "You know what? I think I should go while you get things set up here."

His eyes narrowed. "You sure?"

"If I don't move a little, get some space from him"—she nodded towards the truck—"I'm going to start freaking out. And my freak-outs aren't fun for any of us."

Landon didn't have to say anything to let her know he agreed. She saw it every time he looked at her. He wasn't here for her benefit, even though it was one. Someday she'd make it up to him. Make him trust her, like her again.

But right now she had more important shit to worry about than friendships. She had an organization to take down, a boy to help heal, and a man to bring home from hell.

She hoped her smile was reassuring. "And I'm going to need all your IDs."

CHAPTER XIV

Eden's first stop was the Copy Lobby. Social Security cards were easy to doctor, but just in case they ran into someone with experience spotting forgeries, she stuck to making only a few minor improvements. In their brief and purposefully vague discussion before she left the warehouse, they agreed to change his name as little as possible. Worst case, if flags were raised, it would look like a computer mix-up, not anything more sinister.

His new identity wouldn't hold up for long or under close scrutiny. But it was the best they could do with limited supplies, very little time, and absolutely *no* friends who were criminals. Cop friends are great until you need something illegal done. Hopefully, once Landon was inside, it would only take a day or two for him to find some useful information.

Switching his names around was the simplest, especially with the design of his Florida driver's license. All she had to do was add a comma after 'Landon' and anyone outside of Florida would assume the Department of Transportation put the last name first.

He should keep the goatee. The picture she used was

current. With more facial hair and a little less weight than he used to have, he looked like a different man. A pretty good-looking one.

Already feeling quite productive, she tucked the cards of 'Landon Nicolas' into her pocket, whipped up a gushing letter of recommendation from Chief Fuller, had it printed out on fancy paper, and moved on to the next order of business—the one she hadn't mentioned to Landon because she knew how angry he would be. And it's easier to ask for forgiveness than permission. Although, she wasn't going to ask for forgiveness either.

Their plan hinged on Landon getting a job as a security guard for Malvers Labs' building. Things were already in the works. A friend of a friend of his ex-partner from Atlanta had a friend who worked at the rent-a-cop company that supplied the building's guards.

Eden needed more friends…or *a* friend. A normal one.

But it was a big jump to assume there would even be an open position. And that had led to Eden realizing what she could do to help. She might not be able to get too close, but she had to do something. It was going to be hard enough to stay on the sidelines once Landon was inside.

The square was empty when she arrived, everyone having gone home for the day, but she kept her baseball cap pulled down low just in case.

So this is it. It was nearly as impressive as the Florida facility had been—meaning, not very. The Dallas location was set up in a square, three-story building with square, three-story buildings on either side of it, a fountain and grassy quad in front of them.

How completely underwhelming. There were no pitchforks or flames anywhere. The lab wasn't even called 'The Clinic' or 'We Cage and Torture People Inc.' So there was a chance that it was nothing other than a legitimate business working on legitimate shit.

But Eden didn't think so. This was the center of the hive.

Finally. She felt it in her bones.

She walked around the Malvers building and the ones to each side of it, counting exits and ducts big enough to squeeze through and memorizing the names of every business in the square that was actually a triangle. It was all information they needed to keep in their 'just in case' pocket.

While standing at the southeast corner of the building, she heard a door open and a man's voice. She held in a cry of pain when her back hit the stucco wall, and then she peeked around the corner.

Through the slats of the locked fence surrounding a garbage area, she saw a uniformed security guard talking on his cell phone. After tossing a bag into the dumpster, he stopped to have a nasty fight with his girlfriend or wife. Whichever she was, theirs was not a healthy relationship. And Eden was about to make his evening even worse. She waited until he yelled an insulting goodbye and went back into the building.

Then she moved. With a running start, she vaulted over the fence, landing on top of the dumpster with a bigger noise than she would've liked. The thing slid forward slightly as she jumped down. She stopped the door just before it smashed her fingers.

The door opened into a concrete and metal stairway. The guard's footsteps and grumbling echoed from a floor or two above her. But it sounded like he was coming down, probably because of the thump she had made when she landed on the dumpster.

Damn it. She should've come up with an actual plan. Something. Anything that wouldn't expose her but that would involve being productive. Because in the last week, the number of her accomplishments was in the negative.

She slipped outside as the guard came down the last flight of stairs. The space between the dumpster and the fence wasn't big, but then, neither was she. With her hands on the metal, her whole body tense, she waited.

This is a terrible idea. What the hell are you doing? Even if there were an answer, there was no time to think of it.

The door whined as it opened, and the guard whined as he walked out. "That bitch's voice is never going to leave my head." He moved from near the door to directly in front of the dumpster. "Making me hear things."

Eden shoved the dumpster forward as hard as she could, hearing a crack and a yelp of confusion as it hit him. And then nothing. No sound, no movement, no cries for help.

Shit. What if she'd killed him?

He was half sitting, half lying on the ground, completely unconscious. She hoped. After a quick assessment, she felt better. A lot better than he would when he woke up. One of his legs looked broken, maybe a wrist, but he was still alive.

She wasn't sure what bothered her more—the lack of adrenaline coursing through her veins or the lack of guilt filling her mind. Her breathing and heart rate had barely sped up. A normal person would be feeling different. Did it mean she was more determined or more callous now? She backed up for a second and then went to check the guard's pulse again. His uniform didn't say 'I work for your enemy' anywhere on it, but it was still true. She knew it. And she knew the kind of people The Clinic employed.

Do what you have to. That's what she promised herself. She had no reason to feel bad—*they* never did. The guard was still alive, the security company would need to find a replacement, and she hadn't been seen. Finally, a gain at no cost to Landon, Mitch, or her.

So, all in all, she'd done something good. She just wasn't sure that it was right.

By the time she got back to the warehouse, she'd convinced herself that what had happened to the guard was no more than he deserved. He wasn't going to be put in a cage or tested on, and he'd probably *want* the drugs he'd get.

He'll be fine. And so would she.

"What the hell took you so long?" Landon asked.

"I made an extra stop." Heading directly to the reception area, she raised her arms to show him the multitude of plastic shopping bags she was carrying.

"Where?" There was trust and then there was *trust*. And obviously, Landon didn't have both for her. She didn't make eye contact until he was standing in front of her and she couldn't avoid it. Like always, he looked at her through narrowed eyes, suspicious of every word that came out of her mouth.

"Exactly where you think I went, Landon. Why your voice is a few notches lower and your hands are fisted. But I'm fine and no one saw me."

He slammed his teeth together, cutting off what he really wanted to say. After a deep breath, he asked, "Why?"

"To scope out the place." She pushed her hair out of her face and started unpacking the supplies. "Two rear exits, one leads into a garbage area, fenced but jumpable. Parking garage that probably has an internal entrance."

"And what would've happened if they saw you? We already have enough problems."

"I needed to see it. I know I can't go inside, but I had to at least see it. Besides, once you're in, *he*"—she motioned towards the truck—"and a sixteen-year-old boy are going to be my only company, so it was nice to get out."

Actually, she had hated every step that brought her back here. She didn't want to see Hyde, hear him, or sense the hold he had over her. The rage and hate that rolled off him and landed right on her. Seeing him was a constant reminder of who he was holding hostage—the person she wanted more than air. And Justin, as much as she loved him, wasn't that much easier to be around. He was still shaken by his time in the truck, and she was responsible for that almost as much as he was.

"You can't go back, Eden."

She nodded, knowing she would. Knowing what she had to tell him next wasn't going to go over well.

"On the productive side, I think I just gave you a big boost in your job search. You're welcome."

"Thanks," he said tentatively. "How'd you manage that?"

"Since you're the one who's going to have all the fun, I wanted to help at least. And you can't get a job if there are no openings, so…" There was no way to say it without making him furious. "I know for a fact that a position opened up about an hour ago."

He stopped moving. "What did you do?"

"No permanent damage. He's just going to need a little time to recover."

"Jesus, Eden. Are you kidding me?"

"He worked for them, Landon. Tell me one person who works for them who doesn't deserve a concussion…or worse. Even Fields got smacked around, and he had an excuse." She knew Landon considered her relationship with Fields just another unhealthy milestone. He thought that after she'd found out about her own father, she substituted Fields for him without breaking stride. So that she didn't have to deal with her daddy issues.

But she wasn't replacing anyone with anyone. She just wasn't convinced that *now* was the time to deal with her emotional baggage. Eventually she'd unpack, find an empty drawer somewhere in her mind for all of it. But not now. She was strong enough to carry it without even noticing the extra weight.

"Of course," she continued, "you still need to get the job, but at least there's an opening."

"We should've talked about it first."

"So that you could forbid me to go?" she snapped. *Totally unproductive.*

He answered her anger with calm. "Because we're on the same side."

This was the danger of two strong, stubborn, independent people trying to work as a team. And when they added Mitch, it got even worse. But with no idea how to change the nature of their personalities, all she could do was sigh in frustration.

"You're right. Sorry."

"Ditto," he said. "Can I see the IDs?" He studied them in silence, turning them occasionally to catch the light in different ways, glancing at her regularly. "Nice work."

"They're only useful if you can get the job."

"Already taken care of. It's nice to have friends who trust you enough to not ask a lot of questions. I got the job at the security company but still need to be placed. I'll request a spot at the lab first thing tomorrow."

Landon looked just as good on paper as he did in person. He also knew exactly what to say to the woman in charge of placements. One restless night and a phone call later, he hung up with a beautiful smug-ass grin on his face.

"Nice work," she said.

"I need to pick up my uniform and give them copies of my pretty new IDs. And it turns out that a spot just opened up at Malvers Labs. Night shift. Let the fun begin."

"I love a man in uniform."

"Stop laughing."

She didn't. "I'm sure you'll look great, Landon. I can't wait to see it."

CHAPTER XV

The rest of the day was spent organizing themselves and looking up everything they could find on Malvers Labs. With very little other than the GU-121 to connect *this* lab with The Clinic, both Eden and Landon still thought they were on the right track.

A detective's intuition matching up with an Abnormal's had to mean something.

Officially, the entire Malvers network was scraping by. And the employee roster for Dallas was very, very slim in regard to who actually made the decisions. A long list of names with no job titles higher than 'executive assistant'.

Assistant to whom? A ghost?

When the sun went down, Landon caught her eye and nodded towards Justin. While he dragged a chair into the office area, she called Justin over to help her sort supplies that didn't need sorting. But a kid shouldn't have to watch his cage being built, whether it was made from steel bars or from a thick wooden chair and metal cuffs.

They waited for as long as they could, but when it was time, it was time. Knowing it was Justin's first transformation in cuffs, Eden talked while Landon put them on him. As gently as he could.

"It's okay, E," Justin said. "I'm not afraid."

"Duh. I know that," she said flippantly, knowing they were both lying. He'd seen what he might become someday so, from now on, every transformation would be frightening. "It's just nice to have someone new to talk to. Landon's so serious all the time." She spoke about only pleasant things until Landon left for work and Justin couldn't keep his eyes open any longer.

Let the fun begin. She sighed and settled in for another long, unpleasant evening. Alone.

⌁⌁⌁

Landon stood in front of Malvers Labs, taking in as much as he could. In another life, this might've been a good career move—they certainly paid well. Evil doesn't skimp in the monetary reward system. The only obvious downside was the uniform. Aside from being highly uncomfortable, he was still unhappy about Eden saying that his ass looked better in jeans. His body was the only thing he could still be proud of. Not that anyone was looking.

As soon as he stepped through the door, he checked out the weaponry. The guards wore Tasers, but they were nothing like the ones in Florida. These were off-the-shelf, double-pronged, wired ones.

Turner will be thrilled.

His new boss explained how things worked, and Landon answered all of his questions honestly. Because the guy didn't ask the right questions.

No, he'd never worked security before, but being a cop gave him the necessary experience. Yes, he'd been let go, but he'd been highly praised by his ex-chief whose letter of recommendation explained it was because of budgeting issues.

Then Landon was passed off to another security guard

named Rick. Young guy, short, fairly harmless-looking until you looked at the tats on his knuckles. Maybe the company had some kind of prison outreach program. But Rick was full of smiles and info for the newbie, so Landon wasn't overly concerned. People can change.

During the tour, he tried not to appear overly observant. He'd have time to really check things out later. He noticed the basics and listened intently to schedules and protocols and typical workplace gripes, reading between the lines and learning everything he could.

The security was strong, but there were always weaknesses, flaws, fissures. Their office was just off the lobby, behind the reception desk. Long hallways led to the labs, and all the upper floors were either storage or offices. Supposedly.

Landon clipped the keycard to his belt loop and followed his tour guide to each door, being told what was inside but not going into any of them.

"*This* one you should see," Rick said, stopping in front of a door marked 'Lab 4.'

Landon glanced at his watch. "People stay this late?"

"She's always here—works at night so people won't bother her. Dr. Danielle Sinclair. She seems okay most of the time, but don't ever cross her. Or talk to her. Or look at her too closely."

"Okay."

"Really, man. Don't piss her off. She's not the head of the department, but she should be. Very serious and very hot." Rick swiped his keycard and opened the door. "So I'd suggest you admire her from afar like the rest of us do."

He nodded, even though he had no intention of admiring anyone here. He was a guest in his enemy's home, and the last thing he planned on doing was—

"What do you want?" She whipped her head up, a glare narrowing her dark eyes, a tendril of light brown hair falling loose from her ponytail.

Landon rocked back a step. Okay, fine. Maybe there was a little admiration to be had. But a black mamba is beautiful, a leopard is graceful. And getting too close to either of them isn't good for your health.

"Well?" she asked, her fingers tapping the counter.

"Sorry, doc," Rick said. She grimaced, probably a reaction to the derivative title he'd just used. "I was just showing the new guy around. Didn't mean to interrupt you."

"And yet, you're so good at it." After a quick glance at Landon, she looked back to whatever she'd been working on. "Are you leaving now, or aren't you done gawking at me yet?"

"I'm not quite done yet," Landon said without thinking. Rick elbowed him in the side.

"Excuse me?" she snapped, looking up again.

"Never ask a question if you don't want to hear the answer, Dr. Sinclair." So much for staying under the radar. But she was obviously a direct person and would probably respect someone who was the same. He'd learn more from her and about her with a straightforward approach than with tiptoeing and ducking. A woman, especially an attractive one, often has to fight to get where she wants to be. Then she has to fight to stay there.

Rick had already conveyed how her male coworkers felt—it was fine to ogle her but not okay to talk to her. Landon's mother and two sisters would've castrated him if they ever saw him do that. Hopefully Sinclair would see his bluntness and the way he spoke to her as a sign of respect—something that seemed to be lacking in her coworkers.

She leaned her hip against the counter, spreading her arms out. "Please, help yourself. I needed a break, and there's nothing I like more than being objectified."

He shook his head. "I'm not objectifying, I'm appreciating. A completely natural reaction to beauty."

"It's unfortunate that keeping your opinions to yourself isn't a natural reaction as well."

"And that wasn't an opinion."

She *was* attractive and, unless she'd never looked in a mirror before, she knew it. She looked away briefly, blood filling her cheeks. But her embarrassment was gone a moment later. "I hope you've enjoyed your tour because you're not going to last very long here."

"They hired me to be observant." He shrugged, smiling. "And I'm good at what I do." When he heard Rick moan behind him, he realized he'd moved towards her.

Shit. Back off, dickhead. What was done was done, but he needed to keep an eye on his own behavior as well as hers.

He didn't back up, but he *did* apologize. "I'm sorry. I didn't mean to be rude or embarrass you."

She looked at Rick, and Landon saw a quick flash of hurt in her eyes. "Anything's better than being snickered at and talked about behind my back." She focused on Landon. "What's your name?"

"Landon." He looked for a reaction, any sign that she recognized his name. He saw nothing—no flinch, no grimace, nothing. "Landon Nicolas. Most people call me by my last name."

"Well, Landon Nicolas, you're definitely not suffering from low self-esteem. But I need to get back to work, so…"

"Just another minute." He heard Rick curse.

Her eyes widened, but the corner of her mouth curled up. Daring him, challenging him. "Thirty seconds."

He nodded without losing eye contact. "Agreed."

"Shit," Rick muttered.

They looked at each other, communicating without speaking a word. He held her gently. It wasn't about proving dominance—it was about proving equality. But he knew she was testing him. She seemed surprised that his gaze never strayed to her body. Like hers did briefly.

Am I really this stupid? He had to pull back, to blink his way out. Return to reality. Yes, she was beautiful, but she was also poisonous. As a scientist in the company, she knew what they were doing. She might not know about his involvement, but she sure as shit knew her own.

After about thirty seconds, he released her, dropping his gaze and bowing slightly. "Thank you for your time."

She laughed, looking a bit off-balanced. "You're welcome...I think. There's something strange about you, Landon." The way she said his name sounded familiar, as if they'd known each other for longer than two minutes. As if she knew exactly who he was and how to get under his skin.

And that made his pants all the more uncomfortable. There wasn't enough give for a cock that had just been woken up after a really, really long time.

He cleared his throat. "It's Nicolas."

"You said that most people call you by your last name. Science strives for predictability, Landon. People shouldn't."

Why'd she have to be one of the bad guys? Thankfully and unfortunately, he would get to know her. She was exactly who they needed—someone who knew the science as well as the bullshit. With any luck, she was like Fields and, once she really knew what she was a part of, she'd come over to their side of the tracks. So a little finesse was necessary, a casual interrogation style.

But keep your cock in your pants. As attractive as she was, Landon had too much to lose—in the war and in himself.

CHAPTER XVI

One thing Ryan had learned from the Abnormals was that every good thing comes with a bad thing. And that meant that he was due a lot of good things.

He didn't like Alex. In fact, he didn't like anyone. But he was running out of people he could trust even a little bit, and that was a problem.

So he tried to keep the condescension out of his tone. "We've all made mistakes, Alex." *Such as relying on imbeciles.* "But now, more than ever, we need to pull together, take what's left and make something great out of it."

"It would be easier if Newman didn't keep shooting people, though, wouldn't it?"

"He is one of the mistakes I was referring to."

The first time Ryan had hired Newman, it was for a very simple job. Of course, if he'd known that the 'very simple job' was dating a detective—an overzealous, curious, and moderately intelligent detective who was now a huge pain in the ass—Ryan might have handled things differently. And some of the shit he was dealing with now might never have started.

"But, for now, Newman's necessary. He can find anyone.

It's his gift. Everyone has to be good at something, don't you think?" But most of the time those things were useless or just plain stupid. "I've given him very clear instructions so that, once he tracks them down, he won't accidentally kill them."

He could tell it made Alex nervous to know he employed someone who could find her if she ever ran. Her expression was very possibly the highlight of his whole week. When Alex wasn't being an idiot, she was smart. And Ryan needed smart, predictable, and malleable people if he was going to get out of this with something of value.

When his cell phone started vibrating, he checked the time. Hopefully it was Newman calling to say all of Ryan's problems were now solved.

It wasn't. In fact, with one look at the Caller ID, Ryan had a feeling his problems were about to get a *lot* bigger.

Ron Dunlap never called this late, nor did he ever call with good news or compliments. So all Ryan could hope for was something less than terrible.

"Mr. Dunlap, how are you?"

"I've called an emergency meeting of the Board, Whittley. We're all coming to you."

Ryan flinched. "A meeting?" Emergency meetings qualified more as a really fucking terrible thing. "Here?" They met so infrequently, he was surprised they recognized each other. And in Dallas? Never. *Ever.*

"Of the Board?" Alex's voice held all the shock Ryan felt.

"One second, sir. Someone was just leaving." He covered the phone with his hand and whispered, "We'll talk more in the morning." After Alex closed the door behind her, he let his face contort into the expression he'd been holding back. *Fuck.* "I don't think a meeting is necessary, sir. I've spoken to each of you and—"

"That's what makes me uncomfortable. Phillips might get more information because you have a longer telephone conference. Or you might tell D'Apuzzo something and forget to tell me. In fact, I had no idea you hired that man who cleans things until D'Apuzzo told me."

How did D'Apuzzo know about Newman? "I wasn't deliberately keeping anything from anyone. None of you normally concern yourself with that end of things."

"We're all going to sit down in a room and discuss exactly what went wrong in Florida and what you've done to make sure it doesn't happen in Dallas."

After everything he'd done for them, the bastards still didn't trust him. "All of you?"

"Yes. And I'm bringing my son as well. The others already know."

"Great." Another ass to add to the four he was already kissing. Although Dunlap was about as much of an asshole as Ryan's father was, so maybe Ryan and the new kid on the Board would bond over shitty dads. He wondered if Gregory hated the rest of his family, too.

"I'll be meeting with the others first and will need access to the project files. We'd also like to see the ones you have at the Shop. Probably just the big ones, though—the others are less impressive visually."

Completely pointless. They wouldn't understand anything in the files, and Dunlap only wanted to show the Hydes off to his kid and the other Board members.

"Sounds great, sir. When is everyone getting here?"

"Friday, but we'll meet first thing Saturday morning."

Ryan went through the list of lies he'd told them: Turner was dead. Colfax was being transported to Dallas. Landon was no longer an issue. What happened in Florida was due to the staff's ineptitude with Hyde01 and had nothing to do with the three banes of Ryan's existence.

He had a day and a half to make all of that true. The men had to die, Colfax had to be taken, and everyone else's mouths had to be glued shut.

"I look forward to meeting your son, sir."

The line was dead. Just like Ryan would be if he didn't get this shit done.

CHAPTER XVII

Maybe Sinclair was right—Landon might not be around here for long. Four hours in and he was *hoping* someone would try to kill him.

Being at the ass end of the totem pole meant he was stuck with Rick for the entire night. So in addition to this being the most boring place he'd ever been, for an hour he heard how appreciative he should be that Rick wasn't going to tell their boss what had happened, but that the lovely doctor definitely would. Although when Landon got fired, it was no one's fault but his own.

Landon knew Sinclair wouldn't say anything. He wasn't sure how he knew it, but he did. Maybe intuition, maybe a nonverbal cue she'd sent out—one he couldn't identify or name. He might not be a great judge of himself, but he read other people pretty well. Her message had gotten through and, if she wasn't the enemy, he would've been flattered.

After that, he was forced to hear all about Rick's pretend sex life. Bragging about things and women he hadn't done. The guy had to be one of the worst liars Landon had ever met, and that said a shitload.

So, to stay sane, he let his mind wander back to Sinclair.

Maybe it had been a mistake to get noticed like that. He wouldn't know until the next time he saw her. Or until the moment a few guys wearing black and carrying souped-up Tasers arrived to haul his ass away for interrogation. A distinct possibility and the reason his hand never left his weapon and his eyes never left the door.

"Rick," he said, cutting the guy off mid-sentence, "I need to stretch my legs. Maybe wander around a little." Until he found a room with a computer, a file cabinet, or an incriminating Post-it collection.

"I'll go too."

Where are those assholes with the Tasers when you need them? So much for a little privacy…or quiet. Maybe in another hour, he would claim he needed the bathroom and a newspaper. See if little Ricky wanted to tag along *then*.

As soon as they turned down the hallway, he saw Sinclair storming towards them.

"Oh shit, dude," Rick whispered. "She looks pissed. I've done all I can for you." He held his hands up and backed away from Landon as if he wanted to be clear when Sinclair pounced. But she wasn't aiming for Landon.

She started speaking about twenty feet away from them. Loudly. And angrily. "I need to see video feed of the lab and the hallway in front of my office. *Now*."

"What happened?" Landon asked.

She glanced at him. "Something is missing from the pharmaceutical pantry. A lot of something."

"Since when?" Landon took the lead because…because he always took the lead. And Rick didn't argue.

"I don't know. I don't even know why I noticed—I haven't touched the compound in months. And then, with all the issues with the university…"

How many 'issues' could they have with the university? Landon stayed calm on the way back to the security office and as Rick fumbled with the old footage. But since Sinclair had no idea when in the last few months it had gone missing, chances of seeing anything were a hair's breadth above zilch.

"What's the substance called?" Landon asked.

If she wore glasses, she would have lowered them just to scowl. Instead she just scowled. "It's not over the counter, so the name probably won't ring any bells."

"So I should write 'A substance I'm too stupid to even hear the name of' on the report, then?"

She sighed. "I'm sorry. I didn't mean it that way." It didn't matter if she did or she didn't. He would learn more from her if she was flustered. "You can write down 'GU-121.'"

Hallelujah. He'd sing some hymns later. "Could it have just been moved?" *To another location say...in sunny South Florida.*

"No one here would dare touch it because they know how angry I would be." She shook her head. "It must have been stolen."

Rick looked her as if she were nuts, as if his highly toned security skills would keep that from ever happening.

"I understand that happens a lot," Landon said, hoping to encourage more sharing. "Lots of grant and patent money, right?"

"Exactly." She looked relieved someone understood. "If someone took it and copied my notes, I can't prove it's mine. Maybe we should call the police."

"Let's hold off on that for a second." It didn't make sense. Why was she tattling about something that she'd probably just sent over to Florida? "Doesn't this lab have other labs you work in conjunction with? Couldn't it just have been sent to one of them?"

"Not without—" She shut her mouth quickly, her eyes doubling in size. "You know what? Ignore me. It's late and I'm tired." She started backing out of the room, her body language screaming 'panic' louder than a Christian facing a lion.

"What did you just remember?" He followed her slowly— she was spooked enough.

"Nothing. Forget it. I just remembered where it is." She flipped around and hightailed it out of the room, her shoes clicking down the hallway double-time.

Landon looked at Rick. "I'm going to apologize for earlier. I think she's having a rough night."

"All the more reason to avoid her."

But Landon was already out the door. He went straight to her lab. And...she wasn't there. What had made her recant so quickly? So fearfully? Her panic would work for him if he found her fast enough. Before she spoke to anyone or calmed down enough to think of a cover story.

Speaking of covers...His was about to be blown, but it would be worth it. He'd never expected it to last more than two or three shifts anyway. Whatever Sinclair had realized was important had come on suddenly, and it terrified her. So maybe she wasn't burrowed as deeply in The Clinic's scheming as he'd first thought. But she definitely knew more than she was comfortable knowing.

He checked the bathroom and every room his keycard would open. Then he came to a door with her name on it.

That's some amazing detective work there, dickhead. He put his ear up to it but didn't hear anything. So he knocked.

"Dr. Sinclair, are you in there?"

"Go away," she called. "I'm busy."

"Can I talk to you for a minute?"

"No."

"Can I look at you for a minute?"

"No."

His keycard didn't work on the office doors, so it was useless. He could pick the lock—a skill he'd perfected with Eden's help—but Sinclair would notice and call someone. Maybe he could annoy her into opening up. It's what Turner would do. But *he* was a true master at it, and Landon needed a lot more practice.

"Okay, then I'll just talk through the door. Loudly. So anyone can hear what I say." He paused, hoping the threat was enough. It wasn't.

"So…I'd like to buy you dinner sometime. Or breakfast." *Oh shit, that sounded bad.* He was terrible at this. "Not in a seedy kind of way, but since we both work nights, I thought it might work out well." *How does Turner do this kind of thing?* Landon didn't enjoy lying, but he could do it. Normally. But for whatever reason, the skill wasn't translating to this.

"If you're trying to force a reaction out of me," she said through the door, "it isn't working. No one stays this late, so you're speaking to yourself."

He *had* gotten a reaction out of her, although not a big enough one to get through the door. "I'm speaking to you. And I'll continue speaking to you until you open up. If I'm going to be fired tomorrow, I have nothing to lose."

Although it was wrong on far too many levels and his mother and sisters would be livid if they knew, he would use whatever he could. Pride, integrity, and respect were shoved to the side temporarily.

He already felt guilty.

But if he pushed hard enough, if he made her uncomfortable enough, he knew she'd react territorially.

"I'd like to think you don't look at everyone the way you looked at me," he said weakly, but without a stutter or anything Turner would be horrified by. "But I understand if you're not interested in sharing a simple meal with me. So I'd be happy to skip straight to the sex. Here or in your lab—whichever."

She threw open the door, looking down the hall, her mouth tight and her eyes narrowed. "This is my workplace, not a bar. What is wrong with—?"

He pushed her into the room and slammed the door behind him, locking it with one hand, his other holding her arm so she wouldn't run to the phone. He didn't want to scare her, but there was no other way.

Feel guilty later.

"What are you doing?" She yanked against his grip, and

then lifted her knee, aiming at his balls.

He flipped her around, sliding his arm around her neck and twisting her arm behind her back. "I really didn't want to do this." Not his proudest moment and a really bad idea. He should've been more patient. Maybe it was needing to get to her before whatever had pumped her full of adrenaline faded, or that she was the closest thing to an answer he'd seen in a very long time. Or maybe it was just because he couldn't handle talking to Rick anymore. Whatever the reason, he'd created an unnecessary conflict that he now had to remedy.

"You should be very careful what you do now, Landon," she said breathlessly, nervous but controlled. "I'm not the shy type. If you walk away now, I won't tell anyone about this, Landon." She was smart—using his name like that. The more she said it, the better chance she had of getting through to him—if he were a psycho. Since he wasn't, all it did was make the situation all the more real and horrible. "But if you don't…"

"I'm pretty sure they already know." His lips were close to her ear, his body away from hers as much as possible. "Listen, I'm sorry for everything I've said and how I handled this situation, but you need to keep your voice down. How much do you know about the company you work for?"

"Enough." Her volume lowered, although he doubted it was because he'd asked.

"Too bad. 'Cause I kind of liked you."

"What do you want?"

"I'm not going to hurt you. I just need a chance to talk privately." Preferably with some more space between them. "Can I let go of you now?"

"Golly, I'd sure like that," she said, her words slippery with sarcasm.

"I mean, are you going to freak out if I let you go?"

"I don't freak out."

That, he believed. Her voice hadn't changed, even though she obviously didn't think he was just here to gawk. He released her slowly, praying his intuition was as good as it used to be. Back when things were normal and criminals were more clueless than evil. He'd love to come across a good old-fashioned murderous spouse again.

She jerked away and went to the door. "You're *so* fired."

"Figured that." He walked around her office, checking behind every diploma and award on the walls. It wasn't the best way to sweep a room, but it would have to do.

"What are you doing?" She stopped to watch him peek behind furniture, into drawers.

"I sincerely apologize for the vast amount of ways I have offended you this evening." He would keep things vague until he was absolutely sure which side she was on. And he had no problem misleading her until that happened. "But my curiosity was piqued when you said some supplies were missing."

Her eyes flashed, and she closed the door. "I *knew* you weren't a regular security guard. I *knew* it. There's something about you, the way you carry yourself. Plus, you blushed every time you said something obnoxious. So who are you?"

I blushed? Shit. He mimed turning down the volume and said, "A regular security guard…who used to be a detective."

After a pause, she went to her desk, still watching him.

"Nicolas!" Rick's voice came barreling down the hallway. "Where are you?" That guy had nothing but bad timing.

"I think you're needed elsewhere," she said. "What did you ask me earlier? Through the door?"

He scratched his temple, grimacing at the memory. "If you wanted dinner, breakfast, or just sex." *Yes, I really did say that.*

"You're blushing again. Come get me when your shift is over."

It was wrong that all he could think about was if she'd decided on the last option he'd given her.

Don't do it. Don't be a moron and start thinking with your cock. He nodded, hoping he'd make it that long, that she wouldn't pick up the phone and make a call that would guarantee his death.

As long as his brain stayed above his belt, Landon was smart. So before he left, he made one more sweep of the room. Along the way he unplugged the phone and bent the plug so it couldn't be put back in. And then, with no guilt whatsoever, he swiped her cell phone off her desk.

Because he didn't like her *that* much…yet.

✶ ✶ ✶

Eden wished she could forget a lot of nights in her life, but this was by far the worst. Growls and curses coming from both directions. She felt like she was watching a tennis match from the net. An insult shot from the truck, another sent back from the office.

Mitch's Hyde hit harder verbally and, physically, he shook the truck. Justin's was obviously younger, less developed— what Mitch's must have been like years ago.

He was still rough and definitely not someone she'd want to run into in an alley, but, even though he talked a really unpleasant game, he seemed to know he was way out of his league. If the two of them got near each other, they would fight. To the death. And she'd see Hyde do to Justin what he'd done to her father.

She should've bought some earmuffs or at least a book of crosswords—anything to distract her from the noise and the stress of being in between two devils. Instead, all she could do was think. And God knew nothing useful would come of that.

As the night went on, it became more than just stressful. Being so close to two Hydes affected her in a very uncomfortable way, yanking her one way and then the other, although the younger Hyde's pull was far less than the elder's. Her fingers dug into her thighs and her jaw was clenched so tightly, it ached. She focused on breathing through it, past the fear, past the urge to engage either one of them.

When she heard herself whimper, she got up and went outside, pacing in front of the door, then doing calisthenics just to relieve some tension. She didn't want to be this person, walking so close to the edge all the time. Right now she could blame it on the Hydes, but it wasn't just now. The need for relief was continual. Sure, there were ebbs and flows, like any other need or craving, but this wasn't about binge eating or cigarettes.

This was about violence.

All she had to do was get through tonight. Then Justin's Hyde wouldn't appear for a few days and she'd only have one to worry about. No, that wasn't right. She'd have two. With some effort, she could tune out Hyde's rage.

But she didn't stand a chance against her own.

CHAPTER XVIII

Rick's questioning was relentless. He wanted to know everything, including why Landon had taken so long to come out of her office and why he looked so frazzled when he did. Rick didn't get the story he'd wanted. And at this point, neither had Landon.

Other than two trips to the bathroom and a quick patrol, he didn't leave the security room. He barely took his eyes off the monitor with a view of her lab. She'd gone there almost immediately after he'd left her office. She was busy doing something, but it wasn't using the phone.

Point for her. Once he knew what had put that look on her face and made her recant, she might get another point. Or she might be stripped of all her earnings and be exactly who he'd originally thought she was. Only time and a subtle interrogation over a big breakfast would tell.

When it was time for his 'lunch' break, he decided to see if he could start their discussion early. At least he hadn't been killed yet. Did she earn another point for that?

When he knocked this time, she opened the door right away.

"Do you have time for a walk?" he asked.

"Outside? Um...sure. Just let me...I can't find my phone."

"I'll help you look." Shockingly, he found it about thirty seconds later. "This it?"

"I thought I looked there."

"Sometimes what you're looking for is right in front of you, but it takes someone else to help you see it."

She took it from his outstretched hand, having no idea that he'd already looked through it on one of his bathroom runs. No one puts surveillance equipment in the stalls of a men's room.

He hadn't found anything particularly incriminating. Her contact list was short and almost everyone's name had a 'Dr.' prefix. Steve Harris wasn't there or Bradford, Fuller, Jolie, Fields, or Alex. He wasn't sure if he was happy or disappointed that none of the numbers began with a South Florida area code. But he'd copied down as many as he could anyway and would check them out later.

"Shall we?" he asked.

"Skip to the sex? No. You should eat your lunch." Her smile made him need a few deep breaths. The woman exuded confidence without arrogance—maybe because she could back it up.

Knock it off, idiot. If his libido got in the way of reaching his goal, he'd have more than just his conscience to worry about—he'd have to deal with Eden. The idea of getting his ass kicked by his teammate, who was also a girl, who would also have a really good reason to do it, quelled his lust entirely.

They stopped in a lounge area, where Sinclair got a cup of coffee and he grabbed a sandwich and a soda out of the vending machine. Her eyes were probably getting sore from glancing at him sideways so often, but they said very little until they were outside. Once Landon felt comfortable with the distance from the building, they talked. Slowly at first— friendly, getting-to-know-you-type shit. Feeling each other out in a purely platonic way. Landon asked simple questions, building trust, hoping he was coming off as interested and not stalkerish.

When she stopped talking, he knew she was waiting for him to offer up some information as proof he wasn't lying to her. Something made quite difficult by the fact that he *was* lying to her.

But he gave—a mixture of vague truths and outright lies.

From the fairly obvious: Staying undercover is really tough when your badge accidentally falls out of your pocket.

To the vague and fraudulent: References to things about Malvers Labs that anyone with a computer could find, their pharmaceuticals, and most of what he knew about GU-121. But *these* bits of information were whispered, as if they'd come directly out of a file stamped 'FDA'.

All the way to the truth and nothing but: His team had been working on this case for a while, but they were completely out of leads, time, and energy. And office morale wasn't all that great, either.

The things he gave wide berth to were: What happened in Florida and anything involving criminal behavior—which was almost everything. But whatever he said or didn't say seemed to calm her.

Finally, she stopped him. "Why are we really here?"

"Metaphysically? No idea. Although I've always considered the Buddhists—"

"I looked you up. Well, I looked up Landon Nicolas."

Oh, shit. He thought he'd have longer than this—at least another day. Because people rarely do more work than they're required to do. Especially in the middle of the night.

"There is no record of 'Landon Nicolas' being a detective...anywhere. Ever. At least not in this country. So...if you tell me you're Canadian, I'll say, 'Welcome to the country,' and then tell you how utterly amazed I am that the FDA hired someone who so recently immigrated to the U.S. and has no public record in Canada either."

She didn't even stop long enough for him to think of another lie. "While I didn't find 'Landon Nicolas,' I did find this other guy. Let's call him Nick right now because…well, because that's his name. Anyway, until recently Nick worked as a detective in Fort Lauderdale, but I don't think he ever worked for the FDA."

She took a sip of her coffee. And why not? Her throat must have been dry from all that truth.

"So I'll ask again…Why are we really here, *Nick*?"

Because I don't have a friend of a friend of a friend who works at Google. But she'd come out here with him and he wasn't dead, which meant she hadn't told anyone. Was that enough to trust her?

More than anything, he wanted to meet one goddamn person who was honest. Who was doing something simply because it was the right thing to do, without the moral or ethical implications, the rationalizations, and the excuses. Who was normal. Kind of like he used to be—no gray area or things beyond understanding.

More than anything, he hoped that person was her. If he jumped in, it would be a huge risk and could come back on him compounded. It could hurt the people he cared about and end him. But there are times when you really need to believe in someone. That there are still good people in the world.

He would move slowly, from the big picture stuff to the more detailed, until he found out if she'd already chosen the wrong side. "What do you know about the Abnormals?"

"Is it a TV show?" she asked, obviously annoyed that it seemed he was changing the subject. "I don't watch too much television."

"The Hydes. The Jekylls."

"It's a good story," she said, shrugging and looking utterly confused.

He kept going, naming every person he could think of other than Turner and Eden. He studied her face, watching for the reactions nobody could control, but there was nothing. She knew nothing. A time to rejoice and a time to be disappointed.

"The Clinic," he continued. "The research being done at

your Florida facility."

She inhaled sharply. Color bloomed on her cheeks. Eyes averted. The works. Every sign that screamed 'Bingo' was there to see.

Okay. "What do you know about the lab in Florida?"

"Nothing."

He tensed, anticipating a diversion or an outright lie. "A four-year-old could tell that you're lying."

"Fine." She shrugged. "Since you seem so good with the whole truth thing, I'll start. Aside from the stuff you can read on a tourist pamphlet, all I know is that Malvers Labs doesn't have a facility in Florida." They sat down on the cement bench surrounding the fountain. "Now it's your turn: Are you here because of the supply and accounting discrepancies?"

"I...I can't answer that." *Because I have no idea what you're talking about.* But letting her know that would just be stupid. As would his inclination to lean over and kiss her. The look of earnestness on her face, nervousness, concern, frustration. That wasn't fake. It was real. About supply and accounting discrepancies.

Okay. He didn't quite know what to do with that. The woman was honest. She wasn't part of the scheming. She was actually concerned with the shipping. He really wanted to kiss her. *Accounting discrepancies.* He leaned on his elbow and ran his hand over his mouth to cover his smile.

What now? Don't be stupid. And if that fails, lie some more. Damn, that's sad. "Since you already know about me and the accounting..." He sighed.

The most effective way to cover a lie is to reveal another lie just underneath it, preferably one that makes you seem like an idiot. No one admits to doing something stupid if they can help it. So the likelihood of deliberately making yourself look bad? Very low.

"I spent my entire adult life being a cop." True. "I loved it." True. "But I screwed up." True in many ways, but not on the job. "I trusted the wrong person and it ended my career."

Absolutely and horribly true.

"My chief stuck his neck out and got me on a case investigating"—pause for dramatic effect—"the illegal transportation of pharmaceuticals to a certain little country we have an embargo against." Big, obese lie. And it got the ball rolling pretty damn fast.

He confessed to all kinds of things, making them as embarrassing and complicated as he could to confuse her, to make her unsure of anything and so overwhelmed that she stopped questioning it. If it hadn't confused her yet, he should just go home, because he would never be able to repeat it.

But he wrapped it up with the truth. "If I figure out what's going on with Malvers, I might be able to get my life back."

She stared at him in silence, undoubtedly shocked at what an idiot he was.

"Dr. Sinclair, do you know what it's like to have everything you've worked for just disappear? I'm not talking about the material stuff. I mean when your pride and your dreams are taken away because you trusted the wrong people."

He recognized the moment he hit her soft spot. Because it was the same as his. He was exposing it, opening up in a way he thought he'd forgotten how to.

"Yeah," she whispered.

"I think we might be able to help each other get that back. It might not work, but isn't it worth a shot?"

"Please don't screw me over. I worked hard for this job." After she sighed and tilted her shoulders back and forth as if she was weighing her decision literally, she glanced around them. "Obviously, we weren't supposed to publish anything about GU-121 until we were much further along. It was a mistake, and Danvers knew it as soon as it came out."

Danvers, of course. That was why her name had never come up in anything they'd found—because Danvers' name was on it. But why was she starting with him?

"While I was getting my PhD," she said quietly, "I came

up with an earlier variant of what we now call GU-121. Malvers recruited me and Dr. Danvers helped me recreate something just different enough to avoid any future patent dispute. Of course, the university is still trying, and other people might join in at some point, but I didn't do anything wrong."

"Does Danvers still work here?"

She shook her head. "He was killed during a mugging."

Tara's death had been a 'mugging' too. Landon couldn't respond immediately because it took him a second to relax his jaw. "So Danvers leaked what you were doing."

"It was just a brief mention in an article about another compound, but it caused a lot of problems. Then he was killed. About a week later, Louis Bradford, a pharmacologist who used to work here, came to our lab with two of Malvers' Board members. The next day I was told to completely stop working on GU-121. So I got curious." She closed her eyes. "Okay, I got mad and maybe a little bit paranoid. I thought Bradford might try to claim the compound as his, because while he was here, I overheard him say that Florida was going to need a larger budget for tests."

Bradford—the one name Landon hadn't mentioned. How could he have forgotten the guy with a big hole in his head? *Right*—there were too many of them.

"So you started to look into what was happening there?"

"At first, I just wanted to know what they were working on. Then...I may have *accidentally* found some information in the accounting department's database." She paused, waiting for him to break out his cuffs, maybe. After a moment, she continued. "I noticed all kinds of discrepancies, too many to be accidental. Receipts for things we never ordered or received. Shipping logs claiming special deliveries of lab equipment to a post office box in Ft. Lauderdale. And who hires a truck to ship office supplies halfway across the country when there's an office store on every corner? We're constantly running out of supplies, so it sure wasn't paper or ink cartridges."

Maybe it was paper, ink, and a monster.

He leaned forward conspiratorially. "I shouldn't be telling you anything. You already know too much." He paused, letting his lies settle. "Okay, you're in." *Impressive.* One minute he'd been celebrating her honesty and thirty seconds later, he starts using it to his advantage.

Nice. "The facility in Florida is so secretive and has doctored their books so well, it's hard to know where to begin with this case. I'd like to gather as much information as possible before I start ruffling feathers. Because once that starts, there will be no turning back. Once I know what's going there, I'll know what to look for on that end. Do you think you can get any documentation? Who signed for the shipments, how much money is going to Florida and from which sources, who's in charge of its allocation. That sort of thing."

He needed names. Someone had been on the opposite end of the line from Bradford, and that someone would know what he'd been brewing up. It might not be a way to take down The Clinic, but it would help Turner—a priority Turner would probably disapprove of. But once the idiot was healthy and cursing, Landon would be more than happy to tell him to kiss his ass.

"You should talk to the accounting department or—"

"It's been more difficult than you can imagine to find people I can trust, Dr. Sinclair." As her expression saddened, his desire to punch himself grew.

"It's Danielle."

Hell yes, he felt guilty about lying to her. Not that he was averse to lying nowadays, but she was obviously searching for someone to trust just as hard as he was. She wanted to believe in someone too. But coming clean now wouldn't be a smart move, regardless of instinct or gut feelings. Facts always trump feelings. *Always.* And the truth would only get her in trouble.

"How much time do you need to get that info for me?"

She paused long enough for him to know she was about to balk.

"Can you have it by lunchtime?"

"Seriously?"

"I know you're tired, but time is crunching, Danielle. That information could solve a lot of problems for my team."

She took a sip of coffee and then tipped it to drink the rest. "If I want to be productive, I'm going to need more."

"I'll buy." He stopped her before they went back inside. "Listen, we don't know who's doing this, but we know they have a lot to lose. And people with a lot to lose don't always think clearly or logically. So if you get even an inkling that somebody knows what you're doing, I want you to get out." He couldn't live with another death on his conscience, especially not an innocent one.

Her smile worried him, but he couldn't tell her any more unless he told her everything. "I have no intention of getting fired, Nick. But when you know someone is doing something wrong, you can't just ignore it, you know?"

He held up his soda in a toast. "I knew I'd like you."

She held his eyes for a moment too long. "Me too." A smile crept onto her face. "Because you're nice to gawk at. But I *hate* that uniform."

He was going to burn the thing. "I'll be calling you later to check up on things, so don't…lose your phone again."

What he was asking her to do was unfair. He was putting her in a dangerous situation without telling her the truth. Without giving her enough to make an informed decision. She was smart, but was she *street* smart? He didn't know enough about her to be sure. Some collateral damage was going to happen before this was over, but he hadn't planned on being the one to cause it. He needed to reevaluate what he was willing to do and who he was willing to sacrifice.

Besides himself.

Chapter XIX

When Eden felt the hand on her shoulder, she whipped around, catching it and bending it backward.

"Jesus, Eden, stop! You're going to break my hand."

She let go immediately, recognizing Landon's voice. "Sorry. I've been a bit edgy lately." Her vision was still blurred by the minuscule amount of sleep she'd gotten.

"Really? I hadn't noticed." Even this early in the morning, his sarcasm was obvious. "How'd the kid do?"

She shrugged. "Compared to Mitch's, Justin's Hyde is angelic. How was work?"

"Slightly productive, although I won't be able to define 'slightly' until later. I could've told you this on the phone but you never answer."

"Oops. I just don't think about turning it on. The only person who ever called me was Carter and he's..." She let the thought go. Carter had deserved what he got. "But I will from now on." Because it was a trivial thing that might screw up something important.

"I'm going out."

"Where?"

"Out." He looked at her pointedly and then sighed. "I met

someone who might be able to help us." He told her about some woman who was gathering information about shipping and money. "I'm going somewhere that has Internet access...and a shitload of coffee."

"Sounds like a blast." But she wasn't concerned with the money—she needed names, info on how to help Mitch. Bringing down The Clinic was secondary to that.

"Go back to sleep."

As if she could. She had an exciting day planned, and it didn't involve staying here and doing nothing. But it *did* involve being careful. Since she was one of The Clinic's top freaks, her picture had probably been spread around to all the facilities and put on their recruiting poster by now. That and the fact that Landon could grow facial hair made him the less identifiable one. Especially today—he looked like the walking dead.

"You should get some too," she said.

"Later." He hadn't stopped to rest—driving as long as they had and working the night shift with only one night's bad sleep the day before. And now he was going out again. But he was a big boy and could take care of himself.

Before he moved away, she caught his arm. "Landon, I know I've been...difficult. And I'm sorry."

"It's okay."

"No it's not."

"No it's not, but I understand. Now can I have my arm back?"

Instead of letting go right away, she took his hand and squeezed it, trying to convey something that words could never express. Especially if she didn't bother trying.

Tell him. "I want you to know that I think you're an amazing man." She spoke softly—because that was the only way she could say it.

"Thanks," he said with an awkward smile.

Don't stop there—you owe him. "I don't know how you do it, but you've never diverted from who you are and what you believe in."

His lips grew tight. "I keep trying, and it keeps getting harder."

She shook her head. "That's why I respect you so much. Because even when it is hard, you do the right thing." Like she used to do. Long ago. Always doing the right thing, even when it hurt. But the definition she was basing her life on was flawed and made her weak. Landon had figured out how to be right *and* be strong.

"Yeah, well...too much emotion makes me uncomfortable, so I'm going to take off now." He was better than she was—now and maybe before as well. He followed the rules of fairness while Eden made up her own as she went.

And today she would test even those.

She and Landon had the same goal, but his way would take too long. She needed to try something more direct. He was doing what he was good at and so would she. Isn't that what teams did—use their individual strengths to get things done?

As soon as he was gone and Justin was cuffless but still sleeping, Eden grabbed the supplies she'd kept hidden and brought them into the truly disgusting bathroom. No shower, of course, but the basics were there.

Being able to pee standing up was the thing she envied most about men. The rest sounded awful, but she'd gladly take it if it meant she could avoid sitting down on that toilet. The mirror above the sink was cracked, the reflective surface peeling off three of the corners, and graffiti was placed in such a way that it looked tattooed in reverse across her forehead and one cheek.

Interesting look, but not exactly subtle. She took one last look at herself before setting a pair of scissors down on the edge of the sink and tugging her shirt over her head. She took her ponytail out and shook her hair free, running her fingers through it. She loved her hair. It was healthy and strong.

And it had to go. She cut it off in clumps, sawing the scissors until they made it through, tossing the hair in the corner of the room without looking in the mirror once. If she did, she'd probably start crying. One more piece of the old Eden that couldn't hang around any longer.

When she was done, she took out a bottle of peroxide, skimmed the instructions, and went to work. The wait was terrible. Doing something, moving, meant there was less time for thought. Feeling the mild burn of the bleach as it took away the color, she remembered things that hurt. The good memories hurt most, because they might be the last ones she would ever have.

She rinsed and repeated, and then added color back in, rinsed, conditioned, exactly as the directions suggested. Because the only thing worse than being recognized as herself would be to garner lots of attention for looking like a total freak.

When she saw herself for the first time with blond, chin-length hair, she almost *did* start crying. First off, because the cut she'd given herself was absolutely horrible and second, because she looked so different, even Mitch might not recognize her. Or be attracted to her.

She shook off the thought and concentrated on evening out the strands. When that failed, she went to find Justin. He was in the office area, rummaging through a bag for something to eat.

"Holy shit!" His eyes practically vaulted out of his head.

She smoothed down her new hair self-consciously. "I know—not my best hair day."

"You look seriously hot, E. Seriously."

"As disturbed as I am about you saying that, I needed to hear it. Thanks. Can you help me with the back?"

His hand was a bit shaky as he trimmed, sighed, and trimmed some more. Then sighed. Then—

"I'm going to be bald if you take off much more. Just make it straight."

After a few more snips, he was done. She'd never even know how it looked from the back anyway, so that was something.

"Why'd you do it?" he asked.

"So that no one could recognize me as that crazy brunette who screwed things up for them in Florida."

His smile faded. "I'm glad you did. I *never* would've figured out what they were doing. Shit, I sat in that room for two years, thinking I was so lucky." He laughed bitterly.

She understood. If nothing else, Carter had taught her the limits of trust and dependency. Justin had had Alex just like Eden had Carter. Except Alex was still alive, free, and unpunished...for now.

So yeah, Eden understood. "You're older and wiser already. And in a few years you'll look back on this time and laugh. Probably about my hair. But you'll be fine."

She wished she could help him heal, take away his pain, but it didn't work like that. The only way to get through it was alone. As much as she loved Mitch, as much as she needed him and as much as he'd helped her, she'd done it alone. She was still doing it alone. She'd be there to support Justin, but he had to find his own way—she was only a completely biased bystander in his life.

He bit into a granola bar. "You're so different from her."

"Alex? Jesus, I'd better be. That woman sold her soul for a buck fifty. I'd hold out for at least ten."

His laugh was beautiful—so much like a child's. He was still able to separate himself, forget, live in this moment, and enjoy life, as awful as it might be ten minutes from now. It gave her hope that regardless of what happened to everybody else, Justin would be okay.

"I meant my mom," he said, swallowing. "You're nothing like her."

"Is that a good or a bad thing?"

"It's a *great* thing. I think my transformations changed her, too." He grimaced. "Anyway, you're a lot nicer than she was. I wish you were... Whatever." He bolted before he'd even finished speaking.

God help him if he was looking to her to be maternal. Maybe sometime far, far in the future, but right now she was filled with too much spite, anger, and worry to feel anything else.

Maybe with time. "I'm only eight years older than you are, Justin. So think of me as your seriously hot older sister." She waited until he turned towards her. "One that will kick your ass if you do anything stupid."

"I could take you in a fair fight," he said with a smile.

She couldn't smile back. "Fights are never fair, Justin." *Never.* She started gathering some supplies and shoving them into her bag. There had to be a Girl Scout badge for this—A 'Catastrophe Preparedness' badge. "If Landon calls, tell him I'm at the store."

"Where will you really be?"

"Somewhere else."

"What if something happens?" He glanced at the truck. "If—"

"Hyde's locked up. Tightly." She put her hand on his arm. "But I'll check again before I go. I won't be gone very long, an hour or so." She pointed to the syringe on the table. "Worst case—which won't happen, but should always be planned for—is that you have to shove that into his arm. It may take a few minutes, but it will bring Mitch back. Until it does, just keep the bastard talking. He likes to talk, probably because no one wants to hear it. So put in some earbuds and try to ignore him. Okay?"

He nodded.

"You can't live your life in fear, Justin. You have to beat it. Believe me, I spent twenty-four years in it. Definitely not fun. I took my first real breath about a month ago. And you're a lot stronger than I was. Hell, you sneaked into that truck when you could've run. I wouldn't have had the guts to do that."

"Where are you going for real?" Hopefully he wouldn't ignore her directions as well as he did the compliment.

"I want to look around a little bit more." Because she had to do something. She wasn't the type to stay home and darn socks. She needed out, and she needed to move, and she needed to stop obsessively staring at that stupid truck.

She trusted Landon and his expertise, but this was her future, too. And Mitch's. So she would be involved and be prepared to act as backup for Landon or go in after him, if necessary. But until then, she'd stay out of the facility and not talk to anyone.

How much trouble can I get into from fifty feet away? Her spy skills probably hadn't improved much, but the area around the building would be filled with people at this time of day. With her head down and her new hair, she would look like everyone else. Staying here and controlling nothing was slowly making her go insane. Maybe it was an increased pull from Chastity or the overall imbalance Eden felt, but she couldn't shake the pent-up violence within her.

Like an animal born in the wild but forced to live in captivity.

Thankfully, even in haste, she'd packed well. A pencil skirt and a button-down blouse, only moderately wrinkled. Her flats were perfectly suited for the working world, as well as for fighting and running like hell. So yeah, totally appropriate for her day, however it ended up.

Before she left, she checked every lock—the ones around Hyde's wrists and ankles, the one on the truck, and the one to the warehouse. She walked for about a mile before spotting a cab. It dropped her off five blocks away from the facility.

The whole complex was busy—just like she thought it would be. People milling around the large fountain that had iron horses running through it.

Luckily, she was hidden by two men when a woman walked through Malvers Labs' glass door. A woman Eden recognized. A woman Eden would've strangled right here if it wouldn't ruin everything, including the appetites of everyone around her.

Alex, Alex, Alex. She looked *way* too healthy and vertical for Eden's liking. But timing was everything, and Alex would be out of it soon enough.

Alex is here. So this had to be the right place. An extra twinge of excitement went through Eden when she realized that this wasn't just *one* of The Clinic's facilities—this was where Alex came to be debriefed…and hopefully tortured a little bit.

Of course, in addition to this being the right place, it was also the most dangerous place for Eden to be. She ducked her head, turned in the opposite direction, and went through the first door she saw, right into a busy café. She could stay here until Alex was gone…maybe get a muffin.

A man near the front of the line caught her eye, nodding slightly. She looked away—the last thing she needed was some guy trying to get into her pants. That area was locked down—one key only, thank you very much.

When she looked out the window again, Alex was gone. *One more minute just to be sure.*

"Hon, I'm up here!"

Everyone, including Eden, looked in the direction of the voice.

The man was now smiling and beckoning to her. "Come up here." Then he turned to the person behind him in line and asked, "You don't mind if my girlfriend joins me, do you? It'll be on the same bill and she doesn't eat much." After the woman shrugged, he called to Eden again. "It's fine. Come on."

Eden looked around, hoping he was talking to someone else. No one moved. Except to look at her. *This isn't good.* One or more of these people must work for The Clinic and might recognize her, even with her new hair and sunglasses. If the guy would just shut up…

"Come on, honey."

She shook her head. "Really, it's okay. I'm good."

The woman in front of her turned around, smiling. "If you

don't want him, can I take him?"

When a few people started laughing, Eden gave up and went to the front, keeping her head down and tilted away from the line.

"Hi...*honey.*" In another situation, some woman who wasn't her would probably think that what he'd done was charming. He was tall, *very* attractive, early thirties probably, fit, and expensive looking. Perfect haircut, tailored suit, and shoes that didn't look like they came from Payless.

She felt a tinge of the old Chastity hit her right in the crotch. *Oh, shit.* She'd thought she was done with that, *hoped* she was done with that. But the more she looked at him, the stronger the pulse. So she stopped looking at him.

"This is cheating, you know," she mumbled.

"Yep, I know." The volume of his voice lowered to match hers. "But you looked hungry."

"Do you always pick up strays?"

"My intention wasn't to be charitable," he said. "What do you want?"

She looked at him blankly.

"To eat. What do you want to eat?" Smiling, he motioned to the clerk who was waiting impatiently.

"Oh...um...this." She grabbed a salad and water out of the display case, plopped them down on the counter, and reached into her bag for her wallet. When he touched her arm, she only flinched. He looked confused, but not as confused as he'd be if she'd reacted by grabbing him by the neck and kneeing him in the balls.

So all in all, she felt pretty good about it.

"My treat." Before she could protest, he added, "I promised my neighbor here that it would all be on the same bill."

"That's really nice of you. Thanks." She grabbed the food and left, but he matched her speed.

"Don't run away. Please. It's not a come-on—it's just a conversation."

Yeah, right. "Can't. I have a meeting."

"With who, Eden?" he asked from a few feet behind her.

His words stopped her, stunned her. *Seriously?* She had no spy skills at all.

It would be useless to deny it. "How do you know my name?"

"Because I work for the people you're hunting."

Chapter XX

"I don't know what you mean," Eden said tightly.

"You have a lot of talents. Playing stupid isn't one of them."

Eden's back was to him—not a very favorable position. But he seemed to know not to get too close, his voice coming from at least four feet away.

"Wow, the things men say nowadays just to get a girl to talk to them." She stayed absolutely still, unsure what to do. She could (A) whip around, grab him by the neck, and demand he tell her everything he knows. But that would bring an incredible amount of undesirable attention. Or (B) turn around slowly and talk to him calmly. In public. Where she could see his hands at all times. Not nearly as satisfying, but far more intelligent.

She motioned towards a small space between people on the cement bench that surrounded the fountain. It would be a tight squeeze, but it was very public and she didn't think either of them wanted to speak too loudly.

"Why don't we go—?"

"If you think I'm going anywhere"—she used air-quotes— "'quiet' with you, you're an idiot. And dealing with idiots isn't one of my talents."

As he took a seat on the bench, he smiled—not the normal reaction to someone calling you a derogatory name. He was definitely smooth, but not in a sleazy way. More of a controlled power that—unfortunately—was incredibly attractive.

When she sat down, their thighs brushed, an unwelcomed pulse running through her. Chastity had just found someone she wanted to get to know better. Someone who wasn't Mitch. But regardless of how uncomfortable it was to be here, Eden needed to get to know him better as well.

"Name and rank, please," she said.

He smiled again.

"I'm glad you find me so amusing. But how about you put your smile away and use your mouth to answer?"

He straightened but didn't lose the grin. "Ryan Whittley. Minion to the man."

"Minion?" She doubted it. The man radiated power. "You dress awfully well for a minion, Ryan."

He bowed his head. "Thank you. I try. 'Dress for success,' as they say. My inheritance helps with that."

Great. A rich kid. Who worked for the enemy. "What do you want?"

"What makes you think I want anything?"

"Because you're human and you're breathing—the two things that pretty much guarantee you want more than you already have. Plus, since you know who I am, then you also know how much trouble I cause for the people around me. So it must be worth the risk."

"Guilty on all counts." He crossed his arms over his chest. "I want it all. The company and all of its divisions. I dress for success because I will succeed. And you'll help me do it."

She chuckled. "Why would I do that?"

"Because I intend to run things differently, more along the lines of what you want. You showing up here is kismet, serendipity, a sign from up above"—after a quick glance to the sky, his gaze landed on her—"that we would be good for each other."

She caught the innuendo, felt it reverberate through her, and accepted it for what it was—a way in. Her help wasn't all he wanted from her. When she leaned in closer, he inhaled deeply.

"Tell me what I want to know, everything I want to know, and we might be able to work something out."

"Your place or mine?"

"Here works just fine."

He shook his head and then nodded towards the Malvers building. "Too close to home."

As she stood, he studied her. She wanted to fidget, hide from his eyes, but that would show weakness. "Two cars, I lead. We stop where *I* want to. Get your car and meet me at that corner." She walked away, stopping only to toss her untouched salad in the trash.

Thankfully she didn't have to wait too long for a cab. Ryan was waiting in his car—a very expensive, very fast import.

I guess he drives for success as well. She told the cabbie to keep driving until she said stop. She asked to be dropped off at a run-down fast food restaurant—the kind of place that made people like Ryan uncomfortable. She went inside without checking to see if he followed and then chose a seat facing and near the exit.

He walked in a minute later. "Nice place. Next time, I pick." His lips were tight, but other than that, he didn't give anything away.

"I have yet to determine if there will be a next time."

"Yours?" He pointed to the trash the previous diners had left, then gathered it up and walked over to toss it. After he sat back down, he unbuttoned his jacket and looked at her. Studied her really. "Now that we have the room, shall I lay it all on the table, then?"

Without further ado, he started talking. He didn't beat around the bush or give any lame excuses. Eden kept her mouth shut for as long as she could, but eventually it fell open in disbelief. He knew *everything*. Somehow he knew *everything*. About her, Florida, Mitch, the serums, all of it.

"How am I doing?" he asked. "Have we built any trust yet?"

Yes, damn it. More than she was comfortable with. But trust and The Clinic were antonyms, and that went for their employees as well. "You haven't told me anything I don't already know."

"Tough crowd." He leaned back, pausing to stare at her again. "You're the reason he started all of this, you know. He partnered with Malvers Labs to get funding for his research and spent every waking hour to finding a cure. Not for himself or anyone else—for you. Did you ever meet him?"

"Who?" she asked stiffly, knowing exactly who he was talking about.

"Ian. Did you ever meet him before he"—sadness clouded his face for just a moment—"got tied up in his work?"

Chained up, actually. "You knew him."

"I worked with him for a little while," Ryan said, nodding. "He talked about you a lot. His *raison d'être*. Or his *raison d'*experiment." He smiled. "He was so focused on you, I think he forgot who everyone else was, including himself. So did he? Contact you?"

Eden didn't want to talk about this—not now, not ever. She didn't want to know that her father had been human and had feelings and talked about her with his coworkers. Someone like that shouldn't have been able to live in the same city and never contact her. Never try to help Eden's mom, who was coping the only way she knew how. Never let Eden go into foster care after her mom ODed. No, Eden didn't care how Ian was betrayed, not after he had betrayed her and her mom.

"The only time we met," she snapped, "was when he was in the cage two doors down from mine. So can we get on with it?"

"I didn't know it was a sensitive topic. I apologize."

"I don't need an apology, I need information."

"Okay. Ian's research became a side project for Malvers Labs. The facility in Florida was completely devoted to it. All the others stayed legitimate, above-board laboratories and have never had anything to do with his kind. With *your* kind."

He sighed. "However, due to the nature of humanity, somebody at the top thought he wasn't doing it right. That there were more important things than finding a cure for a very small segment of the population."

"Such as?"

"What if there were no criminals? No murderers, pedophiles, rapists. What if there was a way to stop people from accessing their baser natures? To control their all-too-human evil sides? The Abnormals are exactly what Stevenson wrote about in his book, but unlike Dr. Jekyll, Abnormals don't need chemical modification. Instead of needing a drug to separate the evil from the good, nature did it for you."

Well, yay for us. Was she supposed to feel lucky? "So your bosses want to rid the world of murderers by murdering people? Torturing them? How incredibly altruistic of them."

"From their perspective, it's the price of changing the world. Sacrifice is an unavoidable component of change. You're breathing proof of it—your integration made you sacrifice certain parts of the old you. Or am I wrong?"

"Completely," she lied. "So you want to do things differently. How?"

"Well, for one, I'd like to work with you, not against you. If I were in charge—which I'm not but will be soon—you'd have access to everything. Same ultimate goal, totally different tactics. If cosmetic companies don't have to do animal testing, neither do we." He grimaced. "No disrespect meant with the analogy, of course. There should be a good working relationship between your kind and the researchers— no testing without your full consent and approval."

Eden didn't know what to think. Sitting in front of her was the answer to all the prayers she'd never even dared make. A solution to everything she wanted—a way to help Mitch and the others and to stop the war with The Clinic altogether.

Before anyone else had to die.

"It's a lot to think about, I know." He leaned forward, resting his forearms on the table. "But...I need to know how you did it—how you were able to combine your two sides."

"I didn't do anything. It just happened."

His expression soured. But if he didn't believe her, there was nothing she could do to make him and, honestly, she didn't care enough to worry about it.

"Nothing?" he asked. "Nothing over the counter or spiritual or—"

"Nothing. Unless the guards knocked something loose while they were beating or kidnapping me. You could ask them...if any of them are still alive." Nothing he could say changed the fact that he'd worked for The Clinic long enough to know what he was part of. "So this big coup you're planning... How would I be involved?"

His sigh held as much frustration as she *felt*. "I give you names, you...dispose of them. Without exposing the project, of course."

"Why would I agree to that?" A red flag started waving in her mind, coloring her vision. Her muscles tightened as if they were trying to create a wall the idea couldn't get through.

"Because it's the only way I'll get the top spot. And once I have that, you and yours get your freedom and all the answers you want."

Even though she felt like a loaded gun most of the time, she wasn't one. She'd never purposefully killed anyone. She'd told herself she would do anything to save Mitch, but assassinate people? Even her enemies...

What would that do to what was left of her?

"Want a soda? Fries?" he asked, as if he hadn't just plopped a bomb in her lap and told her she had eight seconds to defuse it. He went to the counter without waiting for an answer.

She needed Landon—talking to him would bring her back into focus and help her look for holes in what Ryan said. But a discussion would have to wait until she had more privacy.

So she texted: '*Need U 2 check out employee. Ryan*'…

Shit, what was his last name? With so much junk clouding her mind, things weren't where they were supposed to be.

…'*Whittle? Whitely? Something w/ a W. First name's right tho.*'

Ryan was walking back to the table holding a tray.

'*Text me when U know. W/ him now. Hurry.*'

〜〜〜

Landon stared at the text for another minute. *How the hell am I supposed to look up someone if she doesn't know his last name?* Great, he would cut the meeting with Danielle short and then come up with an excuse as to why he was eight hours early for work. Just so he could check the personnel files for someone named Ryan Something-That-Begins-With-a-W.

"Very helpful." Shaking his head, he walked into the restaurant and saw Danielle at a table near the back.

"You should try the peach cobbler." She pulled the plate closer to herself. "But not *this* peach cobbler 'cause it's all mine." Her smile created a crack from one side of his armor to the other. There was too much honesty in it.

Turner used sarcasm and insults to distance himself from the world. Landon stayed numb. And both had spent years doing it well. Until a woman found a way inside. Eden was Turner's reason for being and also his greatest weakness. Just like Tara had been for Landon—introducing him to a fight that took over his life even after she was no longer a part of it.

Now Danielle was the distraction. Maybe he was being an idiot. Maybe she was playing him. Or maybe he could have another shot at something good.

What the hell, idiot? You've known her for less than twenty-four hours and you're already picking out china and invitations. There was definitely some desperation going on around here. *Sleep deprivation. Yeah, blame that.*

"How'd you do?" he asked her, shaking off the bullshit and replacing it with something useful.

She reached into her purse and pulled out a stack of papers. "Both the accounting and the shipping departments should really upgrade their firewalls."

"Thank you for doing this."

"I love what I do and am proud of what I've accomplished. Plus I'm territorial," she said smiling. "I didn't find anything too impressive, though."

"Sometimes another set of eyes can see something yours missed." He motioned to the file.

"They're copies of the shipment receipts," she said, handing them over. "Supplies that went from our lab to a PO box in Florida and the reverse. But the contents listed aren't right. An accountant might not question it, but a paranoid pharmacologist who has spent almost a decade of her life on something that might've been in the shipment *would.*"

He flipped through the pages, looking for patterns or repeated signatures. "There are a lot of them."

"The weight's off for what is written down on most of the invoices. And when I asked my coworkers if they'd done anything with the GU-121—"

His head popped up. "You shouldn't have done that."

"Calm down. I know how to be subtle."

"You shouldn't have." He cringed inwardly when she held her hands up in submission. Like a perp with a gun pointed at her head. *Shit.* He softened his tone. "I didn't mean to...I can't have you thinking this is a game."

"I know it isn't. And I won't do it again. But I *did*, and none of them knew anything about it. So I think it was in one of those shipments to Florida. But, frankly, that's a huge jump, and I have absolutely no proof I'm right."

He could have told her she was right—that the files he'd found were filled with references to her drug. But that might put her in more danger than he'd already put her in, and that was something he wouldn't do.

"You shouldn't have mentioned it to anyone, Danielle. Until we know who's doing what, you can't trust *anyone*."

She flinched at the intensity of his voice. "Except you."

"Yeah. Except me." *Liar*. He dropped his gaze to the papers. He'd have to check out the names of everyone who signed for a package. "Thanks, this helps a lot. But now you're out, and I'll handle it from here. Understand?"

"So I guess I should thank you too, huh?"

"Why would you—?" He looked up and saw her eyes warm, fill with trust. While on the force, he had seen that look a lot—from victims' families or from abused kids after he told them they would be safe.

He'd loved his job, but he wasn't a hero, and things rarely worked out the way he wanted them to. Regardless of what he did, some of them wouldn't be saved. So he kept his distance. Because if he didn't, he'd be no good to anyone.

Saying 'you're welcome' didn't mean you let them anywhere near your soul.

He should leave now, walk away from that look and everything behind it. But he couldn't. Not quite yet. Because with Danielle, he felt awkward, uncomfortable, and connected in a way that shouldn't be. He wanted to let her in.

But the risk was too high. If he brought her any further into his life, she would get hurt. Not the emotional kind of hurt that makes you feel like you're dying but diminishes over time. This would be the physical kind that no one ever comes back from.

CHAPTER XXI

"Can I get you anything, hon?" The waitress's question registered in Landon's mind a few seconds later.

"Coffee. Thanks." Maybe the caffeine would clear up his thinking.

"None of this makes sense," Danielle said, having no idea that the man in front of her was on the edge of an incredibly ill-timed emotional breakdown. "It's as if Florida is in an alternative dimension—supplies and money disappear and reappear at the state line."

He cared far, far less about the gateway to hell as he did about who the gatekeeper was. "Who ultimately decides which of the Malvers labs gets what?"

"Officially the Board does. Unofficially, and possibly without their knowledge, Whittley does."

A twinge of unease went through him. "Who's Whittley?"

"The big boss. Although I don't think that's what's actually written on his office door." Her smile drooped and then was gone. "Are you feeling okay?"

"I'm fine." He gripped his pants under the table. Whittley was the ghost they were looking for. A man who understood that claiming the highest position meant he'd be the one people would aim for. "What's his first name?"

"Ryan, I think. Why?"

He wanted to scream obscenities, but there wasn't time for that. "I need to go." He slid out of the booth and tossed some cash on the table.

"No, you need to tell me what's going on." The trust he'd seen in her eyes earlier was gone.

"I can't."

Danielle followed him into the parking lot. "What's happening?"

"I'll call you later," he called. "I have to check on something. But thanks, you helped a lot." He dialed Eden's number as he moved. The call went straight to voice mail. "I should staple that phone to her ear." He unlocked the car and pressed redial at the same time, wondering what the hell he was going to do, where Eden could be, and how many ways this was going wrong. When he threw the car into reverse, the passenger door opened and Danielle slid inside.

"Get out of the car."

She glared at him and put on her seat belt.

"This isn't a joke, Danielle. These are dangerous people."

"You can tell me about it on the way to wherever we're going."

He was seething, torn between needing to go and not being able to until she got out of the frigging car. "Since you don't watch TV, I'll break it down for you. This is one of those situations where the beautiful scientist is getting in way over her head and will end up very, very hurt."

"Those are actors."

"Not on *Cops*."

"So drop me off a few blocks away. But until then, tell me what I'm involved in. What *you* got me involved in."

Did he owe her the truth? Probably. Did he have time to talk her out of getting more involved? Not really. Did he have the heart to shove her out of the car? No.

After he backed out of the spot, he slammed the gearshift

to D. But he wasn't driving the car, he was making it fly. "You stay where I drop you. Got it?"

She gripped the door. "I have two PhDs, was at the top of my class for my entire scholastic career, and am pretty hot shit, Nick. So *please* don't treat me like I'm stupid."

"I'll have to take your word on most of that, but I know you're hot shit first hand. What I don't know is if you understand the shit you stepped into when you got in this car."

"I'm not looking for trouble and will stay out of the way. I just want to know the truth. And I promise to keep my shirt on." When he looked at her confused, she shrugged. "No one ever wears a shirt on *Cops*."

"So you *do* watch TV."

"Only cop shows. I have a thing for police officers."

"Of course you do," he muttered.

How pissed was Mitch going to be when he woke up? Probably somewhere between 'insanely' and 'homicidally.' Not that it mattered—Landon needed help, and he needed it from the person who knew Eden best.

He drove in silence, glancing at Danielle occasionally— every time he turned right or left...or went straight. And she stared back, twisting in her seat to face him. He knew the questions would start any minute, so he used the time to come up with an excuse of why he couldn't answer any of them.

Finally, she spoke. "Oh, that makes so much sense, Nick. Thanks for telling me everything."

"I can't tell you everything," he said tightly.

"You have a tongue and vocal cords, therefore you *can*. So why *won't* you?"

"It's dangerous."

"For whom?"

"Everyone."

"I'm already involved. You *made* me involved. So it would be nice to know if I can go back to work and pretend nothing happened or if I should get out of town for a while."

"The latter is probably the better option."

Her frustration matched his. "If this is about GU-121, I'm the best help you could have. I know it and most of the other pharmaceuticals Malvers is developing. You could use me as a consultant."

"Why do you want in on this? Why not just leave it alone?"

"I discovered GU-121, regardless of what anyone else claims. It's mine but I can't prove it, and if it went to Florida, I want to know."

"You want to be a consultant? Then tell me everything you know about Whittley."

She slammed her fist against the door. "I knew it! He's the one, right? He's the one who's stealing it and shipping it out. Does he have a deal going with Bradford?"

"Why would you think that?"

"Because administrators aren't interested in drugs that are years and years away from launch. They don't care what the side effects are until we're further along in development. But Whittley does. He asks in different ways, but every question centers around one thing—how each compound's half-life can be extended."

"*Is* there a way to extend the half-life?"

She leaned back in her seat but didn't say anything. Obviously, his asking the same question as Whittley had spooked her. But he couldn't take it back and he needed to know the answer.

"Let me out." Her tone had the quiet intensity of someone who'd just found out they'd been duped.

"Let me find a café or something." He'd planned on dropping her off anyway, but not in the middle of nowhere.

"Let me out *now*!"

He grabbed her arm just before she reached the steering wheel. When she cried out in pain, he let go.

"Do you want to kill us? Jesus." He pulled over to the side of the road. "Let me take you somewhere safer."

"Now you're worried about me? I didn't think liars did that." She didn't realize she was still buckled in until her door was open and the seat belt yanked her back against her seat. It locked down as if they'd just hit a wall, protecting her from herself. Unable to twist or bend or calm down, she fumbled with the release button.

Landon put his hands over hers. "Let me help."

"Stupid..." She didn't stop struggling, her words breaking up with agitation, panic, and frustration. "I can't even press a stupid button!"

"The more you fight, the tighter it gets. So relax. And remember that I didn't force you to come along—you forced me to bring you."

She took a breath and pressed into her seat, creating a tiny bit of slack. Tears filled her eyes. "I know. But now I'm stuck in this stupid car with this stupid belt, and I feel like an idiot."

"It's not you, it's the car. Until now, the seat belts were the only things that *did* work."

"You lied to me," she said quietly. "You used me to do something illegal or unethical." Her body slumped. "Is it too late for me to get out of this?" She wasn't talking about the seat belt.

"I'm not... I'm not a bad guy."

Her glare would've knocked him backward if he'd been standing. "Forgive me if I don't take your word on it."

He should release her and let her go. But facts are facts and what she'd said was true—she might be able to help. Allies were past impossible to come by, especially ones with her expertise. If she knew all there was to know about GU-121, then maybe she could help Turner. He sure couldn't help himself, Eden was constantly creating or finding trouble, and Landon was going to kill someone—possibly himself—if things didn't improve soon.

But he wouldn't take Danielle's choice away from her. Not any more than he already had. "I'd like to take you somewhere safer, but it's your decision." He unclipped her belt.

She didn't run. "What's this all about, Nick?"

"If you tell anyone what I'm about to tell you, the price

will be very, very high. Do you understand? I don't know which direction it will come from, and I may not be there to protect you. So"—he took a breath—"with all that good news in mind, you have one more chance to walk away." He looked at her expectantly, hoping she took the out.

"Talk."

Damn it. "Put your belt back on, because we need to be somewhere. I'll explain along the way. Feel free to jump out whenever you've heard enough." The fall would be a lot easier than what was coming.

So he talked. About the Florida facility, what The Clinic was doing with her drug and others, who they were doing it to. He didn't look at her—he just drove and spoke as if he was talking to himself. Over the next ten minutes or so, he brought her into his world. A dark world filled with pain, uncertainty, and danger. One she wouldn't be able to leave until the storm was over, if it ever would be. And he wasn't strong enough to look her in the eyes as he did it.

She didn't scream or hit him. She didn't even burst into tears.

"So," he said, badly in need of a drink, "any questions, doctor?"

"No."

Didn't expect that. Of all the things he thought she might say, 'no' wasn't one of them. "Were you listening?"

"I heard every word, other than a few you mumbled." Her tone was scalpel sharp. "And maybe some of *those* were believable. But the rest of it was highly entertaining, and incredibly insulting. Unless you're crazy. So...are you crazy or creative, Nick?"

Yeah, that was more of what he expected. It was also hurtful—it had been a long time since someone accused him of lying...when he wasn't.

"I'll prove it," he said.

"*Really*? How? Are you going to pull a monster out of your pocket? Or maybe you have before-and-after pictures of the woman's eyes. Because that would *totally* convince me."

"You not believing me is understandable. But driving around with someone you think is insane...? I thought you'd know better."

"Well, this *is* Texas."

He shook his head. "Not getting how that helps."

"Doesn't everyone think we're born with guns in our hands?"

Shit. One of her hands was inside her purse. *Didn't expect that either.* "You have a gun on me?"

"Yep."

"That's unfortunate." He paused. "Feel free to shoot me if I attack you. But when that doesn't happen and after I prove I'm not crazy, I'd like that hand to stay out of your purse."

Hopefully Eden had come to her senses and was back at the warehouse but, even if she wasn't, Hyde would be.

And if that bastard didn't convince Danielle that he wasn't crazy, he'd start wondering if *she* was.

CHAPTER XXII

After sitting down, Ryan slid a soda towards Eden. "I'm never sure what to get a woman to drink. If a man orders diet, she'll be offended. If he orders regular, she won't drink it because it has too many empty calories. So I got you half and half."

She looked at the drink warily.

He laughed. "So distrustful, aren't you?" He grabbed it, took a long sip, and then grimaced. "It isn't poisoned—I just hate the taste of diet soda." He held his cup up in a toast. "Here's to reaching our goals, by whatever means necessary."

"I'm not really in a celebratory mood."

"Completely understandable." He sighed and then ate a french fry. "It's a lot to take in. But you didn't think the solution would come easily, did you?"

"Nothing ever comes easily in my world."

"That's true for most of us. There's a man who was sent to Florida to clean things up after you and your people…made things messy. Do you know about him?"

"I heard some things. Not very nice things."

He nodded. "My understanding is that he may do other not-very-nice things in Dallas soon."

"And he's where you're going to start?" She'd listen, get

as much information as she could, but she wasn't even close to signing up for anything.

"Well…he's not looking for *me*, so I thought he's where you would want to start."

I want to start with something that doesn't involve selling my soul. Distracted, she took a long sip of her drink. Then another before realizing it was really, really bad.

"This tastes like ass. I'm going to get something else." Normally she was fine with either diet or regular, but the two didn't mix well.

"It was my mistake, I'll fix it." He moved to stand.

"I think I can handle it." As she stood, she stumbled and had to grab the edge of the table for balance. "What—?" As an awful warmth radiated through her, she dropped the drink onto the floor so she could use both hands to steady herself.

His image wavered, like heat coming off asphalt on a blistering hot day.

"What did you do to me?" The question should've created a sound, but it didn't. So she tried again, louder this time. Were her lips even moving? They were numb, as numb as the rest of her body.

He stood up and calmly wrapped his arms around her waist. And she couldn't push him away.

"She's fine," he told the customers around them. "It's just vertigo."

Impossible. She'd seen him take a sip. But he was fine. *How did he…?*

He leaned in close and whispered, "Don't ever play poker with me, Eden. I always win."

Her legs crumbled underneath her, his arms all that held her up.

"It's okay, honey," he said loudly. "I'll take you home." Then he swept her up into his arms, and she didn't have the power to stop him.

-ᴧ-ᴧ-ᴧ-

Mitch *heard* reality before he felt it. Landon saying, "You better not make me regret this by dying, asshole."

I'll try my best, cop. The tunnel out was long and coated in scalpels, but he'd take any exit he could get to.

"Turner! Mitch, open your eyes."

When he peeled his lids apart, he was blinded by a light. *Not a big improvement.* His eyes adjusted slowly until he saw a piss-cheap wooden roof that matched the piss-cheap floor under him.

Oh, the beauty. When the horrible light moved, he realized it had been a flashlight. Maybe they'd been interrogating Hyde on the cheap because they couldn't find any floodlights or water to go with the boards.

"I don't wanna seem ungrateful, but that really sucked." He did some more blinking and a couple of neck stretches. "How long was I out this time?"

"Three days."

"Anything exciting happen?"

"You could say that."

This was going to get old quick. As in, three-days-ago quick. "Where's Eden?"

"Someplace she shouldn't be, doing something she shouldn't do."

"Why didn't you stop her?" He jerked up and fell right the fuck back down, his brain doing a 360 in his skull, cuffs burrowing their way into his wrists. *Again, major suckage here, folks.*

"Have you *met* her? How am I supposed to stop someone so intent on destroying something that they don't care if they destroy themselves along the way?"

Mitch had no idea. But he needed to find out. He hauled himself up to a sitting position as soon as the metal clicked open. As much as he wanted to jump up and go rescue her from whatever trouble she'd gotten herself into, he should probably wait until he could make it more than four feet before collapsing. So he took a moment to wiggle his head, shoulders, knees, and toes.

"Nice place." Just like he remembered, only it looked even shittier from the ground. He turned towards the haul-up door and—

"Who the fuck is she?"

From the ground outside the truck, the woman looked amazed, watching him as if he were a monkey at a zoo. And sadly, that was a fair comparison.

"This is Danielle," Landon said. As if that explained anything.

"Jesus, cop! I'm out of it for three goddamn days and you start bringing visitors to gawk at me? Did you charge admission, at least?"

She shook her head slightly, though he didn't know if it was in answer to his asinine question or in wonder. Then she came a step closer. "How often does this happen?"

"Mondays, Wednesdays, and Fridays at 6:30," he grumbled. "But if I miss a day, I can make it up the following week without any financial penalty. Wanna sign up?"

"Two minutes in and I'm already regretting giving you the wake-up call." Landon turned to the woman. "It's a long story but, as of right now, it's only when he gets the drug."

"And how long does he—?"

"How 'bout we stop talking about the freak as if he wasn't here?" Mitch shouted.

"Danielle is a researcher…at The Clinic's facility here in Dallas."

Mitch shot off the ground and was out of the truck before Landon could stop him. Danielle stumbled back a step and then pulled herself into a pride-in-the-face-of-inevitability stance.

"Boy, am I glad to meet you." Yep, he'd growled. That had definitely been a growl. At least it was a human one.

Landon yanked him back by the arm. "She's not with them. Well, not with that side of them."

"Did she tell you that, cop? Because no one who works for them ever lies, so if she used those exact words, then I see no reason not to believe her."

"Do you think I'd bring her here if I hadn't checked her out?"

"How many of them have we trusted? Right until they fucked us over." And then, it got even better. All he saw was Converse tennis shoes and a mop of hair, but it was enough to recognize him. "What the hell is the kid doing here? Shit, it's like I slept through half the party—a whole room of unwanted people. Carry on, folks. Have a great time."

"Let me explain, Turner."

"Good idea." Mitch stepped in close to the cop. *Really* close. "Why don't you start with where the fuck Eden is?"

⊸╂╴╂╴╂╴

A rush of adrenaline hit, jolting Eden into consciousness. But she didn't move. Since Ryan hadn't killed her, she'd keep her eyes closed until she knew what to expect when she opened them. She was lying down on her side, coarse carpeting underneath her, her hands tied behind her with thick synthetic rope, her legs bent and her toes pressed up against something.

Nice car, but there isn't enough trunk space. It definitely hadn't been designed with the kidnapper on the go in mind.

"She looks like an angel, doesn't she? So peaceful." The voice came from above and belonged to a bastard. *Ryan.* Poker-playing asshole extraordinaire. She had to give it to him, though—he'd completely outplayed her.

"You gonna keep her as a pet?" asked a voice Eden didn't recognize.

"Of course not," Ryan snapped. "She bites. Wild animals need to stay in cages and be admired through a thick set of bars."

"That's a shame." Footsteps tapered off as the other

speaker walked away.

"And, Newman," Ryan called out, "I'll tell them to expect your call, so keep your phone handy. I'll see you at the Shop."

The Shop? Somehow she didn't think he was planning on buying her a new wardrobe.

"Eden," he whispered. "Are you awake?" He whistled and switched to his normal, hateful volume. "Shit, you are. Already. That's incredible. Really incredible."

She opened her eyes to see him staring down at her. "You're him."

"Possibly. Can you give me another hint?"

"You're the dickhead I spoke with on Jolie's phone and the asshole who told Alex to breed me."

"I…" He feigned offense for a moment before a smile crept onto his face. "You got me. It's nice to finally meet you, Eden Colfax." Then he laughed. "That *was* you I spoke with on Jolie's phone, wasn't it? I wasn't sure—you two sound equally stupid."

"Be as cocky as you want to, Ryan, and enjoy that grin. 'Cause it isn't going to last much longer."

"Thanks for the warning. But if you'll excuse me, I need to make a call. You don't mind if I use your phone, do you?" He slammed the trunk, smothering her in darkness.

Darkness she could handle, tight spaces too. But assholes thinking they're in control? No, that was something that just didn't sit well with her.

"Eden can't come to the phone right now." Ryan's voice traveled through the walls around her, his tone mockingly sweet. "Is that Turner? Great. Tell him to stop yelling—I want to speak to him."

Mitch was awake? Eden rubbed her wrists together, feeling the rough rope dig into her, blood lubricating her skin. So she kept rubbing—it was something her father had taught her. The *only* thing.

Can't go with instinct on this one. She had to be patient, deliberate in her actions, smart. So she subdued the desire to

yank against the rope, because that wouldn't work.
  Instinct only makes the rabbit tighten the snare.

CHAPTER XXIII

Mitch watched Landon close his eyes, his cell phone still up to his ear. When the cop had picked it up, he said it was Eden. And then he looked surprised. Then confused. Then pissed. And now…who the fuck knew what that expression meant?

"Let me talk to her," Mitch repeated, still trying to swipe the phone out of the cop's hand.

Landon shooed him away.

"Give me the goddamn phone, cop!"

"You can talk to me," Landon said to whoever was on the other end. After a few more back and forths, Landon held the phone out, shaking his head. "Ryan Whittley. He wants to talk to you." Then he mouthed, 'I think he has her.'

Mitch had to relax his hand out of a fist before he could take the phone. He was cramped from head to foot. *Deep breath in, deep breath—Oh, fuck it.* "There needs to be a really good reason why you have her phone, asshole. Or you've just run out of minutes."

"I didn't know you were human, Turner," Whittley said. "Welcome back. And, believe me, I have a great reason. But I can't talk long, because in another five minutes or so your beautiful girlfriend and I are going to be…busy."

Mitch felt his chest rumble with an entirely human, entirely territorial sound. "Totally understandable—you seem like a real charmer. So are you calling me to gloat or what?"

"Well, I'm hoping you can follow directions now that you're human. I want you and Landon to meet someone I employ. When that happens, I'll tell your girl to put her clothes back on and leave."

"How about you tell my girl to leave now? That way she'll be home before everything goes dark. And when I say 'everything,' I mean everything for you, Whittley."

The man chuckled. "Don't worry, I like her. She's cute and has a terrific body. And she smells incredible. Like…what's the right word? Like…lust. Yeah, that's it. She smells like lust. So I don't plan on hurting her. Of course, plans can always change."

Mitch could melt steel right now. "When and where?"

"His name is Newman and he'll give you a call. Then— Fuck!" Whittley's cursing was quickly covered up by what sounded like a tornado. Hopefully a house had just dropped on the wicked witch…who was lying on top of Whittley's head. Mitch would give everything he had to see that fucker's legs sticking out from under something heavy.

What the fuck was happening? He heard a scream—maybe hers, but he wasn't sure. It could also have been a wildcat, its call was so raw.

So endless.

"Eden!" When the phone went dead, Mitch did too. He kept yelling into the empty line, knowing how useless it was but unable to stop himself.

"Turner," Landon said softly. "What's happening?"

He dialed her number again and again and then shoved the phone at Landon. "It's not working. Maybe I'm doing it wrong." It was possible—he couldn't think, couldn't function. Not even the automatic shit, like breathing and blinking. He just couldn't do anything. Because none of those things would help her.

Landon pressed the screen a few times, and then he stopped trying. "What did he say?"

Mitch felt his pulse slow, almost stop. Cold. He was so cold. Like a goddamn bear going into hibernation. His limbs were heavy, as if they'd all gone numb.

Knock it off, asshole. Numb wasn't going to get her back. He wasn't hibernating until she could do it with him. Until they were so close together, they could live off each other's heat. So he shook off the doubt and bounced from side to side like a nutcase—which was completely fitting.

"He made a few threats. Wanted an exchange—us for her. Then before he could say where, he screamed like a little girl at…at something."

"Something like Eden?"

"Maybe. I hope so, but I don't know. There was a scream, man. It was..." He looked to his friend, begging him for a solution. "Hostage negotiation protocols. Go."

He sighed, shrugging slightly. "We wait until he calls back."

"What the fuck, Landon? You have never said anything so fucking useless before! We're not going to wait until he calls back."

"What else can we do?"

"Why don't you call the police?" Danielle asked.

Mitch swung around to face her. "You have no idea what you're part of now, do you?"

"We're all just trying to help, Turner."

"Well, we all just need to try harder to think of less idiotic ideas."

"Not helping, asshole," Landon hissed before turning to Danielle. "If we call the police everything comes out. That would be fine if that didn't also include the Abnormals— Eden, Turner, Justin, and who knows how many others."

Be helpful. Mitch nodded, determined to think logically all the way up until thinking was no longer necessary. "If that happens, taking down The Clinic won't do shit. Because another will pop up in its place and do exactly the same thing. It's the nature of the power hungry—use or be used. And there will never be a deficit of power-hungry people in the world."

"The goal is still to bring them to justice," the cop said. "We just need it to be a quiet kind of justice."

"And if that doesn't work, then we'll settle for a quiet kind of mayhem." Mitch took a deep breath, willed his brain to up the RPMs. Because waiting around wasn't going to happen. "So here's what we're going to do. We go in, guns *quietly* blazing and do as much *quiet* shit kicking as we can. Since Whittley doesn't want any attention either, it shouldn't take much to draw them out.

"Whittley's a businessman," he continued. "A personality type I know pretty well. So we go to the place where he pretends to do business, and we knock heads until we know where he lives and where he keeps his porn collection. Because if I know nothing else, that guy has an enormous porn collection. Probably the hard stuff—expensive, not off the rack, not anything he keeps close enough for someone to find."

Mitch finally felt grounded, capable. He knew Whittley because he knew how power-hungry people worked. A full profile would give them something to work with. It had to. Assholes didn't just fall out of the sky. They had histories, weaknesses, and habits.

Mitch kept on thinking out loud, not sure if anyone else had anything to say but not really caring. If it was important enough, they'd make themselves be heard. "He sounded young, so I'm guessing he's not married—claims he's married to his work. But he's cocky, so he probably has a girlfriend— a trophy he keeps on his mantle until she's needed. They don't really give a shit about each other but hate to be alone. Because then they have time to think about what awful people they both are."

He shook his head. "Correction. He sounded impotent, don't you think, cop? If impotence could speak, he's what it would sound like." Or maybe that was just wishful thinking. "If dad's still around, he's got major issues with him—never feels good enough, needs to prove he's not the asswipe his dad thinks he is. Even though daddy's right.

"Whittley's in it for the power, not the money, although that's a definite perk. So his employees are probably afraid of him, or at least intimidated by him. They stay out of his way, secretly wishing they could strap him up spread eagled on a wall so they could practice knife throwing." He whipped his head towards Danielle. "Am I warm?"

"I'm not sure about the porn collection, his dad, or his impotency issues, but it all sounds likely. And the knife throwing is right on."

"Where would he have taken Eden? He wouldn't want to soil the drapes at his place and there'd be too many witnesses at his office. But if he has—hopefully *had*—Eden, he's strong. And he's smart, but then we already knew that because of all the seemingly smart people who do really fucking stupid things for him. But he's a hell of a chess player—better than I am because I'm not sure I could take Eden down. So he must have built her trust. But she's only been gone for what?" He waited. "Justin, how long has she been gone?"

The kid swallowed, his eyes wide. "Um…"

"You can do it."

"Two hours tops."

Mitch winked at him. "Two hours isn't enough time to get Eden to do anything." Not exactly true, but he wouldn't let his mind go there right now. "So how'd he get her to trust him? Or make her think she had no other option?" He stopped. Wiped his face with both hands. Mumbled, "What's wrong with us?"

"What?"

The bait Eden would swallow no matter what. *Me*. They deserved each other. Because it seemed like neither of them wanted to live all that badly. They couldn't go five minutes without offering themselves up for the other.

"He got her because of me," he said quietly.

A team works together, shares info, and doesn't move separately. The fucking Clinic was less dangerous to them than they were to themselves. Right now, they were all too busy protecting each other from danger to be smart. Life was dangerous no matter where they were. And the only thing they would do alone is die.

"I swear to God, Landon. When we get her back, she doesn't move without one of us at her side. She doesn't breathe where we can't hear it." After he got the nod he needed, he continued. "Now I'm on a bit of a time schedule here." Four to twenty-four hours before he got useless again. "So I suggest we get moving."

"Except for you." He pointed at Justin. "Someone needs to stay here, just in case. If she gets out, this is where she'll come. And I don't want her to be alone when she gets here. Got it? Don't answer that with anything other than a yes."

"Yes."

"Great." He didn't want to split up, but there was no way everything would get done otherwise. Probably stupid, but definitely necessary.

"You"—he pointed at Danielle—"for the love of whatever you believe in, figure out how to keep me human. I'll take whatever you got. Consider me a free-range guinea pig. The only thing this four-to-twenty-four-hour shit does is make me grumpy. So get whatever sciencey crap you need and Bunsen burn the hell out of it."

He waited for her to nod and then turned to Landon. "Alright, cop, seeing as you are my oldest and only friend, I will tell you this once and then we can move on. I am very unhappy that you let her out of your sight. You know how...volatile she's been lately. I know she's not your responsibility, so that unhappiness is unfair to you and I'm sorry. That said, I would appreciate you making sure that she's far away from all of this once it gets ugly. Because it *will* get ugly. Because I'm going to make it ugly. But I don't want her to see it—she's seen enough."

He turned his volume down. "I love her more than you can possibly imagine. I've brought her more pain than *I* can possibly imagine. But she would still give up her soul for me, and that's exactly why I can't let her."

Landon nodded. "I'm in this till the end, man. You aren't the only one who cares about her."

He swallowed, nodded, and headed to the door. "Meanwhile, I'll be looking for someone who knows where the bastard would take her. Possibly this Newman guy."

Landon was at his side. "You're going to make yourself bait?"

He nodded. "It's what Whittley is doing with Eden, so we need a counteroffer." Not that he would ever be worth as much as Eden was. "No offense, cop, but I'm more desirable to them than you are. Plus, I'm more pissed off and more violent. So yeah, I'm bait." He didn't actually realize how quickly he was moving until he saw everyone jogging to keep up with him.

"Wait." Landon grabbed him by the shoulder. "You're going to stand outside of the building and scream until someone tips him off?"

"If that's what it takes. Did you find anything on Alex?"

Landon shook his head. "Nothing."

"Wait!" Justin called.

Mitch cursed, sighed, and then turned. "Time. Ticking. Whatever you say needs to be important."

"You're looking for Alex Bertram?"

"Yeah."

"She has a sister who lives around here."

"Anything else?" Landon asked. "Because that's not enough to move on."

"Her sister's name is Desiree, but I don't know if her last name is Bertram or not. She's a kindergarten teacher."

Mitch almost laughed—one sister watches over six-year-olds and the other watches over monsters. Hopefully, that was where the career similarities ended, or those kids were going to need decades of therapy.

"We could look at all the elementary schools in the area for a teacher named Desiree."

"It's Powell Elementary," Justin said.

Mitch looked at Landon, Landon looked at the kid. "How do you know that?"

"It's my last name: Powell. I think Alex told me because she thought it would make me trust her." He laughed bitterly. "Guess it worked, huh?"

"They're great liars," Mitch said. "I think they all have to take classes or go through a degree program for it."

"Whatev." Justin dropped his gaze back down to the floor.

Mitch turned to Landon. "We can find her with that, right?"

He held up his phone. "I'll do it on the way. Then you can drop us off and go find her."

"It's a good thing I didn't kill her, huh?"

"Don't!" Justin shouted.

"You're gonna need to work on the full sentences, kid," Mitch said. "Because 'don't' doesn't mean a lot to me."

"I need to ask her a question. A really important question. So…"

Mitch let the 'so' slide because the kid looked like he was about to break in half. "Okay. I'll make sure she can still hear and speak." But he wouldn't guarantee anything else.

Chapter XXIV

Eden hadn't killed him, despite the urge to do so. Because Ryan was the answer to all her questions. All she had to do was come up with a way to get him to talk. He'd been so forthcoming at the restaurant, not stopping to think about what to say next, so maybe some of the things he'd told her weren't lies. Even for pros like Ryan, good deception takes forethought and planning.

She wasn't worried about the sound coming from the trunk—she knew how to tie a knot better than he did. His hands and feet were as useless, as the interior trunk-release mechanism that was now standard in all vehicles. If he'd broken it, Eden might not have been able to get out. But he would've had to damage his beautiful car, which he probably couldn't do. It really was a beautiful car. With the Jag gone now, Mitch should buy one of these for Landon.

Since she didn't know the city and didn't want to use the GPS, it took her a while to find her way back to the warehouse. "Hallelujah." She pulled up and pounded on the door so Justin would open it. "Justin! It's me!"

His face lit up at seeing her again. Did he really doubt he would? He threw his arms around her, momentarily forgetting he was supposed to be cool and angsty.

"Good to see you, too." She held him for another moment and then pulled back. "Where are the boys?"

"After Landon woke Turner up, they talked to that guy. Then Turner freaked out, and they left." He took out his cell phone. "I'll call—"

"Could you do me a favor first?" She looked at the empty truck and the chains. They wouldn't work—the cuffs were Hyde sized, not man sized. So if Ryan worked at it and wasn't afraid to shed some skin, he might be able to slip his hands out. She should set up something similar to how Justin had been tied.

"I need help lifting a package," she said. "Are you up for it?" She pulled the car into the warehouse, grabbed some rope, a pair of cuffs, and the wooden chair and put them all into the back of the truck.

Justin was looking over her shoulder when she opened the trunk. "Holy shit!"

Ryan squinted his eyes at the change of light. "Can I get some aspirin? I have a hell of a headache. It feels like I got kicked in the head."

"Why don't we hold off on that aspirin? Because your headache's going to get a lot worse." The last few words were drawn out as she dragged him partway out. "He's a gift for the boys," she told Justin. "Can you help me get him into the truck?"

"That's *the* guy?"

"Yep, that's *the* guy. He won't do anything to you. I won't let him. Promise."

Maybe it was a mistake to involve Justin at all, but she was just too damn tired. The days of carrying full-grown men around were a few weeks behind her. Plus...

Evil weighs more than good.

To get him into the trunk, she'd had to drag his unconscious body and chucked him inside limb by limb. It was actually a liberating moment of payback. But there was no way she could lift a full-grown, conscious, and pissed-off man into the truck. No way. Not even if she knocked him out again.

Justin averted his eyes but didn't shy away. Eden was proud of him. They each took an arm. Ryan didn't seem particularly worried, only pulling away because it amused him to see them struggle.

"Who's your friend, Eden?" Ryan asked.

"Since he's my friend and not yours, let's just call him 'None of Your Business.'"

"I'll have that engraved on his headstone."

Justin flinched, and then hopped into the truck to pull while Eden pushed. Ryan's foot landed in her stomach—something she'd pay him back for really soon. When his ass was over the edge, she jumped up, and they dragged him the rest of the way in.

"Do you think no one will notice I'm gone?" Ryan asked. "That no one will come after me? People will miss me."

Eden laughed. "Sure they will. Who doesn't enjoy a daily dose of humiliation from their asshole of a boss?" She shoved him into the wooden chair and began tying him to it with both rope and chain, making sure not to loosen a knot before another was in place.

"There are people far more important who will be looking for me."

"Of course there are. And I bet they're getting their horses ready and setting up a posse as we speak. Or maybe they're on their way already. Why wouldn't they be? They have nothing to lose." She yanked hard on the rope to finish a knot. "Oh wait. No, that's me—*I* have nothing to lose. Do you think the 'important people' would risk their money or power, let alone their lives, for you?"

"We'll see who's laughing at whose grave as soon as they find me."

"And how will they do that again?"

Ryan smirked.

"It's fairly low-tech, isn't it?" She palmed his cell phone, holding it, the battery, and the SIM card out for him to see. She'd crushed it with her shoe. Repeatedly. Happily. "More useful for parents to keep track of their kids than for important people to keep tabs on their asshole." His amused expression faded. "I wouldn't have thought of it if I didn't know Landon. He's taught me a lot."

"Landon's a smart man. Not smart enough, though." He looked at Justin. "If I were you, I'd run as fast and as far from this as I could. But...not before I loosened some of these ropes."

"Shut up." She tried to get Justin's attention, but he was staring too intently at Ryan to notice. "Hey." She finished one more knot and then stood, stepping in between them. "Don't listen to him. He talks a big game because that's all he can do. Don't let him inside your head."

Worry lines had already imprinted on Justin's forehead, making him seem so much older than sixteen. Ryan had made those lines to appear. Not just right now—this was something Ryan had been building for years. By using other people and places and drugs, he'd manipulated all of them.

Justin shouldn't see what she might have to do to force Ryan to talk. He shouldn't know about things like that. Even if she sent him out, eventually he'd come back and see the bloody mess she'd created. Because she would, if she had to.

It can't happen here. "Come on." She ushered Justin out of the truck. "Ryan needs some time in the naughty chair to think about what he's done."

"What happens then?" Ryan called out just before the back door closed.

Eden wasn't sure. But whatever it was would leave both of them wounded.

She flipped the lock. "I need another favor. I'm starving and exhausted. Can you go get some food? The boys will probably be here by the time you get back."

"Sure." He shoved his hand into his pocket and pulled out

his cell phone. "Shit, my phone's almost dead."

"It can charge while you're at the store," she said, handing him a twenty.

"Nah, I'll take it just in case. Landon's an ass about not being able to reach people." He checked the phone again and stuck it and the cash in his pocket. "It's probably good for one more call." After a quick glance at the truck, he nodded, said goodbye, and took off down the street.

How much time did she have? Not enough. It was never enough. She felt like she was walking through a minefield and all the mines had timers on them. Mitch, Landon, Ryan, herself—everyone was ready to explode. They were all so interconnected, she didn't know where to focus. Or which of them would blow first.

Prioritizing was impossible. This entire situation was impossible. She was afraid of doing something, or not doing something, that would make them lose the whole game. If she made the wrong move right now, it would be her fault. Instinct didn't help because self-preservation was integral to instinct. Self-preservation demanded she run for it, and that would mean doing something she'd never do—leave Mitch behind. So she had to think logically in an illogical situation.

She didn't want to leave and miss seeing Mitch again, but she also knew that he and Landon would stop her from doing what needed to be done, Landon because he still held onto the belief that the world was just and Mitch because he didn't think he was worth getting a little blood on her hands for.

Both of them were wrong.

I'll call them when I have good news. She climbed up into the truck's cab and pulled out of the warehouse.

This had to end. She would never have this chance again. If Ryan got free, if he didn't give her answers, if just one of a million things went wrong, she would lose. Her knuckles were white on the steering wheel. Soon they might be red. A whimper made it through the tightness of her throat.

Toughen up. It didn't make her happy, but she couldn't see any other way. It was maddening, infuriating, and awful. But she'd do it. And she'd ignore the part of her that screamed 'stop' and tried to warn her of what she was turning into.

It wasn't hard to find a quiet spot where the truck wouldn't be noticed. She pulled into a small area along a barren strip of road. It looked like a truck graveyard. Before opening the back, she steadied herself with a deep breath.

Ryan had fallen and, with bound arms, hadn't been able to brace himself. He looked dazed. She climbed up and righted the chair, checking that nothing vital was broken. Nothing vital on the chair—she couldn't care less if any part of Ryan was broken.

"How does it feel to be chained up like an animal?" Just like he'd done to her and others. All she was doing was returning the favor. What would he do if she busted out the needles and tested some drugs on him? Unfortunately, he was human...barely, so the drugs probably wouldn't do much, if anything. "Ever been inside of one of the cages you put people into?"

"Humanity is its own cage," he said calmly. "Don't we all feel trapped at one point or another?"

"I'm pretty sure most people would prefer the metaphorical kind."

He licked his lower lip, grimacing when it hit blood. "You'll have both kinds soon." Maybe he enjoyed being tied up, saw it as a sexual thing. Nah, if anything, he was the 'S' in S&M. But not today.

"The problem with screwing people over is that they have a hard time letting it go. You built me a hell of an army— Landon, Fields, Mitch. All mean sons of bitches whose only goal is to scratch you off the planet."

"And yet, you're still afraid."

He was right. She was afraid. But not of him or his people. Not anymore.

Mitch, Carter, Mom, Ian, Landon, Tara, Alicia. The things he'd done to them had left Eden with battle scars that made her skin impenetrable. Her enemy had created a shield for her, one so thick, so tough, not even he could get through.

So her fear was real, but not in the way Ryan thought it was. Because the shield was impervious from both directions, and she was only afraid of the stuff *inside*.

"Sometimes fear makes us do things we wouldn't normally do," she said.

He took a deep shuddering breath. "It's hot in here."

Yeah, it was. She leaned against the side of the truck to separate herself from the thick air around him. The craving for violence wasn't the only thing suffocating her. There was also a craving for sex, and the more time she spent around him, the stronger the feeling became. As if the two things were intertwined, which she knew they couldn't be. There was never any violence between her and Mitch. There was burning heat and intense need, but no violence.

You can worry about how you'll pay for all the therapy you need later. When there wasn't too much to lose and this much uncertainty.

Ignore the tingles and stick to the violence. She grimaced and shook her head. *I mean, getting him to talk. Shit.* What was going on with her? *Yeah, lots and lots of therapy.*

"Is Ryan your real name?"

"Yes."

"Huh."

He sighed. "And to think you don't believe me. After everything we've been through together."

"I thought the devil would've had more originality. You know, something more dramatic for his first born."

He laughed. "He got more creative with his next child."

"Did he beat the shit out of you when you were little? *Please* tell me he did."

"How about I tell you that I'm beginning to question your sanity?"

Her laugh was so bitter, it almost brought tears to her eyes. "I'm doing less than what you did to me and the others. So maybe you should take a minute to question your own sanity."

"'Insanity is doing the same thing over and over again but expecting different results.' Did you know that, contrary to popular belief, Einstein never said that?" Despite having nothing going for him, he looked at her with incredible confidence. It ate at hers.

"The most admirable thing about Abnormals is their honesty with themselves," he said. "They might lie to others, but they never lie to themselves or try to be something they're not. It's something I've tried to implement in my own life. So, no, I'm not insane. And I don't think you are either. Although I could be wrong."

"Your opinion is about as important to me as your life is right now."

"What are you going to do with me, Eden? Keep me tied up forever? You're not going to kill me—that I know. And since I have nothing to tell you, I think this is something referred to as an 'impasse.'"

"I figured we could hang out for a little while, chat, work out some stress, that kind of thing."

"Working out some stress sounds interesting. Are you going to fuck me?"

"In a manner of speaking," She moved behind him, leaning down to whisper. "But I'm the only one who will be smiling afterwards."

CHAPTER XXV

Just another day at the office that isn't. Landon squeezed Danielle's hand as they went inside the building. She was clutching the purse that now held a vial of each of the drugs and all of the files he'd brought from Florida, in addition to her gun.

He peeked into the security office. "Hey, Rick. I came in early to help the doc with something. I'll be back before my shift starts."

Rick popped a brow. "'Help' the doc with something? Wow. Seriously, Nicolas, my hat is off to you, man. I'm in awe." He put his hand on his heart.

Wrong assumption, but one that could work for them. "Yeah, um...listen. Is there any way you could turn off the cameras in the lab for a little while?" He smirked. "It would be better if some things weren't caught on camera, if you know what I mean."

"In *awe*," Rick repeated. "But...if I turn the cameras off, I won't get to watch."

"And *I* won't have to think about why the keyboard is sticky. Turn them off."

"Alright, alright." He swung his chair to the console.

"These things glitch all the time. How long do you need?"

"As long as she wants it."

"Awe!" Rick called as Landon shut the door and followed Danielle towards the lab.

"Sorry about that," he said quietly. "When we're done, I'll tell him I made the whole thing up."

"There are rumors about me and almost every man here. No one believes them anymore. Probably because of the other rumors going around. Honestly, it's a good thing everyone was talking about it or I would've never known I was frigid. And gay."

Shit, I like her a lot. "Slow down," he said, touching her arm gently. "Unless you *always* run to work."

She slowed, agitated but in control. He knew how much potential trouble he was creating for her. But they were out of options, time, direction, you name it. Mitch was a time bomb on its last few ticks, and Eden was in trouble—two more reasons that Landon needed to keep it together. It was something he was good at—years of fruitless searching had taught him patience and self-control.

After verifying that Rick had turned the cameras off, Landon watched Danielle fuss with equipment, shuffle the vials around, and flip through files.

Then his phone rang. "Yeah?"

"It's Justin." He spoke quickly, nervously—nothing like the typical lazy tone of a typical teenager. "Eden came back a little while ago and she had the guy tied up with her. Not tied up *with* her. He's tied up and he's with her. Separate—"

"Slow and easy, kid. Eden's there?"

"She's at the warehouse, yeah."

"Where are you?"

"She sent me out for food."

That just didn't sound right. *She escapes from a kidnapper, brings him back to the warehouse, and sends the kid out for snacks? Not likely.* Especially for someone who barely ate to begin with.

"Justin, call Mitch and tell him that she's back. And also tell him to move his ass. I'll be there as soon as I can. Okay?"

"But my phone—"

Landon heard something across the room shatter.

"Stupid," Danielle grumbled, bending down to pick up whatever she'd just dropped. In order for her to be productive, he needed to calm her down, which also meant he needed to end this call.

"I gotta go, Justin."

"But my phone—"

"Call Mitch. He and Eden can hold down the fort until I get back." He hung up and went to help Danielle pick up the larger pieces of glass. "Take a few deep breaths. I can handle the glass."

She stood and started rummaging through her supplies again, still frantic. "This is going to take time. More time than Turner might have, I don't know. It's like asking someone who's never seen flour to whip up a cake...in twenty minutes...without a recipe. I don't know anything about the other compounds." She'd gone through the files on the drive here, but it was a lot to go through, even for someone who could look at them without her eyes crossing.

"You don't have to understand them. If I tell you what they do to Turner, maybe the files will help you piece something together." Something that would keep him from transforming so abruptly and with so much risk. "All we need is a start. Or a time-released capsule to slow it down."

Really? A time-release capsule. Wow, that was just brilliant. He couldn't believe he'd even considered doing this without her. He lifted up one of the bottles. "This was in whatever they were giving Carter. He was human, not Abnormal, but maybe it would help an Abnormal be less abnormal, you know?" *Another brilliant idea, idiot. Just stop talking.*

"It's not quite that simple."

"Yeah, didn't think so."

She looked back down at the file, flipping pages and sighing a lot. "Whatever they were giving Carter was a composite drug, a mixture of GU-121 and two others—neither of which I've ever heard of." She held up two containers. "All I know is that *maybe* this one brings out the Abnormal side and *maybe* Bradford developed the other one by using them. Maybe. So even with the components and kinda-sorta knowing what two of them do to Turner, there are still way too many unknowns. I can't risk someone's life on that many maybes."

"Even 'maybe' is better than what we have right now."

"Drug testing takes a huge amount of time and research before we even use animals. And human trials?" She shook her head so fast, she became a beautiful blur. "You've got to be kidding. GU-121 alone is years away from human trials. If the FDA found out that someone had been testing it on humans, they'd send out everyone they had with pitchforks. No one in Texas would need to turn on the lights because there'd be so many torches. Really. It's just...so far beyond imagining."

Landon looked at her, hearing the answer leaving her mouth so casually, but afraid to hope. "Is that true?"

"What? The torches? No, of course not, but—"

"What would the FDA do and how long would it take?"

"Um..." She looked up from her work, which entailed putting some kind of liquid into some kind of beaker. "They'd start an investigation that would probably take years, maybe longer, depending on what they found." Then she went back to work, as if she were a swimmer and had only turned her head to take a breath.

Human trials. He wanted to smack his head against the counter. *Damn it.* He should have figured that out before now. Headline: 'Government Agency Discovers Secret Human Drug Trials.' Effect: The Clinic doesn't get taken down by Eden, Turner, or him. It gets taken down by someone entirely different, in public, someone so big and far-reaching that the bastards can't hide. Without connecting any of it to the Abnormals.

He'd been so focused on not exposing them, so blinded by the fear they'd be discovered, that he missed the way around it. The whole truth didn't need to come out, just part of it. That a non–FDA-approved drug was being used on people. Normal people.

"What if the FDA found Carter's file?" *No, it goes to multiple agencies and anyone else who wants a look.* Until there were so many eyes on it, no amount of bribery could cover it up.

"They may take it seriously, or they may not. But studies are faked all the time. The public only hears about a small fraction of them, usually the ones uncovered by competing labs or manufacturers. Because the FDA can't look into all of them." She came back up for air, looking at him intently. "If the drug was found in human tissue, it would prove far more than a bunch of paperwork. Unbiased tests from a reputable lab would be hard to ignore."

There was no chance The Clinic had left a body behind, not one they'd been experimenting on. But Landon called Joe at the Fort Lauderdale precinct anyway, just to make sure.

It was a very short call.

Carter's body was gone and an autopsy was never ordered. So along with all of Carter's drug-laced tissue went their chance of proving The Clinic had conducted illegal experiments. They couldn't use any of the Abnormals as proof, because it would pull an investigation in the wrong direction—towards the Abnormals, not towards The Clinic.

"From the look on your face," Danielle said, "I'm going to assume it's a no go."

"Correct assumption." Landon ran a hand over his mouth. So many people dead, and the one body he really needed was—

Oh shit. The idea landed on him like an anvil in a Wiley Coyote cartoon. *Think, dickhead. Really think it through.*

They needed to recreate what The Clinic had done to Carter: inject the stuff into the veins of a full-blooded human, have a blood-sample taken, and then leak the files and the blood to the FDA.

Provided Danielle could figure out how to brew up a batch of what they'd given Carter, it just might work. Of course, they would also need a normal guy be the test subject.

Just a normal guy. Sure. Luckily, he knew one who was just stupid enough to do it.

"I'm sorry," she said.

Not as much as *he* might be soon. "Could you recreate the composite drug they gave Carter?"

"Within a certain margin of error, probably. But that's not proof, that's just chemistry."

He swallowed. "I could take it."

"What?" She paused, probably trying to figure out why he'd just said something so stupid. "You? No. No, that's a terrible idea. What if I don't do it right? And even if I do, Carter died."

She was right—Carter died. And so did a lot of other people. And, if this didn't end soon, there would be even more.

Landon was healthy, strong, unlike Carter had been. "The kid was close to death before they even got hold of him. He shouldn't have been able to stand but, when we found him, he was walking. They gave him the drug and he recovered freakishly faster than he should have. Then when they stopped giving it to him, he got worse." *And worse. And then died. But don't focus on that part.*

"So," he continued, "since he was dying and the drug helped him heal, it stands to reason that, without it, he just went back to dying. Because I'm healthy, it should bounce me up a little bit and then drop me off right where I started."

She stared at him as if he'd left his brain back at the warehouse. "You know absolutely nothing about science, do you?"

"I passed chemistry…the second time around." He smiled. She still looked worried.

"I know nothing about the composite, and not enough about GU-121. Not yet. And not at *all* for this particular use. Once they're combined, anything could happen. I mean *anything.* And that doesn't even speak to the fact that I may not do it right."

The more Landon thought about it, the less risky it seemed. Less risky than what he'd faced every day as a cop. A shitload less risky than going anywhere with Turner—something he'd done without hesitation, knowing full well that there was a really good chance he wouldn't make it out.

This needed to end. Landon's body was strong, but his mind was so goddamn fatigued. After years of looking for justice, or vengeance, or whatever it was, his career disappeared faster than a nice set of rims with a 'free' sign hanging off them.

As screwed up as they all were, Turner and Eden were his family now, and The Clinic wanted them gone, too. The bastards wouldn't stop until they'd taken away everything Landon valued. Most of it was already gone.

If he did this, it would end all of the bullshit.

Was it risky? Hell yes. But life was risk. Love was risk. Anything meaningful or important carried risk.

Screw it. He was in. "You don't have to give me a full dose—just enough to have it show up in a blood test. We need outside witnesses and unbiased testing." That wasn't going to happen if Danielle drew his blood here, especially not once the truth started coming out about this facility's ugly stepsister who used to live in South Florida. "So give it to me and then take me to the hospital."

She looked at him, then at the vials in front of her. "No."

"Please, it's the only way."

"I can't do that."

He couldn't force her even if he wanted to. She was new to all of this. She hadn't lived through all that he had or seen what he'd seen, and hopefully she never would. They'd find another way. Not sure *what* way, but he, Eden, and Turner would keep looking. Hell, if they could get through today, Landon might have more time to try to change Danielle's mind.

"It's okay. I understand." He held out his hands for the vials, but she tucked them closer to her. A big goddamn red flag shot up in his mind. "I need those. *Now*, Danielle. Give them to me."

"You'll have to wait a minute." Her eyes darted around the file in front of her.

That's not going to happen. He was already in motion when she spoke again, stopping right before he reached her.

"I'll give you what's left after I mix something up, dilute it with saline, fill a syringe with it, put the syringe on the counter, and then walk away with my back to you." Her voice grew softer. "What you choose to do then is up to you."

He took a breath and let it out slowly. "Thank you." He didn't know what he'd done to earn so much trust, but whatever it was, he wanted to hang onto it.

"I don't deserve it," she said. "But I'll do my best and then cross my fingers and pray it gives you what you need without killing you."

He held up his hand, fingers crossed. "I'm way ahead of you."

She pulled an envelope out of the file and unfolded the paper inside of it. "What's this?" Her eyes moved at sight speed across one page and then another and then stopped.

He recognized it as soon as he got a good look. "Carter's confession. He left it on my desk."

What a day that had been. The look on Eden's face flashed through his mind. He saw what might have been her lowest point—disappointment, confusion, humiliation, doubt, fear. The two of them had been sitting in his car. Eden was flipping through all the notes Carter had taken—mood changes, dosage schedule, and sleeping habits. And then she found

Carter's letter. Landon wasn't actually sure she'd ever even read it.

"She inhaled the drug he was giving her?" Danielle asked. "Snorted it?"

"Just once." He nodded. "Her Abnormal side found it and probably thought it was cocaine."

She blinked, tilted her head, and sighed for about thirty seconds. "It was the powder form of something that was normally diluted in her milk, right?"

"Does that mean something?"

"Well, she snorted a highly condensed form. I don't know enough about this particular drug, but none of them come out of pixie sticks. That much of a nondiluted pharmaceutical...it should've killed her."

"Well, Eden's pretty tough. Now more than ever."

"Okay, but the diluted form affected her, so..." She nodded. "I'd like to talk to her."

"I'd like to introduce you." *If I'm still around.* He stepped back, giving her some space while she used pipettes and beakers and various other crap he hadn't seen since high school. All he could do now was watch. And hope like hell this wasn't going to be his end.

Never lifting her head from her work, she berated him with questions, and he answered truthfully. Not only did she deserve it, if he was about to die, he didn't really want his last moments to be built on deceit and capped off with a guilty conscience.

Eventually she filled a syringe with something, sighed, and put it onto the counter. "I have absolutely no idea if this is going to work, Nick. None whatsoever." When she turned towards him, her eyes were wide but tired looking. "If you die, it will be your own fault. I won't feel bad at all because I told you I couldn't do this."

"I would never blame you for anything." He moved closer to her and tipped her chin up, holding it gently so she'd focus her teary eyes on him. "Thank you."

He brushed his lips against hers gently, because he didn't know if he was allowed to, if he was asking too much from someone he was already asking too much from. She had every right to push him away and tell him to piss off. Every right.

But she didn't push him away. She wrapped her arms around his neck and drew him in and made him regret the hell out of not doing this earlier. He held her, feeling her body mold to his, hearing her gasp into his mouth when he picked her up. The kiss deepened, overwhelming him with how right it felt, *she* felt, the whole frigging world felt. In one day she'd taken down something it had taken him years to build.

When he pressed her against the counter, she moaned and her legs tightened around his hips. There were too many layers of clothing between them. How fast could he get rid of them?

Slow down there, idiot. She's letting you kiss her. Don't blow it by ripping her pants off and—Oh, shit. Stop jumping ahead to a place you're never going to get to.

He didn't want to stop. He wanted to take her, feel her, believe for just one moment that she could be his. That they could have something real, something incredible. Even a chance at it.

It had been a long time since he'd let someone in. But it made sense now—he was supposed to wait. For her. For someone who wanted him, even knowing him at his worst. Seeing his world and not being too afraid to step into it. He'd waited for her without knowing he was. Unfortunately, it had taken him too long to find her.

It wasn't meant to be. Not now. Maybe not ever. Because he had too many people counting on him to linger any longer. It wasn't right to feel this good, knowing his friends were in danger.

Not now, man. Timing was everything. And his timing sucked.

He put her down, pulling away slowly because he couldn't let go of her any faster. And she didn't want to be let go of. *You've gotta be kidding me. What are you doing?* The right thing. He gently pried her hands off his shirt.

She whimpered, 'No,' as soon as their lips separated, her eyes still closed, her lips full, skin flush.

So perfect. Okay, he'd kiss her one more time and then step away. *One more.*

It was a long one. And it was really goddamn difficult to step away.

She opened her eyes and looked into his. "You can still change your mind, you know."

He shook his head. "I'm too stubborn." Maybe too stupid.

She brushed her finger along his lip. "I'm not done with these. Or with you. So don't…" Her hand moved to his chest. "Don't die."

When she walked to the door, Landon wanted to call out to her, say goodbye or tell her to stay because he was afraid he might never see her again. Because he might die as soon as the drug hit his bloodstream, and he didn't want to be alone. He'd been alone for too long.

Before he had a chance to wimp out or man up, she stopped and unlocked a large first aid kit that was on the wall. Then she turned towards him.

"Good luck, Nick."

Yeah, he'd probably need some of that.

CHAPTER XXVI

Mitch had never actually made a house call. He hoped Alex would appreciate it.

He pulled up to the security box outside the planned community Alex's big sis lived in. Was there a maximum age to be a security guard at these things? This one looked exhausted, probably near the end of his shift after a grueling day of sitting on his ass and pressing a button to open the fucking gate.

Mitch tried to seem nervous and not just pissed off as he rolled down his window. He held up a bouquet of roses and a small empty box that he'd bought at the florist down the street.

"Who are you here to see?" the kid asked.

"Brennan. But—" *Look embarrassed...and sappy.* "Do you have to tell her I'm here? I kind of wanted it to be a surprise." He wiped his forehead so it looked like he was sweating over popping the question. Of course, in reality, Mitch wasn't nervous and Alex wouldn't be celebrating when he popped *his* question.

The guard shook his head. "Can't do it. Sorry."

"Please, man. It's impossible to surprise the woman—she's always one step ahead of me." Mitch put the flowers on the passenger seat and took the fifty-dollar bill off the dash. He kept it visible just long enough for the guard to see it.

The kid glanced around quickly and Mitch knew it was simply a matter of time. Twenty seconds probably. He was wrong. It was ten. Damn it, his judgment was slipping all over the place.

The guy palmed the cash, nodded, and said, "Good luck," before buzzing him through.

Mitch stopped in front of a house that looked way too expensive to afford on a teacher's salary. Which meant Alex's big sis was either getting a hell of a nice alimony check every month, or there was a chance hubby would be home.

Be careful and try to behave. He walked to the door holding the flowers up to cover his face. He liked the smell of roses—clean, pretty. He'd get some for Eden as soon as he could. Maybe they would tame her a bit. Domestic, she would never be, and that was absolutely fine with him—he couldn't be domesticated, either. But if she was home more, she wouldn't be out getting herself into situations that made him fucking *insane*.

He couldn't help but smile when the door opened. It wasn't Alex, but the woman looked so much like her, he had to be in the right place. She smiled right back at him when she saw the flowers. Huge smile. *Huge.*

If I do this right, I might get a tip out of it.

"Oh my God, they're beautiful! Are they from Curtis?" The fact that she didn't call out to her husband in glee meant that 'Curtis' was probably not home. Great news—one less variable.

"I don't know," he said. "Are you Alexandra Bertram?"

The woman's smile fell into a pout. "Oh, she's my sister. I'll take them."

He kept them just out of her reach. "I need to give them to *her.* Boss's rules." He rolled his eyes. "Is she here?"

Big sis huffed and then yelled, "Alex, you got something!"

"What?" Alex came around the corner, wiping her hands

with a kitchen towel. As soon as she saw him, she freaked. "Close the door, Desiree!" She rushed forward towards her very confused sister.

Waaaay too late. He was already inside. "No worries, I got it." He shut the door with his boot as Alex slammed on the brakes and told her sister to run.

Mitch wasn't interested in threesomes. He'd tried it in college and, frankly, it was a lot of work and too hard to focus. But he'd make an exception for Alex. Of course, everyone would stay fully clothed because the alternative made him want to vomit. If he touched them, it would have nothing to do with sex, and when he tied them up, it wouldn't be kinky.

He snagged Desiree's wrist before she took a step. "I'm not going to hurt you. I just need to talk to your sister." He shoved the bouquet at her. "You deserve these more than she does." As he moved forward, Desiree followed along, stunned. "You two are so different—one docile and another able to torture people and keep them in cages. What are your parents like?"

"Who is he, Alex?" her sister whined.

Alex didn't answer what was a completely appropriate question. She backed away, glancing from him to her sister and then towards the room she'd just come from. Since she was holding a kitchen towel, Mitch figured she was probably wondering which knife to take out of the block.

He looked at Desiree. "I'm Mitchell. Your sister and I know each other from Florida. She put my girlfriend and her dad in cages and drugged them, and she also more or less killed a not-quite friend of mine. Does she talk about us much?"

"Let her go and I'll talk to you."

"You have no idea what she really does, do you, Desiree? All the shit she's involved in. What did she tell you—that she was an office manager in a paper factory?"

"A hospital," Desiree whispered. Thank goodness for open communication and the nature of families. He barely had to do anything.

"A hospital, huh? Very respectable job. But hers wasn't in a hospital and it wasn't respectable. Does she go anywhere, Desiree? Meet up with anyone?"

"Are you going to hurt us?"

Mitch didn't look away from Alex, but he heard the tears in Desiree's voice. And he was sorry—sorry that she had such a fucking awful person for a sister.

"I don't want to hurt anyone," he said. "Okay, that's not true. I want to hurt a *lot* of people. But I won't. Your sister knows the asshole who kidnapped my Eden, and I need to find them before he hurts her. But I'm out of leads and your sister is the only one I can ask."

Then he pulled Desiree closer and lowered his voice. "Help me out and I promise that the next thing I say will be a lie." Before she could reply, he called out, "I'll hurt her if you won't cooperate, Alex. And then I'll hurt *you*. Worse than last time. Which, frankly, I regret. Because it wasn't nearly bad enough." Desiree tugged against his grip. "It was unfortunate but unavoidable. Alex wouldn't give me the key to Eden's cage." Big sis's eyes doubled in size.

"Yep, a cage. Crazy, isn't it?" He picked up his pace as Alex got close to a corner. "And just so we're clear—Eden's a woman, not an animal. I'm not into that at all."

"Let my sister go, and I will tell you whatever you want to hear."

"Before or after you knife me?" He shook his head. "Not that way." He nodded towards a room with two big couches facing a flat screen. Alex stomped into the room with all the maturity of a four-year-old.

"Tell him, Alex. Just tell him what he wants to know."

"Shut up, Des. You're not helping."

"Does she always talk to you like that?" He tsked. "That's not very nice. The sooner you start talking, the sooner I leave and you can call the badass security guard up front. But I know you're not going to call the police because you only like bars if someone else is behind them."

"I don't know what you're talking about," she said, flopping down on the couch.

He laughed. Clueless people were funny. "The problem with being a part-time monster is that you miss things, but you don't have the same excuse. So I'm thinking—no offense to your sister, her lovely home, or the great state of Texas—but I'm thinking you didn't just come here for a steak. I'm thinking you came here because your boyfriend called you in after that little problem you had in Florida. Am I right?"

"He's not my boyfriend."

"Too bad. Breakups are tough. What happened? Wait, let me guess. Whittley woke up this morning and realized he was in bed with a harpy."

"He's my boss. And he's not going to kill your pain-in-the-ass girlfriend." Her face drained of color when her sister gasped. "Des? I didn't—"

"Don't worry, Des, she didn't kill anyone with her own hands...that I know of. But like I said, I miss a lot."

"*Ryan* Whittley?" Desiree's eyes were stuck on her sister as if she'd just confessed to doing something sinister. Which...she had.

Mitch ignored Alex's whining and focused his attention on the more forthcoming and morally upstanding sister. "What do you know about him?"

"She calls him a lot, but always from another room. I thought...I thought he was married or something."

"I don't think he's married, but he's definitely something." He nodded to the cell on the coffee table. "Is that her phone?" Desiree nodded. "Can I trust you?"

Her pause was in millisecond territory. "And then you'll leave?"

He sighed. "You have no idea how badly I want to. Because right now I have no idea what Whittley is doing to my girl and I don't have a lot of time." He met Alex's eyes and then slowly pulled the syringe out of his pocket. "I haven't been feeling like myself lately. I took something for it, but I don't know how long it will last. And I'm a complete bastard without it."

Whatever Alex opened her mouth to say was swallowed, her eyes never leaving the syringe.

"Can you get the phone for me, Des?" He let go of her wrist, hoping he wasn't being a bigger moron than usual. Hoping that she could read the sincerity in his tone because, for once, everything he'd said was true.

Des leaned down to pick up the phone and shook her head at something Alex whispered. When she came back to him, she looked as pissed as he was. Almost.

"You're going to have to stick around for another minute," he told Desiree. Then he went through the recent calls and found Whittley's. "No picture? Is he shy or grotesquely ugly?" Calling the bastard now would just tip him off and might make him do something stupid...er. So Mitch would wait until absolutely necessary.

"Where did he take her, Alex?"

"I don't know. I don't even know if he has her."

"Oh, I'm pretty sure he took her *somewhere*." He leaned up against the wall, holding the phone with both hands. It was either that or wrap them around her throat. "Do you think I'm overreacting? I guess they could've gone out for smoothies. Eden really likes smoothies." He flipped the phone over. "I should call him and check. Let him know I'm hanging out here...with you."

"He has another lab," she said quietly, dropping her head forward. "But I've never been there. All I know is that it exists."

"How many of us is he holding there?"

She shrugged. "I don't know. He wanted to salvage what he could from Florida and bring it here so he could..."

"Make sure you don't screw up again?"

"Florida wasn't my fault. It was yours and it was hers. If you hadn't been there—"

"You would still have your broodmare."

"I didn't mean for it to be like that. I had no choice." Her emotions and tears had zero effect on him. But Alex wasn't looking at him—she was looking at her sister. So he believed. Partially.

"We all have choices, Alex. And you chose the wrong fucking side. The lies, the kidnapping, and the killing are all on you guys."

"I know that now! But if I don't do what I'm told, Whittley will send Newman after me, too. It didn't used to be like this. When I started, he told me it was about making a better world."

"And you believed him?"

She nodded. "I wanted to believe him. And by the time I knew better, it was too late." She looked at her sister, her face filled with regret. "The things they did...I didn't know until I was too far in." And the sobfest began. If Alex was using the waterworks to make him go easy on her, she was getting dehydrated for nothing. Because mercy was never going to happen.

CHAPTER XXVII

Landon rolled up his sleeve. He'd never done drugs and hated getting shots, but here he was and that's what he'd do. Because there was no other way to stop this without lots and lots of people dying.

The needle bit, and the drug stung as it went in. Luckily, his jaw was already clenched, so he didn't embarrass himself by screaming like a little girl. He watched the black ring of the plunger go down, pushing his possible death into his bloodstream.

This was either the best idea he'd ever had or the absolute worst. He took a breath and gave the thumbs-up signal to an extremely nervous-looking Danielle. "Not dead yet. That's a good sign, right?"

"Not funny. How do you feel?"

"Fine. A little warm, but that could be psychological."

"That tends to happen when you poison yourself," she said flippantly. He didn't want her to be angry, but he didn't blame her. She hadn't been living this for years with no solution or end in sight. Well, now, *finally*, he could see an end. Unfortunately, it might be his. Maybe he should call Turner, give him a heads up on the poison front and toss in a few last words, just in case. Before he could, his phone started vibrating—caller unknown.

"Landon."

"You were told to expect my call." Not a voice he recognized, but it had to be Newman.

"Was I? I don't remember. I've been distracted lately."

"We're supposed to make an exchange."

Let's see, Eden was back at the warehouse. Whittley was tied up in their truck. And Turner was probably already on his way back. So…"What do you have that I want?"

After a long pause, Landon had taken all he could. That happened when you could drop dead any minute. "Look, I have plans for the rest of the evening and they don't include listening to static, so tell me what you're offering. And it better be more exciting than a six-pack."

He waited for a reply that didn't come. Maybe the guy was a sensitive clueless-kidnapper and Landon had hurt his feelings. "How about you call me back when you're ready to talk?"

"Nick?" Danielle asked hesitantly.

When Landon turned towards her, he understood why there had been no response. Without thought he dropped his phone and drew his weapon.

"I'm ready to talk now." The asshole had one arm around Danielle's waist and the other resting a gun on her temple. "Is this more exciting than a six-pack?"

Shit. Landon hadn't even heard the door open. And where the hell was Rick? Maybe he'd taken all of the cameras offline instead of just the ones in the lab. "Okay, let's talk. Outside. But we leave her here."

The man didn't move. "She's necessary. You aren't. But I'm not supposed to kill anyone unless they try to escape or to kill me." The man was a psychopath—a simple conclusion determined by years in the police department and the fact that the guy looked fucking *nuts*. No expression. No variance in his voice other than a slight Southern lilt.

Now was a good time to reassess the situation.

"Are you trying to kill me?" the man asked. Danielle whimpered and tilted her head away from the gun denting her skin.

"I don't want to kill anyone," Landon said. "But you're holding a gun on my friend and that makes me uneasy. How about we both agree not to kill anyone and put down our weapons?"

"How about you put yours down and come with me? Or I might think the doctor is trying to escape."

"Okay." There was no other choice. Not now. Maybe soon. Or Landon might keel over the second the drug took effect. If he was close enough to the asshole with the gun, maybe he could drop dead on top of him. As he slowly put his weapon on the floor, he saw Danielle's eyes track to her purse. To her gun. Smart.

Way smarter than I am. "Whittley would want me to bring my stuff." He walked towards it, trying to think of a reason his 'stuff' would be in a purse…that didn't match anything he was wearing.

He was still three feet away when Newman shook his head and said, "If Whittley wants it, he'll come get it."

"If we leave it behind, someone might wonder what happened to its owner."

He laughed. "It's a bit too late to worry about that."

Landon didn't know what the comment meant, but it probably wasn't good. His hand twitched as he passed the purse. Newman held Danielle tightly and stepped back from the door to let Landon go through first. They walked in a line—Landon in front, then Danielle, and the asshole bringing up the rear.

"If you hurt her, some very bad things are going to happen to you." Best and worst-case scenarios ran through Landon's mind. He walked slowly, hoping to be close enough to do something when an opportunity knocked.

He wished he was glad the door to the security office was

wide open, but he wasn't. Newman didn't slow a stitch, even with the 'Security Office' sign facing their direction. As they passed, Landon saw Rick's body half in and half out of his chair, an armrest the only thing holding him upright, a slowly growing pool of blood on the floor under his head.

Poor bastard didn't even have time to pull his Taser. "Did he try to kill you?"

"Nope."

"Did he try to escape?"

"Nope. He was ungracious."

"Don't look." Landon glanced at Danielle, trying to convey confidence that everything would be okay. At least he didn't have to speak the lie. She nodded tightly, her eyes filled with innocent fear, her body trembling. He'd done this to her. And now he had to fix it.

Newman got her moving again by stabbing his weapon at her neck.

Landon didn't move, giving the man time to push Danielle closer to him. She grabbed Landon's wrist, then slid her hand into his and squeezed. A second later, she took his wrist with her other hand. When she closed her eyes, he grabbed her, just in case she was about to faint.

"No," she said, her eyes popping open.

"She okay?" Newman asked as if he actually cared about her. It was a good sign. It might mean she would survive this, even if Landon didn't.

"I get a little stressed out whenever someone kidnaps me," she snapped. "I guess I'm just too sensitive, huh?" Danielle's eyes were still sharp and observant, but her face was ghost white. Not weak, but scared shitless. There was no doctorate for this kind of thing.

The guy tapped his gun on Landon's shoulder. "Carry her."

He wanted to keep his hands free, but his current options were severely limited.

"I can walk by myself," she said.

"Carry her," he repeated.

Landon scooped her off her feet and kept walking. Her fingertips landed on his neck, resting there softly, her other hand on his shoulder.

She leaned closer to him, almost nuzzling his cheek. Nice thought, bad timing. Then she whispered, "Your pulse is different." Holding her hand where Newman couldn't see it, she counted—four fingers went up, and then were clenched into a fist.

Great. An Abnormal heartbeat. The shit he'd injected was starting to kick in. So this was the moment. The moment he found out how bad an idea it had been to take the stuff. But he couldn't die now. Not with Danielle in his arms, Turner and Eden not knowing what was happening, and the answer to bringing The Clinic down surfing through his bloodstream.

Not now. Please, not now. Preferably not ever.

Newman directed them into the parking garage and stopped at the ass end of a classic kidnapper's tool—white, unmarked, windowless, late-model van. *Fucking things should be tracked right off the lot.* Who else needed one?

"Put her down."

As Landon did, he realized his breathing hadn't changed, even though he'd been carrying her for a while. She didn't weigh much—125, maybe 130—but his muscles should've complained a little. Instead there was nothing. No fatigue, no strain, nothing.

Like he could hold onto her forever.

"Get in the truck."

Landon stood back, letting her go in first. Not to be chivalrous, but because he wanted her to be behind a metal door when the fight started. Unfortunately, he wasn't the only one to think of it.

"Not you. Him." The prick grabbed her by the collar and yanked her back. "You get to ride up front with me."

Landon knew better than to let a criminal take them to a second location. But he also knew that the safety on

Newman's gun was off and he'd already killed someone today. So he climbed in and immediately started looking for a way out.

A row of vertical bars divided the passenger area from the back. Even if he had Hyde's strength, Landon couldn't bend steel. And he sure as hell wasn't faster than a speeding bullet. But each bar was bolted into the ceiling and the floor separately, and one of those attachments had to be weaker than the others. He should be able to work one or two loose enough to reach through. And then he'd take Newman out with his bare hands.

"Make sure you wear your seat belt," he warned her quietly.

She nodded, afraid, but confident. In him. As if she had absolutely no doubt that he would get her out.

No pressure. As soon as the door was slammed in his face, he went to the bars, shaking them and looking for weakness. He found it even before the passenger door opened.

Unfortunately, the asshole wasn't as stupid as he looked. He pushed Danielle into the driver's seat, while he sat sideways, keeping his weapon against her neck.

Landon finally understood Mitch and Eden. *How goddamn ironic.* His body was starting to feel different, stronger, better than it had ever felt.

And he was trapped in a cage.

CHAPTER XXVIII

"As much as I'm enjoying your misery, tell me what Whittley wants from Eden." So Mitch could get out of here with some hint of where the fucker might have taken her.

Alex wiped her eyes and cheeks. "What does *everyone* want? What's the motivation for everything a man has ever created or attempted or fought for?"

He thought the word a second before she said it. *Power.*

"Power. Whittley doesn't care how she's used. How any of us are used. Once they can isolate what makes you different, they'll start testing it on people."

"They already did," he said. "You did. On Carter."

"Can you please let my sister go?"

"So she can call the police or so she doesn't hear about what you did?"

She didn't respond, probably because she couldn't pick just one.

"You were saying...?"

When she spoke, it was fast, as if spewing the information would confuse everybody. Or maybe she was trying to make it as quick and as painless as possible for herself. "Carter was a one-off. Not important. He would've died from his injuries in a matter of time—we knew that when we took him from the hospital. So it was just a…a…" Suddenly she had a stutter.

"A game."

She shook her head. "A test. A chance to test a theory without losing anything."

"I'm pretty sure Carter lost something."

"He got better—dramatically better once he acclimated to the drug. When he was taken off it, he started to deteriorate almost immediately. And then…"

"And then he fizzled out." He tried to keep calm because he needed her to keep talking. So he focused on being an attentive listener instead of shoving her into a corner she would never, ever get out of. "So the endgame is what?" No answer. "Jesus, Alex, just say it! Des already knows you're a bitch."

She swallowed, glanced to her sister and then lowered her head. Maybe to cry again, who knew? As long as she kept talking, she could cry all she wanted. "To take the best parts of the Abnormals and recreate them in humans."

Best parts? There *were* no 'best parts' of being what they were. But there *was* violence, strength, and the ability to heal—all of which would be very desirable in an army and would make some dickhead's pockets very, very heavy.

"Eden came the closest," he said. "Naturally. Without you guys playing with Petri dishes, she was your best shot."

"Once they understand her adaptation, it will save years and years of research. With the stem cells of her offspring, the jump will be enormous."

Will be even bigger. She'd said 'will.' So the plan hadn't changed at all, and coming to Texas had just made it easier for Whittley and his crew. That had been Mitch's idea—before he got useless. Of course, right now he was still useless.

Power. Everything is about how much you have and how well you can control it. In a way, he'd always known. Because while he didn't understand a fucking thing about himself, he understood other people, men specifically. "Besides Whittley, who are they?" They might put women like Jolie and Alex on the front line, but testosterone was driving the bus.

"There's a Board of four or five people, I'm not sure. But Ryan's in charge. The Board provides the funding and thinks they're making decisions, but he only goes to them with insignificant stuff. He calls the shots on everything important. If you want to stop this, start with him."

She wants Whittley dead. Probably to keep her own ass intact. But her motives didn't matter. Not this time. Because she wanted the same thing Mitch did.

"You figure out where they are," he said, his voice low, "and I'll take care of the rest."

"Ryan mentioned something about the building being condemned. But...there are a lot of condemned buildings in Dallas."

"I need a map."

Desiree went into the kitchen and rummaged through a drawer. Just behind her was a calendar with a fat red line circling one day and the words, 'Curtis home 12:30.' "What's the date?"

"The third." So Curtis would be home tomorrow. Good news but not nearly enough to make up for all the bad.

Desiree came back, unfolding an old-school map. Her movements were stilted, as if she was so confused and overwhelmed that she couldn't do anything she wasn't told to do. If she didn't have that annoying conscience, The Clinic would've loved her. Another perfect puppet.

"I'm sorry," Alex said.

"Sorry? It's too fucking late to be sorry." There was no snooze button on this alarm, no reset, and 9-1-1 couldn't handle it.

When Alex's eyes widened and she scrambled backward, Mitch realized he was moving. *Idiot.* He forced his legs to stop, quads and biceps twitching. His hands were in the perfect shape to be wrapped around someone's neck, so he drew them into fists. *Not a lot better.*

I think it's time to leave. Before anyone—meaning Alex—started dying. He couldn't leave her here, and he would *never* trust her, but the last thing he wanted was another liability when there was no insurance that things wouldn't blow up in his face.

And then his phone rang—a normally innocuous sound that pounded on his eardrums until it was the only thing he could hear. It took him a while to answer because his hands were immobile. *Great, I've reverted to something without opposable thumbs.* If it was a wrong number, he might lose it. With no time to look at caller ID, he put a shaky finger down on the accept button, smacking his head as he put it to his ear.

"Yeah?"

"Turner?" Tentative, quiet, probably because of the anger in Mitch's one word comment.

"What is it, Justin?"

"I was supposed to call you earlier, but my phone was dead." Pause.

Mitch was definitely going to have to teach the kid to speak properly. And then Eden could undo the damage by finishing it up with a lesson on why using 'fuck' excessively actually wasn't a good idea. And Mitch would agree to disagree.

"Why were you supposed to call me?" Mitch asked slowly.

"She came back. Eden. She was here."

Mitch shut his eyes and felt his stomach go back to where it should be. Until he processed all of the words. "Was?"

"She came back and then she left again."

"You need to hold on for a few minutes. So take that time to figure out exactly what you're going to say. And then, when I get back on the phone, I want complete sentences. Paragraphs even." It would take him at least twenty minutes to get back to the warehouse, so details could happen in the car.

He lowered the phone from his ear and looked at the two women in front of him—one looking like she was about to be seated in the electric chair and the other still trapped in the magical land of disbelief. Should he bring them along? One of them?

Hell no. Eden was already more woman than he could handle, so he'd let Curtis deal with these two tomorrow at 12:30. "I need rope and duct tape, ladies. Now." He motioned with his hands. "If you don't move fast enough, I'll have time to decide this is a bad idea."

The women started scrambling for stuff, running around like two of the three blind mice. He tied them to chairs back to back. Spending the night tied up wouldn't hurt them. He should know—he'd spent a whole bunch of nights chained to a bed. And look how sane *he* was.

"Des, use this opportunity to say everything you've ever wanted to say to Alex but have never had the balls to. Believe me, she deserves it. And I suggest using the word 'fuck' a lot because it's cathartic."

He put a strip of duct tape across Alex's mouth and then leaned in close. "If I ever see you again, make sure you bring the tape. You're going to need it to put yourself back together."

As soon as he was out the door, he put his phone up to his ear. "Justin, are you ready to tell me everything that happened and everything you know?"

"Yes."

"Then start talking...in full sentences."

To prove how in control he was, Mitch stuck his hand out of the window as he passed the security guard and showed him a finger. Not the middle one, though. He gave the guy a big thumbs-up sign. Because Eden was free.

And whatever happened from this point on—no matter how incredibly screwed up it was—was whipped cream and big fucking cherries.

Chapter XXIX

At the very least, Ryan turned out to be an excellent outlet for Eden's rage. It was like taking a kickboxing class, but instead of her fist hitting air, it hit him.

She was exhausted, he was beaten, and neither of them had shared anything other than a bunch of insults and personal jabs. Everyone had a weakness, a button, a trigger. *Everyone*. And even though she barely thought of him as a human being, Ryan had one too. She just had to figure out what it was.

In the back of her mind, a part of her was screaming, begging her to control herself. The only thing she seemed to be able to control was where she hit him.

She and Ryan made the same sounds of pain, but hers came from a much, much deeper place. It was hard to remember how she used to be, but she definitely hadn't been like this.

It's their fault. Even as she thought it, she knew it was a lie. But if she acknowledged the truth, she couldn't pretend this wasn't happening or that it would end. She needed to believe that when this was over, she could be the person she wanted to be and have the life she wanted with Mitch. Everything awful would go away—The Clinic, the pain, the violence. It would all disappear once Mitch was free.

Liar.

Maybe Landon was right—that she was past the point of behaving logically. But she was in too deep to be able to see another way out. Ryan bled and grunted but didn't talk. All she wanted was for him to admit what he'd done, to give her a shred of a hint as to what to do, and to tell her how to bring Mitch back for good.

But she and Ryan were equally stubborn. If their positions were reversed, he would do the same to her. As if the past few years weren't proof enough, you don't drug someone and stuff them into your trunk to go on a picnic.

He deserved worse than she could ever give him. So each blow brought peace. Payback for ordering women raped and people tortured. She didn't want to enjoy it, but she did. No, not enjoy—relish. Shit, she was. She was relishing his pain and her power over him.

If she wasn't careful, she'd kill him. And then where would she be? The world would be rid of one murderer only to have gained another.

Stop! Finally she did. Not because he cried mercy and not because she pitied him—neither of which happened. She stopped because she hated him so badly she wanted him to suffer, to remember who was in control and be able to see who he should be afraid of. He'd taken so much from her, brought her to her knees so many times. She wanted him to experience everything he'd ordered done to her.

The stuff he said about The Clinic's motives and her father's involvement was bullshit. He would never have been that open if he was telling the truth. And the more she thought about it, the less sense it made—there was no money in making people good. Crime paid, prisons made money. And for Ryan, money meant power. And power was his driving force. In order to believe in right and wrong, you had to have a conscience. He didn't. Or he never could've done the things he had.

"Why are you doing this to us?" she asked.

He licked the blood off his lip, grimacing. "It's research for a children's book."

She smacked him. "I got all day, asshole. No plans at all. So make as many jokes as you want. But come nightfall, I'm going to take you to someone who makes me seem like a pacifist."

"Actually, your violence is impressive." His voice held no fear, no hesitation. As if he'd already planned on this happening and had decided hours ago exactly what he was going to say. "It's an interesting development, really. You integrated your sides so beautifully without any medication, and then *this* starts happening."

"I'll stop the second you tell me what I want to know." *Liar. You won't be able to stop.* And it had nothing to do with Chastity or being Abnormal. Eden couldn't stop because she was human and weak and scared and desperate.

Ryan smiled knowingly as if he knew what she was thinking and had just cataloged it in his mind. "I'm amazed I can still talk. Not to tell you anything you want to know, of course. Just to share how much I admire all you've become." His smile was wiped away by her fist.

She may have left her morality at the door, but she would pick it up later. Everything was secondary to finding answers. But she could feel her frustration mounting. She'd gotten nothing from him so far, no matter which way she tried to get in.

"I love your compliments," she said. "So I'll ask him to stay away from your pretty mouth."

Ryan spit out blood. "He listens to you? That's a first. Hydes aren't a particularly agreeable lot. As I recall, they do a lot of grunting and insulting, but very little listening. And no agreeing at all."

"I meant Mitch. I know he'd love to meet you."

"We've already met. I went to one of his seminars a few years ago. The theme of his talk was something about getting your head out of your ass. Good speaker. Very honest. Helpful to me in a lot of respects career-wise. I don't think he'll remember me, though."

"I'm sure he'd be happy to give you another speech. Probably something about how to get your head *back* into your ass again. With interactive instruction." If he'd learned so much from Mitch's seminars, then maybe Mitch would have insight that she was blind to.

Ryan laughed. "I think I can handle him."

"You'd be the first."

"And probably the last, no? A Hyde having gone without any medication for as long as he did is really unpredictable. He could keel over any minute. Staying in the Abnormal form for too long and then switching takes a big toll on the system. The heart seems to be the weak point. We're not exactly sure why, but it's probably something to do with the strange beat." Four beats and then a pause—hers hadn't done it since she had woken up at The Clinic.

"It's terrible," he continued. "They bleed out of everywhere—eyes, ears, mouth, a couple other places that I don't want to mention. Believe me, it's not something you want to see around dinner time." His brow tightened with a feigned look of concern. "Turner hasn't been bleeding out of anywhere, has he? Don't worry, Eden. I'm sure he'll be the exception."

She didn't react or let her emotions show on her face or body. She wouldn't be beaten by a guy tied to a chair.

"But that's boring," he said. "How about I tell you about your father instead? Wouldn't that be more fun? I'm not sure he would approve of the new you, though. But I guess that doesn't matter now anyway. How many pieces did Turner leave him in again?"

She blamed her weakness on the physical exertion and being overwhelmed, anything other than that he knew exactly how to hurt her. Make her want to run away like a little girl into the arms of someone who'd never been there.

Don't let him win. Her boys were right—she had to deal

with it. Someone like Ryan had made her father into a beast, a Hyde who could never come back. Just like he would do to Mitch given the chance. She wouldn't let him *have* that chance.

I don't have to feel. I just have to do.

"Mitch didn't kill my father. You did. What I saw was only his body, a husk he used to live in."

"That husk was very useful. Very, *very* use—"

Oh shit, she might have just broken his jaw. He wouldn't be able to talk with a broken jaw. Or if he was unconscious—which he *was*, his head sagging to one side, mouth slack, eyes closed.

Not helpful, Eden. Not at all helpful. At least he was breathing. She waited. Then nudged his shoulder. Then waited.

"Shit." She started to pace the length of the truck, glancing at him every time she switched directions. "Shit."

"That hurt," he mumbled, slowly opening his eyes.

"Oh man, I would be so sorry about that if you answered my fucking questions."

He shrugged. "Tell me how you combined."

She'd already told him and he hadn't believed her. And it didn't matter anyway. She wasn't tied up—he was. Therefore *he* got to provide the answers. "You like to be in control, right, Ryan? Well, guess what. You're in total control of when the pain stops."

"Fine, I'll tell you what to do for Turner." He took a deep breath. When he spoke it was so quiet she had to get closer just to hear what he was saying. "Give him the J-0026 to wake him up and the RSL-7 to stop his seizure. And every time he transforms he'll get weaker. And weaker. And weaker. And then he'll be gone. Bye-bye, Turner. There's no way to stop it, darlin'. Not that I know of. You're the only one who's ever done it."

"You lying piece of shit." Her foot met his stomach, knocking the chair over. "Tell me how to fix it!"

"There *is* no way to fix it," he groaned.

"Your blood is making my hands sticky. It's disgusting." She pulled his shirt out of his pants and wiped her hands off with it, ignoring his glossy glare. It meant nothing to her. *He* meant nothing to her. "Hopefully, you'll run out of it pretty soon."

After righting the chair to make sure his last tumble hadn't loosened the bindings, she jumped down, flipped the lock, and went to find something that wasn't covered in blood to towel off on.

She didn't realize she was shaking until she was in the cab. It was hot out and she was sweating, but there were goose bumps on her arms. And she didn't know why or how long it had been going on.

After she cleaned up, she would—*You'll what?* Keep beating him. It hadn't gotten her anywhere, so there was no good reason to keep doing it.

But there were a lot of bad reasons.

CHAPTER XXX

Justin might not be able to speak very well, but at least he was honest. All Mitch found at the warehouse was him—no truck, no Eden. After calling her number a few times and then calling everyone else a lot of truly filthy names, Mitch decided to try patience. He'd wait, breathe, and watch the door for approximately five minutes before he went ape-shit crazy. Why not? He sure as hell didn't have anything better to do.

Why did she leave the warehouse? Probably not to hit the drive-thru. Sure, he was glad she was in the offensive lineup now, but he'd only be comfortable once she was in his sightline.

Five minutes, asshole. You can wait a whole five minutes. Then he would do a street-by-street sweep of the area. That would help him calm down. Because even if he didn't find her, he was sure to find someone who needed a good beating.

Justin sat on the ground a few feet away, staring until Mitch turned towards him.

"I know I'm pretty," Mitch said, "but stop gawking at me. It's making me feel like an object."

"Sorry," the kid mumbled, pulling his knees up to his chest.

I hate kids. He didn't know what to say to them. And they

made him feel old. "Not only am I nice to look at, but I can also read minds. Like right now you're thinking, 'Holy, shit. Is that what I'm going to be like fifteen years and fifty pounds from now?' And the answer is"—he drum-rolled his hands on the metal door—"I fucking hope not."

No reaction. "Look, I don't know shit about kids because I never was one, but I know men. And I don't mean biblically." Why was he letting two underage eyes get to him like this? "I made a lot of money by figuring them out. And from what I know about Fields, he'll keep you from ending up like me. And even though Eden seems to like you a lot, you don't wanna piss that woman off by stepping out of line."

He shoved off the wall and started pacing. "Thing is, when it comes down to it, they can't do shit. You wanna be a man? A good one? Then be one. No one can teach you how or do it for you. So either do it or don't do it." He took a breath. "And that's all the peppy talking I have in me, so you can stop staring now."

He didn't.

"Okay." Mitch should be better at shit like this. His mouth had gotten him in and out of much worse situations that this one. "You're still thinking. But now it's more of a 'What the hell does he know?' And the answer is: Nothing. I know nothing."

"It wasn't that," the kid said. "I was wondering if my Hyde will be like yours."

Mitch stopped. More than anything, he wanted to say, 'If he is, you're screwed,' and then walk away. But he'd told himself he'd wait, and there were still two minutes to go.

"Is yours going to be like mine? Huh. Not unless you're as stupid as I am. Are you?"

Justin shrugged.

"It would be a tough thing to match. Plus, not even Eden would be able to handle more than one charity case at a time. So I think you're in the clear. Just take your medicine like a good boy until somebody figures out an alternative."

Wouldn't that be nice? "*Please*, kid. Say something. Anything. Just talk."

A verbal answer would stop the useless lecture coming out of Mitch's mouth. And would cover the silence and all the shit going through his mind.

"What did you do to Alex?" Justin asked.

Oh shit. The kid wanted to ask her a question. Mitch had thrown everything out of the window as soon as he heard Eden was back, and before he heard she left again. But he'd made an almost-promise and he'd blown it.

"I forgot," Mitch said. "But as soon as we're done with this clusterfuck, I'll take you to her. Her mouth's taped shut, so you'll have the added fun of giving her a lip wax when you rip it off. And if for some reason this takes longer than I pray it does, I'll find her again, probably through her sister. Kindergarten teachers are great at the hide-and-seek thing, but the hide-from-a-raving-madman thing is a far more advanced skill."

"Have you ever done something really, really bad while you were Hyde? Like, so bad you can't..." Another unfinished sentence.

"I thought I did." Mitch shifted uncomfortably. "For a long time I thought I hurt someone really...She..." *Oh fuck, it's contagious. Finish the damn sentence.* "I thought I hurt someone I loved very, very much."

"Was it Eden?"

"I've taken a lot of wrong turns in that neighborhood, but ...it was my sister." He still missed her. Some wounds are so deep, they'll never heal. "But then I found out that *they* had done it. Well, someone who was working two jobs—one for me and one for them. I trusted her, and I'm old and jaded enough to know better."

"What happened to her?"

"Jolie? She died. Violently." On a night he'd love to forget. "Can't say I was sad to see her go. In fact, it couldn't have happen to a nicer person." He grimaced, remembering who he was talking to and that, yes, he was speaking out loud. "But I probably shouldn't have said that...to you...now...here..." This was one of those bad situations his mouth got him into. "So, yeah, sorry 'bout that."

"No problem."

"Great. But, if it's okay with you, I'm going to shut up now." Had it been five minutes? *Please,* let the five minutes be up. He looked at his phone to check the time just in time for it to start ringing. Serendipity or more bad news?

Eden's face came up on the caller ID. He really loved that picture—because he remembered the moment he took it.

It better be her and not the asshole again, or Mitch was going to reach through the phone line and rip the bastard's brain out through his ear.

"Mitch?"

Biiiig sigh of relief. "Where are you, babe?"

"I'm..." She sounded so afraid, so tired.

"Are you okay? What's going on?"

"I'm fine. But I feel a little...weird."

"Okay." Weird was better than 'suicidal' or 'bloodthirsty' or any number of other words or phrases she could've used. "What do you mean?"

"I'm not sure. I'm...I feel like...I think I'm losing control."

Shit. 'Losing control' was one he'd hoped she wouldn't use. *One thing at a time.* Now that he knew where her head was, he had to figure out where her *body* was. "Where are you?"

"Is Justin alright? Did you check on him?"

"He's here with me. But you're not, and I'd really like that to change. So how do we make that happen?"

"Mitch?" There was a fear in her voice that he didn't understand.

"I'm here, babe. Talk to me."

"I'm...I'm enjoying it. It's...exciting, and I think part of me...wants him."

When she didn't explain, his mind started filling in the blanks—none of them good. "You remember what I told you, Eden? I'm standing here, still breathing." Gasping for air, more like. "Which means that no one touches you but me, and you don't touch anyone but me. You understand?" It wasn't about being territorial. It was because he had no idea what was going on with her, what she was doing, or who she *was* right now.

"I'm not going to, but I want to. Do you know what I mean?" Her laugh was arsenic bitter. "How could you? *I* don't even know what I mean. Do you think Chastity's back? That it's her fault?" There was hope in her voice, a need to put the blame onto someone else's shoulders.

"Maybe. We'll figure it out, but you need to tell me—"

"I thought it was just you she wanted, but maybe I was wrong. Maybe it's the power, and that's why she wants him so badly."

Okay, now he was jealous. But he couldn't keep going down this road on the phone. While that asshole was close to her and he wasn't. "Where are you?"

"In a truck yard."

"What truck yard? Why didn't you just stay here?"

"I couldn't—not with Justin there. Not with what I have to do."

"What's that, Eden?" He kept the suspicion out of his voice, but he was pretty sure the terror had gotten through.

She'd not only planned this out, she'd implemented it without telling anyone else. People don't hide good news or good deeds. People only hide the bad shit.

"I gave Justin some money, but I'll pay you back. You know, if I ever have a chance to go job hunting." Her laugh was stiff, uncomfortable.

"This isn't about money. You can have all of it if you want. But I'd rather you blow it on jewelry and clothes."

"I needed somewhere private to take him," she whispered.

He wished she meant Hyde, but he knew better. "You still

have the bastard, don't you? Whittley's still alive?" *This is bad.* She was dangerously close to the point of no return, skirting the edge on rollerblades.

"Is that his last name? I wasn't sure he was telling the truth." None of the usual fire was left in her voice. Now she sounded scared, like a little girl. Like she'd just pulled the monster out from under her bed, tied him up, and was now trying to decide how to get rid of him permanently.

"Is he still alive?"

"Yeah."

Just enough time for a quick sigh of relief before going right back to worrying. "Eden, tell me where you are. Then you stay outside of the truck and take deep, calming breaths until I get there. You hear me? Do nothing else."

Silence.

"*Please*, babe. Please don't do anything you'll regret."

"There's *nothing* I could do to him that I would regret. Nothing."

Now Mitch was actually hoping she'd fuck the guy. If she was going to do anything, *please* let it be a meaningless fuck. Mitch could deal with that—eventually—and she would get over it. But the other thing she was considering would change her forever. No do-overs. There was no climbing back to your feet after that one.

"I want you to wait," he said. "Wait for me to get there. Don't...don't do it alone."

"I know you want to be there for me, that you're willing. But you're not able. Not yet. Not until Ryan tells me how to help you. I'm positive he knows, Mitch. *Positive.* And he'll tell me. Eventually, and with enough incentive, he'll tell me. And then I'll make sure he can't hurt anyone else."

Fuuuuck. Stall, asshole. Stall until you can get there. "Then let me be there while you do it. I want to see. I want to help or just..."

Mitch would kill for her. He would. But even though Whittley deserved it, Mitch didn't want to. Murder, the cold kind, let the worst part of their Abnormal sides seep into their humanity. And once it started, once that fissure was created, it only got bigger and harder to control. He had felt it happen when he'd almost killed Landon.

For the most part, Eden had taken on Chastity's strengths, not her weaknesses. But that could change if she killed Whittley. Shit, everything could change if she killed Whittley.

"Let me be there for you, Eden. Please. I...I want to see that bastard in some pain."

Her pause was long, with only a sigh traveling the distance between them. "Okay. But hurry." He was moving before she started giving him directions.

When you see someone dangling one foot of the precipice, you do a lot of praying, babbling, and hoping. But those things don't do shit to solve the problem or to get through to someone who's already decided to leap. The only useful thing to do is haul their ass backward *fast*, before they even feel your hand.

And if you have to lie to get close enough, then you lie. You deceive, you manipulate. Even if you promised yourself you never would. Even if it destroys all the trust you'd spent a lifetime never thinking you'd find.

So Mitch kept her on the phone, saying things that made him sick and pretending he wasn't afraid for her.

Until she hung up.

"Eden!" He called her name over and over. Then he called her back. Over and over. But she didn't answer.

When he turned the key in the ignition, the POS wouldn't start. With an absurd amount of cursing, he slammed his fist onto the dash. "Motherfucking piece of shit!"

His tantrum had no effect on the engine, and he didn't have time to mess around under the hood. So as soon as his feet hit the earth, he started running. Flat out, with one hand in the pocket that held his lifeline—the syringe that stood between him and death. The drug that would send him back into hell. He held onto it. Because if he lost it, his limited amount of options would drop back down to zero.

CHAPTER XXXI

Mitch ran like a gale-force wind, hoping he'd find the landmarks she had mentioned. He did. Even when she was breaking apart, she gave great directions.

When he got to the truck yard, he slowed down and shook out his arms and legs. He wasn't tired, but between his less-than-ideal emotional state and the run, his adrenaline was in the red zone.

Eden stood in between a tractor and their truck. And her hair was blond. And short. But that wasn't why she looked different.

He wanted to haul ass over to her, toss her over his shoulder and carry her away from all of this, maybe even throw a spank or two in there. But he knew her too well to try anything like that—she was a pipe bomb right now.

Approach with caution. Figure out the damage before you try to fix it.

"Is Whittley in there?"

She nodded.

He moved past her and flipped the lock on the door, opening it and seeing nothing but darkness. "You still breathing?"

"Barely."

'Barely' was good enough. Mitch lowered the door and locked it before saying anything to her. He took a deep breath, knowing that without it, whatever he said would come out angry and desperate. Because he was *feeling* angry and desperate.

His normally miniscule patience was gone, and his frustration was equal to his confusion. What should he do with her? For her? After checking the lock again, he grabbed her hand and pulled her away. To get something out of Whittley, they needed to appear as a united front, so he shouldn't hear what Mitch was about to say.

He led her across the truck yard and then let her go, leaning against the side of a busted-up and rusty car. She leaned back against another, a ravine of only a few feet between them that he wasn't sure he could jump.

Start slow. Tread carefully. "What are you doing here, babe?"

"I'm trying to find a way out of this."

"By making a mistake you won't be able to fix?"

Her anger might trump his. The look in her eyes was of determination, not fear or uncertainty. "He's the one who made the mistakes, Mitch. And he's the one who should pay for them."

He hammered his fist against the hood of the car, her mood feeding his. "Can you even hear yourself? You're giving in to it. But you're better than that. *Stronger* than that. This isn't you. This is *them* getting inside your head and making you react like they would. Don't forget who you are." He paused. "Or the prize isn't worth fighting for."

"The prize is us having a life together," she yelled.

"If it changes who we are, what do we win? Don't give in or we'll lose everything."

"*You* gave in. You let Hyde take over. You let him take you away from me."

"Don't you think I would've done it differently if I'd had

a choice?" He lowered his voice, wanting to reach out to her, touch her, but knowing she would smack his hand away if he tried. "I chose you. And I did what I did to save you. So be the person I fought to save."

"She doesn't exist anymore."

"Of course she does. I can see her. I can feel her. Use some of that incredible strength you have to pull her out, wake her up. For me. Because cosmically speaking, you owe me one." Even his joke couldn't pull her out of whatever state of mind she was in.

"You owe *me* one," she spat. "You owe me *everything* because you gave up. And then you went into wherever you were and left me to deal with it. I had to deal with him while I was mourning you." She shuddered with anger. "So don't tell me what to do. And don't tell me who I am. Because you don't know who I am anymore."

"You've never been more wrong, babe."

She moved so quickly, he didn't have time to duck. Her fist connected with his jaw, and he fell back onto the car. Before he could straighten up, she was on him, trying to hurt him. Like he'd hurt *her*. But he hadn't had a choice.

"Stop!" In shock and without thought, he pushed her off harder than he should have.

She stumbled, throwing a hand out to catch herself. The next time she came at him, he was more prepared. When her fist shot out, he caught her wrist and twisted, hoping she would stop fighting before he broke it. She screamed as she flipped around, kicking out and barely missing him. He shoved her up against the car, caging her body with his. Trapping her.

"Do you want to kill me, too?" he said breathlessly. "Do you?" He held both of her hands onto the car's roof so she wouldn't move.

She squirmed but couldn't get out from under his weight. She accomplished something, though—the wiggling rubbed her ass against his cock. A poorly timed reaction and not a useful one. When her back arched, her hips pressed into his, and her exhalation held a quiet moan, he knew she felt him harden.

For a few more seconds, she fought him. And then she stopped, her breath broken. He didn't want her to break. That's why he was here and why he always wanted to be here—so he could make sure that she was whole. And, so far, he was doing a piss-poor job of it.

"Why did you do it?" she asked quietly. She sounded so hurt, he wanted to take back everything he'd ever said, done, or thought. "Why did you give up?"

He accepted her anger and wished that he'd forced her to talk about it earlier, before things got this far. But this was one of those 'better late than never' situations—if he didn't reel her back now, it would never happen. This was Eden. Hidden under pure rage and fear and the need for balance—to have someone else feel the pain she felt.

"I did it because I wanted you to be free," he said quietly. "Because I didn't care what happened to me as long as you were okay." Which was obviously a mistake because she was far from okay. "If I had known—Shit, I don't know what I would've done because there *was* no other way."

She shoved both of them backward and flipped around to face him. Before she could throw another punch, he pushed her into the car, lifting her off her feet. They were both gasping for air. Both so much in need of solace.

"This isn't you, babe."

She couldn't keep going down this road. Because it dead ended with a brick wall. "Don't tell me how to live my life," she said through her teeth. "You lost that privilege a while ago. You have no right to—"

"I have a right to what's mine. And as long as I'm still breathing, *you* are mine."

She inhaled sharply, her eyes on fire. "Then take me."

So he did.

Right there, thirty feet away from their enemy, up against

an abandoned car, he took. He knew the danger of letting her go, even for the few seconds she needed to undo his pants and free his cock. But there was no stopping this. Whatever she needed, however she needed him, wasn't nearly as much as he needed her.

He lifted her skirt and yanked on her panties. When he heard the fabric tear, he froze. But only for a second. He grabbed the other side and ripped them the rest of the way off. Then he put his hands under her ass, lifted her up, and sank all the way into her. She gasped, wrapping her arms and legs around him.

It wasn't slow. It wasn't gentle. It wasn't even loving. It was raw, fast, and rough—their mutual need driving each stroke, each inhalation, each moan. It had never been like this before. When they made love, it was about creating a deeper connection, savoring the moment and each other, even when it started in frustration or anger.

But not now. Right now, they were fucking. Because if they didn't, they would explode in a far more violent way. So he didn't think, and he wasn't gentle. He took. She was his, as he was hers. More than life and beyond death. They belonged to each other.

Her whimpers and gasps were the most incredible music he'd ever heard, keeping rhythm with the movement of his hips as he pounded into her. He didn't release her mouth, not for one second, needing to feel the vibrations of her moans ricochet through him.

It was so intense, it bordered on pain, and it only got better the harder and faster he thrusted. She felt *so* fucking good. He wouldn't have stopped if the sky fell down on them.

Only with her could something feel this amazing. But there was something…Something in the back of his mind that he just couldn't grasp.

When he felt her body clamp down on his cock, her abs tighten, her breath stop, he knew he was done for.

He pulled back to see her face as she came. "You will

always be mine." Then he was toppled by an orgasm unlike any other. It didn't stop, didn't relent, didn't let go, pulsing out of him and into her, connecting them even more. Nothing could ever come between them.

He leaned his forehead against hers and tried to start breathing again. She was limp in his arms, as if all of that fire had been extinguished by a good old-fashioned orgasm.

"Are you okay?"

Her arms came back to life and she hugged him, clutching him desperately. "I needed you and you left me."

"I didn't know what else to do. I just wanted you to be safe. That's all I've ever wanted, babe. To know you're safe."

"No one is safe. It's not safe to be around me."

"We'll figure it out. We'll figure something out." He started talking, letting out all the things he'd been afraid to say aloud—the ones that made him sound like a complete wuss. Things only ever heard in chick flicks, because no man alive would *ever* admit to feeling that way.

Really, it was pretty fucking embarrassing.

After the tension started to leave her body, he pushed off the car and tried to set her down. She only tightened her grip around his shoulders and his hips. So he stood still and held her while she cried, knowing it was the best thing—the only thing—he could do for her right now.

He had no idea how long they stayed that way. How long he watched her shoulders hiccup and heard her muffled weeping. How many times he kissed her hair, rocked her, told her how much he loved her.

He didn't want to let go of her—ever—but there was no stopping the clock. And there was still so much more to do before he had to leave her again.

And then it hit him. Like a wrecking ball. The thought he hadn't been able to grasp before. That was just out of reach of a brain emptied of blood and sense.

You'reamotherfuckinggoddamnidiot! He wasn't sure if he'd said it aloud or if she was reacting to the tension that had just contracted every single muscle in his body, but she sobbed quietly against his chest.

"I'm so sorry, Mitch."

"No," he said, lifting her chin and wiping a tear away with his thumb. Then another. And another. "No, babe, you didn't do anything wrong." Well, yeah, she did a bucket load of wrong but, at this particular moment in time, he was the one who should be sorry.

He took a breath, looking into moist, beautiful silver-blue eyes that held nothing but love for a guy who didn't deserve it. Now more than ever. Not after everything she'd gone through. Not after what he'd just done.

"I came inside of you." In his entire life he'd *never* forgotten to use protection. Never got so far into the moment that he dared forget. Because the last thing the world needed was a mini him, with all the baggage and Abnormalness he would pass on. And as beautiful as a child they might have would be, the kid would be doubly cursed.

"Oh," was all she said.

Oh? He may have just knocked her up leaning against a rusted-out car and all she said was 'oh'? In an unknown amount of time he might die and leave her pregnant with a demon child and all she said was 'oh'?

"Did you hear me?" he asked. "I came inside of you. Without a condom."

"I was here too."

"I came inside of you," he repeated, to make her understand the ramifications without having to actually put it into words. Because, let's face it, words were not his strong suit—proven by the last thirty years he'd been speaking.

If he didn't already have enough to deal with, and there wasn't a good chance he'd be dead soon, this would've put him into a straitjacket for a few weeks until the test came back. Then he'd do the padded-room thing for three trimesters. Then, if it was a boy, he'd have fifteen years to prepare himself for the kid's Hyde to show up. And if it was a girl, he'd have the same amount of time to prepare himself for any teenage boy who came within twenty yards of her to show up. *And her Jekyll, I guess.*

But instead, being the bang-up asshole that he was, he'd probably be dead and Eden would get to have all the really-not-fun by herself.

"I heard you the first time," she said. "But I got an IUD as soon as we left The Clinic."

"Oh."

She didn't need to tell him why—he already knew. The Clinic wanted her to reproduce. So even if he never came back, she protected herself from that.

It made him want to bleed them out slowly and let them feel every chance of life drip out of them. But he wouldn't. Probably.

"And my cycle has been a bit off since all of this started," she said. "Anyway, I'm not sure what we can do about it now. I guess I could jump around and try to shake your little guys out of me, but I don't think that works very well."

Shit, why hadn't he thought of that? "Maybe you should try, just in case."

"Mitch, I'm not jumping around."

"Right, I'm not thinking clearly yet." He kissed her nose. "I didn't know about the IUD, so I should've protected you. It was my screw-up...again. I'm sorry."

"Stop saying that unless you're referring to all the other shit you've done."

"It was. I am. It's all shit. You're right. And I...I don't know what else to say."

"Promise me you won't let it happen again. And then make sure it doesn't happen."

Not only was that a good idea, but it would keep him from obsessively looking at her belly, expecting it to balloon up and a mini Hyde rip out of it a la *Aliens*. "I promise." *I shouldn't, but...* "I promise."

After another minute or so, he whispered, "Babe, I'm

going to set you down now."

She lifted her head off his shoulder and unwrapped her legs from around his hips. He put her down slowly, giving her time to practice being on her feet again. He kept his hands on her waist as she took a very small step backward and then wiped her face.

She was a mess. A sickeningly beautiful mess that he couldn't take his eyes off of. So fucking gorgeous, despite everything that was going on. It hurt to see her with anything other than a smile or a look of pleasure. But he couldn't control the way she felt and couldn't control what she was going through. All he could do was help her stand until she was ready to do it on her own.

"Better?" he asked, pulling off his t-shirt and using it to wipe away her tears.

"Mostly."

"'Mostly' is a good place to start." He kissed her softly. A promise—not of sex, but of everything good he had in him to give. It was all hers. "I'm going to talk to him. Alone. Are you okay with that, or do we need to have another fight?"

"I'm okay. You go play nice cop."

"Think he'll believe I'm the nice one?"

She shrugged. "He doesn't know you very well." A small smile broke through like the first flower of spring, but far prettier than any flower he'd ever seen.

"I was thinking of starting out with a joke. To lighten things up."

"I think it's a bit late for bad jokes."

"What do you mean 'bad'?"

She laughed. "Nothing."

"Thought so." He gave them both one more minute to enjoy her smile. Then it was time to get back to work. "While I'm in there, I can't have you wandering away. I can't even *wonder* if you're wandering away. Because then I might think you're getting into more trouble or someone grabbed you or a bunch of other awful things. So you're going to drive us back to the warehouse while I'm in the back talking to him." As long as they kept moving forward, he'd know her focus was on the road and not on anything more destructive.

"What if you…"

"Seize? Huh. Yeah." That was definitely something to consider. *Four to twenty-four.* "It hasn't even been four hours. Plus, I felt weird a little while before it happened last time." That didn't seem to put her mind at ease.

"Thirty-eight seconds." She spoke with certainty, as if that number had worn a place in the front of her mind.

"Thirty-eight seconds," he repeated. "So if I feel it again, I shove the needle into my ass and keep my thumb on the plunger. Then, when it starts, I either fall on it or my hand contracts and pushes the shit in."

She didn't look convinced.

"I'll pound on the wall as hard as I can. That's your sign to pull over—*cautiously*—and come to the back. Okay? Thirty-eight seconds should be enough time." *Probably.* He slipped his shirt back on. "It needs to happen like this, babe. Because while 'mostly' is a big step, it isn't big enough. Not yet. You need some more time to cool down."

She nodded.

He smiled and gave her a peck on the lips. "Great. Let's go see if the bastard missed us."

CHAPTER XXXII

The second Mitch hopped into the truck, he felt heavier, more drained, and more irritable. Between waking up from hell fairly recently and the orgasm Eden had just given him, he was tapped. He needed more practice recovering from the latter. Lots and lots of practice.

He took a couple deep breaths, circling the asshole strapped to the chair to get a good look at him. Mitch didn't know why he'd been worried. There was nothing to be jealous about. Frankly, he had no idea what Eden saw in the bastard. Sure, his suit was expensive, but no dry cleaner on earth would ever get those bloodstains out. Attractive? Possibly. Good bone structure, except for his nose. His nose was *huge*. Could've been because of the swelling, though.

She'd definitely done some damage. But at least the guy was breathing. Mitch shook off all thoughts of her. It was time to focus, negotiate, and manipulate. Mano a mano. Asshole to asshole.

"How was it?" Whittley asked calmly.

"How was what?"

"You *reek* of sex."

Yeah, that was one of the best parts—a little reminder. "It

was fantastic, thanks for asking. Plan on doing it again as soon as we finish talking."

"It's making me nauseous."

"I felt the same way as soon as I saw *you*." Mitch pulled the chain to close the door almost all the way. It was dark, but he could see what he needed to. And he knew Whittley could as well...or better.

When the truck started moving, Mitch braced himself with both hands. Since Whittley was tied to the chair and the chair was tottering back and forth with every bump, Mitch considered helping him out. By the time he made a decision about it, Whittley was already on his side on the floor. Which was fine because Mitch's decision was not to help.

"*Ooh.* That looked like it hurt."

"What do you want?" Whittley snapped.

"Just checking in." He moved so that he could see the bastard's face, tilting his head so they were at the same angle. "Making sure she hasn't killed you yet."

"She won't kill me."

"You sound awfully confident for a guy chained to a chair."

"You would know."

"Yeah. Thanks to you and the rest of the gang, I know all about it."

"She's not going to kill me because I have all the answers."

Mitch laughed. "Except how to get out of that chair."

"I have all the answers she wants."

"Maybe. Maybe not."

Whittley chuckled. "You sound awfully confident for a guy who has no idea what he really is. All of these years and you still can't control him. Not even a little bit. Your thinking is flawed, Turner—your understanding of what you are...and what *he* is."

Maybe Whittley had hit his head harder than Mitch had thought, because his tone was seriously arrogant, as if he was sharing the secrets of the universe. As if Mitch should be honored to hear his bullshit.

So maybe it wasn't bullshit.

So Mitch would let him talk.

"Your Hyde has power that you should be embracing, not fearing. *Embracing.* Accepting. You think you know him, but you don't. You think he's a part of you but is apart *from* you. He's not. You *are* him. And he is you. Good and evil don't exist without the other. Until you understand that, your life will be just another science experiment."

Mitch took a moment to tuck all of that away so he could think about it later—figure out what was just arrogance and what might be based in truth.

But before he could deal with the existential shit, he needed to deal with the lying-on-the-floor-in-front-of-him shit. "I'm sure you're right, Whittley, but riddles give me a headache. So let's bare bones it, shall we?" He moved closer. "The woman driving this bus is fine. She's integrated or whatever word you guys use, so she can walk away whenever she feels like it. Leaving behind however many bodies she wants to."

"But she doesn't want to leave your body behind, as screwed up as it is. You standing here breathing is all the leverage I need. How long until the J-0026 wears off, Turner? An hour? Two? Are you sure you want to spend that time with me? Maybe you should spend it convincing your girlfriend to be smart."

"Maybe. Maybe I should do a bunch of other things. Like laundry or grocery shopping or taking a tour of the city on a double-decker bus. And I'd kill someone for a shower. But instead of doing any of those enjoyable things, I'm here with you." He reached into his pocket and took out the syringe. "And I have this."

Whittley laughed. "In case you haven't noticed, I'm on the floor and it's a little dark in here. So whatever you pulled out of your pocket is still a mystery to me."

"But you know I pulled something out of my pocket."

Whittley blew out a loud breath of hot air. "You didn't have anything in your hands when you came in—it was a natural assumption."

"Natural for whom?" After a moment with no reply, Mitch leaned down and held the syringe two inches away from Whittley's face. "Can you see it now?"

"So you seize, give yourself over to him, and he kills me before I tell you anything. That's a great plan. Congratulations."

"Thanks. The party's next week. Feel free to drop by if you're still alive." He rolled the syringe between his fingers. "But the thing is…it isn't for me."

Whittley swallowed—a hard, dry, audible swallow. "What do you mean?" There was fear in his voice. Not a lot, but it was there. And it was encouraging as hell.

"It brings a Hyde out, right? *Any* Hyde." He sensed the panic bloom in Whittley. "*Your* Hyde."

If it wasn't so dark, Mitch knew he'd see a faceful of 'oh fuck.' Damn, he'd really like to have an 8 × 10 of that. Signed, maybe. In blood.

"How did you know?" he asked slowly.

"What good is it to experiment on people if it holds no direct benefit to you? I'm surprised you can't feel the push-pull thing between us. My Hyde, of course, is more sensitive to it than I am. I would've guessed you were just an asshole who gave off bad vibes, but he and I are closer nowadays. Eden felt it too." But she'd taken it as some kind of twisted sexual chemistry. "I might ask your Hyde why he doesn't like you enough to share this kind of info."

"He wouldn't give you any more information than I will."

"That's a theory, sure. Another theory, based on everything I know about *my* Hyde, is that he would do exactly the opposite of what you want him to. The bastards are really contrary, aren't they?"

"You're bluffing."

"I don't bluff. It's too fucking tiresome. And frankly, I'd

love to meet your other half. Your better half. How long has it been since he's come out to play, Ry?"

Whittley turned his head away, but said nothing.

"That's not really fair, is it? So, we have two options. Option one: You tell me what I want to know and in a few more hours, I shove the needle into my own arm. But you might have to share your chains with him. Option two: I shoot you up *now* and watch you transform. Hurts like a bitch to do it awake, but it'll be worth it. Well, he and I will think so."

"You can't just pop on over to the pharmacy and get that stuff." It wasn't the lack of light that made Whittley squint, it was fury. The calm starting to crack. "How much do you have left? My guess is not much. Maybe even just what's in that syringe. But even if you do have more, you'd be smart to hold onto it. Because when you seize without it, you die."

"Yep." That one word held a thousand others—that Mitch was fine with whatever happened to him, that he just didn't care anymore, that he would happily give up everything he'd regained for truth, justice, and the American way.

Who the fuck was he kidding? He'd do it for *her*.

"What do you want, Turner?"

"You stop hunting us. You let her and the others go with as much serum as they can carry and recipes of how to make more."

"That's it?"

"Fuck no. You *start* by answering every question I have about your organization." And if it lined up with what Alex told him, he'd finally have a little something to believe in.

"I'll let her and the others walk, but I'm not in the mood to chat."

"You answer my questions and I may be able to convince my girlfriend not to kill you."

"I thought you didn't bluff."

"No bluff. What you know is the only thing that's kept you alive this long. If you're not going to share, then we gain nothing by keeping you alive. But the bonus of you being in the ground is that she'll have one less obstacle to get through. One less force pushing back. And with me gone, she'll have no reason to stick around. So it's actually a win-win." He shook his head. "Nah, I take that back. It's singular. One win. For her. Because no matter what, it's a lose-lose for us, my friend."

"I'm not your friend."

"Truer words were never spoken...by you. So what'll it be?"

Whittley didn't move, not even to blink. Mitch let him stare. He let those wicked plans that were undoubtedly trying to find root in Whittley's mind swirl for a bit. Because they wouldn't find anything to hold onto. Because there was no other way out. For either of them.

If it was the last thing he did, Mitch would get some goddamn answers. This shit had gone on way too long. It was like a piece of coal squeezed so hard and so long that if Mitch didn't end up with a diamond in his hand pretty soon, he would be bulk shopping for body bags.

"I'm not sure how much you know about me," Mitch said, "or how organized Jolie was with her filing. But the thing is, I am insanely impatient. Sometimes it gets so bad I eat the pizza when it's still frozen. It's a terrible thing, a burden I have to deal with. And unfortunately, right now you do too. So what'll it be?"

Nothing but silence.

"That's too bad. I was actually starting to like you." He laughed. "I'm just kidding." He whistled for effect as he went to the door to let a little more light in, but not a big enough space for the asshole and his chair to fall through. Then he dragged the chair closer to the chains attached through the floor, flipped Whittley from his side to his back, and put the big-boy cuffs around his wrists.

The guy still looked confident, still thought he could call a bluff that didn't exist. When Mitch closed the cuffs, he did it especially hard. So Whittley could feel the vibration, hear the horrific sound of metal on metal, of freedom and hope disappearing. He flinched, his head smacking the floor under him, his breath getting faster.

Making sure the syringe was in a ray of sunshine, Mitch popped off the needle cover as if he were opening a bottle of beer. Whittley swallowed audibly, his face contorting in fear. *Ugly.* Since his arms were already bound, that puppy slipped in without any trouble at all.

"Stop! Okay, okay," Whittley said. "Take it out. Take it out! *Please.*" The last word seemed painful to even utter, as if it were tied to a lung or something, and releasing it meant losing the organ along with it.

As much as Mitch would enjoy hearing the guy beg and beg and beg, he wanted to know *why.* Yeah, transforming sucked and was a real buzz kill, but something more was going on.

"You went from stupidly cocky to oddly terrified. What gives? Are you afraid of needles?"

"I can't... I can't turn into him."

"Come on, he can't *possibly* be more of an asshole than you are."

"It's different for me, more dangerous. The last time I transformed, it almost—I can't."

Until now, Mitch had thought the guy was on the same meds Jolie had been dosing him with. But that was a stupid assumption—Whittley wouldn't waste the good shit on someone like Mitch. The suspicion traveled down Mitch's spine and spread into every cell of his body.

"How long has it been, Ry?"

It took a while, but eventually he answered. "Years."

Well now, that was as unexpected as it was promising. But happy reactions should be kept under wraps when negotiating with assholes. "What's your secret? How do you stay looking so fresh and, you know, unbeastly?"

Whittley didn't say anything, but he looked nervous as fuck. No matter how much Eden beat him, he'd stayed calm because he knew he'd heal. But now the guy was scared to death. And death was a tough thing to come back from.

Mitch shrugged. "No problem. I'll ask *him*." He shoved the needle a bit deeper, a reminder of where they were in the negotiations and that Whittley was losing. Badly.

"Stop! Please. I wasn't going to kill you."

"Well, duh. Of course you weren't—you'd have gotten your suit messed up. That's what less important people are for."

"Please. Take it out." Every word was stiff, awkward, scared shitless—something Mitch really wanted Eden to hear. It was proof that things might be turning around for them soon. But he wasn't going to start counting chickens yet.

"Only one way to make it come out," Mitch said. "Your call." He waited for…nothing. "You can stay in here for another day and a half if you want to, but—"

"How long have I been here?" he asked so quickly his words blended together. "How long was that bitch beating me?"

Mitch slapped his own legs and hung onto his jeans to immobilize his hands. If he couldn't handle a little name calling, he'd lose the ground he had. He was too close to the inside of this asshole's head to have a bad reaction blow it apart. He needed to wait a while before that could happen.

"Jesus, Ry, when you say things like that, it makes me think you don't want to be here anymore."

"How long?"

Would anything be lost by telling the truth? Mitch didn't think so. When you're fucking with someone, you stick to the truth as much as possible. That way there are fewer opportunities for your opponent to figure out you're lying, and the more likely he'll be to trust all the things you're actually lying about.

"It's been about three hours since you called me. What were you telling me before Eden took you down? Something about getting her into bed in five minutes, right? Boy, were you off on that one. You got both the timing and the activity completely wrong."

"That's not...I can't." Whittley's self-destruct button had just been pressed, but Mitch had no idea how he'd done it. "I need to—" His exhalation shook his entire body, hopefully a sign that he was about to give up. "The stuff I take, it's...it's not a cure." His fear was encompassing—a control freak dealing with something uncontrollable. At least not here.

"Okay." Mitch knew how badly transforming sucked, how sickening it felt to know it was coming but there was absolutely nothing you could do about it. He waited for more. "This is getting old, so if that's all you got..."

"It's the same thing that Eden's handler was giving her—J-0026. But I inject it and the dose is higher because Hydes work a little differently. Injected every four days, just before he's due. My Hyde. Just before my Hyde is due." He looked like he was forcing down eggs he knew were rotten.

"Nice try, asshole. But I already tried a larger dose and all it did was give Hyde a four- to twenty-four-hour break and give me a seizure. Which is why I carry"—he wiggled the needle around—"this shit around with me."

"What you took was wrong. The dose has to be exactly right or it does more harm than good."

"Yeah, I noticed that."

"And there's more to it than just the drug. For us. For Hydes."

"Like what?"

He didn't answer right away, which gave Mitch the impression that whatever he said next would be either an outright lie or incredibly misleading.

"I don't even know if it will work for you. You're past the point most of us have ever been."

"Okay, then when I try it, I'll make sure my fingers are crossed." *Holy shit.* Was this it? The answer? Fifteen years of transformations. *Fifteen years* of being drugged with something that only reduced them to every five weeks. But to *never* transform again, to never be in another cage or be cuffed, to never fear what your own body might do...

Mitch was speechless for a moment, overwhelmed for another.

You don't have fuck-all yet, asshole. Stop counting the goddamn chickens. "Dosage?"

"It has to be exact, which is why I don't mix it myself. So I can't give you numbers." It made sense—Whittley was the kind of man who saw himself as a thinker and saw other people as lower beings who were there to do everything for him. It must take a lot of time and focus to concoct evil plans and figure out ways to screw with people.

"Who made it for you?"

"Lou Bradford."

"You know he's dead, right? And I believe that was your fault."

"Not mine, but it doesn't matter." His eyes never left the syringe sticking out of his arm. "I have some left. Not a lot but some. The rest was...lost. I'm working on another source, but I have to be *alive* to do that."

"Who's the other source?"

"No one you know. She doesn't even know anything about it yet, and it will take her some time to get up to speed."

"I'm sure she'll be thrilled with the promotion. But back to your current supply—how are you about sharing?"

"Normally, not good. But if you take out the needle and let me go, I'll give you a full syringe."

Sure he would. *Place your bets now, people.* Would it be a syringeful of Drano or something even less pleasant?

"Thing is," Mitch said, "in addition to the patience problem, I have trust issues. I'm working on it, but these things take time. And until then, I can't help thinking that you're setting me up for something worse than you've already set me up for. So...I'm going to have to keep you here for a bit longer."

"You can't. I need it."

"Said every junkie ever."

"I need to inject myself in about four hours, or I'll turn."

"Dang, that sucks…for you. Thankfully, I've made my peace with it."

"I'll give you the drug. Take me to my office, and I'll inject myself in front of you so you'll know it isn't poison. You can leave with the rest of the vial. You took some of the J-0026 from Florida, right? With a sample, any good chemist can figure out the ratio and duplicate it. Then everyone's happy."

Happy. Not exactly the word he would use. "Maybe."

"'Maybe' isn't good enough."

"Neither is any answer you've given me. Tell you what, I need a few hours to think about it. No more than five, though."

"I'll tell you where your friend is."

"Thanks, but I know where my friends are." Because there weren't that many to keep track of.

"How is your ex-detective friend about answering his phone?"

Mitch shoved back, leaving the syringe sticking out of Whittley's arm. "If he doesn't pick up, you have just made things ten times worse for yourself, asshole." He yanked his phone out of his pocket and dialed Landon's number.

"Newman—the man who killed Bradford and the others—was on his way to pick him up." Whittley's confidence was gaining traction, eating away at the ground Mitch had taken from him. "Landon is working as a security guard now, isn't he? It was very amusing to discover that. It was also very disappointing that it wasn't discovered sooner. But what's done is done. And what *will* be done won't be anything you'll like. So take the goddamn needle out of my arm."

Mitch let the phone ring until it went to voicemail. Then he called again. And then he got really fucking angry. "You call your dog and tell him to heel. Or you die. End of story."

"You would lose your chance of getting the drug."

"I. Don't. Care."

After a moment, Whittley sighed. "Can you dial for me?

I'm a little tied up." He wiggled his hands, then paled as he saw the syringe sway to an unheard melody—a death march, maybe. "Take it out first."

Mitch felt the truck stop and then heard a door open. *Shit.* He didn't need to worry about the drugs—that woman was going to be the thing that killed him. Then Eden shouted Justin's name and told him to open the door.

Home sweet shithole. He bent down next to Whittley. "As soon as we stop, you're making that phone call."

"Take the goddamn thing out of my arm!"

"Sure, right after you answer this question: Will Eden transform if she doesn't take any of your tasty drugs?"

Whittley sighed disgustedly. "With as much as they were able to find out in Florida, no, she doesn't need them anymore." His voice intensified to a desperate level. "She's the answer to everything, Turner. A way for *all* of us to be normal, permanently, our sides integrated. It wasn't what we gave her. It was something else. She *has* to know what did it."

"Yeah, I've heard this one. Eden is the answer and all she has to do is stay in a cage and become a one-woman baby factory." He stood. "I didn't think it was funny—there was no punch line."

"She's the answer, Turner. Whatever she did. How can you not understand how important she is?"

I know exactly how important she is. "I'm going to take the needle out now, but if you're not a good boy, it goes right back in." He slipped it out, finding the cap next to Whittley's head and popping it and the plunger guard back on.

Fuck. Fuck and ewww. Hopefully Mitch wouldn't have to use it on himself. 'Cause who knew what Whittley had picked up on all of the trips he took to hell to sell other people's souls.

Of course, Hyde kept Mitch in pretty damn good shape, so anything floating around in Whittley's veins was the least of his worries.

Hyde giveth and he taketh away. Yeah, that second part was the problem.

Chapter XXXIII

Mitch opened up the back of the truck to give Eden the not-so-good news about Landon, knowing she'd probably already paced a groove into the concrete floor. But one look at her made him reconsider telling her at all. She was practically growling. And while he'd gladly offer himself up for another session of 'stress relief,' its effects would probably only last as long as their last session had. That kind of shit could make a guy insecure.

So with sex temporarily off the table and everywhere else, he needed to come up with a more permanent solution. One that didn't involve Whittley's death.

She hissed when he did the 'give me a minute' finger signal.

"Don't come any closer, Eden. Not another step." He went into the office area for supplies. The place looked like a crack house—unused syringes lying around, a bunch of random vials and bottles on their sides. Not very sanitary. If they made it out of this, he'd hire someone to keep all of their drug paraphernalia organized.

"Are you going to just ignore me?" she yelled. But she hadn't followed, as if her feet were glued to floor, just like he wanted.

"No. Because I'm not suicidal. I'll explain everything in a second. Promise." He filled a syringe with something that might not actually kill anyone but looked truly toxic and would be painful as shit to inject. He'd switch the syringes when Whittley wasn't looking.

Justin stayed about thirty feet away from everything.

"Smart to keep your distance from this, kid," Mitch said over the angry sounds Eden was making. He positioned himself between her and Whittley before he told her about Landon. And congratulated himself on his forethought as he caught her mid-pounce.

"He and I have a deal, Eden. And I'll make another with you—if he balks or says anything he shouldn't, I'll let you push the plunger."

"You can't use it on him. You need it."

He turned his back to the truck and kept his voice low. "This one"—he held up the serum he'd now endearingly dubbed the 'Bring the Bastard Back-7'—"is for me. But this one"—he held up the syringe he'd just filled—"is for him." Brown was a great color for pants or dirt, but was a very bad color to see in a syringe.

"What is it?"

"No idea. I found it in a bucket near your little workstation over there. Does it matter?"

She looked over his shoulder. "No." Her voice was cold, venomous. A one-word reflection of her mind. There was still a lot of work to do before she'd be herself again. The woman in front of him, grinding her teeth in anger, was someone else entirely. Almost without conscience and so filled with hate that she'd forgotten who she was.

He leaned even closer and whispered, "When we're done here, we need to have a long talk." And he might have to tie her to a chair to keep her from killing him.

Since there was nothing she could say to stop it from happening, Mitch jumped up into the truck and asked Whittley for the phone number. Before he pressed send, he eased the needle into the guy's arm. He glanced to the edge of the truck where Eden was standing. And glaring.

"Don't fuck this up, Whittley. I'd really prefer not to kill you."

Whittley didn't look down, trapped by the intense hatred in Eden's eyes. "I'd prefer not to be killed." His tone was dull, flat, all ego gone. *Eden* had done that to him. Kicking his ass for hours hadn't done anything, but the expression on her face right now promised death—whether he helped them or not. And now she had the tools and the incentive to do it.

Mitch held the phone up to Whittley's ear and leaned in close so he could hear both sides of the call.

It took a few seconds for someone to answer. "Who is this?"

"It's me," Whittley said. "Do you have them?"

'Them,' not 'him.' Mitch's mind flashed back to earlier when Whittley had mentioned a scientist who didn't know that 'she' would be brewing up more of his special serum yet. *Danielle.* The bastards had both of them. That explained how the asshole on the other end of the line was able to subdue Landon without one of them killing the other.

Getting two people out would be more complicated—especially when one probably couldn't fight her way out of a daycare center.

"Yeah, I got 'em," the kidnapper said. "It was a huge pain in the ass, but I got 'em."

Mitch mouthed, *"Where?"*

Whittley's face squished up unhappily, but he asked. "Are you already at the Shop?"

"Yep. Been here for a while. I brought a few of my boys here too and let them know that I'm not paying them—*you* are."

"Very kind of you to pass on that erroneous information, but we'll discuss it later. Make sure Sinclair is comfortable and don't do anything to Landon until I get there."

"You should be glad I picked up the phone. I didn't recognize the number."

Whittley paused until Mitch wiggled the needle. "It's Colfax's."

"I thought you were bringing her over right away," the man said.

"I made a small detour."

"I hope you kept her strapped down." When the guy snorted, Mitch instantly knew that he wouldn't be able to walk away before making sure that asshole couldn't.

"Don't do anything until I get there, Newman," Whittley said. "Just keep things—"

Mitch pressed 'end' before Whittley forgot the rules. "Address?"

"5734 Lupton Ave."

"It's not an actual shop, is it? Because Landon hates shopping."

"It's a condemned building I own." That aligned with what Alex had mentioned. So even if it was a trap, at least it was in the right place. Whittley looked at the needle. "I held up my end. Now it's your turn."

Mitch slid the needle out and capped it. "Here's what's going to happen: You stay here while I have a quick conversation with Eden. Then we go pick up my friends and make sure they're okay. And then you and I go to your office for the pick-me-up and, if we have time, we can rent a movie on the way home."

"And letting me go will be squeezed in between which activities?" He watched Eden walk away. "You people consider yourselves the good guys, don't you? So aren't you supposed to have some integrity?"

"We'll let you go once all the duckies are in a row and everyone's still floating."

Funny how quickly everything had changed. A week ago, Mitch would've had no problem killing the guy, integrity be as damned as the rest of him. But seeing Eden shift into 'lost' mode made him realize how screwed up his thinking had been. How screwed-up hers was now.

Whittley wouldn't be allowed to live a happy life, but he wouldn't be killed either. There was no way Mitch would ever trust the guy. As soon as he was free, he'd regroup and come at them again. But there wasn't much they could do about it. Unless they killed the fucker. Or caused him enough trouble that he realized they weren't worth it.

So Mitch had to find the high road and decide if it really was worth taking. And if he had to carry Eden over his shoulder and listen to her screaming, he would.

"I don't have a lot of time, Turner. So hurry the hell up, and don't get killed."

Once Whittley gave up everything he knew, Mitch would release him. And then he'd start spreading rumors. Rumors that would inevitably get back to the Board Alex mentioned. And then he'd sit back and wait until the gauntlet was thrown. Right into Whittley's face. And Eden's hands would still be blood free.

"If you're a good boy, I see no reason to keep you waiting too long. But if you're a naughty boy, I'll go old-school on you. And it won't be with a ruler." He jumped down from the truck to go deal with the other troublemaker.

He found her in the office, changing her clothes. In times of war, jeans and tennis shoes are way better than a skirt and those little shoes that always look like they're about to fall off. Plus, the jeans would be harder for him to get into. In times of war, the fewer distractions, the better.

He put his hand up before she said anything that would make this more difficult. "I love you but am very worried about what you might say right now. So let me talk for a minute, think about what I say, and then I'll do the same on the way. Okay?"

She nodded and wrapped her arms around herself tightly, as if it was the only way she knew how to keep herself together. So he helped by tucking her into his chest.

"We need to get Landon and the doc out. That's the only thing we should think about right now. Then we can worry about Whittley. Right now he's leverage and he's scared. And I don't mind leaving him that way for a while. So put him out of your mind and let's focus on Landon. Okay?"

She stiffened. "What about you? Am I not allowed to think about you, either?"

"I'll be fine. Until I'm not. But I should have enough time left to get Landon out and get back here. So thinking about me is fine, but worrying about me isn't."

He let her pull away from him as he called Justin over. "Got an important job for you, man. But it involves only your eyes—not your mouth, your hands, or your ears. Watch him. No talking to him, no listening to him, and absolutely no touching him. Think you can handle it?"

Justin nodded.

"Great. You do this and I'll—You can't drink yet, can you?"

"Not legally."

"Well, since I'd never do anything illegal, we'll have to figure something else out. Maybe…" What did kids do nowadays? *Damn, I feel old.* "Pick something and we'll do it."

Without hesitation, Justin said, "I want to talk."

With *much* hesitation, Mitch said, "Yeah, okay. We'll talk." Whatever the kid wanted to talk about was something Mitch didn't. *Damn it.* He should've offered to buy him something.

Oh, shit. If the kid was looking for a father figure, that had to be the first thing they discussed. *Or…*Mitch could avoid the conversation altogether by buying the kid a father. Someone to talk to, watch sports with, who understood what he was going through, who'd been in his shoes, who'd—

Oh, bigger shit. This wasn't about hormones and girls and peer pressure. This was about hormones and girls and peer pressure and handcuffs and cages and monsters. Things that not enough dads were comfortable discussing with their kids nowadays. What a shame.

Mitch tried thinking positively—maybe he'd get shot after freeing the cop and Danielle. *That'd be nice.* "Yeah, okay," Mitch mumbled. "We should talk." *Huh. The kid has teeth.* And was showing them off. *Oh, man.* "Are you smiling at me?"

Justin put his lips over the pearly whites and slumped away.

"Hey," he called out, feeling like a colossal shit. "You should do it more often. Makes you look like a badass."

The kid's quick glance backward let Mitch know he'd said exactly the right thing. Now, that was a first.

When they got to the car, Mitch stopped and took Eden's face in his hands. "Don't make me regret anything, beautiful."

"What if I do?" she asked, a smile creeping onto her face. "You gonna throw me up against a car again?"

He smirked. "If we weren't on a time crunch, I'd show you exactly what I'd do to you. But unfortunately, we'll have to wait." After a very promising and hard-to-let-go-of kiss, he released her. "Are you ready for this?"

She took a deep breath and nodded. One look and everything settled into place again. One moment and he had hope she was under control again.

"Get in and see if it'll turn over, but be gentle." When nothing happened, he popped the hood, leaned over the engine, and started tinkering, in case something was just loose and nothing was FUBAR. "Again!"

When he heard the engine come to life...barely, he wanted to kiss it. Instead, he shut the hood and prayed the POS would make it to where they needed to go and get them back, even if it had some bullet holes in it.

Eden scooted over as he swung himself into the driver's side. According to the cell phone's GPS, it would take fourteen minutes to get there. Not enough time to have a deep discussion with lots of tears and sighs. But definitely enough time to stew, trade worried glances, and come up with a plan.

And maybe, just maybe, he'd also have a few seconds to think about what else Whittley had said.

Mitch didn't tell her about the J-0026 because too much could go wrong between now and when he got his hands on it. If she had expectations and it turned out to be just more Whittley bullshit, it would destroy her.

So he decided to wait. He'd figure out a way to distract her when they got to Whittley's office and make sure it was legit before telling her anything. Honestly, he wasn't all that hopeful about it. Sure, it would be great. Amazing. A miracle. But like Whittley said—it might not do shit for someone as far gone as Mitch was.

So he'd wait and he'd pray and he'd get his friend back. And then he'd start looking for miracles.

Chapter XXXIV

"I should go in first," Eden said, knowing that Mitch was probably thinking the same thing, including the pronoun. "Once I figure out what's inside, I'll come back for you. If I still need help." With only a sideways glance, she knew he was pissed. "Mitch, think about it—you're still recovering, and I'm smaller and faster. I can take care of it."

"That's not what we need to talk about."

"You said it first—getting Landon out is the most important thing right now. And I can get him out."

He swung the car over to the side of the road and then turned towards her. "Let's get this straight. Yes, you are tough and smart and a hundred other great things. But I'm not a pussy and I won't be waiting in the car while you go into a dangerous place." The intensity of his voice kept her from responding, at least vocally. But it created enough heat in her body to stave off three winters.

"I didn't just return from the netherworld to let you push me around, babe. So don't even try it. Because you will lose. As much as I love you, you will lose."

"Fine." Lame, but it was all she could manage.

He studied her for a moment, making sure she understood

how it would be. "Fine." He grabbed her shirt and yanked her towards him. Holding the nape of her neck, he tilted her head to exactly the position he wanted her in.

She held back until he took her mouth, until his kiss took all control away from her. She relented, leaning into him because she had no choice. Even if her entire being hadn't loved him before, it would now. Because at some point, he'd reclaimed his power, and he'd claimed her.

"I'm glad that's clear," he said, releasing her and pulling back into the lane. Mitch had always been strong, but now? Now she could sense the change in him. The confidence, the direction. Ever since he woke up, he'd been different. She wondered if he even noticed. Another thing they needed to discuss.

Once Landon is safe. She gripped her thighs more tightly, trying to defuse some of her anger. *Landon... Shit.* After everything she'd put him through, he was still out there trying to do the right thing.

Their enemies were people, thinking and scheming people. Even though they lacked consciences and ethics, they thought things through. *Throwing yourself at an intelligently designed wall won't get you through it.* There was a way over, and they needed to help each other find it.

"Now," he said. "Let's talk about you."

"What about me?" she asked, knowing exactly what he wanted to talk about.

"Can you handle this?"

"Handling things isn't the problem, knowing when to stop is." She sighed, needing a moment before she could say a few things she didn't want to admit, even to herself. "I feel like I'm coming apart. Like so much is wrong that my mind is doing everything it can to protect itself. And it's failing."

"No, it's not."

"I wanted to screw the guy who had me caged! I think that counts as a fail."

"What you felt wasn't attraction. It was Whittley's pull."

"What do you mean?" After he told her about Ryan being Abnormal, they were both silent for a while. *God, it makes sense.* And was a huge relief. It lessened her guilt. At least for part of her reaction.

"Is it possible that his Hyde brought out your violence?" he asked.

"Maybe some of it. But I've kinda been a mess for a while now." She laughed with her lips clenched, a physical reflection of her greatest fear—that if she started really letting things out, the purging would never stop.

"I'm afraid, Mitch. Of myself." It was a whispered comment, one she wasn't sure had carried over the sound of the engine. But when he glanced at her and put his hand on her leg, she knew he'd heard.

"I wish we had more time to deal with this right now. But you are incredible—the strongest woman I've ever known. Not with Chastity's side, *despite* Chastity's side. Focus on *you*, Eden. A whole, kind, complicated, amazingly well-loved, and insanely stubborn person.

She understood what he didn't say, the nonverbalized thought that filled his eyes when he looked at her again: *'Don't be anyone else.'* She nodded her agreement, as if any words either of them might use would never be clearer than the knowledge they shared.

After a moment, he said, "We need to stop thinking as individuals and start acting more like a single unit. I tell you what I'm thinking, and you respect me enough to do the same." The smoothness of his voice helped her get a little closer to calm. "Because every time we split up, bad shit happens. Someone's gotta go rescue someone else."

He was right. They were better and stronger because of each other. She'd known it but hadn't been able to really accept it. So she needed to try harder.

"Each of us needs to accept who we are—strengths and weaknesses. And we all know how many weaknesses I have. So if I've accepted the shit that *I* am, you should have no problem. Because you only have about two."

"Two? What's the second one?"

He smiled. "I love who you are, babe. You should too. Sometimes it's—" His head jerked, his brow furrowed, his chest caved slightly.

"It's what?"

"It's…It's just that simple," he said slowly, his voice filled with something like wonder. As if he'd just figured something out or come to a big decision. But if he'd just decided to sacrifice himself for her—if he said anything remotely like that—she'd knock him out and leave him in the car while she went in alone. 'Cause that shit was *not* going to happen again.

She was a long way from comfort or acceptance. But at least she could breathe. *Breathing's good. Easy. Simple. There's no danger in breathing.* But she was also a realist—they were heading into battle. The warm and cozies would have to wait a little longer.

"Did Ryan tell you anything else that might be important?" she asked.

He paused. "Not that I can think of."

"I know when you're lying, Mitch!" She jabbed the jerk in the cheek, right into his lying little dimple. "Stop doing it."

"*Ow*, you have scratchy nails," he said, rubbing his cheek. "Okay, there's something else—the way he kept his Hyde in check. But… do you want the best case or the worst case first?"

"Worst case," she said,

"You didn't used to be a glass-half-empty kind of person."

"I promise to try harder if you promise to be around to see it. Now get to the point."

"Worst case is that because I went through 'the change,' what worked for him won't work for me, and I will die a miserable death."

Her whole body tightened. But the possibility wasn't anything new. "I'd sure hate for that to happen."

"Me too. And that leads me to the best-case scenario,

which is what I should've started with. Whittley's Hyde hasn't come out in years. Because he takes the J-0026—a different dose than the one Carter was giving you and the one that brought me back. Somewhere in the middle, I guess."

Her reply didn't happen immediately, there were no 'hallelujah's or 'golly, that's great news.' Because she couldn't. When she finally spoke, her voice was shaky. "Years. I… Years?" And that was it for a minute.

"It's about a mile away from a done deal, babe. There are a lot of things that can go wrong before we even have a chance to test the theory." He cocked his head to the side. "That was a very glass-half-empty comment, wasn't it?"

She slugged him in the arm. Hard.

"Can we save the hitting for the bad guys, please?"

"Why the hell didn't you tell me that before?"

"It's only been ten minutes."

"Exactly. You should've told me ten minutes ago. If I hadn't asked and if I didn't know you were lying, you would've waited longer. Why?"

"We don't have it yet, so I didn't want to—"

"Tell me the truth?"

"Make you believe in something that might not be true."

"It's a chance we didn't have a few hours ago, so screw you if you think I'm not going to enjoy it." She smacked him again.

"How about we show our enjoyment in more pleasurable ways from now on?" He rubbed his arm.

"You keep anything like that from me again, and I'll be aiming a lot lower."

He laughed. "Threats of testicular injury should not sound that hot. They just shouldn't."

"Don't try to charm me, Mitch Turner. I'm not in the mood."

"I'm going to have to work hard to make sure that phrase never comes out of your mouth again." Even her anger couldn't erase his smile.

She shook her head, feeling the corners of her mouth respond with like. "Is there *anything* that doesn't amuse you?"

"I'm alive and you're next to me, so my glass is already half full. When we get Landon back and some bad guys need a lot of Band-Aids, it will be pretty damn close to the rim." He could die at any moment and his glass was almost full? Amazing...and deeply troubling.

They pulled into a small lot two buildings away from the address Ryan had given them.

"I'll meet you at the front of the car in about three seconds," he said. "You're not going to get in any trouble from here to there, are you?"

"I think I can handle it." She was out before he finished rolling his eyes and sitting on the hood when he got there. "Proud of me?"

"We don't have time for this," he said, pushing himself between her legs and leaning into her until their lips were millimeters apart. "When we go in"—their hips found each other's, an involuntary reaction to being near each other—"I need you to do whatever I ask you to do. No games, no heroics. Can I trust you?"

She swallowed, pulling back slightly. "Last time you went into something like this, you set yourself up to die. It can't happen again. So can I trust *you*?"

"You can trust that I love you, that I want nothing more than for you to be happy, and that I don't want to die while they have us chained. I'm not going to die in a cage." He cradled her face in both hands. "Look"—his voice was soft and masculine and powerful—"if it really comes down to you or me, I will always choose you. But I won't go looking for it. Because I want a life with you. And I will try my hardest not to let anything or anyone fuck that up. Not even me. Got it?"

"Got it."

He held her still and gave her a kiss she would remember until the day she died. Maybe longer. When he pulled away, her breath went with him. And all the other pieces of her that were left.

She would follow him anywhere. Even into hell.

As they walked, Mitch's mind went right back to the unpleasant conversation he'd had with himself on the drive over. This wasn't a good time to be thinking. This was a very good time to be doing.

He needed to focus on the task at hand...with both hands. He let go of hers as they neared the first of three identical buildings, knowing that being too close together would make them more vulnerable to any nasty surprises.

But he couldn't let go of his thoughts as easily. He'd spent his entire life being cut off, pretending his evil wasn't part of him. It was. *He* was. And the longer Mitch ignored the fact, the less control he had.

Sometimes it's just that simple. Maybe he didn't need to give in, or over, to Hyde. Maybe he needed to accept that the bastard was a part of him. *No, that's not quite right.* He needed to accept that he was made up of just one big bastard—good, bad, and sometimes ugly. Because that was life. And even though it sucked shit a lot of the time, it was worth it.

Proven by the woman who, right now, had stopped moving and was staring at him with a look of concern on her face.

"All good," he said in what, evidently, was an unconvincing way. "Good enough."

With that, she nodded and they kept walking towards three shitty-looking single-story warehouses, the farthest one where Landon and Danielle were supposedly being held.

Without discussion, he and Eden headed directly for the closest building. The front door was glass with plywood behind it. Using one of the pins she had on her belt, it took Eden about ninety seconds to pick the lock. They toured the place—noting exits, lots of unmarked doors, and a loading door in back. In the center of the maze of hallways, they found a large open space with two sets of double doors directly across from each other.

"The other building might not be exactly the same," she said looking everywhere.

"It definitely won't be—this one doesn't have any assholes in it."

As they left, Mitch moved slowly, forcing himself to stay as calm and cool as the woman at his side. He could learn a thing or two from her. *Had* learned a thing or two...or twenty. The only thing he wasn't a hundred percent sure of was— when all was said and done and they were lying poolside on cheap plastic chairs with margaritas in their hands—would she still have that violent hunger in her eyes? Confidence he could handle, appreciate, admire. But only if it came peacefully. Only if it came without risk.

He took her hand, brought her palm to his lips, and then let go. This wasn't a good time to hold hands and sign each other's yearbooks. This was the time to get in, cause as much damage as necessary, and then get the hell out.

In a discreet walk around the building they were targeting, they noticed the same five exits as the last. But the front door was chained up from the inside, and not even Eden could pick a lock through glass. The big loading door in back was boarded up, and the other doors didn't have handles on the outside.

But one had a keypad.

"Pretty shiny way to get into a condemned building, isn't it?" Unfortunately, knowing the way to get in was useless without the code.

"Get the door for me?"

"Wha—?" He didn't even have time for a stupid response, let alone a decent one. She'd already grabbed his arm, shoved him into the wall, and downed the guard before Mitch even registered the door being opened.

How come I'm not that fast? How did she even know the guy was coming outside?

"Mitch, the door!"

He grabbed the edge right before it closed.

Eden nudged the guard with her foot before she reached down for his gun. And it was definitely a gun. No fancy Tasers this time around. Either Whittley had forgotten to tell them to keep the guinea pigs alive or he and his crew didn't give a shit what happened anymore. Either way...

Dead is dead. Given a little time and as long as it wasn't somewhere absolutely vital, he and Eden could heal from a bullet hole, but Landon and Danielle couldn't. So if Mitch had to take one for the team, he'd do it. And while he healed, Landon would have to put up with his bitching and let Mitch hold the remote.

She put the weapon into the back pocket of her jeans. "What? I'm not into guns, but better I have it than them."

"I just don't want you to accidentally shoot off your ass— I like it as is."

She smiled. "Safety's on. I won't use it until they know we're here. So let's go find as many as we can before that happens."

Going in search of people with guns wasn't high on Mitch's list. In fact, he'd probably put it somewhere near the bottom, right in between getting his ass waxed and going through puberty again. But since those things were never going to happen, he'd go along with her. But he sure as fuck wouldn't be behind her, no matter how well she fought.

He finally felt like a man again when they happened upon two guards and each had someone to hit. He didn't look to see how she was doing, in part because he didn't want to know if she was doing better than he was. And in the *other* part because, due to the amount of oh-shit-I'm-being-beaten-by-a-girl grunts coming from the guy she was fighting, Mitch *knew* she was doing better than he was.

Luckily, war is like bicycling—it comes back pretty quickly. Even when you've had a long out-of-body experience and are just getting comfortable in your own skin again. So his ego was appeased when his opponent was KOed before hers was.

By at least ten seconds.

Mitch hated guns. There was something too easy about shooting someone. Taking a life should mean something, put blood on your hands so you didn't forget. But since bloody hands were guaranteed if one of these assholes shot him, Mitch took the weapons—one for him and one for Landon.

Having a gun didn't make him more confident, though. They still had no idea how many guards there were or how much longer their luck would hold out. And seeing as this was Texas, he just hoped they weren't being corralled into a pen they couldn't get out of without being branded.

CHAPTER XXXV

Only a few more turns led them to the least healthy but the most useful place to be: the large open space in the building's center. It was pretty similar to the one they'd seen in the other building, but this one had something that looked like a kitchen along one side.

A kitchen for terrorists. There was a small fridge, a sink, and a counter covered with sciencey crap Mitch couldn't name. Probably where Whittley intended Danielle to work on his magical cure that put the 'normal' back into 'Abnormal.' If she could do it for Whittley, she could do it for Mitch. Especially because Mitch would be really, really nice when he asked.

If that's possible, I could—He shook off the thought before it got too melodramatic. There were more important things to focus on and more important people to focus on. And if he didn't get them out of here, *nothing* would be possible.

In the center of the room were two very expensive-looking cages. The steel shone. They'd probably been purchased recently, just for Eden and him. That was thoughtful of Whittley. *Wouldn't want us to scratch ourselves and get tetanus, now would we?* Wonder why he didn't mention it the last time they spoke. *Oh, riiiiight.*

Inside the cage closest to him, but facing the opposite direction, was Landon. Kind of.

Mitch shook his head and took another look. The guy looked brawnier and almost as shiny as the bars surrounding him. A trick of the light that, for whatever reason, wasn't hitting Danielle. She was huddled up against the bars of the other cage, as close to Landon as she could get. And she looked terrified.

Two cages to open was a bit of a buzz kill. As if one wasn't hard enough. Mitch heard a squeak from the side of the room and dared one quick peek to know how many guards they were up against. Four men—one sitting in a chair with his legs up on a desk, the other three looking bored behind him.

As much as Mitch hated the idea, he and Eden needed to split up. Sticking together would make things too easy for the other side. So he started pantomiming, holding up four fingers, then pointing to himself with his other hand and flipping it over, walking his fingers in a half-circle around the four he was holding up and then threw them all up and mouthed, 'Boom.'

He pointed at her, pretended to turn a key, and then waited for her to say, '*What the fuck does that mean?*'

She nodded. *Seriously?* He'd just witnessed a miracle. And he promised himself he'd keep practicing until he could outmime a Frenchman.

All the time I've spent trapped in a box has gotta be good for something.

He pulled her close and whispered, "Remember how pissed I'm going to be if you have any more holes in you than you do right now. I like those. A lot. But only those."

She gave him a quick kiss. "Whatever happens, we meet back at the warehouse."

He moved through the hallways quickly, hoping his sense of direction hadn't become as dysfunctional as the rest of him. As soon as he saw the hazy light of the main room, he slid to a stop.

And thank the devil, he ended up at the doorway opposite the one he'd just left. With his back to the wall, he scooted to the edge and tried to listen for movement.

Getting rid of four men was completely workable. Probably. The bigger and more immediate question was how to get the men to follow him so Eden could open the cages. He took a quick look. Just inside the room was a row of metal shelves that jutted out a few feet. Crouching down, he moved behind them.

He might be able to shoot one, maybe two, of the guards...if he was really lucky. But his goal was to lure the men away from the room, not to start a shoot-out with Landon and Danielle stuck in the middle of it.

So...what was the best way to get someone's attention? *Birdcall? Toss a pebble? What the hell does a rat cough sound like?* He clicked his tongue on the roof of his mouth. Landon whipped his head towards him, as if he'd actually heard it.

After a barely-there smile and a nod, the cop looked at his captors. "Hey, Newman! Am I supposed to pee in the corner or can I take a trip to the little boys' room?" *Oooh*, the cop was smart—one less locked door to get through would save a lot of time and bullets.

The man sitting at the desk briefly raised his head. "Piss in the corner now, or piss your pants when you die. Makes no difference to me."

The cop chuckled. "I think I'll hold it until I'm standing over your grave."

As soon as Landon made eye contact again, Mitch pointed to the other door, then himself and did a few other things with his fingers before giving up and flashing his gun. He sucked shit at charades. He knew it and, from the look on Landon's face, the cop knew it too.

So Mitch stuck to using his fingers to count down. *4...3...2...Let the fun begin.* He stood. "Hey, do any of you dickheads know where a guy can get a decent espresso around here?"

Landon yelled, "Get down!" put his arm through two sets
of bars, and pushed Danielle to the ground. A millisecond
later, the men lunged forward, drawing their weapons. When
the first shot was fired, Mitch had a moment of *you're-so-
fucking-stupid*. He should have shot at least one of them.

It's hard to aim while running, even harder if the target is
running, too. And Mitch never made anything easy on
anybody. So as soon as he knew all the guards were coming
for him, he kicked the shelf closest to him. When it hit its
neighbor, that one fell too, continuing like a line of dominoes
the men would have to hurtle.

Then he ran like a motherfucking Olympian. He'd have
preferred his running shoes, but the boots had great traction—
perfect for slick tile and sharp corners. Corners equaled
good—bullets don't corner well. Men *shooting* bullets do,
though, so he kept up his pace.

He wove through the hallways, trying to remember which
way he'd come. Hitting a dead end would be *his* dead end, but
he had to lead them away from the cage room, preferably
without running into any other guards. Unfortunately, Clinic
employees were like cockroaches. You don't know they're
there, but when you see *one*, you can bet your ass that there
are a million others behind the little bastard.

Mitch slid to a stop as soon as he saw them, fired once, and
then backed up a few feet to take another hallway, hearing the
assholes firing back.

"Shit!" he yelled as soon as he realized where he was. He'd
gone in a big circle, leading all the guards right back to point
A.

At least everyone was outside the cages—Eden talking
sternly to Danielle and Landon holding onto a man who
looked very, very…floppy.

Without turning or stopping, he pointed over his shoulder.
"Good time to go, don't you think?" They all headed towards
the opposite doorway. "The loop-de-loop thing isn't going to

work much longer. So I'm thinking we follow the exit signs."

Mitch shoved the gun at Landon. Eden was in front, and the cop had one hand on Danielle's waist and the other on his weapon. Mitch slowed down to kick open a few random doors, hoping to confuse the guards. Seriously, how smart could they possibly be if they worked for Whittley? The guy didn't like smart people.

"Move faster," Eden yelled at Danielle. Maybe it was the stress of the cage or, more likely, Danielle simply wasn't used to this kind of fun, but she didn't look like she could go much farther. And she was slowing them down.

Mitch caught up with them and tapped Eden on the ass, warning her. "Calm down." A tall order while you're running for your life. But the last thing they needed was more drama.

"You have to get her out, Eden," Landon said. "She's our best chance. She helped create one of the drugs and might be able to figure the others out. For the kids. For Mitch. Whatever it takes, Eden. Get her out."

Looking very, very irritated, Eden took Danielle's arm and yanked her along.

They fell into a groove, finally working as a team—Eden checking corners before hauling Danielle around them, Mitch and Landon watching the rear, shooting when the assholes got too close on a straightaway. They worked in tandem—conserving ammo as much as possible, never firing at the same time. Mitch was pretty sure they'd picked up a few stragglers, because he heard more than four voices and four guns going off.

From the outside of the building, he'd seen five exits, so one of them had to be close. Because there couldn't possibly be a strip of hallway in the entire building that they hadn't run through.

Thing was, as soon as they hit open air, there was nothing to duck behind, no corners to turn. So the ride had to stop for somebody, and it shouldn't be the stronger sex. To give the ladies a chance to make it out, he would slow the assholes down, and the cop would be there for moral support. Or just in case Mitch fucked it up.

Landon smacked him in the shoulder. "You up to helping me out, Turner?" He spoke softly, so neither the women in front of them nor the men behind them could hear. Not that they would—gunshots in corridors made a hell of a loud noise.

"I was just going to ask you the same thing." They slowed down just enough for a tete à tete, privacy during a flee-for-your-life scenario not being a thing of abundance.

"Follow my lead?" Landon asked.

"Right off the cliff, my friend."

"Hopefully it won't come to that." He dropped his voice even lower. "You get the ladies out while I slow the guards down."

Shit. "Not at all what I had in mind." Did *everyone* want him to wait in the car now?

"I can take care of them." Landon pointed a thumb over his shoulder.

"Really? You against, what, eight? You can't even handle *me*. And those aren't water guns they're carrying." Mitch looked at the guy, the way he moved, breathed, and…was that a fucking smile on his face? This wasn't the same man Mitch had dropped off at the lab a few miserable hours ago.

"What's going on with you, cop? You're so…fresh."

"Danielle made up a batch of whatever they gave Carter. Now I'm walking proof of what the bastards did."

"Not getting it. How are you proof?"

"I injected it. It's in my blood."

"You what?" Mitch screamed as he slammed on the brakes. "Carter fucking died, you idiot!" He would have stayed stuck to that spot if Landon hadn't yanked him by the arm as if he were starting up a lawn mower. So Mitch's feet and mouth moved, but everything else stayed in shock mode.

"Damn it, cop! I let you out of my sight for a few hours and *this* is what happens? Between you and Eden, I'm never going to be able to close my eyes again."

"Once my blood is tested, the FDA will find out what The Clinic is doing. Not to you guys, to humans. Human testing, Turner. Illegal research on humans. The Abnormal shit stays completely out of it, and The Clinic goes down like Al Capone. They'll be investigated, prosecuted, taken apart. But not by us. We can watch the bastards go down from the stands."

If his pause was to give a Mitch a chance to shout, '*Hurray. I'm so glad you shot yourself up with poison,*' he was going to be waiting a lifetime.

"Don't worry about me, Turner. I feel great. Amazing. Like I could move mountains."

Mitch swallowed bile. "How 'bout you just move your ass so we can get out of here. Before that shit works its way out of your system." What was done was done. And now was not the time for mourning or telling Landon how fucking stupid he was. That would come later and would continue for a very, very long time.

He gave a silent 'thank you' to whoever made exit signs mandatory. Then another to whoever thought to put those little green arrows on them that glowed whether the building was condemned or not. And another to the cosmos that seemed to be leading them away from the front door. Because if Eden picked the lock to get them out, there was no way in hell Mitch would be able to stop her from coming back in.

Mitch pointed his finger at Danielle, but spoke to the cop. "Are you guys…"

"No!" Either the run was getting to him—which didn't seem likely seeing as how his breath had barely changed since the fleeing began—or Landon was blushing. A grown-ass man blushing over a girl.

So sweet it made Mitch's teeth hurt. "My mistake." He laughed.

"It's not as if I've had a lot of time for a social life lately."

"What's a social life?"

"Thank god it isn't in public, but all the time you spend in bed with Eden qualifies as social." Another reason to make sure the guy got out of this alive, as if Mitch needed another reason. Landon deserved to be bedridden for about a month—by choice, not necessity. With an attractive, intelligent companion.

"We get them out and make sure no one follows, yeah?"

"Why are you boys so slow?" Eden yelled, glancing backward at them.

"Coming, babe," Mitch called back.

"She's going to be pissed, Turner." He wasn't talking about Danielle.

"I know. But I'd rather she be pissed than any of the alternatives."

"If we get out of this, I'll try to keep her from killing you."

He slugged the cop on the shoulder. "If I didn't already have a soul mate, I'd think you were it, asshole."

"Ditto." Landon picked up the pace, easily catching up to the women. Without warning or breaking stride, he scooped Danielle into his arms.

Whatever she'd brewed up for him was some seriously powerful shit. And while that was great for an escape, what would happen once the women were out and the goal wasn't only to run? Mitch had to be very careful, just in case the strength of a Hyde came with some of his less-pleasant qualities.

Eden hit the door first, slamming it open. There was nothing but black outside—no street lamps and no bad guys. She held the door as Landon put Danielle down and shoved her out. Mitch was there two seconds later.

"What are we waiting for?" Eden asked, shaking with impatience.

No goodbyes. No hints of what he was about to do. *This isn't gonna go over well.* She trusted him, specifically told him not to do anything like this. But someone needed to make sure Danielle was safe—without her, there would be no more good dope for anyone. As soon as he and Landon made sure the guards couldn't walk well enough to chase them, Mitch would have a chance to apologize and feel her wrath.

And hopefully, he'd at least *start* the conversation with all of his blood inside his body.

CHAPTER XXXVI

"What are we waiting for?" How many times had Eden asked *exactly* the same question and gotten *exactly* zero answers? "This isn't a bus stop, boys."

"I'll meet you back at the warehouse," Mitch said. "Take Danielle and go. She's important."

If there was any other sound, she didn't hear it. The only things she could hear were the pounding of her heart and the words he'd just said. Words that didn't make any sense.

And then they did. "No!" She grabbed his shirt, pulling him. "You promised!"

"I choose you." His shirt ripped when he shoved her backward. Hard.

She stumbled, caught herself, and ran for the door. "No!" It slammed shut a second too early. A second before she could get to it. She clawed at the edge, trying to get hold of something, anything. But there was nothing she could grab onto.

"No-no-no-no-no!" She pounded on the door, crying out, her breath coming in gasps, her fist denting it. It still wasn't enough. No matter what she did, it was never enough. She leaned her head against the metal, listening to the shouting fade away and watching her tears fall onto the pavement.

He promised. No, he *lied.*

When she heard breathing that didn't match her own, she flipped around. The scientist, Danielle, stood there, shaking, gasping for air, her arms wrapped around herself.

"Come on." Eden grabbed the woman's arm and dragged her around the building to check every goddamn door there was.

Asshole. He'd promised. No heroics, no solo missions. *All bullshit.* When she heard a whimper, she realized her hand had turned into a vise around Danielle's arm and released her. She kicked the front door, but the plywood behind the glass kept her from doing any real damage to it. The only way she'd get through it was with a car.

"We need to get out of here," Danielle said, her eyes darting around the darkness.

"No."

"Fine. You stay. I'm going. Good luck."

As she turned to go, Eden grabbed her by the back of the neck. "How do I get back inside?"

"I don't know." Danielle's voice was confused, pained. "I didn't even know this place existed. That any of this existed."

"Bullshit. You're one of them. How do I get in there?"

"Why would they have put me in a cage if I was one of them?"

"Because that's what they do." She shook the woman by both arms, knowing how close to the edge she was. Any progress she'd made towards control was gone now. And Danielle was the closest punching bag.

Shit! Eden shoved her away. Danielle stumbled, fell, and caught the concrete with the side of her face. Her cheek was scraped and bleeding, her hands too, probably.

Damnitdamnitdamnit! "I didn't mean to—Sorry. You're right. Let's go." After taking one last look at the door, one last chance to find a way in, she dragged Danielle through the parking lot until she saw the car.

Then she started laughing. When Mitch had so dramatically gotten rid of her, he hadn't dramatically given her the keys. But, even though the car was as big a piece of shit as he was, she could hotwire it.

More than anything she wanted to drive right through the front of the building. But Landon had said Danielle was important, that Eden needed to keep her safe. For everyone, including Justin and all the others. And keeping her safe didn't involve testing out the car's airbags.

Nor did it involve giving her a concrete facial. "Shit!"

She should just leave him. That was what he wanted—to push her far enough away so that she couldn't help. The little woman can babysit the scientist while the menfolk take care of the danger.

Bullshit, bullshit, bullshit.

Her phone rang, and she answered with a growl. It had better be Mitch apologizing for being such an asshole. "You bastard!" When he didn't respond, her anger was immediately extinguished by fear. "Mitch? What's going on? Open one of the doors! I can help."

Still nothing.

She looked at the phone—maybe she hadn't accepted the call. But she had. Except it wasn't Mitch's name on the caller ID.

"Justin, I can't talk right now."

Still nothing.

"Justin, are you there?"

"What's wrong?" Danielle asked.

Eden shushed her. She closed her eyes and listened for something, anything that would let her know he'd just butt dialed her and that nothing was wrong. Despite the heaviness of the night air, a chill ran up her spine, as if her body had caught on to something her mind hadn't processed yet.

And then she heard breathing. Shallow. Labored. "Justin, answer me!"

Still. Nothing.

"Ryan?" she whispered. "Ryan, are you there? Can you hear me?" Her fingers tightened around the phone. "Ryan, put Justin on the goddamn phone right now!"

Still. No. Answer.

If Ryan did anything to him... it would be her fault. "Get in the car."

Danielle looked around. "No offense, but I think I'll take the bus."

"Get. In. Now."

Danielle slid into the passenger side and closed the door, staying as far away from Eden as she could. Smart woman.

Eden shoved the phone at her. "Listen for anything." Then she tackled the car's wiring.

"Justin?" Danielle said softly. "Are you there?" She was silent for a minute.

As soon as the engine turned over, Eden looked at her, hating everything about her. Especially the small shake of her head and the tiny shrug of her shoulders.

"Give it to me." She held her hand out for the phone. Barely able to breathe, Eden pulled onto the street without looking back. This was what Mitch wanted—the only card he'd given her to play. Trying not to wonder if she was making another mistake by leaving, she focused on what was in front of her and not behind her, something that she could *do* instead of be hobbled by.

Landon would make sure Mitch was okay. He'd been doing it for weeks, and Mitch would come back to her. Unless he was seizing. *Shit!* No, he wouldn't. He had time left before she needed to worry about that. She had time. And Mitch had Landon and the syringe.

But Justin was alone with Ryan. She steered with one hand and held her phone in the other. Because the line connecting Justin's phone to hers was still live. Like him.

He's still alive. Because she knew how tight those knots were.

She drove fast enough so that Danielle wouldn't get the

crazy idea of jumping out. She wouldn't get far, but chasing her down was something else Eden didn't want to deal with. She didn't press her for information, either. The interrogation could wait until they got back to the warehouse.

Until then, Eden could spend the time going through bad scenario after bad scenario.

"I wanted to ask you…" Danielle sighed. "Do you know how much of the J-0026 your Abnormal side took? In the powder form."

Wow. Great, another memory she never wanted to revisit. "I don't know," she snapped. "As much as she could fit up our nose, I guess."

"She snorted it. Is that when you—?"

"Why are you talking to me?" Eden shouted.

"Is that when you stopped transforming?" she asked, reacting to Eden's anger with control. Impressive control. The kind Eden didn't seem to have any of.

"I don't—" She shut her mouth to think because keeping it open wasn't doing her any favors.

After Eden had woken up with a straw in her hand and powder on her face, Mitch had taken her home and spent the next few days loving her. And then… And then Chastity didn't show, even though she was scheduled to. But she showed the next night, when Jolie almost killed Carter. And then—

Oh shit. She gripped the steering wheel so she wouldn't crash, and then looked at Danielle, hoping she wouldn't see the tears in Eden's eyes. "Is that what did it? What changed me and made me into one person?" *Could it change Mitch?*

"It's just a theory based on the fact that, even if you inhaled a minimal amount of the condensed form, *something* dramatic should've happened. Death being the most likely but, obviously, that didn't happen."

"We're strong—people like me. We work differently."

"I know. Which means testing the theory would take years and years. And believe me, human testing a compound I know nothing about will *never* happen again." After a quick explanation of what she was talking about, Danielle was quiet, regretful.

Eden couldn't lose any of them. Not her boys. It just couldn't happen. Her foot punched the gas pedal even harder. There was nothing she could do for Landon now, but she could make sure Justin was okay. And maybe, just maybe, Danielle could help her do something for Mitch.

"We don't have years, Danielle. We might not even have tomorrow." She told Danielle what Mitch told her that Ryan had told him.

Awesome. Everything was riding on what could be a fatal game of Telephone. "Why would the less-concentrated dose Mitch took have a worse effect than the big one I did?" Although if there was anything worse than death, Ryan would be the one to come up with it.

Danielle shrugged. "Every pharmaceutical has side effects. Most of the time, they're undesirable, but occasionally, they're not. So, yeah, it's possible that a mega-dose of J-0026 would cause a different reaction. Or it could be the delivery method—the speed at which it's absorbed by the body. Given that your metabolism and endocrine systems work so differently, anything is possible. But it's not something we'll know until we test it."

She held up her hand. "Let me repeat that so I'm sure you understand what I'm saying. *Test. It.*"

"Who are we going to test it on? Our physiology is completely different than a human's, and there are no Abnormal rats. So—"

Ryan's Abnormal. And a rat.

"Do whatever you want to do." Danielle chuckled bitterly. "Give the drug to whomever you want to give it to. But I'm not going to be there."

She didn't have to be.

The first thing Eden noticed was the loading door. It was open. Big no-no. Very wrong. Maybe Justin decided to air the place out.

She ran inside calling his name, searching for him. The scent of blood was strong, even stronger than it was in a closed truck with a bloody Ryan.

"Justin!" When she saw him lying next to the back of the truck, his name felt like a brick in her throat, cutting off her air. Inside the truck, there were loose rope, an overturned chair, empty cuffs, and slack chains.

But no Ryan.

As she slid onto her knees, the cement scraped through her pants and skin. Then she reached an area covered with something wet and slippery that shouldn't be there. It was Justin's, and he needed it. *Inside* of him.

His face was splattered with red as if he'd been a painter's drop cloth. His breath came in gasps, hiccups, just like Carter's had when she'd woken up to find him beside her.

But this was different—Carter was human, Justin wasn't. He could heal in a way Carter couldn't. He just needed time.

"Justin, it'll be okay. You'll be okay." She took his hand in hers without looking at it because all she would see was red. When she wiped his face, the drops smeared, spreading across his cheek.

He opened his eyes, the corners of his mouth twitching as if he was trying to smile, as if he was happy to see her. As if this wasn't all her fault.

"I screwed up." His voice was soft, scratchy, and barely audible.

"No, you didn't. Not at all."

"He was so strong, E. Like you are. Said he needed to piss…that he'd…" A tear dripped down, creating a thin line of normality down his bloodied temple. "I screwed up."

"You didn't do anything wrong. Try to relax and let your body heal itself. Okay? That's the best part of being what we are, so let it happen. Okay?" She sat down above his head, lifting it off the cement and cradling it in her lap. "Just let it happen."

Danielle stood a few feet away, her gaze moving around his body.

"He'll be fine," Eden said, smoothing his hair from his face. She'd take care of him until he was better.

Danielle shook her head sadly.

"You don't know us!" Eden yelled. "You don't know what we can do!" When she felt his head press against her legs, she knew she'd scared him, so she dropped the volume of her voice. "We heal fast. He'll be fine."

"How fast?" She raised her eyebrows in doubt, but her tone was kind.

Not fast enough. Not with the amount of blood there was. And where he wasn't bleeding out, he was probably bleeding internally. "Then do something, Danielle! Don't just stand there. *Do* something." *Please.* Because Eden didn't know what to do.

Danielle knelt down next to him, ignoring the pool of blood under her knees, and started her assessment. She spoke to him, asked him to keep talking to her. He tried, Eden *knew* he tried, but his words were fragmented. Each breath was laborious, his face distorting in pain, even though his lungs couldn't possibly be filling. Not with air, at least.

"Hard...to breathe," he mumbled.

"You have some broken ribs," Danielle said. "One of them might have punct—" When Eden shook her head, Danielle stopped. He didn't need a damage report. "You're doing great. And...you'll be fine."

"It hurts, E. Hurts...everywhere."

"I know, honey." She took a deep breath so her voice wouldn't shake as badly as the rest of her was. "It'll be better soon. You're gonna be okay." She bit her lip to stop the whimper from coming out.

His eyes met hers upside down. "He said he would tell me"—a shuddered breath—"if it was me they"—and another—"used. I screwed up. Sssssorry."

"Oh, *please.* Don't give yourself so much credit. *I* was the one who screwed up." Why hadn't she sent him back to Florida as soon as she found him? Why didn't she kill Ryan before he had the chance to do this?

Mistake after mistake after mistake. And she'd left Justin behind to pay for all of them.

"He was so strong, E."

"I know. It's not your fault, honey." She looked away quickly, not wanting her tears to fall on him, to be another weight on his broken body. *He'll heal. He has to.* She pushed a lock of hair off his forehead. "When you're better, I'll do your hair if you want. But you've seen how bad I am at cutting, so we'll leave that to the professionals. What color do you want?" She waited, not looking down because she was afraid to.

The silence bit into her, ripping into her skin, muscle, bone. Through all of her armor. And it held on, its jaw unyielding, tearing her soul apart and leaving a scar she'd carry for the rest of her life.

It hurt. And she deserved it.

Eden caressed his head. Softer now, so she wouldn't hurt him.

Because he shouldn't hurt anymore.

He shouldn't...hurt.

CHAPTER XXXVII

Life isn't always pretty. Fights are *never* pretty. And death? Well, death is really fucking ugly. No matter how necessary, how deserved, how inescapable, it's motherfucking ugly.

But at least it hadn't been either of *them*. Once the guns were empty and the fighting got more intimate, Mitch and Landon had barely been touched—knocked around a bit but nothing too dramatic. And then...

Shit, and then...

What the fuck just happened?

Two against seven. And only two were still vertical.

Like always, Mitch and Landon made a good team—counting bullets that were aimed at them and men who were doing the aiming, taking turns covering each other so they wouldn't waste ammo, and keeping their enemies engaged until the fight became hand to hand.

And oh, what a hand to hand it was.

Mitch wondered if the guilt would set in later, once the adrenaline died down. Or if carnage was just something cops got used to—seeing it as much as they did. Was causing it any different?

"You kill a lot of people when you were a cop?"

"A few." Landon's voice was steady, controlled. Even

more than normal. 'Compartmentalizing' is what a shrink would call it. During a long bout of psychotherapy for dealing with multiple totally deserved homicides.

"This many?" Mitch asked.

His nod was slow. "But not all at once."

In the time it had taken Mitch to down one of them, Landon had taken out the rest. Like a dance, a rhythm unlike anything Mitch had ever seen, the cop had pulled them down one after another after another. No gun, no mercy, no pause, not even to breathe. The stoic look on his face never changed as he did what he had to for survival.

The guy had skills, but this was something else, something foreign. Abnormal. A gift from the drug he'd injected earlier—had to be. At least there'd been one benefit to it— Landon had gotten them through a situation they never should've made it out of.

Human trials. Great idea. But was it worth whatever had changed inside the cop?

"Newman was the guy who tried to shoot me in Florida. And who nabbed Danielle and me in the lab." Landon was staring at the last man he'd taken out. The one he'd spent the most time fighting. The one who, when Landon asked, "Did you kill Tara Somers in Atlanta?" answered, "Was that her name?"

The one who'd been smiling all the way up until Landon snapped his neck.

"I thought he'd be harder to put down," Landon said. "But he wasn't."

"Yeah," Mitch said slowly, starting to seriously worry about his friend's mental health. "We should get out of here."

They needed to make sure the women were safe and to get Landon to the hospital so the stupidity of pumping poison into his veins wasn't wasted. But neither of them moved, as if their minds were too busy processing what was in front of them to send a message to their leg muscles.

Wonder how long it will take? Maybe he should say

something to get their brains functioning again.

"Now that we finally have a moment together, cop, let me run something by you."

"Not another fucking joke. Please, Turner, it's like torture."

"If it weren't for my bad jokes, you'd have given up on me long ago." Neither one of them moved. "But that's not what I'm talking about. Whittley says that a smaller dose of the stuff that brought me back will keep Hyde down permanently."

"Sounds great," he said. "Where are the strings attached?"

"No strings but a few fatal flaws potentially. First I have to figure out if Whittley even knows *how* to tell the truth. Then I find out what dosage to use. And, even if I get past those two hurdles, it might not work for me at all. But it was the other shit he mentioned that really bothers me."

Now more than ever. Because of what had just happened—seeing Landon access something unnatural, evil maybe, but also being able to control it. If he hadn't, Mitch would probably be lying on the ground with the dead guys. *Maybe over*—his eyes darted across the room to an empty spot of floor space—*there.*

"You gonna tell me before I die of old age or what?"

"Whittley said I'm looking at it wrong—this thing between me and Hyde. That I have to accept him—the good, the bad, and the oh so very ugly, or I'll never be in control."

"Kind of like what Eden did with Chastity?"

"Yeah, I guess." Although not even Eden knew how it had happened. "But Chastity wasn't half the pain in the ass Hyde is. So…"

Landon looked at him long and hard. "For an occasionally intelligent guy, you're really stupid. Hyde has more control than you do right now, and there's a big possibility that you're gonna die any second. So why don't you try everything you can before that happens?"

Good question. The idea that Hyde was really part of him

had always given Mitch headaches and heart palpitations, so he'd stopped thinking about it. Looking at Hyde as a separate entity kept him sane, helped him deal…planted him in a perpetual state of fear. "Shit. Like you said, I'm stupid."

"Maybe you should become a Buddhist and meditate on it."

"I tried meditation. All that happened was I got pissed off and my ass went to sleep."

Landon shrugged heavily, as if everything was finally settling onto his shoulders. "Maybe what you need to accept is your inner ass."

"I'm pretty sure I already do."

"Yeah, me too," he said, his eyes never leaving the bodies. "Turner? *This*…what I did…it was *just*, wasn't it? A fair fight? It was so…easy. I keep thinking that it shouldn't have been so easy."

Mitch understood—it wasn't the physical ease of killing so many men that bothered the guy, it was the lack of conscience while he did it. Cops worked on instinct, especially in high-stress situations, but they still *felt*. They still *thought*. Landon was slowly realizing what being Abnormal was like.

"It was either us or them, cop. And you were on the right side. No doubt at all."

Surrounded by the enemy, even though they were all dead, didn't make Mitch feel all that much better. But seeing his only friend fall to his knees made him feel a whole lot worse.

"Damn it, cop!" He grabbed what he could, but Landon was going down. And all Mitch could do was make sure he went down slowly. The asshole couldn't live through *that* and then die by cracking his head open on the concrete.

"Why the hell did you let me chat if you have a hole in you somewhere?" He frisked him, pulling his hands away every few seconds to look for blood. "Where'd you get hit?" He didn't find more than a few scrapes and a busted lip. "Tell me what's going on, asshole!"

"I'm not feeling very well." His face was blank, his lips pale.

"It's that goddamn drug." Had to be.

"Get me to a hospital. They need to take my blood. Make sure they take lots of it."

"Fucking humans think they're immortal," Mitch muttered, hauling him up with both arms. Then he slipped his arm around the cop's waist and followed the signs towards the nearest exit.

When he felt his ass vibrate, he adjusted his hold on Landon and took out his phone. "Eden texted: '*At warehouse. Hurry.*'" Great news. As long as he didn't think about what she might do to Whittley. But between Danielle and the kid, hopefully they'd be able to keep her from gutting him.

Mitch typed one handed. '*No new holes. Don't kill anyone. B there soon.*' Before he went through the same door he'd shoved Eden out of, he shifted to take more of Landon's weight. He knew the cop was trying to hold himself up, but that meant expending energy he didn't have. The guy was in the red, gas tank below empty, cupboards bare.

"How you feeling, asshole?"

"Like Carter probably did. Right before he—"

"No way, cop. That's not going to happen. You're stronger, more stubborn, and an even bigger pain in the ass than Carter was. Plus, I need you around—you're the only one who laughs at my jokes."

"I never laugh at your jokes. And I'm not sure you get a say."

"Of course I get a say. And I'm saying—if you die, I'll beat the shit out of you so badly, you'll come back to life."

When Landon's laugh turned into a hacking cough, Mitch regretted opening his mouth. He dragged the best asshole he'd ever known outside, taking more and more of his weight with each step. When they neared a streetlamp, Landon winced, closing his eyes against the light.

"See?" Mitch said. "If you can't handle *this* light, you

won't be able to handle the white one, so don't go looking for it."

"I can't do this, Mitch."

Hearing his name—the one he thought of himself as, the one Eden called him—brought a certain tragedy with it. Because the only times Landon used it were when he really needed to get through...or when he thought someone was about to die.

"Keep your idiotic thoughts to yourself," Mitch snapped. "I'm trying to focus here."

Landon's feet dragged, slowing them down even more. "Mitch. I. Can't. Do. This."

"Then be glad I can." They both grunted as Mitch almost picked Landon up. He was strong, but Landon was, too. And muscle weighs a lot. "You couldn't have worked out a little less?"

"Say something nice," Landon said softly. "Hopeful."

"I don't do hopeful very well, you know that." But he'd try—if Landon was listening then he wouldn't be dying. "About that pony you want..."

"What about it?" His voice was so damn weak.

"Shut up. I'm thinking out loud." Mitch didn't want him to waste his strength shooting the shit. "I decided the pony was a bad idea. 'Cause you weigh a fucking ton and you'd *crush* a pony. So then I thought about one of those big motherfuckers—the ones that pull the Budweiser trucks. I figured I'd get one for you and one for me. And we could ride around in circles getting wasted."

"They don't come with the beer, asshole."

"I told you to shut up," he snapped, frustration weighing him down more and more. "But then I remembered that you stopped drinking. Which I think is great and I totally support." He saw a busy road up ahead. Hopefully he could find a cab or hitch a ride from the kind of considerate stranger who didn't really exist anymore.

"So," he continued, "as a symbol of you being on the

wagon, I thought I'd buy just one of those horses and get you an actual wagon. One that was strong enough to hold the five hundred pounds you weigh. What do you think?"

Landon didn't answer.

So Mitch freaked the fuck out.

"Cop?" He felt his legs go weak under him, but he couldn't let that happen. He couldn't let them both fall. Not after everything they'd been through together. "Landon, answer me!" The volume of his voice got louder and louder with every word, every syllable, until he was screaming. "Answer, cop!"

"You told me...to shut up."

Mitch sighed, swallowing his fear so he could keep moving. So he wouldn't take too long. So he wouldn't fail his friend. "Don't talk. But don't *not* answer when I ask you a goddamn question, asshole. You nearly gave me a heart attack. Got it?"

After a short pause, a crooked smile appeared on his face, a mixture of pain, uncertainty, and camaraderie. "Got it."

"Goddamn humans."

When they finally got to the street, Mitch waved at a car for help. Unfortunately, two big, scary-looking guys with their arms wrapped around each other wasn't the kind of thing a lot of people pull over for.

"This isn't working. I'm going to put you down, okay?" After Landon nodded painfully, Mitch eased him onto the narrow patch of grass next to the street. "I swear to God, Landon, you better not fucking die."

"I'll try my best."

Mitch didn't say anything as he turned away. *Idiot. It might be the last time you say anything to the guy and you end with 'you better not fucking die'?* So he turned back around, fearing it was already too late. But Landon's eyes were open.

With no time to spare, he crossed the distance between them and leaned down until he was in Landon's face. "Listen, cop. You tell anyone I said this and I will murder you myself."

He opened his mouth to say it, but before he did, Landon spoke.

"I do too."

"Cool." Mitch stepped back and blew out a breath, thankful for the out. And thankful that the guy already knew how he felt, whether he said the famous words or not. "But I was just gonna tell you that if I wasn't already locked up tight with Eden, I think you and I could've had a chance. You know, if I swung that way."

Landon smiled—an honest, shocked and amused smile. "That's another reason to appreciate her—my rejection speech would've really hurt your feelings."

"As if you'd reject me," he muttered. *Shit*. Another great thing to say. *Try, try again. And do a better job this time, idiot.* "I like having you around, cop, so don't fuck this up." After *that* colossal fail, he gave up and ran away like a little girl. But at least it was towards the street where he could flag down a ride.

He tried his best to look docile, kind, and trustworthy. But he was probably doing a shit-poor job of it—some things can't be learned. Ever. Just when he'd come up with some really terrible ideas for Plan B, a gold convertible pulled over.

The woman was all Dallas—the 1980s version—lots of hair, deep tan, and *big* sparkles on her ears, neck, and wrists. When she bit her lip, Mitch hid his scowl, recognizing a predatory look when he saw one. Her gaze ran from his face to his chest to his package. He waited for her to make eye contact again. It took a minute.

"What are you doing way out here, handsome?"

He smiled, playing a game he had no interest in. "You know you shouldn't pull over for strangers, right?"

"I can take care of myself."

"I'm sure you can." He let his eyes linger where they were expected to linger, not really seeing anything at all. And he avoided looking at the ring on her finger that she was trying to hide. Did she really think a stranger she picked up on the side of the road and seduced would give a shit about her vows?

"I'm Mitchell."

"I'm Jessica."

"Great. Now that we know each other so well, Jessica, is there any chance you can help a friend out?"

"A friend?"

"For now." He smirked, hoping it was an I'm-going-to-make-you-come-three-times-before-we-even-get-to-the-hotel-room look, rather than a the-only-thing-I'm-going-to-use-you-for-is-your-car look.

And it seemed to work because her mouth opened slightly, the tip of her tongue darted out, and she squirmed in her seat. "What would my *friend* like me to help with?"

"Somebody hit my car and then ran."

Huh. She even looked like she gave a shit. "Oh, that's awful. Are you alright?"

"I'm fine, and it was probably healthier for him to run away. But here's the thing, my buddy got a little banged up and I need to get him to the hospital." He saw her face sour at the idea. "Then, after we drop him off, maybe I can thank you properly. Wait. Did I say I would *thank* you?" He leaned down and held her eyes. "I meant I would *fuck* you. Properly."

Her smile came with another visual tour of his body. The woman should really be more cautious—he was a stranger and could be completely lying to her. In fact, he *was* completely lying to her.

She did a weird, girlie head wiggle before sighing. "He's not bleeding, is he?"

"No. He's just bruised." Before she changed her mind, he ran to Landon. "You still breathing, man?"

"My eyes are open, jackass."

Mitch hefted him up and started walking towards the car. "I know, but you always have a glossy, out-of-it look, so I was just making sure. By the way, you got banged up in a hit and run."

Landon looked confused until he saw Jessica and her car.

"And any physical activity I may have promised the woman taking us does not need to be mentioned to Eden. Got it?"

"That depends on if you're going to keep that promise or not."

He laughed. "And miss a chance to see a doctor probe you? Hell no! That's a 'must see.'"

"Your sense of humor is what's going to end up killing me, you know that?"

Jessica's eyes widened when she saw them.

"Try to look well behaved," Mitch said, following his own order. When they got close enough and she still hadn't pulled away, he winked at her and said, "I will never be able to *thank* you enough, Jessica. This is…" Did the cop even have a first name? "Landon."

He helped the cop climb into the backseat. "Put your buckle on, Landon. No repeats of what happened earlier." He rolled his eyes dramatically before swinging into the car.

He chatted about stupid-ass things all the way to the hospital, looking in the side mirror incessantly, and ignoring the hand on his inner thigh. There was a possibility that Mitch was in as much pain as Landon was. Biting back every comment he wanted to make was taking a toll on his mental state and made his Hyde flashbacks more palatable.

As they pulled into the ER loading area, he slammed his hand down on the car's horn and pried Jessica's hand off his leg. An orderly came over to help Mitch get the cop out of the car and into the wheelchair.

"I'm okay, Turner. Stop freaking out."

"You've seen me freak out. I get big and occasionally try to kill people. This is *not* freaking out."

Landon motioned towards Jessica, and whispered, "Get rid of her nicely or I'm telling Eden."

"That's what I get for saving your life?"

"You are most of the reason my life was in danger to begin with, so shut the hell up."

"I love it when you bitch at me, asshole. Make sure you stick around to do more of it."

"Don't make her wait around for hours, man. Nice and easy. Tell her you have a rash or something." Though hoarse and sickly sounding, Landon's laugh made Mitch reconsider bringing him here.

"I wonder if you'll be smiling when I tell the doc that he really needs to make sure that dildo isn't still stuck in your ass." He shook his head and grimaced. "I'm telling you, man, you gotta be careful with those things. The wrong kind can go places where nothing should ever go."

The laugh fizzled out rapidly. "You wouldn't."

"He's ready to go now," Mitch told the orderly.

"Turner?" Landon called. "Don't you dare, Turner. Seriously."

"I'll catch up." Mitch didn't want to leave the cop's side until he knew everything was going to be okay, but he felt somewhat bad for using the woman. Shit, where the fuck did he get a conscience? And what was the return policy?

"Hey." He leaned down, resting his forearms on her door. "You did a nice thing by helping me, and I'm sure you're a great person. But, you see, *I'm* not. In fact, I'm a *terrible* person. You invited a terrible person, not only into your life, but into your pants. Picking up strange men on the side of the road isn't 'safe sex,' Jessica—even if the guy looks harmless, which we both know is *not* how I look.

"So go home, kiss your husband, and think about why you're doing it. If you hate him, get a divorce. If you hate yourself, get some therapy. But self-destructive behavior is called that for a reason." He took a breath. *That wasn't so bad.* Maybe he'd turned over a new leaf and was a nicer person. Helpful, even.

Jessica threw the car into drive, called him a few derogatory names, and peeled out, giving him just enough time to avoid her tires.

He waved goodbye. "Yep. I think that went really well."

CHAPTER XXXVIII

Eden had no sense of time as she stayed with Justin, his head still in her lap. Seconds, maybe hours, passed with no movement other than the thoughts and guilt bouncing around her brain. Danielle had left to go somewhere to do something. The air in the warehouse was stifling, thick with the scent of blood and death and regret, so maybe she had gone somewhere she could breathe.

"I'm so sorry, hon," Eden said softly. If she hadn't brought Ryan here…if she hadn't convinced Landon to let Justin stay...

Risking her own life was one thing, but she'd risked other people's, too. She wished everything would stop so she could go back in time and make better choices. But that's not how life works. A person's life is a journey directed by each decision they make.

Eden had made all the wrong ones. She'd put herself here. *Her*, not anyone else. She'd turned into someone just as evil as the man who did this. The entire time she was hurting Ryan, she kept telling herself that he would've done the same thing or worse. And it was true—the boy she couldn't let go of was proof of that.

But she didn't want to be anything like Ryan, to be able to kill so easily, so selfishly. She'd conned herself into believing she was doing this for Mitch and Justin and every other Abnormal. She wasn't. She was doing this because she was hurt and afraid, and anger was easier to deal with. Violence gave her a sense of power. Fear just made her feel weak.

After one last quiet apology, she slid her legs out from under Justin's head, set him gently on the ground, and went into the office area.

"I'm really sorry, Eden," Danielle said as she stood.

"This was my fault—payback for all the wrong I've done. So, thanks, but *I'm* the one who's sorry. Sorry for him and sorry..." She turned and looked Danielle in the eyes, tears overwhelming her own. "I'm sorry for hurting you. I know it doesn't make up for it—and *please* let me know if there's a way that I can—but I'm really, really sorry."

"It's okay."

"No it isn't." And then she saw the empty table—all the bottles, vials, and syringes were gone. "Ryan took it all." Including the J-0026—the drug that might keep Mitch alive. No, better than alive. It might make it so that he never transformed again. She needed to get that drug back.

Right after she said goodbye. She grabbed one of the sleeping bags and went back to Justin. Eden didn't want to be part of this anymore, this thing that haunted and controlled her. Revenge, hate, rage. This wasn't the life she wanted—to cause the death of someone who trusted her, loved her, and had so much left to experience—or who she wanted to be.

She and Ryan were both responsible, and both of them had a lesson to learn. But Justin's death would be the last. She'd fight to make sure Mitch and the others were safe and healthy, but she refused to be the cause of any more destruction—hers or anyone else's.

After covering Justin's body with the sleeping bag, she knelt down beside him. She should say something. But it was too late—what good were words when he wasn't around to hear them?

Danielle stood a few feet back. "You didn't force Ryan to do anything, Eden. No mistake in the world would make what he did right. If you want to blame someone, then blame everyone Ryan has ever met. Didn't we all have a hand in shaping him into who he is, into a man who could do this?"

"No one made him do this. This is on *him*."

"Exactly."

Touché. Eden looked at Danielle, seeing her as a person, not an enemy or a problem or a regret. "But Ryan is a Hyde."

"He always looked human to me." Danielle didn't seem shocked, or maybe she'd been shocked ever since Eden met her. "So his Hyde determines who he is while he's a man, as well?"

"No." She thought about Mitch, the years he had spent believing he had no good inside of him. Even then, he did everything he could to keep people safe. To keep *her* safe...and to love her.

The Clinic thought the Abnormal side determined who they were and what they did. *The Clinic is wrong.* Eden would decide—*all* of her, not just one part. She'd make better choices, be a better person. It was possible. She'd come so far, all she needed to do was switch directions. No more lines crossed, no more destruction, no more violence built on fear. Because she wasn't afraid anymore.

"You're a good person, aren't you?" she asked.

Danielle shrugged. "I try to be."

"That's why you *are*."

"Tha—"

Eden shushed her and craned her neck to listen. Someone was moving outside and, with the day she was having, it probably wasn't a UPS guy.

She couldn't silently sneak out of a squeaky metal door, so she did the next best thing. She listened until she knew exactly where the intruder was, took a deep breath, and yanked the door up just enough to stop, drop, and roll out.

After knocking his legs out from under him, she flipped over so her knee was on his chest and her hand was around his neck.

"Unless we're rationing air here, could I get a little more?"

Eden fell on top of him, holding him, kissing him, feeling his body for injuries and bullet holes. "Are you okay?"

Mitch rolled her onto her back. "Calm down, babe. I'm fine."

"It's been...an awful day." Pinned to the ground and helpless, and so incredibly relieved.

"I'm of the same opinion. But can we talk about it inside? Over a cup of tea...or maybe something I actually *like* to drink?" He sighed, leaning down until his lips brushed hers. "I'm also okay with staying here for a little while. It's nice here. Comfortable." The need in his voice was for comfort and companionship, not sex. The same thing she needed.

Then she realized that he was alone. *Oh no. Not Landon too.* "Where's Landon? Did he—?"

"He's okay. Well, he's not *okay*-okay. But he's still breathing and still being a pain in the ass. I wanted the hospital to sedate him so *both* of us would feel better, but he wouldn't let them. I was hoping Danielle would go over there and make sure they do whatever blood tests we need while we figure the rest of this shit out."

"How'd you get out of the Shop?" She wanted to be mad at him, scream and curse, but she couldn't. *Not now.* Not after Justin. She just didn't have the energy to fight anymore. "What happened?"

"*Landon* happened. That guy's a hell of a fighter now. Saved my ass. I'm not going to pull him off the wagon, so I need to think of something to owe him. How's Danielle?"

"She's...fine." But Justin wasn't.

He pushed off the ground, lifting her up and brushing her off before doing the same to himself. It took 1.4 seconds for Mitch's expression to go from *so*-glad-to-see-you-again to what-the-fuck-did-you-do. He grabbed her by the shoulders,

pushing her away and looking at her body. "Oh no, babe. No."
Even in the darkness, he could probably see the blood. "You
were just supposed to bring her here and wait for us."

"Ryan's gone. Just—" She couldn't even say his name
because she'd failed him so miserably. "Just gone. Danielle's
inside."

He sighed, his shoulders dropping. "Okay, Ryan's
gone…okay. Just tell me you didn't do anything to Danielle."
His fingers dug into her skin, his voice desperate. "She's one
of us."

She shook her head. "There are only three of us. But I…"

"Fuck, Eden. What did you do?" Without waiting for her
answer, he yanked the loading door up and ran inside, calling
Danielle's name. Eden didn't blame him for thinking that
she'd killed Ryan, maybe Danielle too. Until a little while ago,
she probably could have.

"I'm over here," Danielle called. Somewhere behind her,
still shrouded in darkness, was Justin's body.

"Are you alright?" he asked, moving towards her, turning
her head until her face caught the light.

"It's okay," Danielle said. "What she did to me. It's okay."

Mitch didn't let go of her. "It's *not* okay."

"I'm fine. But I'm not sure *she* is. Not after Justin—"

He jerked. "Where *is* Justin?"

Eden couldn't breathe, let alone speak, with them staring
at her like that.

"Where is the kid?" Mitch asked again, with even less
patience.

"Over there," Danielle mumbled.

Every step Mitch took was heavy, lethargic. Eden
understood because she'd felt the same way. The sense of
foreboding. Your mind frantically trying to find a reason
powerful enough to overwhelm the knowledge you feel in
your chest. Anything to turn something real but unimaginable
back into something you *couldn't* imagine.

Mitch stopped. The stillness was universal—not even the

crickets outside dared to move. Then he bent down and pulled back the sleeping bag. It was all she'd had to give him, and it was inadequate. Mitch mumbled something incoherent, something only for Justin, and then covered him back up.

"Whittley did this?" His question rang out, bouncing off the cement walls, the steel beams of the ceiling, shaking the air around all of them. Like a battle cry. His strides were long and determined as he came to her, his face filled with more rage than she'd ever seen in him.

"I can't look at you right now."

"Okay," she whispered, her head low, her eyes stinging with tears again. She couldn't blame him for this either. It was her fault and—

"Jesus, babe, you're covered in it. I can't think while his blood is all over you. Go change your clothes." Justin's blood. He was upset about the blood, not about her.

She ran, relieved but still trembling from the adrenaline of the last... Wow, how long had it been?

Mitch followed her into the office and changed his shirt while she ripped all of her clothes off and slipped into jeans and a tank top.

"We do this together because I'm never letting you out of my sight again." He spun her toward the door, his fingers digging into her biceps. "But I swear to you, Eden, if you die, I'll make sure a huge chunk of the world dies with you. So don't let that fucking happen."

His free hand lashed out to grab the edge of the door like an anchor, his body pressing forward with anger-infused momentum.

"Danielle," he yelled before blowing out a breath and relaxing the grip he had on Eden's arm. "I would greatly appreciate it if you could go be with Landon." Every word was controlled, monotone, as if it was the only way he could get it out. "He's at Baylor Medical Center. Please make sure he doesn't die and that they test for whatever shit he injected himself with." He swallowed. "Justin had a phone. If it's on him, then I'm sorry, but you need to get it. Use it to call a cab and then call me with updates. *Lots* of updates."

"If you're going to Malvers," Danielle handed him a lanyard with a card hanging from it, "This will get you into the building and all the labs, but it won't work on any of the offices."

"Thank you." He took a deep breath. "If you don't hear from us in a few hours, tell Landon he's an asshole. A well-loved asshole."

Mitch took Eden's hand, kissed her palm gently, and said, "Your chariot awaits, my love." Her heart broke a little more when he smiled. So beautiful. "And by 'chariot,' I mean some guy's Mercedes I car-napped from the valet line. He's probably already reported it stolen, so we might need to switch it out. But from now on, I'm sticking to things and people I trust, so we're not taking the POS." He tilted his head, slipped his hand into his pocket, and pulled the car keys out. "You are pretty damn amazing."

"A girl's gotta be prepared for anything."

"Hopefully for some good things soon, too."

As they drove, Eden felt his anger slowly overtake the calm he'd had just a moment ago. It had been the eye of the storm, and now he was heading back in. About halfway there, he slammed his fist onto the dash so hard, she heard it crack.

"He doesn't die. Got it? He *feels*. He feels every evil he's ever done come back on him. Until he has no choice but to understand what he is."

CHAPTER XXXIX

Ryan used the office building's side entrance and kept his back to the camera so the security guard wouldn't see his injuries and the incredible amount of blood covering him.

Because that kid sure knew how to bleed.

The entire trip here—on foot and then in some woman's car—all he could think about was getting to his serum. That's it. Everything else could wait until he had that shit in his hand. Even though he couldn't inject himself for another hour yet, having it near him would make him feel safe.

As soon as he got to his office, he booted up his computer and accessed the building's security cameras. If Turner didn't die at the Shop, he'd be coming here. So Ryan didn't plan on staying long—just enough time to grab the serum and clean himself up a little.

It had been a huge risk telling them where the Shop was. Maybe it was even a mistake. If they somehow overpowered Newman and his men and found out what was in the basement...

"Damn it!" Ryan had handled himself beautifully the whole time Eden was beating him. But he'd lost control with Turner. That prick had figured out something Ryan had kept hidden for years. From everyone.

And threatening to force Ryan to transform… For that alone he deserved to die. If Newman hadn't already taken the bastard out, Ryan would. Happily. And that went for Eden, too. But before she died, Ryan would show her how right she was about him. Because, to find out how she'd integrated her sides, he would do ten times the damage she'd done to him.

Control yourself and you can control others. It wasn't working—he'd never felt more out of control.

Newman didn't answer his phone. After the third try, Ryan's arm twitched with the desire to throw the phone at the wall. Two possibilities—Newman couldn't pick up because he was too busy doing what he was supposed to do. Or…Ryan's problems were only getting bigger, and it was time to switch into damage-control mode.

Control yourself first. He took his remaining supply of the serum and a pack of syringes out of his safe. Two vials, one of which was practically empty. The shelf life on this shit wasn't great. He wouldn't stake his life on the dregs at the bottom, not with the way he was feeling today, so he put the almost-empty one back. There was one more vial at the Shop. Two vials would last for months, but he still felt naked without a guaranteed source of more.

Sinclair better be all she's cracked up to be. She would make a gallon of the stuff for him, even if he had to keep her chained up for the next fifty years.

Next, he called the basement's emergency number.

One of the zookeepers answered. "Mr. Whittley?"

"Yeah. Tell me what's going on."

"I've been trying to call you, sir."

"Presumably so you could tell me what's going on. So do it."

"Something happened upstairs. It sounded like lots of shooting, but I'm the only one here, so…should I go upstairs to check?"

"No, lock the basement down completely." With the phone

in the crook of his neck, he filled a syringe on the way to his private bathroom and then set it and the vial down on the counter. "I'll be there as soon as I can. Don't open the door for anyone."

"Yes, sir."

"How are the animals?"

"They got really riled up when the shooting started, but they're calming down now."

"Don't sedate them yet, but make sure the darts are ready." He hung up. After tossing his bloody shirt on the floor, he accessed the damage in the mirror.

Shit. He'd heal but not fast enough. Not with the meeting with the Board members scheduled for tomorrow. How was he going to explain his face? Mugging? Bar fight?

Bitch who needed to learn her place?

She'd really worked her magic on him. The pain was worth it, though. It had been fascinating to watch her struggle with herself, giving in to the darkness and then pulling herself back out of it. As much as he detested her, he had to admit that she was amazing. The only one who knew how to integrate her Abnormal side with her human side—something Ryan would be more than happy to kill for. He couldn't let her slip away.

Once he found the right people, he'd turn the Shop into a better version of the Florida facility. *Better* because he'd be there to monitor it. He was done trusting something so fucking important to idiots.

Sinclair would produce the serum he needed and then start working on something better. Something so that he would be more like the bitch who'd been so precious to Ian. Beyond everything and everyone else. Something so that Ryan would never be dependent on anything or anyone ever again. So that he didn't have to report to the Board because there wouldn't *be* a Board. It would be just him, a miracle the world would never see coming, and whoever would pay him what it was worth.

He was so close, his mouth was already watering.

You wanted soldiers who never tired, barely ate, were always happy to kill and were fucking *good* at it? Sure, he could make them for you. Or maybe—small chance in hell of this actually happening—but maybe someone would want *peace*. To free the world from psychos and killers and rapists. Ryan could make that happen, too.

And everyone else could go screw themselves. Control— that's what he was offering and that's what he would receive. He'd been paying his dues to evil since he was fifteen—to his Hyde, to Ian, to the Board.

I fucking deserve this. And no bitch in the world was going to take it away from him.

He carefully slipped a clean shirt on and buttoned it up slowly, his fingers still sore and swollen from his time with Eden. After slipping the syringe into his pocket, he went to his wall safe, trading the vial and everything he'd taken from Eden's warehouse in for his gun.

Now to find out what the hell is happening at the Shop.

It was silent, deathly silent. The Shop's basement was well insulated, so if the Hydes were making any noise down there, Ryan wouldn't hear it. But he'd hoped that on the ground level there'd be some crying, at least. Turner whining to be let go, Eden whimpering. No, they'd probably be stoic, standing strong in their delusions of mortality. If they were still alive— which Eden had better be—he'd know soon enough.

As he walked down the hall, he noted the occasional bullet hole in the wall, crumbled drywall on the floor. But no blood. Was that a good sign or a bad one?

Bad one. The inner room that held the two cages and lab equipment was now a tomb. What a mess. There were bodies everywhere, and not a single one of them was someone he *wanted* dead. After kicking the dead idiot who was supposed to control this shit for him, he contemplated his next move.

It was late, and there was only one zookeeper on the overnight shift. He could help Ryan move the bodies and clean up the blood, but that wouldn't be enough. Not with

Turner, Eden, and now Landon out there somewhere.

They'd probably found that kid's body already. Great, yet another reason for them to come after him. And they knew where this place was.

"Fuck!" His voice echoed off the ceiling. It needed to be shut down. All of it.

Calm down. Control yourself. His movements were slow as he took Newman's cell phone out of the dead man's pocket and dialed Alex's number.

"You're needed," he said as soon as she answered. He listened to her grovel for a bit, tell him that Turner had found her but she hadn't told him anything. *Yeah, right.* Since she still didn't know what Ryan was, Turner must have figured that out on his own. But the man was persuasive. If he had gotten Ryan to talk, Alex hadn't stood a chance.

"You can shut up now, Alex. What you need to do is listen carefully to the instructions I am about to give you. Then you will follow those instructions to the letter. Do you understand?"

"Yes."

"Good. You will come meet me at the Shop." Since she'd never been here before, Ryan gave her the address and the key code to get inside the ground level. "We need to get the files together, get the Normals ready to go, and terminate the other projects that live here."

"What about the Board meeting tomorrow?"

He paused. He had no intention of meeting with them looking like a punching bag, and there was no way to lie his way out of all this. No fucking way. So he'd end the operation in Dallas and start again somewhere else. Maybe California. He was glad he hadn't let Newman kill Alex. He was going to need her.

"Ryan, are you still there?"

"Yeah," he said, snapping back into the game.

"What about the Board?" she asked. Not a single question about all the other things he'd said. Instead, she was just worried about the Board.

Clueless. "You worry about dismantling the facility. I'll take care of the Board."

CHAPTER XL

Mitch knew exactly where the bastard would go after leaving Justin in a puddle of blood. Whittley probably hadn't even washed his hands yet, only worrying about the serum that would save his own ass, at every other ass's expense.

His rage had settled a bit but not his anger. He forced himself to focus on his emotions without giving himself over to them. Hyde would gladly come out to help murder someone, and Mitch accepted that in a way he'd never been able to do before.

Admitting you have a problem is the first step to solving it or some shit like that. And to accept something truly evil in yourself, you first have to acknowledge that it's part of you. And like it or not—way closer to not—Hyde was a part of him.

He glanced at Eden to make sure she was alright. Not that he'd be able to see that, but it made him feel a bit better to know that she hadn't clawed through the seat or, possibly worse, stopped feeling anything. Even though he never wanted her to feel sad, he needed her to feel *something*. To not push down her emotions so well they couldn't come back up.

For a few minutes, neither of them spoke—too much to say to know where to begin. He owed her an apology for what happened back at Whittley's Shop. But since then something even worse had happened. Something that both of them felt to their cores. He'd barely known the kid, but...

'*I want to talk.*' Justin's one request for doing what Mitch had basically ordered him to do. The same thing that got him killed. As much as Mitch hadn't wanted to have that conversation an hour ago, he'd give his goddamn balls for the chance now.

Fucking kid. Fucking stupid-ass—No, it wasn't the kid's fault. It was *his*.

And Eden had known the kid, had felt something for him. So whatever Mitch was feeling right now was nothing in comparison to what she must be. So the little control she'd garnered since beating the shit out of Whittley was probably completely gone now. *Huge* do-si-do right back into hate and violence.

By killing Justin, Whittley had signed his own death warrant, put a seal on that fucker, and sent it out by FedEx. But Mitch was *not* shopping for caskets today—not for his allies and not for his enemies. It would take everything he had in him to stop her from doing to Whittley what Mitch had done to Hyde01.

Please let this end well. And soon. Neither of them could take much more.

"Where are we going, Mitch?" He was so deep in his own barely functioning brain, her voice made him flinch. She'd probably been wondering about it since they left, trusting his judgment. But his judgment was *seriously* flawed right now.

"I thought we were supposed to be a team," she said. "Teams share information. Like, why one member seems so confident about where the bad guy is while the other team member can think of a whole bunch of places to check."

"Whittley needs to shoot up soon. He's a workaholic and probably prefers to leave the work at work. Thinking of new ways to torture and manipulate people isn't conducive to a calm home environment. It fucks with the feng shui of the place."

"His office." She nodded and took a deep breath. "If that stuff works, I don't want to hear a single word about your pride. Or I'll start doping you secretly. Understood?"

"If it works, you can poke me as much as you want to while we're celebrating on an island somewhere. All I ask is that you kiss the injection site and put a Spider-Man Band-Aid on it."

"The Hulk hits a little too close to home, huh?"

"Funny girl. I look way better in green."

"Yeah, you do. Okay, now it's my turn."

"For...?"

"Danielle thinks the J-0026 is what changed me." She reminded him of the mega-dose Chastity had snorted. He thought it was strange that he'd forgotten—until he remembered what came after that. Four days of utter perfection. The moment his life had started being something other than total shit.

"That high a concentration should've killed me, *would've* killed me if I were totally human. Danielle's theory is that it integrated my sides instead." She paused. "So it's an option for you."

"Why don't we consider that option two, with option one being the dose Whittley's using." Because option two might be something that would kill everyone but her. "Plus, there is nothing fun or hot about shoving something up your nose." He grimaced. "Yeah, I'm not sure I could pull that off."

"If it would work, I'd shove it up your ass."

"Language, babe! Language," he said, laughing. "You're not shoving anything anywhere. Especially not there."

Mitch kept his hand on her until they reached the last bit of cover. From here to the building's front door was open space.

Eden peeked. "All clear." They already knew Newman had

taken out the guard, but there were worse things than security guards.

He took the 'Bring the Bastard Back' syringe out of his pocket. "I'm gonna hang onto this because it's all we have for now. But you should probably know which pocket it's in, just in case you need to stick me. If that happens—hopefully in a room with Whittley—run fast and lock the door behind you."

She fisted his shirt. "Don't you dare die." Damn, she was beautiful. And so strong. Yeah, she was pissed, but he'd take her any way he could.

He wrapped his arms around her waist and pulled her into him, resting his forehead on hers. "I love you, Eden Colfax. You *made* me love you. Thanks for not listening to me until I stopped being an idiot." Lifting her off her feet, he kissed her. As if it was their last, as if everything was about to end and they would never have another chance.

He lowered her slowly because she looked a bit wobbly. Maybe he'd squeezed her too tightly. "Shit, babe. I didn't mean to make you stop breathing."

"Every time you touch me, I stop breathing."

"Me too. So let's make sure we keep doing it. And that touching each other is the only reason either of us do." He took her hand and ran for The Clinic's front door. One swipe of Danielle's keycard and the door slid open. If getting out was as easy as getting in, Mitch might start believing good luck actually existed.

They didn't need to check the sign on the wall to know where Whittley's office would be. "Southwest corner, third floor." Big man on campus always got the top corner with the best view.

There was a big chance that Whittley had already limped here and limped away, but aside from Jessica, people didn't stop for strangers anymore, especially when they were covered in blood—theirs and a sixteen-year-old boy's. So it must have taken him awhile to bum a ride.

"What happened to Whittley's phone?" he asked as they

headed upstairs.

"I tossed the battery. He could've gotten another, though, stolen it or something. Do you think he called for backup?"

"I think all his backup is lying on the floor of his Shop. Or they'd already be trying to shoot us."

As soon as they got to the third floor, he stopped her. Even though he wanted Whittley to pay just as much as Eden did, he wouldn't let it happen at the expense of either of their humanities. He needed to subdue the bastard before she 'accidentally' fatally wounded him.

"I'd like you to wait outside," he said. "I don't think it will happen, but if he kicks my ass, you'll be there to stop him. But if you go in first, then the fight will be over before it begins and I won't ever get a chance to hit him. And I haven't gotten to do that yet. So…pretty please?"

It didn't take her long to see his point. And that was slightly depressing. "Two minutes. But leave him conscious."

"You had *hours*." He sighed and then smirked. "And you know I can last a lot longer than two minutes."

She gaped at him. "Your focus is exceptionally bad."

"You're exceptionally distracting."

They wound through the third floor hallway, always turning left. And what they found was really fucking disappointing: Whittley's name on the door of an empty office. While Mitch cursed, Eden used one of her safety pins to pick the lock, but all they found was his bloody shirt.

"The wall safe won't be easy to open," she said, studying it. "It'll take some time. Do you think whatever's in there is more important than finding him?"

"He would've taken his meds with him. And, other than a dirty magazine or two, I don't think he values anything else."

"Would he go home?"

Mitch shook his head. "I think he'd go check to see if we were hanging out with Landon and Danielle in those pretty cages. Plus, there was a mini lab set up at the Shop. If I was wrong and he didn't keep his stash here, it would be there.

You up for another car ride?" Preferably a quick one. It was nearing the four-hour mark since he'd been woken up from his big-boy nap.

CHAPTER XLI

When Ryan heard the short alarm bell, he tossed another handful of files into a large rolling bin and glanced at his watch. *Took her long enough.*

"Keep going," he told the zookeeper. "When we're done with the files, we'll move on to the Normals." He brushed his hands down his thighs and went upstairs to get Alex and bring her down to the basement.

He found her in the center room. And the bitch wasn't alone. Tasting blood as his teeth slammed together, Ryan forced his lips into a smile.

I guess that's what took her so long to get here.

"What the hell is going on, Whittley?" Dunlap stood with his hands on his hips, dead bodies in front of him and Board members behind him. Three other Board members—D'Apuzzo, someone who looked like he could be Dunlap's son, and Mary Taylor.

"Who are these people?" D'Apuzzo said, motioning to the bodies.

"What are you all doing here? Alex?" He knew exactly why she'd brought them—to cover her ass by fucking *his*. Smart actually. He probably would've done the same thing if their roles were reversed. But their roles *weren't* reversed, and Ryan didn't like getting fucked.

Alex kept her gaze averted, pretending she gave a shit about the dead bodies on the floor. Well, she should—hers was going to be there, too. As soon as Ryan could make it happen.

"It was an internal issue," he lied. "We all know how stupid people are. This had something to do with money, I believe. But, as you can see, the problem took care of itself."

D'Apuzzo looked at Ryan's face. "Were you involved?"

"No. Somebody jumped me in the parking garage at my office."

"I hope your cleanup crew is better than your security."

"It is." He couldn't even bring himself to nod. "Why are you all here?"

"While the four of us were having dinner, Alex called and told us there was something we should see." He raised an eyebrow. "It's a good thing we didn't come any earlier, or we might've been involved in the fight."

If only Ryan were that lucky. "Where is Phillips?"

"Heart attack," D'Apuzzo said. "It's not looking good for him."

"I'm sorry to hear that." Finally, there was something to smile about... inwardly. Phillips was the loudest and most demanding out of all of them.

"It shouldn't affect this project at all. My son, Gregory"— Dunlap nodded toward the younger man—"will take his place."

Ryan looked at Gregory, another man to lie to, another ass to kiss. He looked nervous, so maybe he'd be easier to handle. Until Ryan didn't need to handle any of them.

"Since we're here anyway and have things to discuss," Dunlap said, "why don't you give the others a tour of the basement?"

"Now's not a good time for me. Why don't we do it tomorrow?" *When I'm in another city.*

"My question was rhetorical." The severity of his voice cut through any residual hope that Ryan had.

So it came down to this—the best day of his life had turned into the worst. And now Eden's beating was one of the high points.

"Alright, but please excuse the mess. If I'd known you were coming I would've made them pick up their rooms." He was the only one laughing, and even he was faking it. "If you'll all follow me. Alex, you're coming too?"

She hesitated until he mouthed, '*It is what it is.*'

"Of course."

"Great." *Let's get this over with.* He felt the pockets of his coat. On the right, he felt his gun and on the left, the syringe. It was too early to inject himself. He'd do it after the tour was over and the Board was gone. As he led them down to the basement, he fantasized about the time when he wouldn't need these people's financing and would be free to wrap his hands around Dunlap's fat neck.

At the bottom of the stairway, he held the door for them. Dunlap took the lead, heading straight for the observation room. Ryan felt his pocket again, like a child holding onto his security blanket.

This was going to be excruciating.

The observation room was in the center of the building, directly underneath the room that was littered with bodies. Along one side of the room was a holding area, where a very long chain that had thick cuffs on both ends was threaded through numerous O-rings bolted into the wall. On the other side was a row of cabinets and a small fridge.

But the room's most prominent feature was an enormous glass room, completely closed in except for the top, which was open for ventilation and had I-beams running across it for additional stability. The glass was the kind they used for shark tanks, allowing for unobstructed viewing while able to withstand literally tons of pressure.

"When the Abnormals are brought into this room, they are

sedated."

"They're too hard to move if they aren't," Dunlap added. "They have a mini fork lift to haul them around."

"For security purposes," Ryan said, "they're never fully conscious and unbound outside of their cages." He picked up the chain. "In this area, we can hold them or give them additional pharmaceuticals—whatever is needed." He walked across the room to the fridge but didn't open it. These people didn't need to know how low on supplies they currently were. "We only keep a small stock of the drugs we're testing on hand."

"What is that for?" Gregory pointed at the cage.

Ryan's guilty pleasure. Something he wished no one knew about. But aside from needed help to bring in the Hydes, he'd also acquiesced to Dunlap and Phillips' nagging and shown them exactly what he used it for.

He chose his words carefully. "The Abnormals have all been medicated for different amounts of time—either in their human form or their Abnormal one. Therefore it's important to observe any changes as they present themselves."

"Cut the crap, Whittley," Dunlap said. "Tell them what it's really for."

"Yes, sir." He took a deep breath and let it out slowly but subtly. *Control yourself and you can control others.* "This is where we watch them fight." Tear each other apart, more accurately. Unstoppable until one or both were dead. Just how he imagined the fight between Turner and Ian went down.

Dunlap turned toward the group, Alex didn't lift her eyes off the floor, and the only one who had the decency to look afraid was Gregory. "We watch them fight, rip each other apart with their bare hands. Test the limits of their violence and hatred of each other. Some of them are stronger than others, more violent, but they don't know why yet."

But Dunlap wasn't done talking. "This is an instance of survival of the fittest. And we want to use the absolute fittest for the serum we use on the Normals." He looked at Ryan with all the excitement of a kid at a carnival. "Right?"

"Yes, sir." Ryan kept the disgust off his face. He had the right to explore the Hydes' capabilities, even to take pleasure from watching them kill each other. These people didn't.

They paid in cash, not in fear and pain and anger. Not like he had.

But it might be time for that to change.

After the group was done gawking at the glass cage and Dunlap promised them a fight later on, Ryan took them to see the contestants. The zookeeper stood wide eyed in the hallway until, with one look, Ryan told him to buzz off. He punched the code into the keypad and held the door open for them to pass.

As each entered the room, they gasped, mumbled, or cursed. The Hydes responded by growling and rattling the bars of their cages.

When Alex went through the door, Ryan grabbed her arm and whispered, "I understand why you felt the need to cover your ass, but you created more problems for both of us. We need to talk once the tour is over."

She swallowed but said nothing.

"I'm not angry, Alex." *I'm furious.* "But I'm going to need a sincere apology and your help when I ask for it. No questions asked."

She nodded. "I'm sorry. I didn't think you would get into any trouble that you couldn't handle."

"Well… you were right." He could handle anything.

"Can I have a second to regroup?" Her voice was annoyingly shaky. If she didn't pull her shit together soon, he'd do it for her.

"Bathroom's down there on your right." He didn't know if it was an excuse or not. He could force her to stay, but almost every door down here used a key code. And Alex didn't know the code. She took off as soon as he released her arm.

"And here they are," he said loudly, with his hands tucked in his pockets. "The space between the bars is sized so they can't get their arms through, but I wouldn't get too close, just in case. If they see an opportunity, they'll take it."

He hated being in this room. The Hydes, kept in a perpetual state of transformation, pulled his Hyde—their power feeding the strength of his. Especially right before he took the serum, right before his Hyde would come out if Ryan let it. So he stayed by the open door, breathing deeply. *Control yourself.* It was getting worse—the more things went wrong, the harder it was to control. And almost everything was going wrong.

Shaking himself off, he addressed the Board. "Now I imagine you're wondering about the muzzles. Understandable. And the reason is simple—when they speak, it isn't nice. It is the basest part of humanity, the lowest form. It's disturbing for their caretakers to listen to, so we muzzle them. It doesn't hurt them—it just keeps them quiet."

"Why are there so many empty cages?" someone asked.

"We've lost a few and haven't replaced them yet. And, unfortunately, we also learned a hard lesson on why it's so important to keep them separated. If they're next to each other, they'll fight until one of them gets a good grip on the other or they pick each other apart. It isn't pretty." And it was hell to clean up.

After a few more minutes of explanation, Ryan took the key to the cages off the wall.

One shot. Make it a good one. While all four Board members were busy antagonizing and laughing at the Hydes a bit farther down the line, Ryan got as close as he could manage and tossed the key into the closest cage.

As soon as he saw the beast palm it, he whispered, "Have fun," walked out of the room, and closed the door. He didn't need to manually lock it. Security protocol meant that a four-digit number code was needed to unlock the door from either side.

He leaned his forehead against the metal—a moment of silence to mourn the loss of so much of his time and energy. But he could take what he needed and start again somewhere else. With another Board.

A few seconds later he heard the first scream.

It melded into multiples, until it sounded almost like music. A four-part harmony of terror. Beautiful in its own way.

A moment after that, he felt the vibration of someone pounding on the door, rattling the knob, scratching to be free.

Aren't we all?

CHAPTER XLII

What seemed like a good omen made Eden shiver. One of the side doors was open. Just a crack, but enough for her to grasp with her fingertips. And that meant whatever was behind the door would be very, very bad.

She jumped to the side just in time to avoid getting smacked in the face as it flew open. A guy, no more than twenty-five years old, came barreling out right into Mitch's chest. He bounced back, stopping when Mitch grabbed him by the shirt and steadied him.

"I...Who...I..." He didn't look dangerous...

"Who are you?" Mitch asked.

...about to pee his pants, but not dangerous. "It's...I..."

Mitch looked at her. "Am I what makes everyone under twenty-three stutter?"

She shrugged. "You can be intimidating sometimes."

"Huh. I'll work on that as soon as it stops coming in handy." He turned his attention back to the guy. "What do you do here, and why are you leaving Roadrunner style?"

He squirmed and tugged against Mitch's grip. "I...I just watch the animals. That's all. I don't know *anything*."

The animals. "We were here earlier and we didn't see any

animals. Where are they?"

The guy stopped moving, his eyes wide, scared. But not of them. Or not *only* of them. He was afraid of whatever was happening inside.

"For once could someone just be a *little* cooperative?" Mitch looked up for a moment and then adjusted his grip to the guy's neck and marched him back inside the building. "Tell us what's going on or I'll park you right in front of whatever you were running from."

"Whittley. He's…" And then the words came pouring out of him. "He locked people in with the animals. They were screaming. Like, *dying* screams. They were dying. The other lady might still be alive, but I don't know."

"Where are they?"

"In the basement." He kept talking, still referring to the 'animals.' They were contained in one room, probably with a number of dead bodies by now. And then he said something else.

Something terrifying.

"What did you just say?"

"The Normals," he repeated. "They're all still locked in their rooms."

Normals. Not *Ab*normals. *Normals.* "They're regular people?"

"Not even close. But they're not like the animals."

Mitch took a deep, broken breath. "They were given a serum, right? Regular men who were given a serum." After the guy nodded, Mitch's eyes darkened and she got it.

Landon. "We can't deal with that yet," she told him. "Whittley first. Then we find these… Normals, talk to them, and figure out what to do. We need to help them, Mitch."

He ignored her, staring at the man in his hands, his grip tightening.

"Mitch, stop! Stop now!" She yanked the guy back and put herself between them. "Freaking out now will do nothing but cause more trouble. We can't help Landon if we don't even know what we're dealing with." When he still didn't respond, she shoved him back a step. There wasn't time for this. If he couldn't deal, then she would.

"Show me how to get downstairs," she said to the guy.

"No way."

"Look at my eyes." Her voice never raised or changed pitch, but he listened. "Have you seen that color before?"

He swallowed.

"And do you know what *he* is?" She flicked her head towards Mitch, who was seething so badly she could almost hear him crackle. "He's a functioning version of what you call the 'animals.' But he's not always *well* functioning. So show us the way downstairs before either of us gets grumpy."

She kept one hand on him and another on Mitch as the guy led them through the building. They stopped at the only door with a keypad and, as he typed the four-digit code in, Eden memorized it.

"Is it the same for the doors downstairs?"

"Most but not all. The ones to the fight cage and Whittley's office are different."

A tremor went through Mitch at the mention of a fight cage. Not good on many, many levels.

She tightened her grip on both men but spoke to the scared one. "You know the kind of people you work for. So I'd suggest you pack your bag, throw a dart at a map of the world, and head straight to wherever it lands without ever mentioning this to anyone."

"Nicely said, babe." Mitch kissed the top of her head. "And handled."

Before she knew what was happening, he reached around her, took the guy by the neck and slammed him into the wall. He crumbled onto the floor.

"No man left behind," Mitch grumbled. "Unless they're dead or unconscious." She almost wished she had a problem with that.

On the way down the stairs, they heard the echo of a

woman's voice. Whimpering. Crying. Then Ryan cursing. When the crying turned into the sound of running footsteps, Eden and Mitch picked up their pace, still not knowing what they were moving towards.

Mitch's strides were longer, so he got to the door first. "You've got to be kidding me. Did Des's hubby come home early?"

"What?" Eden ducked under his arm and then stopped. Ryan held Alex by the hair, her head tilted back painfully.

"Alex," Mitch said, "I thought I told you to stay home. In fact, I distinctly remember using enough duct tape to make sure you did." He shook his head in wonder. "I don't know why no one listens to me. I know shit." Something about his ill-timed humor gave Eden confidence. If he was being sarcastic, it meant he felt somewhat in control of the situation—*obnoxious* control, but still control.

They went in slowly, watching Ryan while giving themselves time to take in the room. There was an enormous glass room in the center, like a tank you would see dolphins in at an aquarium. Except this one was empty and there was a door with a key-coded lock on it. Along one side were a fridge and cabinets, and on the other was a lot of chain hanging from a cinder-block wall.

"And I thought *I* was screwed up," Mitch said under his breath. He understood something Eden didn't. Until he whispered an explanation. "The kid upstairs said there was a fight cage. Whittley must think them brutalizing each other is a spectator sport. Probably gets off on it."

Eden tasted bile. She knew Ryan experimented on Hydes, but she'd thought the torture was psychological or something that fit into a syringe. This was…

His own kind. People suffering from the same curse he did. He enjoyed watching something that would haunt her dreams for the rest of her life. The images of Mitch's Hyde tearing apart Hyde01 would never go away or diminish, and Ryan had a special viewing cage set up for fun.

How sick does a person have to be to do that?

Mitch's whistle yanked her back into the conversation. "Super kinky in here, Whittley. I had a feeling you'd be into feet or women's clothing, but *this*? Nah, *this* is impressive. But if we interrupted you two, we can wait in the hallway. He doesn't last more than a minute or two, does he, Alex?"

Ryan sighed disgustedly, his gaze moving from Eden to Alex to Mitch. "I wish I could've seen you and my father fight, Turner. My old man was a lot of things, but 'easy to deal with' wasn't one of them. How much damage did he do before you took him apart?" He wasn't talking about a guard, he was talking about...

"Hyde01 was your..." No, she *couldn't* have heard that correctly.

Mitch's hand slipped around her waist, jostling the safety pins, and pulled her back a step while he took one forward. "I just had the weirdest moment. I thought I heard you say that Hyde01, formerly known as Ian"—formerly Eden's dad— "was your father." His grip tightened protectively.

"You heard right." Ryan yanked on Alex's hair when her ineffectual squirming increased, her eyes red and terrified. "Fucking terrible one, frankly. Kind of like yours, Turner. But, *unlike* yours, Ian took his drugs...until somehow they stopped working." He looked at Eden and opened his eyes in feigned shock. "Oops."

The idea that she and this monster shared even one strand of DNA was impossible. *Impossible.*

"I'm sorry, babe," Mitch whispered. "So sorry." He held onto her, slowly easing her behind him as if she would break if he moved too quickly. But she wouldn't. Her body felt like it was being entombed by cement—hardening as odd things Ryan said pieced together.

"It's..." *Not okay.* Not by a long shot. But what could she do about her DNA? She had a brother. A psychotic, serial-murdering, patricidal brother whose life mission included drugging and caging his little sister. And while she would've preferred him taking that secret to his grave, he looked happy about it. As if his confession had taken the weight off his chest and slammed it into hers.

"We had different shitty moms but the same shitty father," Ryan said. "Be glad you didn't know him, sis."

"You must have had a tough childhood...*bro.*" Her voice was calm, icy, but inside she was burning. "I'm sorry he hated you." Her lip curled into a disgusted smirk. "About equal to how much he loved me, right? You said he did it for me—his life's work to find a cure. Not for himself, not for you. For *me.*"

"And what's not to love?" Mitch asked, shoving her farther behind him. "She's amazing."

"She probably got that from her trash heap of a mom."

"It's understandable that you're hurt." But there was no pity in Eden's tone. "He barely knew me, but he still cared more about me than he did you. You worked alongside him for, what, years? Knowing his reasons and knowing you weren't one of them."

Whatever Ryan was feeling stayed internal. She knew what he wanted from her, why he hadn't killed her years ago—she was pureblooded and female, and that made her useful. Singular. But all of that was nothing compared to how important she was to him now.

"And then you find out that dad was right—your little sister actually *is* better than you are. She did something that you couldn't. Something that *he* couldn't. Without drugs or transformations, she became a better version of herself."

Ryan's eyes ignited with rage as he chuckled. "I had time to rethink that while you were beating the shit out of me." Alex's whimpers increased, probably because his grip had tightened. "Would you actually consider that 'better'?"

"Enough, you two," Mitch said. "We didn't come here for therapy." They had come here to end this, however they had to. "If this is going to be two on two, I think you should explain that to your teammate."

"No need." Ignoring her cries, Ryan yanked Alex towards him and adjusted his grip.

Her neck gave way with a crack. The crying stopped but her expression never changed. Not even when he let go and her body slumped to the floor.

"Wow, what did she do to deserve that?" Mitch's laugh held absolutely no humor. "Oh right. But what did she do to you?"

"I'm assuming you didn't come here to chat or take a tour. So let's do this."

Ryan's calm made Eden even more uncomfortable. He'd already proven he was a better poker player than she was and that he knew how to stack a deck. With Alex dead, Ryan only had two opponents to consider, but both were equal to or stronger than him. So he knew something they didn't. Some trick up his sleeve or in his pocket.

As soon as she saw his hand move, she knew which it was.

"No!" She spun around Mitch and lunged, but Ryan was too far away.

It happened in slow motion, or as if there was a strobe light that only showed blinks of chaos. Ryan's hand coming out of his pocket. The glare of overhead lights on the metal. A loud pop. A flash of fire. Mitch crying out her name. The bullet slamming into her, its force disrupting her flight. Pain. *Oh god, the pain.*

Everything stopped by a tiny piece of lead. And then things started flowing again—time...sound...her blood.

⎯⎱⎰⎯⎱⎰⎯⎱⎰⎯

"Eden!" As soon as he realized what Whittley was doing, Mitch had moved. But it all happened too quickly. He'd only been a half second behind her, and that was a half second too late.

When Eden went down right in front of him, something broke. But he stayed absolutely still because nothing he could do would stop Whittley from putting a second bullet into her, somewhere more vital. So Mitch only *imagined* the pain he was going to cause the fucker.

Each quick exhalation came with a quiet whimper as she tried to gain control over the pain.

"Back off, Turner."

The hardest two steps he'd ever taken. Because they were away from her. "Eden?"

"I'm okay." She rolled onto her back, cursing when she saw the gun pointed at her face. "I'll be better when he's dead." Blood slowly seeped through the left shoulder of her shirt.

"If either of you move an inch, a millimeter," Whittley said, "the next one goes through her forehead."

"I'm going to kill you *twice*, asshole," Mitch growled.

"No. You're going to shut up. And she"—he kicked her right where the bullet had gone in—"is going to tell me how she integrated her sides."

"Is that all?" Mitch asked. "Shit, I'll tell you that."

"Don't," she warned, her gaze never leaving the gun.

"If you know, why haven't you done it?"

Mitch tried to appear relaxed. Because nobody thinks a relaxed person is actually planning out every possible way they can slaughter you. "I don't have what I need. *You* do."

"What do you mean?"

"Let her go and I'll tell you."

"No!" she cried. "I'm not leaving until you do."

"That's so grotesquely sweet." Whittley's gaze played Ping-Pong between the two of them.

And then Mitch saw something horrible. Shit-brown irises became a shit-brown-over-chlorinated-pool-blue swirl.

No fucking way. Mitch squeezed his eyes shut, opened them again, and blew out a breath of relief. Whittley's irises were shit brown again. *Hallelujah.* It must have been a trick of the light or a trick of Mitch's paranoia. Because even *this* asshole wasn't stupid enough to skip his meds.

"I only need one of you to tell me how to do it."

Mitch nodded. "That's one way of looking at it. But the *not*-incredibly-stupid way is that if you kill either one of us, you lose leverage over the other. Think, Whittley. What will get you what you want?" He paused. "Okay, let me tell you what I would do if I were you. Thank fuck I'm *not* you, because the only thing the world needs even less than you is two of you." He looked at Eden, worried that this might be the note things would end on.

Just get her out. Whatever you do, make sure she's out of it. Big breath and…"She's bleeding all over the floor, which is unsanitary, as well as being a major slip-and-fall hazard. So I would shove her out the door and then torture the asshole in front of me until he gave up what he knew."

"Mitch, no."

"I'm not letting her go." Damn his even moderate intelligence.

Better come up with something quick, asshole.

And then he did. And she was going to be so pissed.

"Fair enough. Then chain her up over there in those cuffs."

"What?" she screamed.

"Would you please stop interrupting, babe?" he snapped and then turned back to her brother. Her fucking *brother*. What the hell? Did she have any other family members Mitch could kill? Because he seemed to have a real knack for it. Something he would prove as soon as she was safe and he had his hands on Whittley.

"I'm assuming you have a key to the cuffs," Mitch said.

"Of course."

"And since she bites her nails, she won't be able to pick the lock with them." He looked at her pointedly and put his thumbs through his belt loops that *didn't* have the get-out-of-cuffs-free pins hers did. "It's a terrible habit, babe. Really." *Aaaaand* back to Whittley. "Then I'd play a little game." He nodded towards the glass box. "With my fists."

"Meaning?"

"We play for the key to her cuffs and the cure." Of course, it had nothing to do with either of those things. It had to do with getting her away from the gun and getting that asshole trapped in something until either Mitch or Eden beat him soundly. As long as the bastard got exactly what he deserved, it didn't matter who gave it to him.

Mitch yawned. "I name the drug but hold onto the dosage info until after I've killed you."

"I have the cure and you still expect me to put up the key?" He shook his head. "What are *you* anteing up?"

Mitch didn't want to ante up anything. Primarily because he didn't need the key. Eden would do her little trick and be out of those cuffs in a minute and a half. Whittley was unknowingly calling Mitch's bluff before the game even started.

He reached into the pockets of his jeans, felt around dramatically, and pulled out nothing. "I only brought my winning personality. Maybe I could come up with a joke or two."

"The RLS-7. *That's* your ante."

"No," Eden hissed.

"No worries, babe. I can take him." Not only was Mitch taller, bigger, and heavier than Whittley, he also had a visual reminder of what he was fighting for. Sure, she looked pissed, but if he *really* squinted his eyes, her expression looked a little like the one she made when she came. *You gonna ask her to moan occasionally, too, asshole?* That might actually help.

Whittley didn't look convinced.

"I don't get why you're still confused, Ry. Either you win and I die via seizure or I win and you have—what is it?— thirty-eight seconds to high-tail it out of there. And it will *still* be a win for you because you'll have my Hyde to entertain you through four inches of glass."

By Mitch's figuring, if this human episode was anything like the last, he had a bit more time. But honestly, his figuring had been proven totally fucking wrong for about the last…oh…fifteen years or so.

Mitch spread out his arms. "All of today's prizes will come into the cage with us. He who is still breathing takes all."

Without a word, Whittley hauled Eden off the ground and shoved the gun to her temple. He held her so tightly, she couldn't hurt him faster than he could curl his index finger. He pushed her toward the chaining station and ordered her to put the Hyde-sized cuffs around her ankles.

Attaching chains around your body holds its own kind of torture. The sound of metal coming together and the feel of cold enclosing your skin make every other sound and sensation disappear.

And from the look of satisfaction on Whittley's face, he knew it, too. Mitch should've killed him while he was still attached to the chair. Probably should've killed Alex, too.

Live and learn. Live and learn to kill your enemies at the first opportunity because they always come back for more. *Persistent little fuckers.*

The cuffs were so wide they covered a third of her calf. The chain clanked against the O-rings it was threaded through. Whittley yanked on one end, pulling one of Eden's legs out from under her. She fell to the ground, catching herself in a push-up position. Then her injured shoulder gave out, and she rolled onto her back, groaning.

Mitch was on his knees right in front of her when he saw the gun in his peripheral vision.

"Keep your hands off her."

Mitch held them up at three and nine, staring into her eyes, seeing anger and pain in them but not fear. "Great." The word barely made it through his clenched jaw.

Buddhists *lie*—deep breaths didn't cleanse, calm, or harmonize *shit*. Not like caressing this dickhead's face with a fist would.

She climbed to her feet slowly, glaring at both of them. Hopefully not for the same reasons.

"Quick kiss for luck—but not from you, Whittley—and

then we'll make this happen." He moved closer to her before the prick could refuse. "How's your shoulder?"

"It won't kill me. How's your idiotic brain?"

"It won't kill me." *Hopefully.* He leaned towards her, not to kiss—although he'd get to that in a second—but to whisper in her ear. She balked, so angry she didn't even want him to touch her.

"Knock it off, babe. This all rests on you slipping out of those cuffs, grabbing that gun, getting to the top of that cage, and shooting him." The walls were high but she'd figure out a way to get up there. She was resourceful like that.

"Oh. That's not as stupid as I thought it was."

"Gee, thank you so much. Now give me a goddamn kiss."

She did, and it was as far from damning as anything could be.

"Do I need to shoot someone to break you two up?"

She pulled back. "Don't let him kill you."

"Do you really think I'd give him that honor? If anyone's going to kill me, it'll be you." Because that bastard's face would *not* be the last thing Mitch saw. "I'll see you soon." *Uncuffed.*

CHAPTER XLIII

Mitch clapped his hands and rubbed them together. "Well, this is exciting and barbaric, isn't it? Oh, the gun stays out here and, since I'm guessing neither of us wants to go in first, we can hold hands."

"I can't wait to shut you up." Whittley flicked his head towards the refrigerator and row of cabinets along the opposite wall. "Which one are we playing for?"

Oh, right. The drug. He went to the fridge. "Shit! Don't your people know that whoever drinks the last beer restocks the fridge?" He saw it right away—J-0026—in a big bottle. But he took his time, saying anything insulting he could think of to stall. He straightened, holding the J-0026 and a bottle of something else.

Whittley put the gun down on a table near the door of the cage.

Mitch knew his strengths, as limited as they were. He could fight pretty well, especially against someone who spent most of his time ordering people to do things for him. But what Mitch truly excelled at was annoying the shit out of anyone with functioning ears. Fifteen years of perfecting his technique, figuring out which areas were the most sensitive and heading straight for them. And if that not-so-high road failed, he had no problem aiming lower.

This might actually be fun. "So this Board…"

"The Board doesn't matter anymore."

"Oh my, I think someone's been naughty." Mitch walked to the door of the cage, Whittley following cautiously. And hopefully, Eden was working on those cuffs as quickly as she could. "Damn, Ry. When are you going to figure out that there will *always* be someone who's willing to spank you?"

"Not if you're in the top spot, which I am now. But don't worry, Turner, I'll be glad to spank you."

"Thanks, but I'm not into spanking or guys. Although…" He sighed. "Okay, I admit it—I've had more than a few fantasies about all the years the Board had you bent over."

"I should've put you down a long time ago."

"That hurts my feelings, Ry-ry." They walked in side by side, both ready to pounce if the other even thought about closing the door from the outside.

Mitch put his precious syringe on the floor next to the unnecessary key to Eden's cuffs. *Huh.* That didn't seem quite fair.

Did you just set yourself up to be fucked, you idiot?

Rattling off the door's key code, Whittley stared greedily at the bottles Mitch set down. "You're going to share the recipe?"

Mitch nodded. "Tell me a story first, Ry. I want to hear all about why your dad hated you so much. His eldest child, right? Following in his beastly footsteps. Were your parents still together when he decided he liked Eden's mom better? Or did your mom run for it as soon as she figured out that her son was actually nicer to be around when he was in his Abnormal form?"

He shrugged. "All I remember is how good Ian looked through bars."

"That had to be satisfying for you—turn the man who probably could have cured all of us into an unthinking guinea pig." He winked. "You sure showed him, right?"

They stood on opposite sides of the room, equidistant from the door and the items anted up.

"Ian was a very useful guinea pig. Until you tore him apart." He whistled. "How mad was she about that?"

"Well, she wasn't happy—that's for sure. But I think she has more of a problem with what you did to him... and her, and me, and all those other people. If I ever have a son, Whittley, I hope like hell he's nothing like you."

"If you ever have a son." He laughed. "Too bad Eden isn't as fertile as your sister was."

Mitch felt the comment hit him low, right on his most sensitive area—Shelly. Until she had been killed, Shelly was everything to him, the only person he'd ever loved, cherished. He wished she could've met Eden. She would have loved Eden. But nothing this asshole could say about her would hurt Mitch more than he already did.

He took a deep breath and laughed. "Game on, motherfucker."

"That'd be 'sisterfucker,' wouldn't it?" Whittley asked, smiling. "Yours was a pleasure, but I'm not going to fuck my little sister—half or not. And since you couldn't get it done, I'll have to find an Abnormal who can."

Mitch had been wrong—there *was* something that could make him hurt more. And *that* was it. The room chilled as, one by one, all of Mitch's defenses were knocked over until there was nothing left to protect his heart.

When he'd found out Shelly was pregnant— posthumously—he assumed she'd had a secret boyfriend she thought he would hate. And she would've been right—no man was good enough for her. And the man in front of him...

Nah, that's impossible. "You're such a goddamn liar."

"Often yes, but not right now. Even if I gave a shit about my sister, I wouldn't be upset about you fucking her. Because I fucked yours. And—I forgot her name. Shelby? Sheila? Whatever. She was an amazing fuck."

Mitch felt like he'd just been punched in the gut from six feet away. He wished it had been a physical punch. 'Cause that hurt far less than this.

Whittley was the bastard who got Shelly pregnant. Another science experiment performed on a wonderful, innocent soul. Mitch knew his sister—she had been everything he wasn't. Everything Whittley wasn't. Shelly was not a one-night-stand kind of girl. So the only way Whittley could've gotten her pregnant was if he got her so drunk she couldn't say no. Or if he didn't listen to her nos.

He raped my sister. He fucking raped my sister. The only way to stop his body from shaking was to move. So he launched himself forward. Whittley jumped out of the way, and all Mitch grabbed was shirt. When that ripped, the asshole ran away. Did he know they were both stuck in a box? Not too many places to flee in a box.

"Was she conscious?" He asked the question before he realized that he didn't want to know. It wouldn't change anything. This was just something else to hate him for. And knowing what he'd done to her only reminded Mitch of all the ways he hadn't been able to protect her.

"Mostly." Whittley shrugged. "She wouldn't have been able to suck my cock if she was *totally* unconscious."

"You sick fucking bastard." He hit low, like a football player, using Whittley's body instead of one of those plush pad things. The momentum sent both of them onto the floor. At least the other asshole was getting the brunt of it, acting as an unwilling crash pad.

"You and I have a lot in common, Turner."

"Same curse, totally different coping mechanisms. You torture, rape, and kill people. I irritate them. I don't see the similarity."

"Tomatoes, tomatoes."

Mitch shot back onto his feet, dragging the other man up by the waist. He didn't let go and he didn't stop striking. He did, however, have a hard time ignoring the fist that hit him right in the solar plexus. He lost his grip as he tumbled backward, fiery pain in his chest and his breath knocked out of him.

With absolutely no thought for himself, he came back and, after grabbing the collar of Whittley's shirt and squeezing, he landed a few satisfying punches. One in the jaw, another in the cheekbone. The last one was so hard, it knocked the guy out of Mitch's grip.

Something felt...wrong.

Whittley was panting, blood on his forehead, lip, hands, and everywhere else Mitch had touched him.

"I'm going to castrate you," Mitch said. "You realize that, don't you? And you'll *definitely* be conscious." In order to do that, he had to stay in control. Of himself and of Whittley.

But whatever the hell was going on inside the asshole was deeply disturbing. Mitch's body was stiffening up, his muscles locking as the pull grew stronger. Just like in Florida around Whittley's old man. That damn pull—like a siren's call. A perverse, evil, ugly siren that would get metaphorically fucked if it was the last thing Mitch ever did.

The only way out was through pain. He wouldn't let the asshole win the fight *because* he was unworthy. Because he wasn't beating Mitch enough.

A kick to his abs that normally might have knocked him back a step put him on the ground instead. Mitch wasn't the kind of guy anyone would put on a pedestal, but it turned out that he'd be great at falling off one. His back hit the floor first and then his head, but not with enough force to do any damage or even to release him from the pull.

The only thing that would make this more fun would be if Mitch started seizing now. Not that anyone would be able to tell, of course—rigor mortis had already set in.

Whittley stood still for a minute, heavy breathing, confusion on his face. "What's wrong with you?"

"Just giving you a breather." If he wasn't going to die in the next few seconds, he would have the time to feel humiliated.

Instead of kicking Mitch while he was down like any sane person would do, Whittley ran in the other direction. Right to the syringe Mitch had anted up.

Oh, shit.

His head tilting and a melodramatic frown on his face, Whittley pressed his thumb on the plunger, sending all of Mitch's salvation raining down, down, down.

Wonderful. I get to lick the floor after I kill that motherfucker. Unless the motherfucker killed him first, which seemed the more likely scenario when Mitch looked at it…from his back.

"Oh no, Turner. Did you need that?"

"I would never have pegged you as a cheater, Whittley. You seem like such an honest guy."

"I'm honest with myself. No one else matters." He took a few steps closer. "But how about this—I *honestly* thought you'd be a better fighter."

I used to be. Mitch was almost out of smack to talk, so he had to move on to something deeper, something that would cause him a lot of emotional pain. And hopefully, it would get Whittley to turn the pain physical. *No pain, no more Mitch.* In times like these, you aim low—physically, psychologically, and verbally. Whittley had already proven the damage it could do. But he had sore spots as well, two sore spots—his Hyde and his family.

Mitch looked at the I-beams that ran across the ceiling of the cell. "So to recap: You…knew my sister once, and I know your sister frequently, and right up until I killed him, I think your dad and I were getting along great. So we're practically a family—a seriously dysfunctional, incestuous family."

"Get up."

"Did I ever fuck your mom, Ry?"

Whittley's shoulders tightened even further as he came towards Mitch. "Fight with your hands, not your mouth."

"Sure. Just one more question: Did *you* ever fuck your

mom?"

When Whittley's boot hit Mitch's side, he gained some control over his body. *Oooh, feel the burn.* He snagged the guy's foot and shoved hard. All he had to do was keep up the motivational speeches and he'd be fine.

"I didn't hear your answer. Can you repeat it?" Mitch relished the control gained by the pain. And he wouldn't have to worry about the pull once Whittley was dead.

"I wanted to drag this out and enjoy it, but you've made that impossible."

"Right, you're on a timeline. Things to torture and people to kill. What are you going to do when you run out of them?"

Whittley spun around and did some kind of jujitsu move that ended with his foot on Mitch's abs again, shooting him backward onto his ass. He blinked, trying to find air, but either his lungs had shut down or the room wasn't giving any up.

"Thanks for your concern, but I'm fine."

"Really?" he asked, concentrating on expanding his ribcage and belly to force his goddamn lungs to start working again. "Because you don't *seem* fine. You *seem* like you've lost all your fucking marbles." He looked up and saw something that would've made him laugh...if he'd been on the other side of the glass.

Whittley's eyes were now entirely blue.

Big fucking game changer. "You idiot. You didn't take your meds, did you?"

"Got distracted. I'll do it just as soon as I'm done with you."

"It's going to be too late by then, asshole." And with no drug to stop a seizure and bring Hyde back, Mitch's time and luck gauges were both blinking 'E.'

He climbed to his feet. "I've been thinking about what to put on your headstone, Ry. What do you think of: 'Even though he was a crappy son, a terrible boss, and a shitty lay, he was the best monster *ever*'? And then it could end with a smiley face." He shrugged. "But if you want to change the order around, I'm okay with that—put 'shitty lay' first or something."

Mitch needed to get out. Now. But the walls were too tall to climb, and he doubted that Whittley would give him a boost. So the door it was. The door that was on the other side of the asshole transforming right before his eyes.

He threw all of his weight into Whittley, knocking him to the ground. Then he lifted him up by a fistful of shirt and slammed his head against the floor as many times as he could. Dazed and wobbly, Whittley still managed a good jab right under Mitch's ribcage. Mitch rallied with a punch so hard, it was a miracle he hadn't broken his hand along with Whittley's jaw.

But a Hyde didn't need a working jaw to kill. Or to follow Mitch out that door as soon as he opened it. His only chance was to knock Whittley so unconscious, it might have some effect on the monster crawling out of the asshole's skin.

In not nearly enough time, he felt Whittley's body change, his own body lifting a little farther off the ground. Hyde Jr. was ready to play. Now would be a good time for Plan B. If he *had* a Plan B. What could he do against a beast that outweighed him by about a hundred pounds and whose knack for destruction was unparalleled by any other primate? Well, it would be nice to start by getting off the bastard. But that wasn't exactly possible with Mitch's entire body in statue mode.

Blood was leaking out of places it shouldn't—the Hyde's ears and eyes. *Well, isn't that particularly disgusting?* And it was a great sign that the bastard's body was failing. Unfortunately, it wasn't happening fast enough.

Not wanting to excite the animal while they were in the same fucking cage, Mitch spoke slowly and calmly. "Okay, big guy. I take back the shitty lay comment. And any of the others you want me to. I'm sure you're a *great* lay. Not that I actually want to know."

"Move!" Eden's voice came through the open ceiling.

Boy, he'd really, really like to. And then, when the Hyde wrapped his hand around Mitch's neck and squeezed, he could. Now he had to do something before he passed out. He aimed for something he could reach, jabbing his fist right into the creature's throat.

"Get out of the way!"

What did she think he was trying to do? Coughing, the Hyde tossed him backward, and Mitch kept going, scrambling backward on his ass because it would've taken too long to get to his feet.

Eden was standing on a table and straining to reach the top of the wall, the gun raised above her head. Props for trying, but it wasn't going to work from that angle. As the monster slowly climbed to his feet, Mitch glanced at the empty syringe that would've brought out his own Hyde. And given him a chance of getting out of here.

I'm gonna die in a fucking fishbowl.

CHAPTER XLIV

Eden fired as soon as Mitch was out of the way. Once. Twice. Then a third time. Each bullet hit a different area, jolting the Hyde back a step and then knocking him to his knees. Then he climbed back to his feet and ripped off what was left of Ryan's clothing.

Damn it. She'd just wasted three shots. Firing from outside the glass while hanging on the wall by her arms was just stupid, especially with the slug in her shoulder. She was never going to hit him somewhere fatal unless she fired from one of the beams running across the top of the cage.

The Hyde was tossing Mitch around, playing with him, enjoying the incredibly unfair fight.

"Get out, Mitch!" She jumped down and grabbed a chair to put on top of the table.

"No can do, babe! He'd come out with me." 'Me' was elongated and then cut off abruptly at the same time Eden heard a thud and a moan. "But you feel free to shoot him whenever."

"You stupid, stubborn, idiotic…*man*. Just get out!" From her makeshift pyramid, she aimed directly at the Hyde's head and pulled the trigger….of a gun that did nothing but click.

Not now! She pulled it again. And again.

Stupid, idiotic, piece of shit. She threw it at the Hyde and jumped down, hearing him grunt when the weapon hit. *Hurray—he'll have an itty-bitty bump on his head when he murders Mitch.*

Think, Eden. There had to be a way to either kill the Hyde or get Mitch out of the cage. *Think.*

She saw the chain and cuffs she'd just gotten out of. The chain was long, long enough to hang over one of the beams and give Mitch something he could use to climb out. She pulled the chain hand over hand until it was free from the O-rings on the wall and then dragged it to the cage.

Eden tried to separate herself from what was happening behind the glass, because if she focused on Mitch dying, she couldn't make sure he lived. It was impossible to ignore when his body hit the wall in front of her and she saw the pain on his face. Only four inches separated them.

Without looking at her, Mitch turned around dazedly and stretched his neck. "You hit like a girl...who's asleep."

The Hyde chuckled. "The more you talk, the more I want to kill you."

"Really? Who would've ever thought my mouth would get me into trouble?"

She slipped her hand through the cuff at one end of the chain and pulled herself onto the top of the wall. Then she let herself fall forward, grabbing the closest I-beam with both arms as she hit. Her shoulder screamed in pain, but the muscles didn't fail. Once she was straddling the beam, she wrapped the chain around it twice and attached the cuff to secure it.

Groans, moans, and slams echoed below her, but Eden couldn't lose focus now. When Mitch coughed and said, "Do you know a good Chinese place around here? When we're done with this, I wanna take Eden out for dinner," she wanted to laugh. As long as he was being an ass, he was still breathing.

He landed a good kick right in between the creature's legs that sent him to his knees. It also sent Mitch stumbling backward awkwardly. He was too weak right now. There was no way he'd be able to use the chain to climb out. She crouched down and then made a decision Mitch was going to hate. But there was no other way, and he wasn't going to last much longer. Plus, he did stuff she hated all the time. The Hyde looked disoriented but deadly as he gathered his legs under him, readying to stand.

When the unattached end of the chain hit the cage floor, Mitch looked up, his eyes finding hers almost immediately. "No." There was such finality in that one word. No room for negotiation or discussion. Neither of which she was interested in.

"No!" he yelled as her feet hit the floor next to his. "Get out of here!"

"Shut up and distract him. Then pull when I tell you to pull."

Without any further explanation, he understood. "This isn't going to work."

"It *has* to," she said, already running for the opposite side of the room, the chain in her fist. She was faster than Hyde, but speed might not be enough. He turned towards her, but she kept moving, circling him. Mitch wrapped his arms around the Hyde's waist to hold him back. The creature was so strong, Mitch's feet slid on the cement floor.

Eden's only focus was avoiding his hands and getting the chain onto his shoulders. He didn't seem to even notice the extra weight, probably because he was so focused on trying to kill her. When his nails stripped grooves into her back, she cried out but kept moving. Pain could happen later.

One more loop and she ran into Mitch. "Now!" With his hands almost on top of hers, they pulled. The chain tightened, sliding from something like a necklace into a noose. When the links snagged on each other, they had to give it slack and shake it free. And that meant getting closer to the beast. He lunged towards them and they jerked backward—each action serving to tighten the noose. Gagging, he swiped, desperately trying to reach them.

He fisted the chain and pulled, but their combined weight and strength stopped him from dragging them closer. As long as they and the I-beam held, he was stuck. And his desire to get his hands on them resulted only in cutting off more of his air.

Straining from physical exertion and emotional fatigue, Eden held the creature's eyes. The color was so familiar to her. What was behind them was so foreign. Her voice never rose above a whisper as she told him what he was. So many things—son, brother, liar, manipulator, abuser, torturer, rapist, murderer.

All in his human form.

―᠕―᠕―᠕―

Don't seize, don't seize, don't seize. Because Eden's plan might actually work. The bastard was losing with every second that passed, getting closer to the white light that would turn into hell as soon as he walked through it. Something no one had ever deserved more.

But everything would go to hell if Mitch had one of his super-fun seizures and dropped the chain. When his hand slipped, he shoved his wrist through the closed cuff, using his forearm as a bar he could hold with his other hand.

Could the fucker please just *die* already? So this would finally end. Blood dripped from Mitch's arm where the cuff was slicing into his skin. But if either of them let go, that would be the least painful thing he'd ever feel.

Until today, Mitch had never killed anyone. Wanted to? Yes. Fantasized about it? Innumerable times. There was a big difference between thinking it and doing it. But a rabid dog had to be put down. It was the humane thing to do for the inhuman and evil creature. And Mitch hated every motherfucking second of it.

Even though it felt like they'd been pulling on the chain for hours, days maybe, it had probably been less than five minutes. But five minutes was too long for a man or beast to go without oxygen. So after a few more ugly twitches, the bastard's thick arms fell limply to his sides and his body sagged. Eyes that had been a piercing ice blue a minute ago were now a *dead* ice-blue.

Neither one of them relaxed. They waited and watched for any sign of life. Eden understood it first. She dropped the chain and turned to bury her head in Mitch's chest. He held her as she wept, knowing she wasn't grieving Whittley's death. She was grieving all the shit caused by his hands or on his order. Finally. She needed to grieve.

He held her tighter as he watched the Hyde change. Just like his father had fifteen years ago. The Abnormal became a man again. A dead man who'd been just as evil as his Hyde was. Maybe more.

There was no way Whittley was still alive, but Mitch was feeling like Santa—he'd be checking that shit twice. Because the only thing he had any faith in was the woman he held in his arms.

Chapter XLV

When a shudder went through him, Mitch prayed it was just fatigue, the effects of a truly shitty evening. But in their world, bad things didn't happen in threes. They happened in hundreds. And this was number one-*oh-shit*-one. The thirty-eight-second countdown might not have started yet, but something was off...*more* off.

Has it been four hours already? If he made it out, he should buy himself a celebratory watch. Get it engraved with *'Congrats, asshole. The world has to put up with you for a little while longer.'*

Eden went to verify the asshole was dead with a capital 'Fucking.' Since Whittley was wearing a chainmail turtleneck, she used his wrist to check for a pulse.

"Babe?"

"Just shut up a minute." Bitter words spoken with nothing other than fatigue and sadness.

He knew she was at least as tired as he was, but they had to keep moving forward. Having lots of dead enemies meant the external threat was gone, but there was still that itty-bitty other issue—Mitch's internal, time-released one.

He picked up the now-empty syringe and held it up to the

light. How many drops would it take to do the job? Probably more than three.

When she saw it, she moaned, "*Nooooooo.* What did you do?" She barreled into him, knocking him onto the ground. "What did you do?" repeated over and over as she slammed her fists into his chest, straddling his waist. As if her violence was still unfulfilled and needed a new outlet now that the old one was dangling from a chain.

Tears spilled everywhere. "Why, Mitch? Why?" Eventually her crying overwhelmed her screams, and she collapsed onto his chest. He kissed her hair, her temple, her forehead, anywhere he could reach. For as long as the world would let him.

"You bastard," she cried, clutching the empty syringe in her fist. "Why did you let him do it?"

"I didn't exactly *let* him, babe."

"I can't take this anymore. I can't."

When she lifted her head, he realized he'd never seen anything more beautiful. Sure, she was ugly-crying—red eyes, runny nose, the works. But she was *his.* And her eyes, as puffy as they were, still had hope in them, love in them, trust in them. And those were things he could work with.

"Don't give up on me yet, babe."

"I can't handle any more. I don't know what to do." She stood on shaky legs and helped him to his feet.

Unfortunately, the shock was over, the adrenaline was waning, and his entire body was feeling the effects of being tossed around like a dog's chew toy. And now, he could start worrying about *other* fun things. If he started to seize, the worst-case scenario would *definitely* happen.

Being a moron is really inconvenient sometimes. For instance, when you need to whip up a syringe of something and the only person who knows the recipe is at a hospital a few miles away.

Yep, I'm a moron. "I probably should've asked Landon to write down the recipe, huh?" So he'd have to go with option two. He picked up the bottle of J-0026 and then took Whittley's wallet out of his shredded jacket. The guy wouldn't mind—what's a benjamin between friends? Or enemies? Especially dead enemies.

Mitch had never snorted anything because he'd always seen his body as a temple. A satanic temple that didn't need any more bad shit put into it—the place was already packed to the rafters.

She watched him roll the bill up. "So you're just going to take it and see what happens?"

"Yep." What was the worst that could happen? Death. And if he didn't take it? Death. *Yeah, tough call.*

"And you think you're going to make me leave, don't you?"

He grimaced. "It would be safer for you and make me a little less neurotic, so yeah."

"Until you're standing in front of me big and hairy, I'm not leaving."

"Wow. That's incredibly superficial of you." He looked at her, thinking about how much she'd changed from the woman he'd found on his doorstep so many times. "So it's for better or for worse, in sickness and in health, till death do us part until I get big and hairy?"

"I'm going to wear white."

"Of course you are. You look great in white. Is it for a special occasion?" Her glare made him smile. Made him oddly happy and inappropriately hopeful. He looked around the cage that might be the last one he'd ever be in—whether the drug worked or not.

"Come here." He wrapped his arm around her. "I've decided something." He ran his fingertips across her jaw, down her neck, and to her heart. "This isn't my favorite part of you anymore."

"No?"

He shook his head. "All of you is. Every piece from your head to your toes." He cocked his head to the side. "Except your ears. You have funny ears."

She poked him in the cheek. "Liar! You *love* my ears."

"Yes. Yes I do," he whispered, nibbling on one, feeling her shiver. "Your ears, your new hair, the works. Except the part that's bleeding." He turned her slightly to look at her shoulder. "Promise me you'll take care of that. Because I told you no more holes."

"Shut up." Her smile was a sign of her strength and resilience. And it was beautiful.

He rested his forehead on hers. "So, I'm going to try not to die, but if I do...you're going to be okay, right?"

Without specifics, she seemed to know exactly what he was referring to. "A few hours ago, everything would've been different. But I didn't come here to kill Ryan. I didn't even really want to hurt him more than necessary. Because that's what *he* would've done. I don't want to be like him, Mitch. I *won't* be like him." She was calmer than she'd been in a long time. Maybe resolved, maybe just tired. But things were much closer to 'o-kay' than 'oh-shit'.

"Are we sure this is the only way?" she asked.

"No. But it's the only option we have." And it needed to happen now. He wasn't quite ready for the countdown to start, but his body was definitely doing some preseizure warm-ups. He tapped the code into the keypad and opened the door.

"There could be some RLS-7 in here somewhere. In one of those cabinets. I think we should wait."

"For what exactly?" The only thing he was waiting for was her to leave.

"For Danielle to test it somehow. On someone else."

Another lab rat. Nah, Mitch was the perfect rat for the job. So before she could start negotiating, he kissed her.

And then he shoved her out the door.

"Damn it! No, not like this!" She scrambled to her feet and rushed to the keypad.

"Don't, babe. Please. You can't help me now. All you can do is get hurt. Don't open the door until we know one way or another. There are other people—here and in other places—who need help, and they won't get it if both of us are dead."

What he said barely made her hesitate before she started typing numbers in. "No, Mitch. Not like this."

As soon as the makeshift straw and the probably toxic powder met, he inhaled as hard and as much as he could. Before she could stop him or stall or make him reconsider.

Fuuuuuuck. There were a lot of reasons he'd never done drugs. And now he could add one more—that shit *stung.* He suddenly had a new respect and disdain for anyone who willingly put anything up their nose. His head shook, trying to rid itself of the poison and the pain, his hands wiping his face like a kid forced to eat broccoli.

"I wasn't ready yet," she said frantically.

He was. He was done being angry and frustrated and unsure. Whatever happened now would happen. For both of them. She looked at him with so much fear it rocked him back a step.

He loved her more than he'd ever loved anything. More than he'd known was possible. Really understanding that made him want to cry. He wouldn't, but he wanted to. *Oh shit.* Really? *Come on.* He tried to hide it from her, but her expression stopped him. From moving, from breathing, even from tearing up like a fucking wuss. Mostly.

"Why are you smiling?" she yelled, smacking the glass. She was anxious, angry, and scared, and it would only make her madder if he admitted that he'd never seen anything sexier. Her passion was beautiful because it was for him.

He felt a tear slide down his cheek. Saw her face change to concern, apprehension.

"Does it hurt?" she asked so quietly, he wasn't sure if he'd heard it or just read her lips.

"No." *It's embarrassing as hell, though.*

She reached up as if to wipe it away, pulling her hand back when she realized she couldn't touch him. "What's that for?"

"You." He took a deep breath. "Everything good inside me

is for you. *Because* of you."

"You know the expression 'For better or for worse'?"

"Sure, I think I've heard it before." He raised an eyebrow. "Wait. Are you hinting at something?"

"Maybe later. What I meant is that we get the bad with the good. You once told me that it was okay to be bad every once in a while, and you were right." She cocked her head to the side and a sad smile flickered across her lips. "But just about that."

"My bad isn't exactly average." And his ratio of wrong things to right things was probably about five thousand to four. Well, four might be too generous.

"True. But your good isn't average either. Your good is incredible."

He'd always thought he knew who he was—an asshole going through life punishing himself for being an asshole. Afraid of his transformations, of being like his father, of allowing Hyde to hurt someone.

All real things. All things that, until recently, were preventable. If he hadn't been so stupid. He'd spent the last fifteen years hurting people so they'd stay outside the danger zone. But he'd been way more dangerous than Hyde ever had.

Stick a bastard in a cage, and he's fine. Give a bastard too much time to think, and you've got problems.

And then *she* came along and refused to be affected by his best insults. Until then, the idea that he was actually worth anything hadn't even occurred to him. But she believed he was worth something, so it had to be true.

And he had to stop trying so fucking hard to prove her wrong.

He'd spent his life keeping the wall separating man from beast intact. But there *was* no wall. No wall, no war, and no victor. There was just him—the jackass, fighting this other side of himself that he would never be able to beat. Not two separate beings. *One.* But there was good in that one. A nice-sized chunk of it. And Eden had made it bigger. Stronger.

He pulled away from the glass just enough to take a breath, the first deep breath of a new life, a new him.

You're still a long fucking way from nice, but—

Oh, shit. Something shifted in his brain, like he'd blown a fuse or something. Another traumatic injury caused by positive thinking. He shouldn't have done it. *Stick to the hard stuff, asshole.*

Oh, fuck. He did *not* feel right. And no amount of aspirin was going to help. Nothing would help him now. You finally get used to who you are and then you're over. He'd laugh if it wasn't so tragic. *And* if he didn't think laughing would pop a gasket in his head.

He felt a wave of heat, then nausea, and stumbled backward. Aw hell, *please* let this be a good sign and not another really fucking bad one.

"Look at me, Mitch." She pounded her fist on the glass. "Focus on me."

He tried. As pain ravaged his insides, he tried. "You're so beautiful. Thank you for choosing me." He could look at her forever. And he did.

Until everything disappeared.

Chapter XLVI

Eden screamed when he fell. She kept her hands pressing against the glass, forcing herself not to touch the keypad and open the door. There was nothing she could do for him now.

Thirty-eight seconds passed.

Then a minute. And another.

No seizure. No Hyde. No movement at all. From either of them.

When the speed of her tears slowed to a manageable level, she unlocked the door and went inside. She knelt down and brushed the hair out of his eyes, even though they were closed. She talked to him for a while, not really knowing what she was saying. It didn't matter.

"It's not like you ever listen to me anyway."

He looked like he was just sleeping, as if any minute he would raise his arms above his head, stretch, and then feel around for her before even opening his eyes.

But that didn't happen.

After what seemed like forever but was probably just an hour or so, she kissed him gently and stood up. "I'll be right back, babe."

As she walked down a long hallway of white doors, her

steps were heavy. Her left arm was getting harder and harder to move. *Finish this. Pain can happen later.* Crying too.

She stopped in front of a room marked: 'Normal #1.' She couldn't fight anymore so, before opening the door, she had to find out if 'Normal #1' was human. A little test. If he said something vile and repulsive, she'd... Well, she didn't know what she'd do.

"You in there!" she called. "I'm female and I'm naked. So tell me what you wanna do to me."

"What did you just say?" asked an irritated voice.

"Do you want to fuck me?"

"Shit, you bastards really get off on this, don't you?" He sounded disgusted, not disgust*ing*. "Why don't you go fuck yourself?"

She unlocked the door and swung it open, expecting and planning for the worst. The man was big, long legs, very muscular, but definitely human looking. Blue scrubs, messy blond hair, and a face like a fallen and pissed off angel. He was sitting on the bed, but his entire body was tensed, as ready for something to go wrong as she was. 'Normal' was a misnomer. This guy wasn't normal.

"Who are you?" Her hand stayed on the door, ready to slam it closed again.

"Lost my file?" He laughed without smiling, bitterly. "Or is it your first day on the job?"

"I'm not one of them. Which is kind of a good thing because they all seem to have died. So if you're not one of them either and you're not insane, you're free to go."

Not even his eyes moved.

She didn't have time for this. "Look, jackass, I'm not posing for any pictures today. You want out? Then get out."

He lifted his hand, exposing the cuff around his wrist, a weird-looking chain attaching it to the wall.

"Are you kidding? I have *necklaces* thicker than that."

"I didn't know they used palladium alloy for jewelry. I'll have to get some—there are a few necks I'd *love* to see something wrapped around." There was no inflection in his voice, no fear or surprise either. But Eden knew that behind the calm was a storm. A big one.

She walked towards him slowly, taking a safety pin off her belt. The closer she got, the more she *felt* him—he had a pull, but it wasn't a huge one. He seemed to feel it too, getting slightly uncomfortable, more edgy, as if he didn't understand where the feeling was coming from. He probably hadn't been around too many others like her.

"What's your name?"

"You can call me Fox."

"That's your name?"

"That's what you can call me."

"Okay...*Fox*. You touch me, even by accident, you die. You move too quickly, you die. You say anything inappropriate, you hurt really badly."

He watched her in silence, his brow furrowed, still on edge. Rightfully so, if he'd been on the receiving end of the only thing Ryan was good at.

"No joke—you move, and you're dead. Do you understand?"

"I'm not sure." His voice was controlled, like everything else about him—absolutely still until movement was necessary. "I think you're trying to tell me not to move. But if I'm wrong, maybe you could say it a few more times."

Amusing. That comment almost made her smile. "I think you got it." She gestured for his hand and went to work, still standing. He was right—impressive metal. The lock was definitely the weak point.

"You're really going to let me go." He seemed shocked. Maybe he had PTSD. *Maybe I have PTSD too.* "I didn't mean to sound unappreciative."

"After a little while in this place, it's hard to believe anyone *isn't* screwing with you, right?"

He nodded slowly. "You took all of them out?"

She shook her head and leaned closer to the lock. "Just

Ryan. He'd already taken care of the others."

"Thank you."

"I didn't do it for you."

"Doesn't matter. I got something out of it." His voice was deeper than it had been a minute ago, more guttural.

She took a step back. "Yeah, well. Don't start thinking you're going to get anything else out of it because I'm not in a great mood."

"Sorry." He looked it—sorry, frustrated, confused, disgusted by things he couldn't control. "Everything feels different now. I'm still trying to figure it out." He hadn't touched her and he was only reacting to the pull, so she wasn't worried. He might not be normal, but he was human. And humans shouldn't be caged.

"There's a lot to get used to," she said. "If I let you go, are you going to be a problem for me?"

"If I am, I'll cuff myself. Or you can kill me."

"Try not to make that necessary." When the lock clicked open, she straightened and stepped back.

"Thank you." He rubbed his wrist but waited until she was across the room before he stood. Smart man.

"You should know that if any of this comes out, everybody loses—you, me, your family, everybody. All that will happen is you'll end up in another room in another building with another cuff around your wrist. Because people suck and will want to know how you function now. So until we understand it, don't do anything stupid."

"So you're saying I can't use the story to pick up women?" he asked dryly. "Damn it. Alright, you win—I'll try not being stupid." He shrugged. "It might work."

"Try hard."

"Have you seen the other men?"

"No. Don't let anyone out until you know they're safe and sane." God, she hoped they all were sane, because she had no idea what they would do with any who weren't.

"I'll take care of them."

She could tell he wanted to get out of the room—who likes to stay in their prison cell any longer than necessary? But he waited. She didn't think it was because he was a gentleman. Or even because he saw her as a threat.

Okay, so the guy has some trust issues. Who doesn't? "If you think I'm with Ryan, I'm incredibly offended. I'd hate to think I look that stupid."

One corner of his mouth curled ever so slightly, but only for a second. "What did they do to you?"

She paused. "Everything they could."

But not anymore. When she realized it, the knowledge didn't have the impact she thought it would. She was free, Ryan, Alex, and the Board were gone, but she was still scared. *For Mitch.*

"Once you've freed the others," she said, "meet me in the fight room. All of you. Because we need to chat." After giving him the code for the doors and the lock pick, she started running down the hall, back to Mitch.

"What will you be doing?" Fox called.

"Praying." *And crying.* She would be doing a whole lot of both.

CHAPTER XLVII

Hope.

It had been so long, Eden almost didn't recognize it. Or understand why she was so overwhelmed with the feeling. Mitch was still unconscious and hadn't moved in days. But he was *Mitch*. Stunning to look at, even more so in slumber. Maybe because he couldn't ruin it by saying something obnoxious.

Jesus, she loved how obnoxious he was. He was stubborn and snide and wicked and one hundred percent male. And she knew he'd wake up soon. His breathing was steady and his pulse was... perfect. Because it was *his*. The normal rhythm of the man, not of Hyde.

She was perched at the foot of the mattress, never looking away, expecting his eyes to open any minute and not wanting to miss it. She wasn't stupid—the cuffs and chains stayed where she could grab them quickly if necessary. But she didn't think he would need them.

After she'd left Fox and gone back to the fight cage, there was no seizure. There was no Hyde. Just Mitch, lying completely still with his head in her lap, her hand smoothing his hair like she'd done for Justin. It was the most fearful moment of her life, sitting there waiting. Hoping. Praying. But he hadn't even twitched. Not even when Fox helped her carry him to one of the 'Normal' rooms. And she'd definitely dropped her half a few times.

Since then...nothing. But their time together had been good for her. It would've been better if he were conscious, but the quiet helped her focus, to think about things she hadn't allowed herself to think about—those she'd lost, who she was, what she wanted their lives to be like after he woke up.

Aside from certain areas, Eden actually liked living at the Shop. Since they'd changed the codes for all the doors—on the building's ground floor and to the basement—and only a few people knew the new codes, it was incredibly secure. Even though Mitch was unconscious and Landon was still recovering and didn't leave his room much, Eden felt safe. Because her family was here.

Strangely, Danielle had become part of that. She came to check on Mitch—and maybe Eden too—frequently since she'd brought Landon back here. But most of her time was spent in the small lab. They were quietly excited about using the J-0026 in all its forms. But it was taking time, and, after what had almost happened to Landon, Danielle wouldn't let them use any of The Clinic's drugs until she understood them better. *So* frustrating, but the smart thing to do.

Fox and the four men referred to as 'Normals' stayed away from Eden if they could help it. They were all really uncomfortable with the pull, even though she'd explained it to them a few times. All she knew about them was that Ryan had hired the team for a job that had actually been a setup. Everything else was even vaguer. But how many kinds of teams agree to do secret jobs for evil people and whose members are all built like brick walls and move like panthers?

Thankfully, they all seemed to fall right in line under Fox's leadership, tracking down the 'zookeepers' and visiting the other Malvers labs, but checking in daily. Of course, a huge part of that was because, until further notice, they would keep taking The Clinic's meds.

Eden heard Danielle's voice in the hallway, a laugh, and then a knock on the door. She opened the door for them. "How are you feeling, Landon?"

"Better." He *looked* better, but he still wasn't back to normal. "The guys said it took them at least a full week for their bodies to adjust to the drug, so I guess that means I get to feel like shit for another couple of days."

His room was just down the hall, but Eden rarely saw him. Because she couldn't leave Mitch. If he woke up while she wasn't here, she'd hate herself. And that was a place she was never going again. Hate, gone. Rage, gone. Replaced by the parts of herself that she loved, and that Mitch loved too.

Landon was in good hands, though, and one of them was currently holding his. "How is he?" He looked over her shoulder into the room. "Can I see him?"

Eden nodded and let them both into the room she'd been keeping vigil in. There was no reason for her to leave—Mitch was here. Ryan was dead. And Justin was gone. She leaned against the doorjamb while Landon sat down next to the bed.

"Here," Danielle said, holding out a Styrofoam box. "You need to start eating, because I already have too much to worry about." She waited until Eden ripped off a piece of bread and shoved it into her mouth.

As soon as it hit her tongue, Eden realized how hungry she was and really dug in. "Thanks." She tried to focus on the food and not what Landon was whispering to Mitch. Words of friendship and curses of impatience—guy talk.

Not wanting to intrude, she turned to Danielle. "It's none of my business, but are you guys…?"

Danielle's smile was answer enough. "I don't know exactly what we are yet, but we're definitely *something*."

"I hope it works out. He deserves something great. A whole bunch of great things actually. And you completely lucked out—he's amazing."

"I might agree with that once he's done his penance for all

the lying."

"That's fair." Because she imagined that penance would be something he'd enjoy paying.

Danielle's smile faltered when she looked at him. "I'm not sure he'll be able to come off it." She didn't have to be more specific. The drug Landon and the other Normals were on seemed to be an all-or-nothing kind of thing. If they stopped taking it, what had happened to Carter would happen to them.

But Fox had offered to be the guinea pig for all of them. His doses would get smaller and smaller until he was back to a *true* normal...or was dead.

"Come on, Danielle. With your brain, Fox's insanity, and Landon being such a baby about the needles, it's gonna happen." And if not, they had a large supply of it and, since Danielle was close to understanding where she'd gone wrong with the batch she made for Landon, she'd be able to reproduce it soon.

"Hope so. I'm still not even done going through all of the files. That will never get old." Danielle rolled her eyes. "*So much fun.* But you know how I feel about testing before injecting." She closed her eyes. "Ugh, that's like my mantra around here. 'Test before you inject.' That's just sad." She paused. "I worry about the long-term effects, too."

"Well, if it makes you feel any better, Ryan and I were on J-0026 for years and look how well adjusted we both were." She laughed and then looked at Mitch. "I know you can figure it out. You were right about the big dose—he hasn't transformed."

"He hasn't woken up either."

"I took a two-week-long nap, so he's not due for a few more days." But he would wake up, she was sure of it.

Landon turned towards them. "The guys called from the other facilities. They seem legit—no Abnormals or Normals found in any basements yet. Fox told them to stick around until the labs get word of Ryan and the Board members' disappearances."

Another point for Fox. Eden didn't ask what he and his men had done with the bodies—Ryan, Alex, the Board members, all the Hydes who'd taken each other apart after taking apart the Board. She wasn't even sure she cared what happened to the zookeepers they tracked down. If it were up to her, she'd never hear the word 'clinic' again.

But she understood the necessity of watching to see who stepped up to lead the business end of the operation. Because people are people, and business is business, and money is money. The Clinic knocked down only to rebuild itself under new management? That was *not* going to happen—there was no way any of them could do this again.

A few days ago, Eden had gone back to Ryan's office and cracked open his safe. No secret drug stashes beyond the stuff he'd stolen from *them*, but she *did* find a shitload of cash and an envelope. She'd already sent the money to Fields. It was only fitting that Ryan's blood money went to support those whose blood he'd earned it from, and Fields would put it to good use.

What she'd found inside the envelope proved to be far more interesting—a list of names with dates next to them. She knew better than to think it was Ryan's version of a little black book, although there was a good chance he'd been screwing them metaphorically. No, the people whose names were on that list were involved, Eden just didn't know how. They could be investors, handlers, or Abnormals.

Eden sat down on the edge of the bed. "What about the list?"

"That's where you come in," Landon said.

"How's that?"

"You can sense them, right? If they are totally human or not?"

"Yeah." She felt the pull around every Abnormal she'd met and, to a lesser extent, Fox, Landon and the other men. "But I can't leave." And frankly, she didn't want the responsibility. Not now. Maybe not ever.

"I think right now we all need a chance to recover, so it can wait. Maybe until Turner can go with you." The confidence in his tone verified what Eden already knew— Mitch *would* come back. It was just a matter of time.

"Maybe." She'd try to do what Landon wanted—get close enough to sense if they were like her—but that was it. She didn't just need a chance to recover—she needed a chance to *live*. A regular life—no fighting, no evil, no drugs.

The next few hours were the most relaxing Eden could remember. She sat in her regular spot at Mitch's feet with her hand on his ankle just to feel his warmth while Landon and Danielle told stories about odd memories of normalcy. They laughed like good friends might do over wine and cheese. The only thing that would make it better would be if the fourth member of their group could laugh along with them.

But he didn't laugh. He didn't move.

Did he...?

"Did he just move?" She scrambled onto her knees.

They stared down at him, waiting. Waiting for another sign.

He grimaced.

Eden sucked in a breath and heard one, or both, of the others do the same. *Calm.* It could've just been involuntary. It would still be incredible, but it didn't mean he was just going to—

She fell on her ass when his eyes opened. They were different—not hazel anymore but not silver-blue either. They were light blue, like an unpolluted ocean or a pristine swimming pool. Absolutely beautiful.

"Mitch?" Landon said hesitantly.

Eden stayed still, knowing there was a chance she'd have to jump for the chains, not sure if she could believe in the eyes that stared back at her. She *really* wanted to believe.

"Hey there, beautiful," he said softly. "Why aren't you naked?"

She threw herself on top of him, relishing the heat of his

arms as they wrapped around her. He held her so tightly, she could finally breathe.

"Did it work or am I dead?" His voice was muffled by her kisses.

"You're alive, Mitch," she whispered. "And you'd better fucking stay that way."

EPILOGUE

Two and a half months later…

Unfortunately, just because Hyde wasn't around anymore didn't mean Mitch had any more patience than he used to. They stood in the master bedroom of yet another house. Mitch would give anything to go back to bed…with *her*. But he kept his mouth shut…because he wasn't stupid. And because he didn't want anything to take that look off Eden's face. Ever.

"What do you think?" she asked.

"It's fine."

She tilted her head in annoyance. "That's not an answer."

"It's a perfectly fine answer."

"No. It's a perfectly *useless* answer. Because it's the same answer you've given the last four times I asked you."

Oh, it had been *way* more than four times. Four times per house, at least. So it was more like sixteen times. Today.

He sighed. "I like the walls—they look strong enough to bolt some heavy-duty cuffs onto." From behind him, he heard the realtor gasp.

"He's just kidding," Eden said quickly, throwing a glare his way.

"Could we have a minute?" he asked the woman.

"Take whatever time you need." She looked as tired of showing them houses as he was of looking at them. "I'll be downstairs."

He followed Eden into the bathroom and shut the door behind him. "We need to talk."

"Do you like the shower?" she asked, sliding the glass door open and closed, open and closed, open and closed, open and closed, open and—

"Please, Eden! Can you just stop for a second?"

She flipped around and waited for him to explain himself.

"The shower's great. Obviously the door works *really* well, and it's big enough for both of us, so I think it's...great. But that's not what we need to talk about."

She sighed, went to the vanity, and leaned back on it, her arms folded across her chest. "What do we need to talk about?"

Patience—was it a virtue or a vice? "Look, I know why we're doing this—why it's important to you to put down roots and have a real home and all that shit. But in case you haven't noticed, we're not normal. As big as this property is, you could spy on the neighbors without trying, and I'm still getting used to sleeping outside of a cage." He shook his head. "That's not normal."

"So you're worried we're going to bring down the property values?"

"I'm worried that you're trying so hard to forget that you actually *will*." He wasn't complaining—the last two and a half months had been better than anyone had a right to. Watching things get cleaned up without lending a hand or a fist, minimal fighting between the two of them, and lots and lots of incredible sex.

With no more danger, she'd mellowed—and he'd make sure she stayed that way—but there was more to it than that. They'd gone through a shitload of really bad stuff—her more than him. And her inability to talk about it was taking a toll on both of them.

"When's the last time you spoke to Fields?" he asked. "Danielle? Landon? Anybody?"

Landon was in Dallas with Danielle and the others. Still trying to understand how the Normals worked and if there was a way to make them un-Normal. Thus far, Fox had almost died six times. Maybe seven. That guy had huge balls and was a tiny bit scary. Danielle continued to look for the right way to use the J-0026. And, for some crazy reason, she didn't think Mitch had followed proper scientific protocols when he'd taken whatever amount he'd taken whenever he'd taken it.

All of them had agreed that Eden needed time to heal and that Mitch was the only one who could help her. But it wasn't going very well.

"If I wanted to talk to Landon," she said, "he'd have to get off the phone with *you*."

That was true. Mitch missed the bastard. So he and Landon talked on the phone like teenage girls—minus the giggling and gossip, and plus a lot more cursing and insults. He needed to talk this shit out with someone, and Eden didn't want to hear it.

She and Mitch discussed everything else—he knew all about her past, her life, her hopes, her thoughts. But whenever he tried to broach one of many touchy subjects, she balked.

She told him about her dreams but not her nightmares.

"And I talk to Danielle a lot," she said.

"I want you to be happy, babe. And if the only way you'll be happy is by having a house in the 'burbs, then that's where I'll go. That said, I sleep next to you, and I hear you talk in your sleep."

She tensed. "What do I say?"

"Justin's name," he said quietly. "And you cry. You cry a lot."

"Oh."

He saw her start to shut down, felt the air between them shift. "Hey, there'll be none of that." He wrapped his arms around her. "You wanted to know what I think, right?" She nodded. "Well, I think we should go downstairs and make what's-her-name's day. Buy this house and the last two we saw, if you want. Then we should go furniture shopping or hire a decorator or whatever ordinary people do." He took a deep breath. "Then I get your extraordinary ass on a plane. We get hitched on a deserted island somewhere, and after a week of doing *indescribably* dirty things to each other, we come back here to do laundry." *Need more oxygen for this part.* "Then we pack up and keep going."

"Where to?"

"To get back in the game." Because they were never going to be sideline type people. "To help Fields and the others find all the kids like Justin who are still out there. Who are like us when we were that age—scared, alone, and potentially dangerous."

"Then what?" She edged out of his arms, turning towards the mirror as if looking directly at him was too intense.

"We tell them who they are and give them what they need—drugs and a home with strong walls and Velcro straps." He grimaced. "Wow, that's not going on the brochure." Then he waited. Uncomfortably.

He'd been planning this since a few days after he woke up a new man and realized they had a future to work with. Shit, he'd even learned how to use a computer well enough to start a database of places to start trolling for young pretransitional Hydes and Jekylls. And that last part would sound incredibly seedy if he said it out loud, so he didn't.

But she hadn't been ready two months ago. She'd needed a break, and he'd needed to know if she could ever go back into that world. He still wasn't sure she could, but not bringing it up wasn't doing her any favors.

So he'd wait for an answer. And if she said no, he'd accept it, put in on the shelf, and revisit the idea in a few months, lathering, rinsing, and repeating for as long as he had to. Because to do it right, they had to do it together.

He waited.

And he waited.

And hell, at this point, he'd even take a facial expression.

After a while he started wondering what the realtor was doing downstairs and when she'd come back up to find out what the hell they were doing. A person can only check their email for so long.

Eden just stared at his reflection. Her eye color had changed from brown to an ethereal blue. His had gone from hazel to a darker, far less stunning blue. And then—strangely for the first time—he wondered what color their kids' eyes would be. After a brief moment of panic at the thought of actually *being* a father, he settled into the idea. In a terrified sort of way.

Now everything in his life was uncharted territory, every moment unexpected. First, because he was still in shock that no one had killed him yet. Second, because he didn't need a steel guestroom every five weeks anymore. And third, because he still couldn't quite believe that the woman in front of him was, and always would be, his.

When he saw her body soften, relax, he thought it might be a trick of the glass or the sunset. She'd outlasted the sun. Impressive. But then she turned around, took his shirt in her fist, and pulled him towards her.

A good sign. A hopeful sign. But not a done deal.

He was never, ever going to get tired of looking at her. *This is important stuff, asshole. Don't get distracted.* He shouldn't think about the way her body pressed against his or how easy it would be to slide her skirt—

Nope. He shouldn't think about what color her panties were, if she was even *wearing* panties. *Stop getting distracted.* Until she said something, he'd stay here and think about nothing. *Oh shit, is she wearing any? Idiot.* He shouldn't think about panties or how the counter she was practically sitting on would give him excellent leverage when he—

"Okay." She nodded, a look of satisfaction, maybe even

peace, on her face. "I think I'm ready." A single tear fell. "Thank you."

"Okay." More than okay—perfect. He closed his eyes, thanked the heavens, and grinned like an idiot. Until she kissed him. First lightly, then more deeply. Until everything else went away—the house, the walls, the world. A shudder went through one of them, but he didn't know who. It didn't matter—they were *one* in everything that mattered.

She sighed, pulling away only slightly. "You're a very good man, Mitch Turner."

"But not *too* good, right?" he asked, kissing her forehead.

"Just the right amount of good."

"I like that." He went to the door and flipped the lock. "Because a *too*-good man wouldn't even *consider* leaving that poor realtor downstairs while he made love to his woman on the bathroom counter of their new house."

She laughed as he came back to her. "And just the right amount of bad."

~The End~

AUTHOR'S NOTES

Dear reader,

The way I look at it, *characters* don't have happy endings, *books* do. What characters have are happy *beginnings*. So Mitch and Eden are now heading into another tough battle—having a healthy relationship. But they know their love is real, lasting, and worth more trouble than they've ever run into.

Though *Strange Case* marks the end of the Hyde trilogy, their lives will continue as I explore other characters and conflicts in this world. Mitch and Eden may even show up from time to time, because I'm never going to be ready to say goodbye to those two. Plus, Mitch makes me laugh, especially when he's with Landon. And I've found a new infatuation in Fox, a very focused, very secretive man who doesn't allow himself to get distracted and who would sacrifice anything or anyone to protect his team. Anyone, huh? Um...Yeah, about that...

May you all find, or continue to live, your own happy beginning!

Lauren

ABOUT LAUREN STEWART

Lauren Stewart lives in Northern California with two of the most amazing children that the world has ever seen. She reads almost every genre so, naturally, her writing reflects that. With every book, every story, you'll find elements of other genres—fantasy, mystery, romance, paranormal, suspense, YA, women's literature, all with a touch of humor because what doesn't kill us should make us laugh.

CONTACT LAUREN

Sign up for my newsletter to get:
Behind the Scenes Looks at Your Favorite Characters
Updates about Coming Soon and New Releases
News about Contests and Giveaways
Teasers and Sneak Peaks
Book Signings, Conventions, and Appearances
Just go to: www.ReadLaurenS.com

Find me at:
www.facebook.com/LaurenStewartAuthor
Twitter: @ReadLaurenS
ReadLaurenS@gmail.com

OTHER TITLES BY LAUREN STEWART

Darker Water, Once and Forever #1
Unseen, The Heights Vol. 1
Unearthed, The Heights Vol. 2
Hyde, an Urban Fantasy
Jekyll, Hyde Book II
Strange Case, Hyde Book III
The Complete Hyde Series Box Set
No Experience Required, a Summer Rains Novel
Second Bite